CONQUISTADORS

BLACK AUTUMN BOOK THREE

JEFF KIRKHAM
JASON ROSS

Black Autumn
Conquistadors

Black Autumn Companion Series

Book 3

by Jeff Kirkham, Fmr. Army Green Beret
& Jason Ross

© copyright 2019

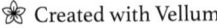 Created with Vellum

"The liar's punishment is not in the least that he is not believed, but that he cannot believe anyone else."

George Bernard Shaw

CHAPTER 1
TAVO CASTILLO

If Tavo knew he would be using an assassin to murder his daughter, he probably would've picked one with a different name. Sending a "mongrel dog" to murder his spotless darling struck him as a profound sacrilege.

"I've pre-positioned *El Chucho* in Hermosillo," the assassin's handler repeated.

The voice over the satellite phone came through warbled and spackled, like a demon reaching across an ice-bound solar system.

"Sir," the man on the other end of the phone interrupted his fugue. "Please confirm. *El Chucho* to prosecute target Sofía Castillo Sausa in Hermosillo, Sonora."

The roaring ache in his severed toe rose like boiling water at the mention of her name. Tavo steadied himself with deep breaths and gripped the rotting lawn chair so tightly he feared the brittle armrests might shatter. After an eternity, the pain receded.

"Sir. I need you to confirm," the satellite phone chirped.

"Confirmed."

There was nothing else to say. The other man disconnected,

as though saying "goodbye" might be an inappropriate way to end the call.

The shack where Tavo rolled between pain, malice and regret must've been a guard shack in a previous life. The walls were decaying adobe, but someone had recently replaced the roof with gleaming, corrugated metal. It radiated the sun's relentless heat like a stone pulled from the fire. Whoever had replaced the roof hadn't bothered to pull down the 1980s porn calendar, hanging on a rust-chewed nail. A big-breasted Latina stared back at Tavo with a vacant smile, her face yellowing from decades hanging there.

Such a strange room for an emperor, Tavo brooded. Again, his ruined foot throbbed so powerfully that it made his ears pulse with a dull thrum. Somewhere in Hermosillo, Mexico the daughter he had once lived to serve had now been marked for death. She was likely dressed in white today, like most days—a crisp breeze cutting the desert heat. At that same moment, her father sweltered in a mud shack, wounded, swooning and spattered in his own blood.

Maybe all great men faced solitary moments in windowless rooms like this one. Maybe all great men committed deeds that only fierce men could.

CHAPTER 2
TAVO CASTILLO
FILADELFIA HOTEL, ANTIGUA, GUATEMALA

Three weeks earlier.

Whoever said "crime doesn't pay" must not have known many smart criminals.

Gustavo "Tavo" Castillo drifted in and out of thought as the coming dawn filtered through the coffee plantation and quieted his restless soul. The rich light touched off the emerald greens of the leaves and the brilliant white of the blossoms one degree at a time, like an awakening after too much sleep.

Each of the hundred million blossoms granted a minuscule breath of fragrance, mingling in the slight breeze and washing the hillside in alternating waves of vanilla and jasmine.

Nothing in the world touched Tavo more deeply than this place, during this time of year: the flowering of the coffee in Antigua, Guatemala. Tavo had set the annual business meeting with his daughter for this place and time—the Hotel Filadelfia in late September.

"Buenas dias, Papi." His daughter kissed him on the head, careful not to jostle his coffee, and took the seat across from him at the wrought iron patio table.

Well, Tavo corrected himself, there was one thing in the world that touched him more deeply than the coffee bloom. He looked at her and felt mesmerized by his daughter, as Latin American fathers had for eons.

Somehow, even without makeup and at the cusp of dawn, she lit up the patio like a Roman goddess. Her airy white blouse floated around her shoulders and set off her rosy, latte-colored skin and her blush lips, delicately closing on the edge of her coffee cup. She smiled at Tavo silently, as if to acknowledge the perfect morning.

Loving his daughter was one of the few ways Tavo felt human. Mostly, he didn't. He felt like an alien wearing the skin of a man; an infiltrator, passing through the world, harvesting the weakness of humans. Tavo preyed upon them—except for this gut-punch-beautiful woman.

He pulled his eyes away from the coffee bloom to watch her pour half-and-half into her coffee. Were it not for her, he would be no different than any other predator; living only to kill and eat. Because of Sofía, his predations meant something: that the spoils of his life would pass to this light-dappled creature. As far as life purpose went, Tavo knew that many men had far less.

She waited on his pleasure. She sipped her coffee without a sound, honoring his enjoyment of the dawn and the mist-dusted coffee flowers. It was something he might do, himself, to soften a target of manipulation—feigning grace and openheartedness. Pretending to respect the other man's pleasure and taking time to indulge the petty contentments of his target. Tavo was ninety-nine percent certain that his daughter did it because she sincerely cared for him. Either way, he respected her self-mastery. It was a rare trait among twenty-nine year old women.

He set his coffee cup quietly on the patio table and straightened in his chair, signaling his willingness to get to work.

"Will you tell me me what you think about the troubles in America?" she began.

Good, Tavo thought. *Always start with a question. Draw the other person in. Make them feel heard before maneuvering toward your objective.*

"We've seen big swings in the stock market six times in the last year," Tavo recalled. "This could just be one more of those."

"Yes, but the dirty bomb attack on the Saudi oil pumping station might make this stick. We haven't seen the New York Stock Exchange circuit breakers close trading until now. The market troubles in the past have been herd panic. This one's founded on an actual loss of capital infrastructure."

He couldn't help but take pride in her nuanced understanding of the global financial situation, but it also unsettled him. She'd done her undergrad at Vanderbilt and then whipped through her MBA at Wharton. Since then, she'd been building her way up to running all his legitimate enterprises, and she'd had unbelievable success. Of course, his legitimate businesses could never compete with drug trafficking for profitability. But until she'd taken the helm of his corporations, they almost all lost money. They were money laundering schemes more than anything else, so losses hadn't been an issue. But she'd turned that around. Now they were making money on their money laundering.

He wondered how much her analysis of the stock market had been lifted from a class she'd taken at Wharton. The alternative—that her genius approached his own in magnitude—brought with it another set of problems. He'd made it a personal mantra: never work with anyone as intelligent as him. A smart enough person would see through his well-manicured humanity and peg him for the sociopath he was. Had his daughter already turned that corner?

"American financial trouble has always been good for us," Tavo threw out the statement, more interested in keeping her talking than anything.

She chuckled. "It's been good for *you*. My businesses take damage when markets fall. They're only worth what people will pay for them and that depends on private equity funds and the cash they have on hand, which relies heavily on their investors' stock gains."

Tavo received it for what it was: an intellectual parry. She was fully aware of the drug trade that had funded all the family's legitimate enterprises. At the same time, she had worked tirelessly to firewall the two sides of the family fortune. In theory, her policy fit perfectly into his empire strategy. In practice, her relentless fence-building between his "dirty work" and her "clean work" tasted like last night's garlic.

And yet, he reminded himself, it had always been just the two of them. Father and daughter, forever driving toward the same outcome; her long-term wealth, and hopefully, the well-being of his grandchildren at some point. The thought of grandchildren made him think of a male counterpart for Sofia. *Just another person I would have to eventually kill,* he worried. He knew everything about every man she'd ever been with, and thankfully, she had never taken any of them seriously. There hadn't been one equal to the challenge of becoming a Castillo.

Tavo realized that his long silence had revealed his discomfiture and he regretted his lapse in control. "I'll make sure you have the capital to weather any storm, Sofi. If American investors take losses, that's our time to buy. Did they teach you at business school about how the industrialists expanded their empires on the back of the Great Depression? We should be so lucky."

She enjoyed her coffee and her eyes lingered over the plantation.

She's suppressing her first response, Tavo noticed. *Her first response had probably been to take a jab. But she didn't go with that. She refrained.*

"We may not need the expansion. I'm getting close to our exit threshold," she reported, returning to the agenda. "Our net worth is running just above thirty-five million on my side. We can cut over to purely legitimate businesses and we'll be good."

Tavo leaned back in his chair and chuffed. *Thirty-five million.* The glacial pace of profit accumulation in the corporate world always amazed him. He could generate thirty-five million in three days with narcotics. It'd taken her four years.

Sofía always came back to "the exit threshold." *Our* exit threshold, Tavo noted. She presumed his consent to her strategy —that someday they would abandon his drug operation in favor of legitimate enterprise. When they hit their "exit threshold" of clean cash, they would move off together, Tavo and Sofía, respectable business partners, welcome to walk among the elites without any taint of criminality.

Every time she said it, his disdain for "the elites" arose. Tavo ground his teeth, eager to pulverize the useless upper class between the twin stones of his formidable intellect and his hatred for aristocrats. He had sent his daughter into their world to study at their schools and master their markets, but he had never ceded one inch to the oligarchs. In the end, he longed to see them burn.

She must've noticed the foul wind pass across his face because she tacked an anxious footnote to her statement. "Papi. Nobody survives forever as a *narcotraficante*. You need to get out while you can."

He held up a finger, hearing something in the breeze. A dog barked at the edge of the plantation. After a moment's pause, he replied, "Nobody *yet* has survived. Everyone who has tried, so far, has been a fucking idiot. I apologize, *mi amor*, but you need to leave right now. Don't pack. Go to your helicopter now. I'll see you in Los Mochis soon. Go." He stood and lifted her from her chair, her face beset with momentary confusion. He kissed her on the forehead. "Go."

Sofía left her coffee cooling and walked back into the hotel without another word.

As soon as she disappeared around the plaster-spackled columns, Tavo slid the Glock G26 from the low-viz holster on his waistband and reflexively press-checked the chamber. Brass glinted back at him.

He moved to another patio table, this one surrounded by stone and adobe columns, the same columns that once ringed the hacienda of the Filadelfia before it had become an ultra-lux hotel. He left his coffee alongside his daughter's and dragged a wrought iron patio chair from behind a table and over to a column. To the staff, Tavo would look like he was being discrete. To another shooter, Tavo would look like he was taking cover and concealment.

There were no other guests. When he visited the Filly—one of his few, secretly-owned Latin American holdings—he ordered all other guest reservations cancelled, if for no other reason than to protect his quiet time in the morning. It was one of the few financial indulgences he allowed himself south of the American border.

This visit to the Filly had been a close call. Tavo's personal "Egghead," as he jokingly called his pet millennial Octavio, had flagged an up-tick in Guatemalan electronic chatter around one of Tavo's nicknames, "*El Mentor*." "*Mentor*" was a common enough word in Spanish, but *El Mentor* was a term worthy of note. The fact that the phrase had been bouncing around the Guatemalan Ministry of Defense had elevated the possible threat sufficiently that Octavio had raised the red flag. That, together with the barking dog, had set off Tavo's finely-tuned situational awareness.

Something was wrong.

Later, he might feel bad about possibly losing the Filly to the Guatemalan government. For the moment, his heart rate picked up and his endocrine system flooded with one of the few highs he actually enjoyed: *combat.*

Someone had quieted the dog.

Tavo knew the grey and brown mongrel the manager of the plantation kept at his shack along the southern wall. Tavo had threatened the dog half-a-dozen times with a stick when he walked the rows of coffee on his morning strolls. He had seen the *gerente* beat the living shit out of the dog for barking, to an early morning chorus of yelps and whines. This time, the barking had simply gone silent.

His Glock held at the low ready, Tavo considered his options. There was a good chance this was a false alarm, but if the blood pounding in his ears could be trusted, it was not. If the Guatemalan Ministry of Defense had anything to do with this interruption of his annual meeting with Sofía, they would come at him hard. Anyone who knew of his existence would also know that he was a formidable adversary. No petty criminal could maintain his level of secrecy and preparedness.

He had invested hundreds, if not thousands, of hours in American combat shooting schools. He also became indistinguishable from an American—without any Spanish accent whatsoever. He justified the allocation of time by telling himself that the training eliminated the need for personal security, which would otherwise increase his profile. But in reality, there were other reasons: Tavo took great pride in being one of the toughest gunfighters in the country. Maybe one of the top hundred in the world. That truth placed him in another universe as a man, set apart from the paunch-belly narcos and golf-playing oligarchs he so despised. He had honed himself into a hunter of men and had mastered the sword of the modern age: the firearm.

Tavo considered his first impulse; to slip deeper into the area of operation and engage the threat. He could move along the outside of the south wall—detecting security they may have posted at their rear. Then he could double back into the plantation at the big drainage grate, about halfway down the six-hundred yard wall. Given good timing, he would probably come up behind any assault force. Odds were better than ninety percent that he could pull off the buttonhook and backdoor the assaulters, racking up a few kills before they reset their OODA loop and figured out a way to come at him from a new angle. By then he would be gone, and he'd have a row of new notches on his leather gun belt.

The words of his pistol/carbine instructor at the DARC School of Combat Shooting, rang in his ears: *"When you open the Pandora's box of combat, no matter how good you may be, you release forces that cannot be controlled. The smart gunfighter walks away from an ambush, every time he can."*

Tavo was nothing if not smart, and he'd walked away from unnecessary risk scores of times. The words of his old instructor settled the debate. He would withdraw to his secret gun locker, hidden in the bowels of the Filly, quickly upgrade his weapons, and then exfil by the route he'd prepared when he first acquired the hotel.

He caught a glint of burgundy, many rows back in the coffee, and recognized it as a beret. *Kaibiles*. Guatemalan special forces. They were approaching this like an urban mission, maybe even like a photo op. *Otherwise, why would they wear the berets?* His thoughts swirled and his ears rang from the massive hit of dopamine surging through his endocrine system. Seeing the flash of the burgundy beret launched his hunter's impulse. Predatory chemicals pinged through his system like a trillion red hot ball bearings, heating up his reflexes, his muscles and his senses. His right hand shifted up the Glock and forward, sliding instinctively into his combat grip—high into the tang and his hand canting forward. From that grip, the shots would find their mark almost without aiming.

The thundering of Sofia's helo, rising into the air, released Tavo from any responsibility he had to restrain himself. He knew the Guatemalans had no air assets capable of downing her helicopter, other than a few World War Two P-51 Mustangs that the Americans had given them. If the Mustangs were in the air, lifting off from Guatemala City, half the country would've heard their massive engines by now.

With his daughter aloft, he was free to do some killing, if killing needed doing.

For now, he'd do the smart thing and withdraw. Later...perhaps.

Tavo re-holstered his Glock, massaged the tension out of his gun hand, and walked through the halls of the Filly while he worked down the initial rush of adrenaline, consciously lowering his respiration and heart rate, even taking a second or two to give *saludos* to the housekeeping ladies in the open-air passageways. He had seen nothing to indicate an assault other than that flash of burgundy. That's all he would ever see from professionals, and that had been a fortunate slip. Despite his calm, he tasted the storm that gathered.

The housekeeping ladies blushed at his attention. Tavo stood six-foot-two, stock-straight and of noble bearing, even in his early fifties, when one could expect a man to begin to stoop.

The ladies couldn't resist him, but Tavo never took advantage of the attraction. It amused him. It made him smile. But he had little interest in sexual conquest.

He channeled his mind toward musings about women. He forced himself to think about anything other than combat. It was a trick he'd been taught by another DARC instructor, Evan Hafer.

"Focus on your latest fuck buddy. Focus on the book you're reading. Focus on the running shoes you need to order from Amazon when you get back to base. Focus on anything other than the fight that's coming, and get your mind back to smart-mode before it kicks off, if the Gods of War give you that option. Your brain doesn't work for shit jumped up on adrenaline. Bring it down. Get back to stone-cold-killer mode. The guys who consistently win gunfights are the guys who don't get too spun up about winning gunfights."

Tavo smiled. With his hazel-brown eyes and salt-and-pepper close-cropped beard, the women soften as he turned his moneymakers on them. He enjoyed watching the cleaning ladies melt as he graced them with his approving gaze. Tavo had been ruthless about working out in the gym since his early forties. He alternated between sweat-drenched cardio and ass-busting weight-lifting. He was formidable, and even in his fifties, his virility would give a younger Sean Connery a run for his money.

Of course, Tavo understood himself; he knew he was a sociopath. Unlike most people imagined, it didn't mean he was without human emotions. He clearly enjoyed the pleasure of the cleaning ladies blushing and fidgeting under his attentions. He loved his daughter with all his soul. He enjoyed winning at the game of money. He wasn't a machine. He was a more efficient model of human being.

He descended the stairs into the old basement of the hotel. The detour in his focus had done its job and he found himself exhaling away the jitters. He sucked through his teeth and forced himself to smile as he stared into the retina lock on the gun locker. The lock responded by quietly clicking, and Tavo opened the thick, teak door and stepped into the closet. The LED lights flickered to life and revealed the load-out Tavo kept oiled and ready, everywhere he spent more than a couple days: two Heckler and Koch 416 AR15 rifles, a Crye AVS plate carrier with detachable chest rig, six loaded mags, a full-sized Glock 17 on a battle belt with extra mags and a white phosphor PVS-14 night vision monocular on an OpsCore bump helmet. He left the night vision and bump helmet on their hooks, but strapped on the rest with practiced efficiency. Within thirty seconds, he was set to go to war.

―――

Before leaving the gun locker, Tavo turned back inside and hunted around in a drawer for a final piece—a suppressor for the AR15.

The smart play would be to drop into the huge storm drain that ran under the plantation and pass right beneath the Special Forces team. He could abandon his combat kit in the tunnel and emerge on the edge of town without a shot being fired, free as a *quetzal* bird.

Tavo lifted the steel grate set in the patio tile and lowered himself into a six-foot clay tunnel. Antigua was like this everywhere—threaded throughout with artifacts from the earliest Spanish settlers. Only God knew why the Spanish had built such a huge storm drain in the middle of a hacienda. When they built it, the native Kakchikel Mayans frequently attacked and slaughtered the Spanish invaders. They made excellent slaves, right up until the moment they went berserk and murdered their overlords. Maybe the oversized storm drain had been built for escape even then.

Tavo trotted down the huge drain counting his paces, his feet pattering through the sheen of water trickling along the bottom of the old tunnel. He'd marked a feature in the escape tunnel at two hundred and seventy-five paces—an access grate at the back of the plantation. He found himself counting down.

Two-nineteen, two-eighteen, two-seventeen...

He knew he should keep going. The professional gunman in him insisted that the pro move would be to keep walking, right out into the sunshine of town. He should drop his $10,000 worth of combat gear in the mud at the bottom of the storm drain and drift away into another perfect, emerald morning. The green-shrouded volcanos towering over Antigua would welcome him with open arms, sociopathic heart notwithstanding.

Nothing good could come from stopping at that access grate.

One eighty-six, one eighty-five, one eighty-four...

He regretted not grabbing the bump helmet. He hadn't thought about how dark the tunnel would be even in the light of morning and the helmet had an LED flashlight clipped over the left ear. He was more afraid of tripping over a dead rat than anything. If he fell face-first into the muck, a low-profile escape into town would be harder. People would stare.

Again, the professional in him shook its head, preaching that the smart play was to walk away. Tavo always took the smart play. Yet, still he counted down his steps to the access grate.

Ninety-six, ninety-five, ninety-four...

The glint of light ahead, coming from the access grate, drove his primal urges forward, like reluctant lambs, and forced them to become thoughts.

He wanted to fight.

Such a stupid thing, but primal urges could not be ignored. Again, he was no machine. His bits of humanity demanded their due.

Ever the smart sociopath, Tavo had a system for this. He

pictured his emotions coming from his gut: as though his bowels were the bottom of a well and the emotions burbled up from below. By catching his emotions down low, Tavo found that he could identify them and deal with them. There would be no stopping his emotions—they would bubble up to his conscious mind regardless. But once identified, he could wrangle the feelings with a modicum of control. The trick would be to *not* let the feelings become thoughts. Thoughts—and decisions—generated by un-inventoried emotion were the Achilles Heel of human beings.

Tavo told himself no lies, and therefore, he lived as a lord among men; a god in man's clothing.

He reached deeper than his desire to fight and found...nothing. So, that was it. The originating emotion. He supposed the lust for combat was nothing new to mankind and that a faceless urge to kill had been making decisions for men for tens of thousands of years.

Now standing beneath the big iron grate, with green-tinted light of the plantation dripping down from above, he shrugged, conceding to a part of his brain that operated on chemicals rather than electrical impulses. Without really thinking about it, Tavo reached around to the pouch at the back of his battle belt and withdrew the little bottle of gun oil. He reached up and squirted oil on top of each hinge and let it sink into the crevices while he weighed his options.

Not all emotions were unproductive, he reasoned. This would be far from his first gunfight. He generally avoided killing since it drew so much attention. But in his line of work, killing was always on the table, and his competitors routinely overused the tool. Tavo had never gone to war against government troops, and if he was right about the burgundy beret, these were American-trained Guatemalan Special Forces. Rather than give him pause, the thought struck him as a rare opportunity.

He reminded himself that the originating emotion—his lust for combat—colored his judgment. With that realization in hand, he weighed the benefits.

For one thing, he was ready. Over the past three years, he'd slipped into dozens of classes at the best combat shooting schools offered by American Special Operations Forces veterans: DARC, Blackwater, Gunsite, Lamb, Haley, Costa, Yeager. He had been just another handsome Latin American man, welcome and befriended in the highest circles of American gun culture. Nobody had any inkling he stood at the head of the largest drug cartel north of Panama. His desire to fight wasn't just a primitive impulse; he had made ready for fifteen years, and fighting against American-trained adversaries would be his final validation.

Guatemala and the Filadelfia were lost to him. He already knew that. He wouldn't be fighting to regain his property. The Guatemalans probably didn't even know his real name or his face, but they had somehow connected the Filly to drug trafficking. Somewhere in his organically-designed organization, security had slipped and the Guatemalan Ministry of Defense—ever eager to appease the Americans with drug seizures—had sent a professional team to root him out. His security breach would be a puzzle for another day, and he would most certainly get to the bottom of it, no matter how deep he had to go.

No, the Guatemalans were making an exploratory incursion based on a speculative notion that the Filly, and its VIP guest, were connected to the Mexican cartels.

If Tavo ambushed their finest soldiers from behind, it would send a shockwave through the Latin American Special Forces community. The Kaibiles were considered some of the best, and they frequently trained other troops in the region. Killing even one of the Kaibiles would have a chilling effect on Special Forces, even in Mexico.

Somewhere between his bowels and his mind, the decision was made, and Tavo silently lifted the grate and peered out. He emerged against the stone wall deep inside the plantation. With only a hundred and eighty degree threat angle, it would be a good place to insert.

He enjoyed the sensation of lifting his body weight up and out of the storm drain. Five thousand hours of upper body work in the gym was a small price to pay for the gratification of using his body as a weapon in combat.

He crouched low and scanned the columns and rows of coffee, seeking any shape that did not belong. Fifty yards down a row, he found a Special Forces soldier, facing toward the west boundary, apparently on security. Tavo lowered himself to the ground and took his time setting up the prone shot. From his position, the coffee blocked his shot. He knelt and shifted back and forth until a window opened.

Zzzz-snap!

The 5.56 round passed through the neck of the Kaibil and dropped him to the ground.

With that single shot, Tavo had racked up ninety percent of the advantage of conducting this assault. He could lower himself back down the storm drain and call it a win. The rational justification for engaging the Kaibiles disappeared like the mist over the coffee.

Ambushing a Special Forces unit with a single man wasn't combat training. It was stupid.

Tavo popped off the ground into a crouch and Indian-stepped over to the dead man, scooping up his beret while scanning for threats. He jammed the too-small beret on his head and went hunting for the remainder of the team's rear security.

Stupid, stupid, stupid—the mantra rang in his head. Still he hunted.

He made his way toward the west wall, his ultra-expensive,

German AR15 at the ready, scanning down each row of coffee as it arched into the distance.

A man, a fine killing machine and death; the trifecta of a human predator's trade. Tavo smiled despite the objections clanging in his mind.

He almost passed the row, but something snagged at his consciousness. He stepped back and picked out the shape-that-didn't-belong and recognized it as the front three inches of a Tavor rifle. He could've tracked the shape back into the leafy, green coffee and sent a barrage of 5.56 into the man. Instead, Tavo waited, occasionally checking his back for threats.

He could *feel* the distance between himself and the metal storm grate, like a cave diver with a safety line, stretched to its limit, scratching across dozens of sharp rocks. Tavo would either need to withdraw back to safety or decide on a new path of egress. He concluded that the Kaibiles had inserted over the south wall. If he exfilled in that direction, he would risk coming face-to-face with their command element. He'd either need to fight through to the north or withdraw to the storm drain.

The Kaibil stepped into the open. Tavo's rifle rose of its own accord. The young man's death had already been written on the wind, and a series of automatic actions took over. Tavo sent a round, quickly followed by two more. The soldier hadn't even turned in the direction of the gunfire before crumpling to the ground. The rows of coffee echoed with a sound like three, quick snaps of a bullwhip.

Stupid, stupid, stupid...

Finally, Tavo's intellect regained full control and he retraced his steps back to the storm drain, his eyes hunting for another adversary.

There was no reaction to his suppressed rifle fire. The mist and the coffee plants must have absorbed the sound of his bullets, or more likely, had deprived the assaulters of a sense of where the shots had originated.

The Kaibiles would return to find their security element dead; probably the youngest members of their team. Psychologically, nothing would scare the forces of law and order more than this. Some part of every fighting man longed for a head-on fight. But the kind of opponent who murdered your security element would seem supernatural, as though the bullets had come from the clear, blue sky.

Fighting men could kill what they could see and understand. What really terrified them was dying without ever knowing the threat.

Maybe not such a stupid play after all.

Tavo dropped down the storm drain and quietly pulled the cover closed over him. The round grate settled into its steel collar with the crunch of rust-on-rust.

He pattered through the thin mud at the bottom of the tunnel toward the circle of light at the end. Now, with the animal carnality of combat behind him, questions flooded his mind.

Who had set him up?

Only one person had known he would be at the Filidelfia Hotel that morning, and she had just taken to the skies in a helicopter.

CHAPTER 3

NOAH MILLER
MILLER CATTLE RANCH, RIO RICO COUNTY, ARIZONA

Noah Miller counted thirteen trees on his property, and they were all cottonwoods. His daughter's tire swing had nearly rotted off the nylon rope on the big cottonwood by his stock watering pond.

Used to have, he reminded himself.

Used to have a pond.

Used to have a daughter.

The pond had been dry since July and the daughter had been gone for two years, three months and thirteen days.

Noah took another long pull of his Dos Equis, but it'd take a lot more than beer to put down the gnawing in the back of his throat. Noah knew this from ample experience; beer was good for ending the day, not putting down heartache.

He'd seen enough John Wayne and Liam Neeson to know that he was supposed to be going balls-out on a revenge plot. He knew it the same way he knew he was supposed to vote in the primaries and buy life insurance. It wasn't like he didn't know who had killed his family. It'd been one of the cartels. Zetas maybe. Quite possibly one of the smaller bands of smuggler-thugs. He would've recognized the head man, but probably not the others. He was too busy that afternoon trying to think of a way to keep them from murdering his wife and daughter.

But Liam Neeson would've tracked that shit down and sorted it out by now.

Two years, three months and thirteen days. Plenty of time to find five Mexican cartel soldiers among the thousands in Northern Sonora. Noah hadn't even tried. In the movies, the bereaved father came away from the funeral on fire to murder some sonofabitches. Noah came away from the funeral feeling like his flame had been snuffed out under a flood of remorse.

"Enough," Noah said aloud to the dirt lawn and the rotting tire swing. He took another pull of beer, happy to get a head start on the bottle of whiskey that would undoubtedly round out his evening.

His porch faced east, so he couldn't watch the sunset from there. But the sunset painted Miller Peak gold like an Aztec pyramid which was almost better. Leah had insisted he build the homestead facing east. She'd been a woman who always looked to what was coming and never what had passed. She preferred the sunrise to the sunset.

Maybe she'd used up all her sunrises. Maybe that's why Grandfather Death had come for her so young. Noah couldn't remember Leah ever sleeping in. Not once in all those years of courtship and marriage. He was pretty sure she woke to watch the dawn the day after she gave birth to their daughter Katya. He couldn't know for sure, because he'd been asleep.

Everything in the world had been a fucking wonderland to that woman. If Leah got punched in the face, she popped right up and celebrated the bruise. She'd been unstoppable, but this place—this dried-up desert ranch—had soothed her restless heart; right up until it killed her.

"Enough," Noah repeated. He didn't need another night of drinking by himself. Nobody ever needed a night of drinking by themselves. Drinking by oneself amounted to *prima facia* evidence that a man was doing a shit job of handling his affairs. He hadn't arrived at that conclusion himself. It'd been one of ten thousand pearls of wisdom imparted to him by his adoptive father.

Bill McCallister lived just fifteen miles northwest of Noah's ranch, on the backside of Wrightson Mountain. Noah had grown up on Bill's ranch and had learned the ways of manhood digging in its crumbled granite soil.

His actual father, who had given him these two sections of the family ranch in his will, lived in Ciudad Juarez with his three wives. He'd died five years ago. Noah never cottoned to his birth family's brand of religion, so Bill McCallister had taken him in at twelve years old. The old, broken down Green Beret needed young arms and a young back for the hundreds of chores on a cattle ranch. Noah's asshole birth father had been right about one thing: he would never conform to the stifling guilt and endless sermonizing of the fundamentalist Mormons in Ciudad Juarez. After Noah healed from leaving his mother, he'd come to see Bill McCallister's ranch as his rightful home—a stepping stone of fate and a waypoint of destiny.

Marrying Leah and making little Katya had only strengthened his sense of being at the right place at the right time. It was a fairy tale saga for a rough man with a stone-etched heart. The mornings when Noah awoke to share coffee on the porch with Leah—the two sipping and grinning as Miller Peak gave birth to the sun—felt like God winking at their family and tousling their hair.

It had been perfect, and Noah's cowboy heart had drifted away from the rodeo of barfighting and hard living and out to the pasture of honest work and gentle sunrises standing beside a woman who smelled like vanilla and looked like a rodeo queen.

And then it had all been ripped away. Two years later, Noah

had become just another dried up rancher, sitting on his porch, his past life dwindling in his rearview mirror.

He'd hashed this out ten thousand times, sitting on the decaying porch watching the rope swing die its slow death. The result was always the same: the hardness in the back of his throat tightened into a bony fist and the bottle of Jack Daniels in the kitchen cupboard started calling his name.

Before he could muster the will to go into the kitchen, Noah saw someone on his land. He sat up a little straighter and followed the man ducking in and out of the cattle in the south pasture. His loneliness hit him so hard that he didn't see the illegal as a trespasser or a Mexican or even a possible cartel smuggler. He saw him as salvation.

Noah whistled loudly enough to hurt his own ears. The man froze behind a cow. The cow got nervous and shuffled forward and the man shuffled with her.

Almost every night he saw illegal immigrants crossing over on his land. His ranch house was just a mile and a half from the border, and the border was nothing more than a chain-link this far from a town.

"*Doze Eh-keys!!*" Noah shouted, articulating an offer in the universal language of beer. "*Ven aca!*" He grabbed a second bottle from the bowl of ice, stood up and held them high.

Families rarely crossed on his ranch. The terrain was too rugged—too likely to end in death by heat stroke. But the men sometimes took their chances alone or in small groups. The kind of man who took his chances with the desert might take his chances with an American vaquero offering an ice cold bottle of beer.

But not this time. The illegal skittered around the cows and made a mad dash for the creek bottom.

"Damn. That's one fast Mexican," Noah remarked to himself. "The Mexican olympic team's loss is America's gain." He dropped back down into his chair. "No luck tonight. Guess I'll have to drink them all."

He helped himself to the Mexican's beer, popping the top off with a slight hiss. Noah didn't give a shit about the issue of illegal immigration. He didn't give a shit about anything people yapped about on Facebook or Instagrammar. In fact, he didn't give a shit about much at all. Everything he'd cared about had died in the space of five minutes, two years ago.

On second thought, that bottle of Jack sounded like a prayer. Like angels singing and little babies cooing. It sounded like a nap on a warm summer afternoon. It sounded like a bargain downpayment on all he had lost.

He got up from his chair, grabbed the bowl, tossed the ice water off the porch and went inside.

His half-full bottle of Dos Equis sat on the old wood of the deck, warming by degrees as the sunset reflected off the back of Miller Peak. The mountain, named after Noah's great grandfather, turned purple, then gray, then faded to black.

CHAPTER 4
TAVO CASTILLO
THE CITY OF LOS MOCHIS, SINALOA, MEXICO

Regardless of where he was in the world, Tavo never missed Catholic mass, nor did he ever go a week without confession and absolution. After narrowly avoiding arrest in Antigua, he called his lieutenants back to home base and they joined his family for Sunday mass.

Father Andrade sang the entrance hymn under his breath as he passed the Castillo family pew in procession, the young crucifer carrying the cross before him.

Like a bird that could never land, Tavo felt faith around him, but couldn't touch it. He accepted Catholicism completely, like he accepted the physics of the internal combustion engine. He knew himself as a sinner. But the same was true of all men in the eyes of God, he reasoned. For that purpose, God had given men the Church. Tavo had no compunction taking the church at its word, accepting without concern the forgiveness that the rites and absolutions offered.

The Catholic mass continued, and the men watched their sinful pasts float away on wisps of incense. Father Andrade moved into the liturgy, sonorously reciting the Psalm from memory. Tavo believed it to be the ninety-first:

"He who dwells in the shelter of the Most High will rest in the shadow of the Almighty. I will say of the LORD, 'He is my refuge and my fortress, my God, in whom I trust.' Surely he will save you from the fowler's snare and from the deadly pestilence."

Tavo accepted the words as personal direction, as he always accepted the liturgy. God gave instruction, somehow to every person in the mass at the same time. He didn't see this as mystical—rather as ultimate competency; God was the master manipulator of men.

As the Psalm said, Tavo had been lately "saved from the fowler's snare" and by offering Psalm Ninety-one, God was telling Tavo to prepare for the "deadly pestilence" as well.

"Surely he will save you from the fowler's snare and from the deadly pestilence."

Tavo had indeed prepared—far beyond anything ever conceived by government or cartel. The simple math of pestilence, for someone as emotionally detached as Tavo, had been easy. Collapse of society—due to pestilence of the viral, economic or ideological sort—came every generation or two, and those scourges reset the counter of civilization. He had no problem imagining the suffering that would come. He'd inflicted enough suffering that he could feel its proximity and taste the bitterness on his tongue.

It'd been almost a hundred years since the Great Depression, and there had been two close calls since then: the Cuban Missile Crisis and the Crash of 2008. By his reckoning, large civilizations took major hits every fifty years. The comfort and abundance in the western world stacked the odds against them, making them soft and stupid until something broke. The more drugs they sold, the more likely a collapse, and they were selling an awful lot of drugs.

Tavo had invested five percent of his American profits over the last five years to prepare for the next cataclysm. He'd resisted the urge to pull money out of America and bring it back to Mexico. There was nothing his money could do in Mexico that it couldn't do in America. Most drug lords needed the money at home to pay off corrupt politicians, police and judges—and to satisfy their desire to live like sheiks. By living under-the-radar, he had no one to pay off. He was like the mouse that shit inside the walls rather than on the kitchen floor. Nobody would ever know it existed.

His three lieutenants did the same. None of them had ever paid off a corrupt politician because all of them lived like well-to-do veterans instead of idiot egomaniacs. They had reinvented the *narcotraficante* lifestyle, and so long as nobody discovered their play, they would continue to rule their chunk of the world, fueled by the despondency of feckless American addicts.

But somebody had made a move on him. Odds were high, that same person sat in the family pew, reciting the mass with Tavo and Father Andrade. The thought made Tavo look down the bench, left then right.

Tavo's wife—Isabel—stood on his left. She'd come from money and Los Mochis had been her family home for over a hundred years. Like other oligarchs, she lived in a walled compound checkered with courtyards, fountains and gardens. If it hadn't already been her family residence, Tavo wouldn't have permitted the display of wealth. He'd learned from the grisly deaths of *narcotraficantes* before him: lavish spending drew politicians and bureaucrats like flies to a rotting corpse, each one seeking his maggot's bite. Virtually every narco Tavo had ever known had been taken down by corrupt politicians, each one inevitably dissatisfied with their bite of the profits. Tavo lived above that fray, choosing to leave the vast majority of his money in the United States and to wave the stink of wealth away from him and his family. As far as anyone knew in Los Mochis, except for perhaps the priests, Tavo was nothing more than a handsome husband who had married a wealthy heiress.

When Tavo looked at her in her Sunday dress, he could still see the beauty she'd once been, but it took a bit of imagination. She'd gone from being a stunning bride to a thickening mother to a slow-moving grandmother—though they had no grandchildren yet.

It'd been a long time since Tavo and Isabel had sex. Still, he hadn't violated his marriage vows. They slept in the same bed, sat together during the mass and he kissed her on the head when he got up to leave the dinner table. But a quiet, simmering enmity had been born of their separate lives. Tavo might suspect her of wanting him gone. Yet, there were things a Mexican oligarch family would never do, and sending the father of one's child to prison would bring dishonor to the family name. There was simply no possible way that Isabel had conspired to have him arrested. Family meant more to her than suffering through an ice cold marriage.

Their only child, Sofía, hadn't joined them for mass. Her plane hadn't arrived from the States in time to join them for church. Of course, Sofí knew of his criminal enterprise. She was its primary beneficiary, and every cent that poured over into her businesses was washed of any connection to drugs. Sofí had nothing to gain and everything to lose by her father being arrested. She constantly lobbied Tavo to leave narcotics, but her intention was to keep him out of jail, not send him to jail. As Tavo considered a betrayal of that magnitude, he shook his head —like a dog shaking off a scare. The strange reflex drew a disapproving look from his wife next to him in the pew.

Could Sofí have betrayed him?

Father and daughter had loved one another impeccably, and not even the turbulence of her teenage years had rocked that peace. Isabel had handled all childhood discipline with Sofí, on the rare occasion it had been necessary, and that'd left Tavo free to be a doting father. She was the ideal daughter and he was her picture-perfect father.

Unimaginable. The idea of her betraying him to the police was literally impossible for him to imagine. He moved on to likelier candidates: Beto, Alejandro and Saúl.

The three men sat on the right end of the family pew, half listening to the liturgy and half playing grab-ass with each other. While he watched, Alejandro poked Saúl in the ribs with a knuckle, causing Saúl to bobble like he'd sat on a pin. These three men managed almost a billion dollars of criminal enterprise, but given five minutes together, they devolved into the fraternal antics of bored soldiers. Somehow, the focused violence of Special Forces operators came part-and-parcel with a compulsion toward fuckery. It was as though the men counterbalanced the deadly seriousness of their craft with an equal measure of practical jokes, degenerate insults and raw stand-up comedy.

Tavo didn't understand it, but he knew to expect it—he'd killed plenty of men, women and children himself, and it hadn't made him one bit funnier. He didn't necessarily find the compulsion entertaining, but it played into the brotherhood he'd carefully engineered, so he let it pass. It made him wonder, had the bonds of brotherhood been strong enough to prevent at least one of them from trying to remove him?

He would never have called the three men "lieutenants"— not to their faces. It would violate the fabric of the relationship; a rapport he had woven with exquisite care over the last fifteen years. He played the role of their "counselor," casting himself as the obliging father of the group; the senior man in a brotherhood of equals. *El Canoso,* they called him in jest, exactly as Tavo wanted: *The Gray Hair.*

The "military" assaults they'd done together had been

orchestrated to some degree by Tavo. He'd dressed the operations up with staggering investments of cash, making the men feel like Navy SEAL DEVGRU operators hitting Al Queda strongholds rather than four drug dealers murdering their competition.

Tavo had studied the psychology of killing, war and brotherhood, and he knew the bonds that tied men together in clans. Nothing galvanized loyalty more than going to war beside another man, and Tavo made certain he and his lieutenants went into combat together every year or two.

As the liturgy moved into the New Testament, Tavo recalled the last assault he and his lieutenants had executed together, three months prior. If one of these three men had been set to betray him, the signs would be there, buried in the stripped-down truth of combat.

Tavo had gone all out for this assault. He'd contracted a civilian C-130 for a HALO jump—High Altitude, Low Open—over their target outside Guadalajara, Mexico. They'd come together to eliminate a threat to Beto, his longest-standing lieutenant.

Mostly, Tavo's job in the brotherhood consisted of deconflicting the three lieutenants. Inevitably, three strong-willed men would compete with one another over territory, profits and even over Tavo's favor. His primary job, for which he received fifty percent of each man's take, was to keep them working together like blood brothers.

His first lieutenant had fallen into his lap back while Tavo hunted for deer with wealthy Americans outside of Hermosillo, Sonora. Tavo had married well and dabbled in his father-in-law's tequila business. But he'd been looking for a big score—something that'd launch him from family money to *real* money. Even in his thirties, he knew that meant drugs and guns, which inevitably drew him toward the borderlands of Sonora. Big game hunting in Northern Sonora blurred the lines between drug runners and legitimate American business, and Tavo knew the right opportunity would find him there.

Beto Navarro had spent seven years as an American Navy SEAL, mostly serving in Iraq. He'd been an invited guest of a rich, American hunter in Sonora to pursue mulies, Coues deer and desert bighorn sheep.

A second generation Mexican-American, Beto hit it off with Tavo while they wandered the sprawling desert ranches, searching the hills and draws for trophy deer and sheep. Most of the ranches were owned by *narcotraficantes*, with small runways that serviced a fleet of single-prop airplanes.

It hadn't taken long for Tavo and Beto to befriend one of the biggest narcos in the area, drinking rum and Coke in all-night dirty joke sessions on the porch of the man's hacienda. Within a year, that same narco was buried under the desert sand and Tavo and Beto assumed operational control of his network of drug traffickers.

Over the next two years, Tavo and Beto grew the enterprise and added two more operators to their family. Saúl had been a Mexican *Fuerzas Especiales* and Alejandro served in the *Xatruch* Honduran elite commandos. None of the men had served in the same unit which allowed Tavo to build a team without previous loyalties complicating their four-way brotherhood. But something had gone wrong. A squad of Kaibiles didn't show up in the middle of a posh hotel in full battle-rattle for nothing. Someone had screwed him and Tavo would find the telltales of that betrayal if he looked closely enough.

He recalled his three lieutenants sitting in the cargo compartment of the ferociously-loud C-130, lit only by the red glow of the bay lights, loaded down with tactical equipment and smiling like boys on their way to the swimming hole.

The four operators drifted into the target field from higher than was really necessary and left their parachutes on the ground. Tavo had stashed twenty other parachutes under a trash pile, and they dug those out and tossed them around, making it look like an entire squad had landed in the night. With their ruse prepared, they moved toward the small compound of the federal police commander.

As planned, Beto climbed to the top of a nearby water tower and supplied overwatch with his suppressed LaRue OBR rifle. Just in case, he'd lugged a F&N 249 SAW up there as well, with a hulking drum of 5.56 rounds.

The other three men rolled over a dark corner of the wall, spreading out and pointing in with their H&K 416 AR rifles as they crossed the open danger area all at once. The two junior policemen who served as nighttime security for the police commander were posted on the front corners of the hacienda, giving Tavo and his men plenty of space to circle them from behind. They found both men sitting in plastic chairs, no doubt taken from the servant's quarters. One of them chain-smoked cheap cigarettes and the other dozed. Both of them cradled FN/FAL rifles like anchors around their necks.

Tavo and his men planned to hit the guards simultaneously in two teams, since Beto's overwatch couldn't cover the man on the far side of the house. Tavo went solo and was to give the "go" signal over the radio before taking down the guards.

A split second before he keyed the mic, a woman staggered out of the servant's quarters, slamming the door. Both police guards jumped to attention, probably afraid of being caught slack-jawed in their chairs. The woman stumbled across the courtyard, half asleep, and headed toward a building that must have contained the toilet. The fact that the servant's quarters had no toilet had been missed by Tavo during his recon of the target.

He called in the new threat over the radio.

"One straggler in the courtyard. Three threats total. Execute on my shot."

His AR15 spat two suppressed rounds hitting the young sentry in the head both times. He shot the sleep-drugged woman three times in the chest. The woman's thick legs folded to the side and she collapsed in the courtyard. Her ample bust heaved as she struggled for life even as her blood sieved into the crabgrass. The woman keened a loud, dying breath and he lined up for another shot—this one to the head. But, the sentry on Tavo's side—gushing blood from a double head wound—wobbled to his knees and fired a thundering burst of 7.62 from his FN.

Tavo dove back around the edge of the house. Within ten seconds, Alejandro and Saúl circled behind the wounded man and ripped him full of holes. But the cat had been let out of the bag. The big FN rifle had undoubtedly woken up half the town.

Three minutes later, Beto radioed from the water tower, "Two trucks approaching from the police substation. Permission to engage."

The combat rifle training Tavo had received in American shooting schools hadn't offered him much in the way of force-on-force scenarios like this one. He'd read a couple books on mission planning, but fighting in a three-dimensional threat matrix was different than reading about it.

He pictured the federal police commandant still alive in the hacienda, probably arming himself. He factored in additional guards inside. He considered the police truck. He saw each of his men on the tactical map, spread out in the courtyard and hovering over the battle space from the water tower. With the chess board arranged in his mind, Tavo acted.

"Negative, Raven. Hold for now." Once Beto opened up with the SAW, the forces on the ground would focus on his muzzle flash. It'd be a bitch for Beto to climb down out of the tower. Tavo decided to save his wild card for later.

"Jaguar One is breaching the side door," he informed his team. "Jaguar Two and Three, engage hostiles at the front gate."

Given the compressed timeline now forced on them by the police response, he would have to kill the wife and teenage daughter. Tavo preferred to keep that brand of killing off his mens' conscience whenever possible, so he went in alone. He suffered no qualms about killing women and children. A murder was a murder, and he hadn't seen anything to convince him that women and children cost more penance than a man.

He changed his mag, kicked in the side door and cleared the hacienda in a relentless, fluid movement. From room to room, Tavo repeated the same cadence taught in American close quarters battle schools: throw open the door, step to the position of dominance, sweep from the area of greatest threat to the center of the room, check behind any obstacles, kill anything that moves, withdraw to the hall, check his six, then move to the next room. It was far from a perfect system—a person hiding in a closet could blast even a proficient shooter. But extreme violence of action gave the assaulter a distinct advantage.

Tavo burst into the master bedroom and found the police commander partially hidden behind his wife, pointing a revolver at the door. Tavo stepped inside so quickly that the man shot the doorframe. Before the commandant could work the sluggish, double trigger again, Tavo placed two shots in his chest and two into his wife's chest. Both slumped to the ground. Tavo leaned forward and placed one more round into the commandant's forehead.

Ever the meticulous professional, he finished clearing the room—behind the bed, the closet, the armoire—then stepped back into the hall. He cleared all the rooms in the hacienda, but the daughter never appeared. Either he'd missed her or she wasn't home.

He shrugged. "Jaguar One. House clear. Exfil, exfil, exfil."

"Good copy," all three men replied. Gunfire boomed from the front gate as the police response arrived.

Tavo updated his mental chessboard. The police at the front of the hacienda would be grossly outgunned and out-skilled and leaving a yard full of dead policemen would have long-term benefits for him. Journalists would attribute the assault to a much larger force than just four men.

"Belay last," he radioed. "Jaguar Two, maneuver to the west and let the cops into the courtyard. Raven: hit them with the SAW once inside the wall."

For the next two minutes, the bloodletting raged. Alejandro swooped over the front wall of the compound and chewed up several of the policemen before they knew they'd been flanked. The surviving police fled into the walled courtyard where Beto and Saúl ate them like a steak dinner.

When the *mad minute* subsided, Tavo radioed, "Jaguar One: exfil, exfil, exfil. Route Alpha."

They climbed out of the compound the way they'd come—over the back wall—and jogged a kilometer through the fields to where Tavo had stashed four powerful BMW motorcycles. Their escape would've been less conspicuous on light bikes, but Tavo's primary purpose for the mission was better served with burly, 1,200cc road monsters. Putting that sort of shine on an op would be money well spent.

As dawn broke, the four warriors roared through the town of Ixtlán del Rio, grinning like fools, dodging in and out of early morning truck traffic. They hurtled back to Tepic to offload their gear at a safe house and do some serious drinking and storytelling.

Three of the four men lived for moments like this—time

shared in company of warfighters, the blood of their victory still on their hands. Only one of the four understood the real purpose. Only Tavo could stand above it all—the grand chessboard of life—and enjoy the brotherhood for what it truly was: four men harnessed to one man's ultimate goal.

But thinking back to that time in Tepic after the raid, drinking, playing cards and telling war stories, Tavo saw no clues to who might betray him. The four had prospered together. They'd gone to war together. And they seemed to sincerely enjoy one another. Not only was Tavo not seeing who might betray him, he had no idea why anyone would betray him in the first place.

Everyone benefitted: Isabel, Sofi, Beto, Alejandro and Saúl. Everyone, for the most part, had everything they wanted. They were all rich beyond their wildest dreams, and except for a few details, they all had the life they desired.

But as someone once said, when you have eliminated the impossible, whatever remains, no matter how improbable, must be the truth.

———

As his family and his criminal brotherhood stepped out of the whitewashed Sagrado Corazón church, Tavo blinked back the relentless Sinaloa sunshine. His meticulous recollection of the last six months had yielded nothing. All three of his lieutenants had behaved like professionals and friends. His wife, though slightly perturbed by her husband and his guests, was the furthest thing from a conniver. His daughter gave no sign whatsoever of treachery. He was no closer to understanding the Kaibil attempt to arrest him in Antigua than he'd been two days before.

Tavo's three lieutenants walked onto the stone steps of the cathedral together, stretching their limbs, slapping each other

on the back and ruffling one another's hair like muscular boys; puppies happy to be free from the hardwood pews.

The assault on the police commandant outside Guadalajara had been two months previous, and it continued to pay rich dividends. Their fondness for one another and their joy at being reunited buzzed with their secret life as professional killers—locked behind their smiles and their teasing. They were battle-field-tested operators. The four of them had served the Reaper, ridding the world of another hypocrite and scaring the hell out of corrupt politicians and cops throughout the region.

He couldn't care less about all the self-congratulatory nonsense, but he was happy with the shockwaves the assault generated. Anyone the federal police commander might have told about Tavo's organization had undoubtedly read the same newspaper articles. The all-caps headlines blared about an elite force of at least twenty paratroopers who had descended on a federal police commander's home, killing everyone around the compound, including eight policemen. Eleven were dead and not so much as a drop of blood or a single hair had been discovered from the assault force—just empty magazines, shell casings and a bunch of used parachutes.

The message had been clear to anyone looking to profit from their shadowy group: the juice wasn't worth the squeeze. Tavo's danger with the federal police were buried with the commandant and his wife.

But that message hadn't reached Guatemala. Or, maybe it had. Maybe it explained why the Guatemalan Ministry of Defense had employed top shooters to take down Tavo at the Filadelfia Hotel. But Beto's and Tavo's aliases lived in a different universe. Tavo was Beto's son's godfather, and other than their family get-togethers two or three times a year, there was nothing to tie Beto to Tavo. No financial or corporate linkage existed between the men.

Tavo toyed with the idea that the American FBI had gotten involved but that seemed unlikely. The FBI would've picked him up last week in Charleston instead of using Guatemalans and hassling through the extradition process.

The most likely leak would be a back-channel whistle-blower, mouth-to-mouth, from Tavo's organization to the Guatemalan Ministry of Defense. In his experience, that was usually how things worked in Latin America: somebody's cousin talked to his uncle's *padrino* who was drinking buddies with the Guatemalan Deputy Minister of Defense. Nine times out of ten that's how things got done from the Mexican border down to the Amazon River: people shot off their mouths and weird connections were made. But that meant someone had shot off their mouth in the first place, and Tavo only connected to the organization through these three men.

Tavo sincerely doubted that Beto, Alejandro and Saúl were the source of the leak, since their egos prevented them from seeing Tavo as their leader anyway. They had no reason to talk to anyone—even each other—about how Tavo's fifty percent added up to a bigger piece of the pie than any one of them received individually. People generally avoided seeing things that made them feel small. "Fifty percent" had a very nice ring to it, and the split had been engineered to keep friction between him and his lieutenants to a minimum. Even one more percentage point in Tavo's favor would've increased the risk of jealousy tenfold. He'd structured the deal perfectly, managed his lieutenants perfectly and he'd comported himself without error —never saying or doing anything that would sow jealousy toward himself. In his experience, people were predictable, and the rollicking Special Forces operators goofing off on the steps of his cathedral were more predictable than most. Tavo looked out over the square in front of the cathedral as he struggled in his mind to see what he might have missed.

Tavo's wife, Isabel, stepped up to his side after paying her respects to Father Andrade.

"How long will they be staying?" she asked about the men screwing around down by the street. "How many do I need to feed?"

With their Sofi now grown, the couple rarely had anything to talk about other than family logistics. These days, it seemed like Isabel did little more than cook and watch television.

"They'll be leaving tomorrow morning."

'Very well." She ambled down the stone steps toward their waiting SUV.

———

When they returned to the hacienda after church, Sofía was there, perched on a barstool in her mother's kitchen, leaning toward the small television, where most days, her mother watched *telenovelas*.

Sofía launched off the barstool when she saw the men.

"*Tios!*" She hugged and kissed each man on the cheek, greeting the men who had been her "uncles" for half her life. All eyes drew back to the little TV.

"Someone hit Los Angeles with a nuclear bomb," Sofía explained after giving her father a quick kiss.

It only took Tavo a few moments to revise the meeting agenda in his mind. They probably wouldn't be talking much about their leak. Much greater concerns had arisen.

———

For the first time, Tavo asked if Sofía could join them for their meeting.

"*Amor*," Tavo started the meeting by turning to his daughter.

"Tell us about the American economy."

"They're in trouble." Sofia gestured toward the TV in the kitchen. "With this nuclear bomb, I don't know if they can recover. It seems like an isolated terrorist thing, but the markets were already coming apart a few days ago. I don't think they can take two hits in a row. At best, they'll slide into a depression like the nineteen thirties. At worst, the economy will collapse. The bomb will zero-out hundreds of billions, maybe a trillion, in real estate values in California. They can't absorb that kind of loss. It's bigger than insurance companies. It's even bigger than government."

Tavo shared a knowing look with his three lieutenants. They'd invested heavily to prepare for an economic disaster, but their preparations were nothing to discuss in front of his daughter.

Beto smacked his hands together and jumped out of his chair with a big smile, like a man who just hit twenty-two black on the roulette wheel. Sofia raised her eyebrows and jumped from face to face, one-at-a-time, looking for an explanation as to why Beto would celebrate a calamity.

"How does this affect us?" Tavo asked her, drawing her attention away from Beto.

"Many of my businesses will get wiped out by a depression —they're too young to survive a market collapse. But my Mexican petroleum play could make millions, maybe even billions. The Iranian attack against the Saudi pipeline made my investment in Mexican gas look like a winning lottery ticket."

Tavo had secretly assured the success of her investments in Mexican petroleum. What she had been chalking up to good fortune and smart investing had actually been a masterstroke engineered by her father. Three years before, the Mexican government changed their national constitution to allow American energy companies to return after over eighty years of being exiled. The Mexican national oil company, Pemex, pumped almost a billion barrels of oil per year, but more than half of Pemex' production was being stolen—some by illegal taps drilled into their sprawling network of gas pipelines, but most stolen from within the rotted-out bureaucracy of Pemex itself. As a result, Mexico was forced to import seventy-five percent of its oil and gas even though they had billions of barrels just off their coast.

Tavo didn't give two shits about Mexican energy independence, but he knew an opportunity when he saw one. The other Mexican cartels had captured most of the gasoline graft, building oil and gas theft into a criminal industry as profitable as drug trafficking. Rather than fight for a slice of the criminal pie, Tavo architected a scheme to stamp out the corruption, channel the profits toward his daughter and launder hundreds of millions of dollars in the process.

In a pact with the Zeta cartel, Tavo redirected his chunk of drug profits from the states of Texas, New Mexico, Arizona and Colorado to the Zetas in exchange for backing out of gas theft. The Zetas had been the biggest gas thieves of all, so he choked the theft issue down to a minor nuisance with that one swap. To have his cartel pay tribute to the Zetas sweetened the deal for those idiot egomaniacs. It made the Zeta boss feel like hot shit.

Simultaneously, Tavo paid Alejandro, his lieutenant over the southwestern United States, to train and equip a team of Mexican-American assassins, turning them into a professional hit squad on par with any Tier One military unit. He spent lavishly on the project, resulting in a razor-sharp team to conduct ambushes against the white collar gas thieves within the Pemex bureaucracy. After a dozen assassinations of the most corrupt Pemex executives, word got around. The tie-wearing crooks stopped stealing almost overnight. Once Alejandro's team finished its intimidation kills against Pemex executives, Tavo sent them to teach paramilitary tactics to their gang soldiers. The shadow cartel claimed thousands of young dealers; surprisingly disciplined, armed and now, militarized.

Sofia moved into the gap left by the retreating thieves with a legitimate energy corporation, and took over a huge chunk of oil and gas distribution. It made her look like the hero of the hour. Tavo shut out the criminal enterprise and then set Sofi up as a catcher's mitt for Mexican petroleum profits without having to move a single dollar across the U.S./Mexican border. Both her energy company and the Mexican military were winning big points with the Mexican president, the news media and the Mexican public. The oil shortages lifted, and Mexicans could buy their own gas again.

In the gas scheme, Tavo had weighed much more than just profits, money laundering and public approval. His Pemex shell game had been part of a larger plan—an opportunistic strategy to dominate the region if anything should shake the American economy. Controlling the distribution of Mexican gasoline gave him a stranglehold on trucking. Trucking gave him a stranglehold on food. Food gave him a stranglehold on *everyone*.

These were exactly the kinds of bets Tavo liked—and the kinds of bets his psyche armed him to win against lesser men. Human beings were beset by psychological fallacies: irreparably broken thinking patterns that ignored long-odds risks and focused on the here-and-now. Tavo didn't mind placing scores of long-odds bets against unlikely outcomes, especially since those bets were usually cheap to place. The Mexican gas bet had been the perfect example of a long play with good short term gains and a chance to sweep the table if things went really bad. Not only had it paid off in the medium term, but it looked like it might make him powerful beyond his wildest predictions.

Tavo fancied himself as a modern-day J. Paul Getty—the man who made billions by investing in failed stocks during the

Great Depression. Tavo planned a much bigger play than Getty—the ultimate "bear market" hedge. He would corner the gas market and set himself for massive gains in a *future* depression. Beto had jumped out of his chair because their longest, deepest bet looked like it might pay off. Their cartel had everything to gain by the American economy going south.

"Is there civil disorder in America?" Tavo asked his daughter. Civil disorder would be the precursor to total meltdown—the point of no return.

"Los Angeles is a mess, of course. People are fleeing like refugees—by car, boat and motorcycle. There were already some inner city riots last night because of the stock market trading halt and because of some power problems in L.A. No word yet on whether all this is a terrorist attack or not. So, yes. There's definitely civil disorder."

It sounded precisely like what they'd been hoping for. He thought the attacks were likely terrorism accelerated by some old fashioned bad luck. Random chance worked like that.

Even in Vegas, a craps table can crap out ten times in a row. The odds are on the order of sixty million-to-one. However impossible that seems, it happens once every three years. And that means it *can* happen twice in the same week. Random chance doesn't work like people imagine. Very strange events, like a dice roll of seven ten times in a row or like two nuclear attacks in the same week, are certain given enough time. In this universe, the strange is commonplace.

Tavo took the long bets that nobody else could see. He was the kind of bettor who kept a stack of chips on the Hardways, stepped back from the craps table, and waited for the big payday. He didn't mind losing money in the short term, and he certainly didn't mind watching other people lose it all. He and his boys had placed a big bet on the Hardways—betting against the western economy—and odds were looking good. The nuke in Los Angeles had put them over fifty-fifty. If the civil disorder spread, they'd be in the big money.

"How's it going with General Bautista?" Saúl asked Sofía. Tavo noticed that Saúl tucked his hair behind his ear.

She brightened. "Thank you for reaching out to him for me. He's got patrols accompanying sixty-five of our most problematic gas delivery routes. Robbery of our trucks have dropped to nothing."

The men shifted in their chairs, crossing their legs and flexing their arms. Alejandro leaned forward and added, "He's one of the good ones. He was base commander when we cross-trained with Mexican Special Forces. Bautista would hammer back drinks with us at the enlisted bar on weekends. When he got shit-faced, he'd shout, 'one tequila, two tequila, three tequila, floor!' All the SF guys would join in. He's probably the highest ranking officer I've ever seen close the bar with the Joes."

Tavo watched his men preen for Sofía; married men, all. He couldn't blame them. She was one of those women whose magnetism multiplied by ten when she started talking. Her eyes blazed hazel and her cheeks had that rare, Spanish-Mexican rosiness. Her quick wit, expansive intelligence and indefatigable optimism vibrated with *goodness*. If she weren't his blood, and if she didn't despise his criminal enterprises, he'd worry about her taking his place at the head of his organization.

"The General and I have shared many drinks, and he's always been the perfect gentleman." She smiled.

"Well, my darling. What comes next you won't want to hear." Tavo sat up and reached for his glass of *agua de jamaica*.

"I assume it has to do with the men I saw crawling around the Hotel Filadelfia as I flew away?"

"I'm sad to say that it does." Tavo took a sip.

"Uncles, please talk sense into my *papa*. You've done enough. I would be thrilled to work with the four of you in *real* business.

Actual business. You'd be marvelous successes and it'd be the same thrill as...what you're doing now. Please talk some sense into my father."

The men shifted in their seats and their eyes wandered. Tavo guessed what they were thinking: Sofía had no idea what it felt like, doing what they did.

She apparently read the room and knew she had said too much. "I'm sorry *tios*, I love you all and I want you to be safe." Sofía stood, went to Beto, pinched his cheek and kissed the other. Then she moved to each of the men, hugging and kissing them on their cheeks in turn.

"Nos vemos al almuerzo." She waved as she left. "See you at lunch." Tavo noticed her shoulder's slump a little as she went back inside to help her mother in the kitchen.

"Who fucked us, *Canoso*?" Beto's eyes caught fire as soon as Sofía stepped out of earshot. The meeting had been called to talk about the hit on the Hotel Filidelfia.

"I don't know yet," Tavo admitted. "It smells like someone from inside our circle. The assaulters were Kaibiles, so the hit had to originate from the Guatemalan Ministry of Defense."

"Maybe American agencies pulled the trigger?"

"No, I don't think so." Tavo shook his head. "The CIA or the FBI could've picked me up any of a dozen times in the U.S. If they could've, they would've. This is something else."

"How'd you escape and evade, Boss?" Alejandro asked.

"I'm nobody's boss," Tavo corrected. "I had to shoot two of the Kaibiles," he lied. He shot them because he wanted to. These were professional soldiers and they knew the game of life and death. They would be okay with killing their brothers-in-arms, so long as it was necessary.

"I don't think the hit on the Filly is our biggest concern right now," Tavo changed the subject.

"Really?" Alejandro furrowed his brow. "How could a hit on us not be our biggest concern? Isn't that why you called the meeting?"

"Yes, but if America keeps on this downward spiral, government threats might not be a problem for us anymore. They'll evaporate."

The men nodded and stared into their corners of the hacienda courtyard. It wasn't the first time they'd talked about a collapse of the western economy. They talked about it every time they'd met for almost a decade. Their slack jaws and silence belied the truth: they never really thought it would happen. It just seemed so *weird,* like waking up to discover that aliens had landed. Even though they'd made a game out of preparing for the *Planet of the Apes*, they hadn't actually believed it.

"What's the point of no return?" Beto asked, watching the little water fountain in the courtyard burble its endless loop of water. "When do we know if the U.S. economy has flipped for sure?"

"End of the week. Maybe sooner," Tavo considered the rumors of bank closures he'd heard that morning. In 1929, that'd been enough to tip the U.S. into the Great Depression, but now with the Federal Reserve and the stock markets being smarter, maybe the U.S. economy could absorb the hits. There was a chance they could pull out. "We should know by Friday," he repeated.

"We have more than a brigade of trained guys. We have weapons and ammo. What are we going to do with them, besides bunker up with our families at the ranch?" Alejandro wondered out loud. The three lieutenants hadn't thought much past initial survival. Tavo, on the other hand, had much bigger plans.

Their ranch in Hermosillo—the first property taken by Tavo and Beto from a drug lord—had been built up as a survival retreat for these four men and their families. Tavo never visited the ranch because the buildings looked exactly like what they were: a castle. It was a classic "drug lord" thing to do—build a thick-walled compound that fairly screamed "criminal mastermind."

Tavo paid his twenty-five percent to see the ranch built and stocked without complaint, but he'd never stepped foot on it. Over the years, the lieutenants had packed the ranch with military vehicles, light and heavy weapons, food, ammunition, water systems, solar systems, cattle, pigs, chickens and even an old attack helicopter. The only good thing Tavo could say about the high-profile project was that they'd placed the compound dead-center in the middle of 100,000 hectares of land, well away from prying eyes. In northern Sonora, one more narco compound was barely a blip on the radar of the local gossip network.

"I think we may need to look at being in a different business." Tavo let the news sink in while he furrowed his brows like a concerned father. "Are any of your families overseas at the moment?"

The men shook their heads. Beto's son—Tavo's godson—had recently started college at the University of Pennsylvania, and it'd be easy to get him back to Mexico even if flights stopped.

Tavo stood from his chair. "Maybe it's best if our families all head to the ranch, at least for the weekend."

The men nodded and dug their cell phones out of their pockets, drifting to private corners of the courtyard to call their wives.

Fifteen minutes later, they regrouped in the hacienda. The shadows stretched and the Los Mochis heat broke for the evening.

"Tavo—you were saying something about going into a

different business. What's that?" Alejandro's voice went up an octave. He didn't like change and was bound to object.

Tavo worked this conversational strategy even with his closest friends: he dropped bits of information and then backed away, forcing them to come to him for more.

We pursue that which retreats from us.

Tavo never pursued. Even as a young man with his wife, he would never initiate sex. It was a miracle they had a child at all. As far as pursuing other women beside his wife, Tavo would never expose himself like that. Sex wasn't worth the vulnerability that came with it. He enjoyed being admired by women and his interest stopped there.

Now that he had the men on the edge of their chairs, Tavo explained. "If the economy goes down, the narcotics trade will fold. It will be like trying to sell cocaine to Africans. Nobody will have anything of value."

Saúl picked up the counterpoint. He had a habit of playing the devil's advocate in the group. Tavo didn't mind. Saúl rarely debated with any conviction. "They might still want the coke and heroin to avoid reality—you know—to get away from their worries."

"I don't doubt that people will still want drugs. I doubt they'll have anything we want in return. The value of a dollar will be highly dubious after this week." His words sent the men back to their thoughts, just as Tavo had planned.

After listening to the fountain for a moment, Beto broke the silence. "We have everything we need to weather the storm at the ranch. How can we make profit *after* the storm?"

Tavo enjoyed moments like this; moments where his lieutenants were reminded how much they needed him. "Like always, we find a market gap and exploit it. If the American economy collapses, what *thing* will be in greatest demand, least supply and that we're already prepared to deliver?"

"Food?" Beto posited. "Northern Sinaloa could feed half of America."

"Maybe," Tavo agreed. "As of now, we have no distribution system. Food would be a thousand times the volume of drugs. We'd have to build a new distribution system or take it from someone, and that would require time. The summer harvest ended in July and the winter harvest doesn't start again until January. We're in late September, so there's nothing to pick for another three months. Maybe that'll work out perfectly, or maybe half of America will have already starved to death by then. Still, if we figure out a food distribution system to feed America, how would they pay us? What will they have that we want?"

He already knew the answer, but the cat-and-mouse served as a reminder of how much his lieutenants needed Tavo to do their thinking. He wanted them to see him as *the man with the plan*.

"They'll need protection..." Beto declared. All eyes turned to him. "They'll need to be controlled and protected, especially if their government shits the bed."

"Excellent, Beto." Tavo nodded. It was clear that he'd already reached the same conclusion. "If we lost our government here in Mexico, it wouldn't be a big deal. Local governments, old families, cartels, and even gangs would fill the gaps. The cartels are already governing in a lot of places. If America lost its government, though, it'd be like a herd of cattle set loose in a china shop. It'd be total destruction. Americans don't know how to feed themselves. As Beto pointed out, they're counting on Sinaloa to supply ninety percent of their fruits and vegetables this winter. With our army, and our gasoline, we have what Americans want: *to be protected.* And to be told what to do. Our control would be the new drug—and they would welcome us with open arms...*if* their government fails."

CHAPTER 5

NOAH MILLER

MCCALLISTER RANCH, FIFTEEN MILES OUTSIDE
PATAGONIA, ARIZONA

Noah cranked the windlass stick through the wire until the wire sang with tension and the old man's gatepost stood straight up and down. He checked the plumb with his bullet level. It still leaned a bit north to south. He put his shoulder to the post and shoved hard. The bullet level confirmed that he'd nailed it—the gatepost stood plumb and true. He started thinking about doubling up on the tension wire for good measure.

"Stop," the old man shouted. He carried two red, plastic cups in his hands, probably iced tea. "You never did know when good was good enough. And I could've repaired that gate myself."

A neighbor of Bill's had backed into the gatepost while picking up a calf almost two weeks back. While waiting for his tea, Noah had gone to work fixing it for his adopted father.

"How long were you going to leave it like that—all catawampus?" Noah stood back and admired his work.

"It's in the nature of youth to criticize one's betters." Bill sighed and handed Noah the cup.

This was one of their favorite games—talking as though Noah was still a boy and as though Bill was a decrepit old man.

Noah was thirty-five, and Bill McCallister, despite his injuries from military service, was a ramrod-fit sixty-two years old.

When two men spent as much time together as these two had, they devised their own means of self-entertainment. Noah and Bill employed at least ten standard routines of good-natured ribbing.

"Well now," Bill admired his son's repair job. "You sure you don't want to concrete this all in and replace the gate posts with some of that well pipe in the east pasture? Then we could build the cows a little cabana inside the corral. We could hire some boys to serve them umbrella drinks and give them massages."

"I apologize for fixing your gate like a real man should. You probably had a roll of duct tape set aside for the job." Noah sipped the iced tea.

"Do not ever disrespect duct tape." Bill pointed a finger at Noah's chest. "A real man knows that duct tape is one of the greatest inventions of the twentieth century. It's what truly and finally separated *homo sapiens* from the Neanderthals. To real men, duct tape is sacred and you best watch what you say about it."

"I stand corrected." Noah bowed his head and chuckled.

"Did you catch the news about Los Angeles?" The old Green Beret changed the subject.

"No." Noah glanced about the ranch, searching for other projects he could hammer out. "Why should I care about Los Angeles?"

"Hmph." Bill gave Noah a disapproving look. "The least you can do, while you're trying to find the bottom of that bottle is to listen to the news while you're doing it."

"I prefer music. I drink with the Man in Black--the only recording artist who pairs perfectly with Tennessee whiskey. Jonathan R. Cash."

"Apparently, you learned at least one thing from me," Bill

nodded. "And that's not his actual name. Don't go saying that to someone who knows better... You're not going to ask about Los Angeles, so I'll just tell you. The *durks* hit 'em with a nuke, son. It didn't do much damage, but those bastards attacked 'em with a no-bullshit nuclear weapon."

"It finally happened? So, did we hit back?" Noah looked off to the west, as though he might see a mushroom cloud two thousand miles away in Los Angeles.

"They don't know who to glass. The nuke came in on a sailboat and any evidence is either underwater or floating around in the stratosphere."

"I'll be damned. Just like that? Out-of-the-blue?" Noah found himself caring more than usual about the outside world. This bit of news could actually reach the borderlands.

And it could give him a window of opportunity.

Bill studied his face. "You really didn't know, did you? I worry about you, Noah." Bill gave him a look that meant *all bullshit aside.* Hard drinking wasn't something one cowboy brought up with another cowboy. Not until it became an issue with the law. Drinking oneself to death in the safety of one's own kitchen fell into the category of "none of anyone's damn business."

"How about you?" Noah fired back, steering the conversation into safer waters. "Did you wake up today caring about the fate of the United States of America? I thought you'd sworn all that off—the red, white and blue and all that. Didn't you fight under that flag? Didn't you take a bullet for them?"

"Hmph," Bill shrugged and stared at the mountains surrounding his ranch. "I'm so close to Mexico and so far from all that yap, yap, yapping about transgender bathrooms and free college. Americans and me aren't even the same species anymore... But don't think I don't know you're trying to throw me off your trail, son. Have you been listening to the news or haven't you?"

"You know I don't listen to the news, so why are you sheep dogging me about it?"

"Well, you should. You can't maintain situational awareness without knowing the damned situation." In thirty years, Bill had taught Noah as much about combat as he had about ranching. Phrases like "situational awareness" and "OODA loop" were as common to them as "I'm going out for a bit" and "where'd you leave the truck keys?"

"Someone hit a Saudi oil pumping station with a dirty bomb. That made the stock market run into a high-speed death wobble. Today, they're not cashing checks at the bank. Electricity's going off around the country, especially in California. Then that nuke went off in Los Angeles Harbor. Things are good and supremely FUBARed. Just as I predicted."

Noah sucked his teeth and considered the news. "How many dead?"

"From the nuke?" Bill shook his head. "Just a handful. It's the rioting and civil disorder that's the major shitstorm. That's what'll kill America. The snowflakes are going bucknutty."

"When did this happen?"

"The nuke in L.A. was just this morning, but the Saudi thing was two days ago. America was already on-the-ropes with the jump in the price of oil, the stock market and the power grid failing. I can only imagine what a nuke strike is going to do to those silver spoon ass clowns."

"Will illegals come pouring over the border if they think ICE is tangled up?" Noah's mind shifted back to the borderlands. He didn't waste much worry juice on the fancy half of America. Californians were the self-centered assholes who consumed the drugs that attracted the cartels that killed his wife and daughter. Californians were the festering bait that brought in the wolves.

"I think the illegals will do the exact opposite," Bill reached down and plucked up a bit of long grass and picked at his teeth with the dry stem. "Mexicans know there's shit for food growing in the southwest. They'll either go east toward the cornfields of the Midwest or south towards the vegetable fields of Sinaloa. Illegals understand hunger way better than most Americans. They're not going to run toward starvation. They're going to run to where there's something to eat. I wouldn't be surprised if we get overrun with illegals crossing in the opposite direction. They'll be heading south." Bill pointed the stalk of grass toward Mexico.

"If the shit hits the fan like you're thinking, when does the sheriff stop answering 9-1-1?" Noah wondered out loud.

"Why? You planning on robbing a bank?" Bill cocked his head.

"No. But if this is turning Wild West out here, there are a couple narcos I might like to put in the ground." Noah took off his cowboy hat and rubbed the sweat out of the hair under his hatband.

Bill looked at his son side-eyed. "Ain't it a little late for that? All this time I thought you were being smart about that whole thing. You know what they say about going after revenge: dig two graves first."

"Smart? You wouldn't have let it go if it'd been your family."

"No, I wouldn't have," Billy shrugged. "But then again, I'm a godforsaken old soldier of fortune and you're the kind of man who can hold down a family—a beautiful family. We aren't the same, you and I, and thank the Almighty for that."

Noah stared at the gatepost and gave it a light shove as though testing his work. "I'm glad someone's thanking the Almighty, because it sure seems like you and I landed on the same square after all."

Bill shook his head. "When you get to be my age, you realize that not one damn thing lasts forever. When you have something beautiful then you lose it, only a fool would waste time regretting it. Having it at all was manna from heaven—no matter how long you had it."

"Yeah, if you're so damn wise," Noah pointed at his dad's left eye, "how come you got one gray eyebrow hair sticking out six inches like a damn donkey?"

Bill's hand reached up and hunted for the offending eyebrow. "Youth is wasted on the young, that's for damn sure."

CHAPTER 6
TAVO CASTILLO
VILLAGE OF EL AMAPAL, SINALOA, MEXICO

Earlier in the morning, Tavo drove up the mountains bracketing Los Mochis to El Amapal, one of the hundreds of tiny villages ringing the broad valleys of Sinaloa. He'd chosen his Toyota Hilux, more concerned with managing the mountain road than with comfort. Truth was, he didn't much care for his "narco car" as he thought of the black Mercedes SUV. The air conditioning worked on the Hilux and it wouldn't break a tie rod in a pothole going up the mountain. What more did he need?

The phone vibrated and Tavo snatched it up. "*Diga*," he ordered. The man on the other end wasn't somebody he liked, so he dispensed with his usual pleasantries. "Talk."

"Salazar drove from Guatemala City to Antigua last week, as you suspected."

"What day?" Tavo asked.

"Sunday."

"Any more information on the primary?"

"The old man? Nothing new. We think he lives in Guatemala City and that he's an *OG* shot caller for MS-13. MS-13 is hardened to surveillance, so it's taking time to isolate his location. We don't normally operate in Guat City, so we're still developing local assets."

Tavo thought about hanging up, since he had nothing else to say. The man on the other end of the burner phone, Samuel Ortiz, had been working for him for five years—the handler of a vicious and resourceful *sicario* known as "*El Chucho*," the Mongrel Dog.

Tavo knew the *sicario's* real name: Tomás Valasquez. Before he'd hired the assassin, he'd learned everything about their two-man organization. Samuel Ortiz did the yapping and Tomás Vasquez did the killing. They fronted as a private detective agency in Mexico City. They'd proven equally good at getting information as they were at getting people dead. Competent or not, Tavo found them repulsive because he secretly despised gay men. His early investigation into Ortiz and Velasquez had been accompanied with photographs of the aging men engaged in sex. Every time he saw their number on his phone, Tavo's face picked up a sneer. He'd watched Ortiz and Velasquez for five years to make sure they hadn't been talking to police. That's when he discovered that both men were homosexuals and probably pederasts. He knew the depravity of pederasts, firsthand. Someday, Tavo would kill them both and it would give him great pleasure. Until then, he'd continue to use them for his side projects.

For five years, He'd been calling Ortiz on the burner phone and mailing him diamonds every two months. Tavo wore two gold rings back and forth to the U.S. and they carried two carats apiece. His watch held numerous smaller stones. Several times a month, he returned to Mexico with about $150,000 in untraceable diamonds—enough to fund small operations like this one.

Ortiz cleared his throat on the other end of the phone line.

"Begin monitoring secondary comms channels," Tavo

ordered, thinking the cell networks might fail and he may be forced onto satellite phone or amateur ham radio.

"I need to charge an extra eighth carat per month for that," Ortiz reminded Tavo.

"I know what was agreed." He dismissed the man and hung up the phone.

He pulled the battery out, slipped the phone in one pocket and dropped the battery in the other. Tavo climbed down out of the Hilux and walked across the street to the cart that was wrapping up midday food service.

"*Buenas tardes,*" Tavo greeted the *taquero*. "Two of tongue and two of carne asada." The man nodded and went to work on the tacos. Tavo reached over to the cooler and pulled out a Coke. He'd run a 10k at dawn and his just-coffee breakfast had given way to a gnawing hunger on the drive up the mountain.

"The Target," Agusto Salazar, had visited Antigua the same day Tavo had been hit at the Filly Hotel. Why would his half-brother—who didn't know Tavo even existed—be part of a hit on him? He couldn't make the connection. Well-to-do Guatemalans frequently left the city for Antigua on the weekends. It could be a coincidence.

Tavo mulled it over in his mind while he waited for his taco meat on the sizzling grill.

Then, he thought about the last time he'd seen his father.

1974
City of Tepic,
Nayarit, Mexico

. . .

The mostly-collapsed stone ruins crawled with trees and vines. To Tavo's six-year-old imagination, it was an ancient Mayan city and he was a Spanish conquistador. Except, instead of a lance and sword, he carried a revolver.

His father had given him the revolver and taken him to play in the ruins of the clothing factory owned by his mother's great-great grandparents. These days, the Sausa family made tequila instead of clothing. None of this mattered to Tavo, except that he was the only boy at his school allowed to play in the ruins. Today, he got to play with his father and a gun as well.

"Bang. I got you!" Tavo shouted as he clacked the hammer on the tiny gun, using both his hands to cycle the stiff trigger. "Bang, bang, bang…"

"I'm hit!" his father feigned a mortal wound and sunk to his knees. "There's more on the walls!" Tavo's father pointed to the top of the thick stone, long stripped of the roof that once hung over the massive space.

"Bang, bang, bang, bang." Tavo unleashed a fusillade at the walls, felling imaginary Mayan warriors by the dozen.

"Watch out! They're shooting arrows back." Tavo's father laughed and pantomimed dodging back and forth, scanning the walls for the enemy.

This is the best day of my life, Tavo remembered thinking. Finally, something had changed, and now his father cared to play with him.

His parents had shouted at one another earlier that morning. It hadn't been the first time, but Tavo gathered that they were shouting about bad things, like ending their family. Tavo had no idea how a family could end.

His mother's parents, Papito Juan and Abuelita Guadalupe, owned nearly everything in town, and Tavo was old enough to know that his family was better than his friends' families. Even though they attended the same private school, everyone treated Tavo like royalty. How could a family like his end?

"Don't shoot!" Tavo's father shouted. "I am the King of the Mayans and you have conquered us. Your amazing weapons have swept us from the land and taken our gold. We will work for you forever if you will let us live." Tavo's father knelt down on one knee, making Tavo a little nervous.

Tavo softened, no longer so hearty about his conquests. "Maybe I will let you live if you promise to be nice from now on." Tavo lowered the revolver and stepped closer.

Tavo's father leapt up and seized the gun. "Ha! Now YOU will die," Tavo's father shouted. "You're a very stupid boy. See how easily I tricked you?" His father pointed the gun at Tavo's face and clacked the hammer. "You die for being so weak."

Fear gripped little Tavo. The play with his father had taken a turn he didn't understand.

"I'm just joking." Tavo's father ruffled his hair with one hand. "Let's go show your mother how good you are at shooting the gun. Your hands have become strong. We'll show her. Come on."

Tavo's father turned his back for a moment and worked the revolver. "Let's go, Tavo."

Father and son laughed and chatted as they mounted the steep road back toward their home in the family compound. They stopped at an *abarrotes* and Tavo's father bought them both watermelon popsicles.

When they neared their front door, Tavo's father turned playful again. "Tavo. The Indian queen is inside. Repay the treachery of the King and slay the old hag. Prove that you cannot be defeated. Sneak up behind her and shoot her in the head. Then you will rule the Indians forever."

Tavo basked in his father's attention, and in his imagination, he became the ruthless Spanish conquistador, seeking revenge for the dishonorable acts of the Mayan king. He stalked into the kitchen and found his mother cutting vegetables, her back to the doorway.

Thrilled to see his mother, and to tell her about his morning of adventure with his father, Tavo lost track of the game.

"Mami!" he shouted.

She turned around, glowing at the sound of his voice, her smile instantly vanishing.

"Papi taught me how to use the gun. My hands are so strong now." He pointed the gun at her face and demonstrated. "Bang!" he shouted.

BOOM!

The gun thundered in his hands and his mother fell back against the tiled countertop, sweeping the knife and a pile of cabbage onto the floor. She teetered a moment, then followed the vegetables to the ground, hitting with a loud, wet slap.

"Mami!" He dropped the gun and fell to the ground. "Help! Mami? Help!"

The bottom of her jaw had been blown off along with a chunk of her ear and pieces of her face, scalp and the back of her head. Blood gushed from the tattered wound. Her eyes lulled in her head while she moaned deep in her throat.

"Help! Help!" Tavo screamed. His father had disappeared.

Finally, Marta, one of the housekeepers rushed into the kitchen and began screaming, "Dios, mio! Dios, mio!"

Tavo ran into the courtyard howling for help.

———

Tavo's eyes glazed over as he chewed his tacos.

His mother hadn't died, at least not right away. She'd lived another twenty years in a wheelchair, her face a scrambled parody of her former beauty. She could barely speak, and her mental capacity had been severely impaired. He visited her only twice before her death.

Tavo spent the next five years in and out of orphanages, finally turning to street life at eleven years old, after deciding that anything was better than the physical and sexual abuse he endured in the orphanages.

Tavo's grandparents refused to speak to him. His father had refused to leave Tepic until the grandparents paid him a sum of money. Eventually, they must've paid, because his father disappeared while Tavo was incarcerated in reform school.

For the millionth time, Tavo wondered what people did those kinds of things to a child. One day, he was a beloved young prince, the next, he woke up locked in a room, a hated wretch, abused and abandoned.

Soon he'd need to put his childhood back in its box. Tavo didn't allow himself the luxury of emotional forays into stupid questions like fairness, regret or vengeance. Those kinds of emotions gave people power over him, and he preferred to be the only one with power over himself.

If his grandparents hadn't already died, he might actually like to cut their throats in bed. That would be nice. But they were long gone, the arrogant monsters.

And, if he could find his father...well, that would get messy. Messy like his mother on that tile floor, half her face blown onto the cupboard doors.

Tavo kept the investigation—with the *sicario* and his rat-faced handler—partitioned from the rest of his life. It was the only way he could justify the risk of hiring them to find his father.

Based on what Tavo knew as an adult, he was sure his father had manipulated him into shooting her—playacting that day in the ruins to get Tavo groomed to murder. Then his father loaded the gun and sent a six-year-old boy to kill his own mother. Even after five years, the search for his father had gone nowhere. The man had intentionally vanished, probably working other scams under other names.

The rat-face pederast had suggested an idea six months previously: that Tavo do a DNA test and check the online databases for hits on other children from his father, or even on his father himself. Given his likely occupation as a criminal, Tavo didn't think his father would be doing online DNA tests, but Tavo gave the test a shot anyway using a false identity.

The report had returned a half-brother in Guatemala City: Agusto Salazar, who sold corporate training to Guatemalan multi-level marketing companies. For some reason, Salazar had been in Antigua the same day the Guatemalan Special Forces attempted to capture Tavo.

Tavo drained the last of his Coke and paid the *taquero*.

No matter how much he wanted to believe his search for his father hadn't bled over into to his business life, he couldn't afford to write off his half-brother being in Antigua as coincidence. That'd be one emotion fueling another. Cascades of emotion—wishful thinking—got men in his business tortured, arrested or killed.

Tavo assured himself, he was nothing like those other narcos.

And he was definitely nothing like his father.

CHAPTER 7

NOAH MILLER
MILLER CATTLE RANCH, RIO RICO COUNTY, ARIZONA

> The wicked flee when none pursueth.
>
> — Proverbs 28:1

The old men of Rio Rico County passed DVD movies around like a bad cold. None of the old men had any internet bandwidth to speak of—Bill maintained dial up for the sole purpose of logging onto SurvivalistBoards.com and telling the other survivalists how stupid they were. So, in the crustiest sense conceivable, social media had come to Rio Rico County via Bill McCallister. In that dried up county with a population just south of two thousand souls, Bill was a trendsetter, and he usually introduced the next great movie to Rio Rico, often decades after the film's release. As a result, ninety-five percent of the movies watched in Rio Rico County were either action flicks or westerns.

Bill showed up on Noah's porch without calling ahead, holding a DVD and a bottle of Leadslinger's whiskey. They both knew full well that Noah had no other plans.

At first blush, the movie looked like a western—a redux of

John Wayne's *True Grit*. In his obscenely self-involved way, Bill probably thought the film would be a perfect candidate for movie night with his son. He'd shown up with a revenge movie and a bottle of whiskey to help his son; an alcoholic grieving the murder of his family.

Noah sighed. He loved his father and he felt protective of all the old men of Rio Rico County. Brittle and dusty, they were his tribe. But moments like this grated on him. His father had been right. Noah would never quite be like these men. He was like a fish who'd been raised by tortoises. They possessed an outer shell that Noah simply did not possess, a simplicity that eluded him. Even before he married and started his family, Noah looked deeper than Bill would ever care to see. And when the slings and arrows of life struck, Noah felt the wounds more deeply than those men as well. Every man in Rio Rico understood the cause of Noah's pain. None of them understood how deeply it'd wormed its way into his soul.

As the movie progressed through young Mattie Ross' plan to avenge her murdered father, Bill hooted and hollered—waving his whiskey tumbler at the screen and offering commentary and counsel that, perhaps, the producers might take into consideration during a future re-filming. In particular, he had much to say about Matt Damon playing the part of a Texas Ranger. Apparently, Bill had never forgiven the physically-unimposing Matt Damon for attempting to play Jason Bourne. Bill had known many real-life assassins, after all, and most of those men were bulls. In consideration for that oversight, Bill deposited his disdain for Hollywood cleanly at Matt Damon's feet.

Noah bit back his irritation with his father, buoyed up by approximately ten fingers of booze. He knew that nothing under heaven and earth could shut his father up when he got on a roll, so he didn't even try.

Afloat on a sea of whiskey, Noah felt a confluence between

the movie, his irritation with his father and the truth about his own life. He took another sip of his dad's whiskey and watched the movie from behind the tumbler.

On the screen, young Mattie Ross explained to Marshall Cogburn: *"My mother is indecisive and hobbled by grief..."*

Was that what Noah had become? Hobbled by grief? If it were true—if he'd become hobbled by grief—maybe he was drunk enough to finally admit it.

"If you'd shut the hell up, we could *both* enjoy the movie," Noah cut loose and shouted in the middle of Bill's next rant.

"Well, excuse me, son. I'll keep it to myself, then," old Bill sulked. He poured another slug of whiskey in his glass and sat back on the couch with arms folded.

Noah knew his dad deserved better. For the millionth time, he reminded himself that the old army Green Beret hadn't been forced to raise him. He'd taken Noah in out of the kindness of his heart when it became clear that Noah would never fit in with his whack job polygamist family. The movie and his misgivings about his solitary life had gotten the better of him and Noah had no business taking it out on his old man.

He knew what it was that'd sent him off, and that bugged him even more. Something about the damn revenge plot, the whiskey and his dad's blathering had broken through a dam. Nobody liked seeing things about themselves they'd been avoiding and Noah had run smack into the thing he wanted to see the least—that he'd abandoned the fight. He'd run from life and holed up in his dying cattle ranch.

As he watched the wrestling match between a girl, a Texas Ranger and an old bounty hunter play out, Noah felt himself pulled gently off the rocky crag of grief and self-doubt that'd hung him up for the last two years.

He knew he had more grit than this. He had loved and lost before, and he'd not only survived but he'd made the best of it.

1999
 The Mormon Colonies,
 Ciudad Juarez, Chihuahua, Mexico

"I hope you understand someday, but you're not cut out for this family," Noah's father explained. "The kindest thing I can do as a father is to send you to a more suitable place. There's nothing here for you."

"I don't understand. You're sending mother and I away? Just because I brought a gun to school? I didn't even know it wasn't allowed. I only brought it to show my friends."

His dad stood up and looked out his office window. "Your mother isn't going with you."

Noah's eyes spilled over with tears. It felt like having his guts ripped out and fed to the hogs. His father had two other wives. Why did the sonofabitch need more than that?

"Son. This life in the colonies isn't for everyone. The longer you stay, the more painful it'll be when you finally leave. I'm doing you a favor. I don't expect you to understand."

Noah had one father, three mothers, eight brothers and four sisters. Noah knew even then, he would eventually get over leaving the two "sister wives" and he'd miss his brothers and sisters awfully. But the thought of being sent away from his mother struck his heart like a thunderclap. Noah struggled to breathe.

"I promise, I will not bring a gun to school ever again. I swear, I won't ever touch a gun, if that's what you want," he pleaded. Noah normally did everything he could not to cry in front of his dad, but this time, he couldn't control it. He was sobbing so hard now, a rope of snot ran down his face.

His father looked away in embarrassment.

"I can't go away. I'm TWELVE." Noah stood up from the chair, gripping the armrests so tightly his kunckles went white.

When Noah had been called upstairs to his father's office, he knew it would be bad. He'd been expelled from school over the gun. But he'd no idea that it'd be this bad. No idea at all.

His father shook his head, looked at Noah and turned away. "It's not about the gun, Noah. You're not doing well in Sunday School, and this isn't the first time you've been in trouble."

Noah searched his memory, sorting out the trouble he'd been caught in and the trouble he hadn't. Maybe it was when he tried to fill the window well with water to make a pool and it flooded the basement. Or maybe it was when he scratched his name on the pickup truck fender. But all the boys in the Colonies got into trouble like that sometimes.

"I swear. I'll be good. I'll study the scriptures and do better at praying. Don't send me away from my family. From my mom."

His father shook his head, folded his hands behind his back and refused to look Noah in the eyes.

"You'll be okay among the gentiles. I've made arrangements with a client across the border in Arizona. If you like guns so much, you're going to like Bill McCallister."

"I don't care about guns. I need to be with my...family. Please, father. *Please*," Noah implored. "*Please*."

His father hesitated, glanced at Noah, and then walked out of his office, leaving him to put his feelings in order by himself. At twelve years old, Noah would be driven away from the only person he had ever loved—his mother. Maybe forever. He felt like digging out the hunting knife his father kept in his desk and stabbing it into his own throat. He was being sent to live with the gentiles, which meant he had failed his mother and everyone else.

Noah eventually choked back his tears, wiped his eyes and steeled himself to face the family. Everyone would already know that he was being sent away and their judgment of him would pile on top of his grief like pig shit on top of a load of corn husks. Already, Noah could feel the distance between he and his once-family growing. He barely suppressed the urge to run from the house and never turn back.

"I'm big enough," Noah convinced himself. "I'm going to show them. I am big enough." Noah bent over, wiped his nose on his shirttail, straightened his back and walked out of the office with red-rimmed eyes steady as a prizefighter.

Noah's dad had left the house after the movie, still sulking over his son's reprimand. Nothing made old Bill more butthurt than having someone point out that he talked too much. Still, Noah felt guilty for having opened his mouth.

After offending his old man, Noah had stopped drinking the whiskey and by the end of the show, sobriety crept up on him. Still holding his tumbler--filled with water from the sink--he stood on the porch and watched his dad pull away from the ranch in his old Land Cruiser. A part of Noah wanted to call him back and apologize, but the conversation would probably cost them both too much. A man got only so many words in any given day, and Noah had run dry.

Despite the screw up with his dad, the rope around his gut had loosened, maybe for the first time in two years.

Since Leah and Katya died, he often found himself marooned on Fuck-it Island. Some days he could barely get his ass out of bed to feed the cattle. He'd been the furthest thing from a wussy—riding bulls in high school, working cattle his whole life and hammering out PT circuits six times a week with his old man. He'd even coached the high school football team back before the girls died.

But with the death of his family, it had felt like a mesquite stick punctured his fuel tank. All the gas had dribbled out of Noah, and he'd been running on fumes these last two years. Some days, the lowing of hungry cattle had been all that stood between him and lying in bed staring at the ceiling all day.

Standing on the dark porch with a glass of water and the stars burning overhead like a billion distant souls, Noah discovered that he cared. He cared about his dad. He cared about all those dipshits running around scared out of their minds in California. Hell, he even cared about himself.

The time had come for his first conversation with Leah—the first one since she'd left him to join the stars.

"Hey Babe. I sure as hell miss you," Noah spoke into the black night. The fist in the back of his throat rose, turned into a palm, then became a caress. Tears sprung up in the corners of his eyes.

"I guess I've been a prick about this, haven't I? I had you all to myself for five years and that mighta been five more years than I deserved. But I got to have you with me on this porch all those mornings and I got to have you in my bed all those nights and that was more than I probably deserved. And it was sure as hell enough.

"So I've been wondering, Babe. What's next?... I could off myself. That'd get me heading toward wherever you and Katya are up there, but that doesn't feel right.

"I'd love to know--if you could spare a minute sometime-- what's my next play? I'm lonely. I'm just a dumb cowboy, but I've got you and Katya up there on my side. That's gotta count for something. I'm willing to bet my life on it."

Noah raised his glass to those billion souls and he picked out two.

"Goodnight, my lovelies."

CHAPTER 8

TAVO CASTILLO
RANCHO SANTIAGUITO, 65 MILES OUTSIDE OF
HERMOSILLO, SONORA, MEXICO

Detroit burned on CNN. For the hundredth time, Tavo struggled to understand Americans. Even though the lights were on in Detroit, people were rioting over "Fair Power" to *other* inner cities that weren't getting their share of electricity. Cities thousands of miles from Detroit.

Power was out in Los Angeles, Washington D.C., Atlanta and several other large cities, and those idiots were also rioting. But Detroit rioted because of the *idea* that inner city poor people in *other states* weren't getting power while rich people in the suburbs supposedly were.

Tavo sipped a beer as he watched the insanity on the big-screen TV, in the family room at the survival compound in Sonora, two hundred miles north of Los Mochis.

The absurdity on CNN reminded him of a joke he'd heard about Oprah Winfrey, supposedly the richest African American woman in the world.

"What if Bill Gates woke up one morning and all he had was Oprah Winfrey's money? He'd throw himself off a building and cut his throat on the way down, screaming 'What happened? I can't even put gas in my plane...'"

What if America woke up one morning and it had Mexico's money?

Hypothetically, America would be just fine. America's food production would still stand. They'd still have the finest infrastructure the world had ever seen. There wouldn't be any reason for the trucks to stop running, the trains to stop delivering or the ships to stop dropping shipping containers at the ports. America could dial back to being like Mexico and scrape by until they figured everything out. After all, nobody starved in Mexico. Not even in the worst of times.

But that wasn't what Tavo saw happening on CNN. America was throwing a fit. Like a rage-drunk child, America punched itself in the face and ripped off its clothes, just one night after their power grid began having problems.

Tavo knew what he wanted to do next, but it'd be better if his guys thought they'd arrived at the conclusion on their own.

"Good evening, Papi" Sofía put her hand on his shoulder and kissed him on the head. Tavo turned down the news with the remote. He'd heard her helicopter arrive thirty minutes before—a big military bird—but she must've taken time to clean up before coming to find him.

"Any trouble with flights?" Tavo asked.

"No. I got into Hermosillo okay, but things were a little scary at the airport. I decided to get a ride from my military friends instead of trying to über."

"I could've sent a car for you," Tavo said. His daughter definitely shouldn't be taking an über from Hermosillo to the ranch. Nobody in Sonora knew their family controlled the three largest cartels in Mexico. That was one downside of being a ghost. Nobody knew enough to fear him.

Sofía's access to the military—a helicopter, no less—snagged in his mind. She had been the only person to know he would be in Antigua, Guatemala the day of the Kaibil strike. Like an invisible mosquito whining in his ear, the thought of Sofía betraying him would never quite leave him alone, but he hadn't been willing to confront it directly either.

"Who'd you have to blow to get a helo ride?" Tavo asked, already regretting the coarseness of the words.

"Papi! ¡Que verguenza! Shame on you!" Her huge hazel eyes narrowed and her face reddened. "Why would you say that? Are you angry with me?"

Something in Tavo's chest broke loose and sank, but his mind caught it, reminding him that he would've feigned innocence too if he were her. It was the age-old question of kings and Greek gods—*is my child a threat to my throne?*

"I'm sorry, mi amor. The news has me on edge," Tavo said. Nothing could've been further from the truth. The news enchanted Tavo with dreams of vast opportunity.

She sat on the arm of her father's chair. "Are you worried about your business? If this keeps up..." she nodded at the riots playing out behind the news commentator on the screen, "there won't be money for narcotics. There won't be money for anything."

Then there will be no reason for you to try and have me thrown in jail, his mind barked.

While she tittered about the news, building a case for this as an opportunity for him to leave the drug trade, he mentally ticked off her motives for wanting him in jail.

So she could have power over his syndicate.

Maybe all this innocence she pretended was a cover for her own sociopathy. Maybe she was his progeny in *that way* too. Maybe power, in and of itself, fed her the way it fed him.

So she could free the family of the stink of drugs.

Maybe she was just another aristocrat like her dead grandparents. Maybe, she preferred him hidden away in another country, leaving her and her mother to take possession of the money he had earned.

So she could gain retribution for what he had done to her mother.

Tavo knew that his wife despised him for what she'd become in the shadow of his disinterest. She had been the town beauty, with suitors calling on her home like doves to the pea fields. Tavo swept in, captured her, then locked her in a life of lies. Once he'd secured his association to her respected family, his interest in her elementary intellect and lusterless imagination waned. As the romance starved, her waistline grew. He became the dashing man married to the frumpy, former beauty. Sofía never accused him of crushing her mother's dreams, but she worked tirelessly to redeem what had been stolen. Sofía dedicated her young life to making her mother happy. Tavo suspected that Sofía resented him for selling her mother on a life of bounty only to watch her starve for attention. Maybe that had been why Sofía hadn't yet married. Maybe she carried her mother's wounds. Maybe Antiqua had been payback for what he'd done to Isabel.

"Papi. What're you going to do?" Sofía interrupted his grinding thoughts. Tavo tilted his head, casting free from the paranoia that'd seized him.

He motioned to the muted news program. "I'm waiting to see how this plays out."

"Nonsense. I know you. You have plans on top of plans. You don't wait."

Tavo smiled and leaned his head back in the chair. "The Americans might need help. I can't imagine their government failing, but I can't imagine it maintaining for long without reliable electricity, either."

"And their army?" she asked.

"Most of the American soldiers on American soil aren't full time. The majority are doing military service for school tuition or a paycheck. I'm not sure how much different the army is from any other government job."

"How would you help if their government fails?"

Tavo pretended to consider the question. In truth, he had decided long ago. "We could help restore order. Keep the criminal element under control."

Sofía snorted. "With your own criminal element?"

Tavo took a deep breath. "Do you have a better plan?"

She shook her head.

Beto interrupted them, charging into the family room, projecting intensity like a lion closing in on his prey.

"*Los Negros* have taken the archbishop. Let's go get him back."

"Whoa..." Tavo considered the implications. Fortune might be serving him an opportunity. "Are you saying that the *Los Negros* gang rolled up the archbishop?"

"Yep. And the vicar and several padres. They've got them in the state offices across from the Señora de la Asunción Cathedral. There are only thirty *Los Negros*, give or take. Let's get our gun on, brother. I've got thirty *Caballeros Templarios* standing by."

Beto had been the instigator of the "*Caballeros Templarios*" movement among their drug soldiers. When they'd begun training drug soldiers to become commandos two years back, Beto had argued for a faith element to the training. He pitched it as a way to control the men—and a much less expensive way to extend influence than paying the men top dollar. To Tavo, it'd seemed like a harmless salve to the rumbling conscience of Beto and the commandos. It made drug running feel more Catholic, which couldn't hurt. "*Templarios*" had become organizational shorthand for drug commando. With communications crumbling and control of his men becoming less and less reliable,

Tavo hoped the *Templario* thing would help maintain cohesion. It couldn't hurt.

Tavo nodded to Beto. "Okay, hermano. But let's do this right. Call in your *Templarios* and let's flex our muscle."

Beto shook himself like a dog, releasing his pre-battle jitters. "I like it. I'll get a recon team over to the cathedral now. But, what's to keep the Mexican military from launching an op first? It's not like we're the only Catholics in town who know how to shoot."

"They might." Tavo considered. "That'd save us the trouble. Does Hermosillo have a police paramilitary unit?"

"No. Half the cops work for *Los Negros*." Beto clearly wanted to assault tonight, but he folded into Tavo's more deliberate manner.

"Let's plan on assaulting tomorrow night. Score some solid intel tonight, get your guys from Tucson here by morning, and we'll do a couple rehearsals at the ranch before we go in. We'll hit them when they're dead asleep and hung over tomorrow night. Good?"

Beto smiled and nodded. "That's why you get paid the big bucks, Canoso. Always using your melon. Fucking rehearsals... Who even does that?"

"Just the professionals." Tavo gave him a sideways glance. There had always been an operational tension between him and Beto. A former SEAL, Beto liked to rely on hard-hitting violence of action. He liked to throw himself into the meat grinder and let the adrenaline flow.

"Yeah. We didn't do a whole lot of rehearsing, downrange," Beto admitted. "We left that shit to the ODA guys."

Tavo had watched Sofía out of the corner of his eye during the entire exchange with Beto. She stood with her arms folded, observing her father and his lieutenant like a biologist watching gorillas in the wild.

"So, you're going on the warpath," she summarized, cutting through the military bravado.

"We can't let rabid dogs like *Los Negros* run this close to home," Tavo explained. "And someone needs to protect the church."

Sofía was a devout Catholic. She attended faithfully, did confession regularly, even volunteered at the parroquía. Much the same could be said about Tavo himself.

Was her faith part of her ruse? A white cloak over a dark heart?

It felt alien to doubt her—the girl he'd known her whole life, and half of his own. Flesh of his flesh. When he winnowed down the purpose of his own life, it could be reduced to one word: *Sofía*. The last thing in the world he wanted to consider was that she had betrayed him.

But above all else, Tavo would not lie to himself, and that made him unique. Tavo understood the keystone of the human psyche. He knew the lie upon which all of humanity predicated their hundred years of life. Tavo had been born with a flaw in his brain and while that flaw had stripped away most human emotion, it also revealed a gaping, secret weakness within nearly every other human being.

Every man, woman and child on the planet endlessly persuaded themselves into a fantasy they longed to believe. From birth to death, they layered stone upon stone in a monument that described who they were, why they should be loved and *why their life mattered*. Those stones of belief—the fictional tale of each human life, erected tirelessly in the human mind—became an altar of devotion to the fantasy that the person *belonged*. That their life mattered. With that at their back, they could live another day, inveigled by their own specialness.

But most people were not special. Most people were average, and many were much less than average. Mumbling prayers to self-deception guaranteed that their life would be consumed defending their fantasy rather than discovering the uninspiring truth—that every person was just another flesh popsicle, grubbing their way through a handful of decades, leaving almost no mark on the history of man.

Tavo would leave a mark, of that he was certain. He would not dedicate his life to propping up a fantasy of specialness.

He would dig into the truth about Sofia, regardless of the damage to his self-concept. Perhaps he'd built a castle in his mind—an empire, a fortune, a story that involved his daughter. And perhaps she was nothing like he had imagined.

Tavo's stomach twisted in on itself as he regarded her open face, framed by wisps of tawny hair. He could see his Castilian, Spanish genes in her highlights and in the rose-blush of her skin when she disagreed with him.

Could a lifetime with his daughter have been a carefully-architected lie?

Sofia put her hands on her hips and said nothing.

Tavo stared at her, wondering what thoughts were clicking and whirring behind that stern expression and perfect face. His suspicion that his own daughter might have set him up for arrest needed to be locked down. It was a binary consideration—either it was true and he would have to rebuild the purpose of his life from scratch, or it was false and he would have to let it go. But would it matter if the U.S. fell?

Maybe it didn't matter if she had betrayed him.

Tavo ground down the agony churning in his gut, pushed it aside and replaced it with the hard metal gears of reason.

Sofia controlled two assets that might be crucial to Tavo: Mexican gas and the Mexican army. His daughter's opinion of her father and his drug business had been a curiosity until this moment. With the U.S. collapsing, and endless opportunity opening up north of the border, her opinion of his drug business could get in his way. Whether she was his deadly nemesis or the blood-of-his-blood, either way, enrolling her into the direction he wanted to go should be his next gambit.

"If the government is tied up with other problems," Tavo soothed, "we should help with peacekeeping, shouldn't we? If we maintain order in the region, everyone benefits. Especially the common people."

Sofia chewed her lower lip.

Tavo continued, "You wanted us out of narcotics. With what's happening in the U.S., we're probably out of narcotics." He glanced at Beto and his lieutenant shrugged, as though saying *it's over my pay grade*. "We have over 250,000 street soldiers under our command if we count the affiliated gangs in the U.S., and that's just the pledged guys. If the American and Mexican armies fragment, we'll have the largest organized peacekeeping force in the region. Should we disband them because they used to sell drugs?"

"I don't know your business—I don't want to know your business," Sofia finally spoke. "But are you seriously proposing that your street gangs will stop preying upon people and help maintain order? Will they wake up tomorrow morning and suddenly become shepherds instead of wolves?"

He had maneuvered her exactly where he wanted her. "There's no way to get our soldiers to be entirely compliant, and we'll lose a lot of them to communication breakdown and chaos in America, but we can still probably maintain a hold on a significant percentage of them. We have over 20,000 soldiers in our organization with paramilitary training and those men will follow orders. With this op tomorrow, we move in a new direction. We become the church's protector."

Beto shifted on his feet, struggling to cover his astonishment.

Tavo pressed, "We're all Catholics, at least on this side of the border. We can help the church take back the whole region."

Sofia stood, wide-eyed. "You can't be serious. The church

won't do that. The church hasn't wanted to govern in a hundred and fifty years."

"But what if that was the only way to stop millions of people from dying?" Tavo held out his hands. "What if the church was the last, remaining organization? Would the bishops and archbishops step up? From what I see on that television screen, we might be within forty-eight hours of that exact scenario."

"I'm going with you." Sofía sat down on the couch. "I need to see it."

Tavo recoiled. "No. You don't. You don't need to see this." He could think of a hundred reasons why Sofía joining an op was a bad idea. "You're not coming."

She leaned her head back on the couch. "If I'm going to support you in this, I need to see it with my own eyes—men killing and dying. Because that's what this is: men being killed to save other men from death. That barely even makes sense... and I've never seen a man die."

Tavo sifted through her possible motives and came up with nothing. What could she possibly hope to gain from coming on the op?

"I don't even know why you're trying to talk me into this," she continued, staring at the ceiling. "You've never cared what I thought about your criminal activities before. Why now?"

It was a good question and Tavo knew the answer: *Mexican gas.*

But his doubt circled with storm-darkened curiosity: *Was his daughter trying to take him down?*

Like an itch on his back he couldn't reach, it vexed him. He kept reaching for it. There was nothing he could do but worry and prod—and time would eventually tell—but he goaded the festering question: w*as she a super-human creature like him?*

...and could he survive the answer?

CHAPTER 9

NOAH MILLER
RIO RICO COUNTY, NEAR LOCHIEL, ARIZONA

"9-1-1. State your emergency."

"Hey, Glenda. How're things up in Sierra Vista with my favorite sheriff's deputy?" Noah didn't need to lay on the charm, but he did anyway. He and Glenda had gone to school together. At six foot-two, blond hair, just now fringed in gray, and with six-pack abs that could still be recognized beneath his slight whiskey gut, Noah was the designated bachelor of Rio Rico County. But because of the violent death of his wife and daughter, the three ladies who knocked the edge off their loneliness with Noah's company kept it on the down low. They were in their late thirties, and given Noah's circumstances, maturity won out over possessiveness. Nobody asked too many questions.

"Is that Noah Miller?" Glenda's voice brightened. "You're supposed to use the *landline* for chitchat, Noah, not 9-1-1. Every kid knows that."

"Yeah, but nobody's answering the landline."

"Hmm." Glenda hesitated. "I'm not surprised. The sheriff gave everyone the option of working from home until things got back to normal. 9-1-1 calls are being forwarded to my cell."

"That makes sense," Noah said.

He had learned what he needed. Now he wanted off the phone. "You take care of yourself, Glenda. Lock your doors at night. No telling how the cartels are going to react to the Border Patrol pulling back."

"Will do, Noah. Did you need something from the Sheriff?"

"Nope. Just checking in on you," Noah lied.

"Such a gentleman. Good night." Glenda disconnected.

Noah hung up his cell phone, stuck it in his pocket and turned back to watching the caravan approach the border fence through his Schmidt and Bender riflescope. Even with just a half-moon, he could see them as though it were daytime, even at eight hundred yards. And he could tell they were cartel.

Noah had been watching the Zetas cross this point in the fence for over two years. He knew which men were the mules and which were the mule drivers. He recognized most of them—had even given them pet names.

Tonight, El Mustachio was in charge of the slave labor. Sixteen men carried bulging backpacks and four men carried just enough kit to survive a couple days in the desert. The four guys with light loads also carried AK-47 rifles.

El Mustachio favored a big FN/FAL rifle, as though the larger gun lent him greater authority. He walked in the middle of the formation, like any officer should. But this mean sonofabitch was no military officer. He was a smuggler. El Mustachio might die tonight, and maybe one or two of his drug soldiers with him.

The formation moved slowly. Even before the Border Patrol turned to dust in the collapse of the banking system, the fence between the United States and Mexico had always been a natural danger zone. Competing cartels, American vigilantes, pissed off landowners and Mexican opportunists showed up like chimeras in this twilight margin of law and order. Sometimes, they even left with some of the millions of dollars of drugs strapped to the mules' backs. A lot of anger and greed got pulled into this five hundred yard section of fence, and that godforsaken place bordered his ranch.

Noah would've expected to show up with his own stewing anger at the border tonight. With all the conditions ripe for some old fashion revenge killing, Noah felt strangely serene. His conversation with Leah the night before hadn't done much for his bloodlust.

He watched El Mustachio move up the column as his men halted at the border fence. El Mustachio always led at the crossing.

This drug crossing didn't employ bulb-lit tunnels or anything so romantic. Rather, the narcos had cut the fence with bolt cutters and every time they crossed, they wired it back together. It helped that the hole had been cut behind a mesquite bush on the bank of the dry wash. The Border Patrol had driven past a thousand times in the last two years, and they'd never noticed the break in their fence. Simple solutions usually worked better than romantic solutions—it was one of the hundreds of fieldcraft tidbits Noah had been taught by his father.

El Mustachio unwired the breach and held the fence open while his men crossed, then he slid through the gap, rewired it and trotted back to the middle of the column.

The group continued their steady movement north toward the choke point Noah had prepared in the bottom of the empty streambed. He'd been watching this spot so long now, he knew every rock, every bush and every jackrabbit in the dry wash where the narcos would pass. Noah knew right where he'd set off the ambush, and he had planned a perfect escape route.

Bill had taught him never to ambush with less than a three-to-one advantage, but Noah reasoned that there was more than one way to gain an advantage besides more men. He had the advantage of terrain—he lay on a rocky crag at least four hundred yards away and above where the men would pass. He had the advantage of superior intel—he knew everything about the column and they knew nothing about him. And, he owned the first five seconds of the mad minute. When Noah sent his first rounds, it'd be at least five seconds before the narcos would even *think about* plotting countermoves. Before they did, he'd dash into the hills and down a path he knew better than the route from his bed to the shitter.

But the narcos weren't likely to chase him with a quarter million in cocaine strapped to their backs. Noah could shoot them at will and they probably weren't going to move more than fifty yards from that dry wash. His biggest concern had always been the American cops, but they'd all taken the night off. It'd been the window he'd been waiting for.

As the first narcos in the column passed the tamarack bush that marked the forward edge of the ambush zone, Noah shook his head, but it did nothing to clear the cobwebs.

Now was not a good time for a surge of conscience, but that was exactly what was happening. He'd hoped killing a few shit bags would put a little spring in his step, but as he watched El Mustachio walk into the ambush, Noah knew it wasn't true. El Mustachio hadn't killed his family, and even if he had, Noah didn't think blasting him would make him feel any better.

Who was he to judge the hard-hearted, anyway?

Like a blacksmith hammering carbon into steel, Noah had hardened his own heart. Most days, only ferocious bouts of loneliness could get him thinking of anyone beside himself.

Some nights, adrift in booze, he would remember when they lowered the caskets—one big and one small—into the ground of the Rio Rico cemetery. Halfway between a Mexican cemetery and an American cemetery, the Rio Rico County Memorial Park didn't offer a single blade of grass. Half of the graves were faded blue, pink or purple mausoleums. The other half were American-style stone grave markers surrounded by nothing but sand and dust. In the booze haze, Noah would often obsess on the dust and wonder if it had seeped into Katya's casket. Was her face covered in a thin layer of grime for eternity? Her little nose? Her dishwater blonde hair?

Noah shook off the familiar loop of images and returned to the night and his predations. His grief had begun to turn, and along with it, his desperation. The mental pictures of his wife and daughter in the Rio Rico cemetery didn't cut the furrows in his soul that they did just a few nights previous. The horror had lost its hold and gratitude had begun to rise in him.

He held the big Schmidt and Bender scope on El Mustachio and centered the crosshairs on his chest.

"Pew, pew, asshole," Noah whispered. "You can thank Leah you're not facedown in the dust, *hombre*."

Noah ran the bolt of his Sako rifle and caught the fresh cartridge as it hopped out of the chamber. He poked his pinkie into the breach to make sure it was clear. Old habits die hard and no matter how little he cared about the criminals downrange of his rifle, he still cared plenty about firearm safety.

CHAPTER 10
TAVO CASTILLO
CATHEDRAL METROPOLITANA DE NUESTRA
SEÑORA DE LA ASUNCIÓN, PLAZA ZARAGOZA,
HERMOSILLO, SONORA, MEXICO

Cradling the heavy rifle, Tavo leaned against the low concrete wall atop the OXXO mercantile building. Across Plaza Zaragoza, he watched the state office building where the *Los Negros* gang had been partying. It was five a.m., and true to her word, his daughter stood beside him, wearing workout clothes and a dark jacket.

A woman had been shrieking for over ten minutes in a dark corner somewhere near the state building. It seemed like she would never stop; shrieking, shrieking, shrieking.

Tavo came out from behind his rifle and cast a sidelong glance at his daughter. She stared into the darkness, covering her mouth, searching for the suffering woman. Tavo had already told her once not to speak, so Sofía glanced back at him, the white around her eyes visible in the dim light.

The gangbangers held the archbishop, the vicar and several priests inside the state building, doing God-knew-what to them. Why the gang had taken the priests was beyond Tavo's comprehension. Street gangs like Los Negros were little more than packs of feral dogs. Kidnapping priests made no sense, even for them. It wasn't like the gangbangers were going to rape the old men. Maybe they had some vague idea of using them as hostages for ransom.

Either way, mopping up gangbangers gave Tavo something he would soon require: moral authority. He didn't give a shit what people thought about him personally, but if he could cover himself in the patina of law and order—and maybe add an implied partnership with the Catholic Church—he could prop himself up as the protector of the region. For that to happen, he'd need the Mexican army and the local government to settle down long enough for him to slip into the gap. This mess with Los Negros was just the window he required.

A man emerged from the deep shadows, dragging the shrieking woman by her hair. She screamed and whimpered. She shuffled and stumbled, her pants dangling by one leg, tangling her up. The woman was naked from the belly button down. The gangbanger dragging her toward the building paused to punch her in the mouth and to stomp on the pants, freeing the writhing woman from her entanglement. Maybe the man meant to hand her off to his compatriots inside. After the punch in the mouth, her shrieking gave way to mewling. The man dragged her through the glass doors at the front of the building and the woman's cries ceased as the door swished closed.

"Why didn't you..." Sofia began to speak and Tavo jammed his finger to his lips. His daughter stilled, the question still swirling in her eyes. She reached for his binoculars sitting on the low wall beside the rifle and looked from window to window. Tavo thought he heard the slightest whimper from his daughter.

"We're at the state building," Tavo's radioed blared. He turned it down and replied, "Overwatch confirms. Roadrunner at Overwatch. Situation nominal. You've got one sentry on each corner facing the plaza. Several tangos are passed out on the sidewalk. Unknown combatants inside." The reminder that they didn't know what was inside was probably unnecessary. Beto had done more door kicking than Tavo by a wide margin.

Fifteen years ago, Beto deployed four times as a SEAL right in the middle of the "get some" years of the Global War on Terror. He had assaulted buildings like this probably dozens, if not hundreds of times.

Now she understands, Tavo thought to himself, switching his thoughts to his daughter. The scene in the plaza with the raped woman slammed home the brutal truth— the world had always been a more monstrous place than they taught in business school.

Tavo suddenly regretted his decision to let his daughter come with him on the op. He never would've permitted her to see this side of the world if not for his suspicions that she betrayed him. It'd been an error of judgment caused by his cynicism.

He had been wrong. She almost certainly had nothing to do with the assault on the hotel in Antigua. He flicked a look in her direction. His daughter covered her mouth with one hand and searched with the other, scanning the building across the plaza for any sign of the woman.

Sofía was an innocent...

Tavo settled his riflescope on the first sentry, keeping his finger away from the hungry trigger. He'd humped the thirty pound Barrett 82A1 to the top of the OXXO building, thinking he might need to send rounds through concrete. But hanging over the little Plaza Zaragoza, he realized that the Barrett was way too much gun for this op. More importantly: it was way too much gun to kill men with his daughter present. Tavo felt a shock of foreboding—the cocktail of emotion that marked a rare mistake.

Foolishness. Regret. Consternation.

The Barrett would be like shooting gangbangers with a deck cannon on a warship. If he pulled the trigger, he'd unleash a six-foot tongue of flame that'd paint them as the most inviting target in the entire area of operation. And it would obliterate anything on the other side of the battle space. His daughter might see the carnage the Barrett and its master intended.

He reached out his hand, as though he needed the binos. Sofia passed them and Tavo pretended to examine a target. Then he slipped them into the big pocket on his plate carrier vest. At least she wouldn't see the carnage up close.

Tavo had come on the assault to command and to provide overwatch. With his daughter present, he had no intention of joining the fight. Even so, his trigger finger stroked the side of the Barrett's lower receiver.

This was war, and anything could happen.

He didn't hear the *whip-snap* of Beto's suppressed round as it passed through the gangbanger sentry's head. The man slumped deeply, not even falling out of his chair. Tavo strained to hear the rifle shot. His men materialized from the shadows, passing the dead sentry.

Watching his trained assaulters work was like watching a TV show. They flowed through the sentry positions, eliminating threats and drunken men alike with their M4s. Tavo felt pleased with the money he'd invested in training. He wanted to be on the ground with them, skirting death and dealing oblivion.

Beto's second element must've closed on the state building from the west side. The guard suddenly stood, then folded to the ground like a puppet with severed strings. Again, Tavo heard nothing.

He knew from the evening news that many of the big cities in America burned at this moment in the darkest part of night. Hermosillo probably wouldn't be far behind, but the street lamps still glowed in Plaza Zaragoza just like any other night.

Tavo didn't need night vision to see his teams make entry into the building. The pools of light from the street lamps poured almost all the way around the building, painting the scene in grayscale. His men disappeared through the doorway and the night hushed. A peal of drunken laughter echoed about the plaza from the state building. A silent twinkle flashed in a first story window, then another.

Suddenly, the windows of the first floor lit up like a lightning storm. The thunder of unsuppressed gunfire boomed across the plaza, startling the drowsy town. Tavo pictured the gangbangers inside the building groping through their drunken fugue in a vain attempt to defend themselves.

He monitored the front door, the side entrances and the roof, peering over the top of his giant rifle. His unaided eyes would pick out movement a lot better than through the big Leupold scope.

The access door on the state building roof slammed open and four *Los Negros* gunmen spilled out, driven like rats before the flood tide. Tavo rested his weight on the stone wall of the OXXO building, two floors higher, and steadied himself. He held the pistol grip with one hand and cupped the other hand beneath it, flexing his fist to make adjustments to his point of aim. Two hundred meters across the plaza might as well have been point-blank for the Barrett.

WHOOMP! WHOOMP! WHOOMP! WHOOMP!

The Barrett barked like a bull mastodon, unleashing one-tenth of a pound slugs that shredded the men across the plaza like piñatas. As he resettled his optic on the rooftop, the first thing he noticed, as his eyes recovered from the flash, was a blue-sleeved, severed arm, draped over the roof wall. Tavo could hear his daughter whimpering. She'd been wearing ear protection, but the violence of the fifty cal was enough to unsettle anyone.

"Overwatch to Roadrunner."

"Go for Roadrunner."

"I just wasted some local PD on top of the building."

"Yeah," Beto responded. "There are police partying with the gangbangers."

Tavo snorted. His recon guys hadn't said anything about cops. They probably hadn't thought it worth mentioning. Local police in Hermosillo ran with gangs as often as not.

His command radio crackled to life. "Overwatch, North security. Six army Jeeps entering town from the north. Requesting permission to engage."

Tavo rubbed his face with his rough shooting gloves.

The dogs of war had bolted off their leash.

Enter the Mexican Army, too soon for his liking. Tavo closed his eyes and pictured the threat. He mulled over ramifications. The battle space and his long-term game plan commingled in his mind. He sorted through the big chess pieces, the players of influence, his pile of toy soldiers. He considered the malleable people of Sonora. The Catholic Church. The local army commander. He thought about his daughter. He weighed his doubts. He measured his power in drams of lethal force.

"Engage the Jeeps hard, then withdraw," Tavo ordered his men at the north end of town. "Stop them on the road."

He needed a half-hour. He wasn't ready to get into a fight with the army. His soldiers were still filtering into Sonora from the roiling stew of America. At the present moment, he could only field two hundred men. He needed just a couple more days to consolidate.

As Tavo watched the state building flicker with rifle fire, he wondered what had awoken the army. They didn't usually get off their bureaucratic asses for anything short of the promise of a cash bribe. Had they come to rescue the archbishop? Maybe the base commander was waxing brave tonight. Maybe a junior officer hadn't gotten laid in a while and he was feeling his oats. Sometimes weird shit happened. The world wasn't a chess game, Tavo reminded himself. It was more like a fishing derby with currents and tides, spawning seasons and moon phases. He couldn't hope to capture all the myriad elements in his calculations. Some fish would escape his genius, no matter how meticulous.

"They broke through, sir," the radio blared. "The Jeeps pushed past our ambush."

Another fish through the net.

He should've set up a roadblock between the army base and town. The last thing he wanted was a shooting fight with the army this morning. Not yet. This little assault was supposed to position his cartel as the peacekeeper, not the invader.

"North Security. Withdraw to the plaza," Tavo ordered and switched radios.

"Overwatch to Roadrunner."

"Go for Roadrunner," Beto answered.

"Mex military approaching from the north. We need to exfil. They might be spinning up birds."

Helicopters would throw the battle space into an entirely new level of chaos. Tavo felt the presence of his daughter, exposed with him on the roof of the OXXO building.

"We're *jackpot* here," Beto called over the radio. "Archbishop and the priests are free and we're escorting them outside. Forty dead Los Negros inside. We have two down. The vicar got killed in the crossfire. Coming out the east door. Acknowledge."

"Acknowledged," Tavo spoke into the radio. The priests and several assaulters poured out of the side door of the state office building, making their way west down the sidewalk.

"Exfil, NOW, Roadrunner." Tavo coaxed into the radio as the angry whine of the speeding Jeeps filled the plaza. "Let those priests go on their own. I don't want the army guys to see our assaulters. Everyone needs to vanish."

As he said it, he already knew it was wishful thinking. Nothing in battle ever conformed to wishful thinking.

The knobby tires of the Jeeps howled as they flew into the Plaza Zaragoza. Tavo swiveled the Barrett and thunder-clapped a .50 caliber round through the front grill of the first Jeep. The passenger compartment exploded with dark liquid—engine oil, blood or both. The Jeep careened over the curb, across the plaza grass and smashed, full speed, into a tree. The impact knocked the tree askew and launched a body through the window.

BRRRRRRRRR!

The second Jeep was still rolling when the Rheinmetall MG3 opened up on Tavo's position. Tavo dropped behind the concrete wall, leaving his Barrett on top. Sofia had already curled into a ball against one of the air exchangers. She and Tavo stared at one another as she prayed with her rosary beads, muted by the roar of the belt-fed machine gun tearing up their rooftop.

Was she praying for their lives? Was she praying for the woman being raped?

None of the machine gun fire was particularly effective—the machine gunner had sighted in on the vanished burst of flame from the Barrett. The night brimmed over with whizzing chips of concrete and buzzing chunks of lead, enough to humble any hard-bitten warrior. In his daughter's eyes, even in the milky dark, Tavo beheld her amazement and fear.

Her wide eyes and open mouth gaped at him—surely bewildered at how her father could live in two worlds: the fairytale citadels of wealth and the gristmill of combat. It was not the face of a sociopath. This girl, praying the rosary under the scythe of a machine gun, could not plot the destruction of her father. A person could pretend to be someone they weren't in the light of day, wrapped in human drama, but nobody could playact under a barrage of suppressing fire. Nothing revealed a person like combat.

BRRRRRR...

The machine-gun fire shifted away and Tavo lifted himself slowly up to the Barrett and searched for threats. He spotted the machine-gunner, now crumpled in the back of the second Jeep, probably killed by one of Beto's men. Movement at the edge of the reticle caught his eye and he swiveled to a new threat, a soldier preparing to fire another MG3 from a third Jeep, probably at Beto's squad. Tavo fired another round from the Barrett.

WHOMP!

The scope jumped with recoil and Tavo tracked back, searching for the target. He found the man dangling over the side, cut nearly in half below his breastbone. Intestines and offal hung over the side wall and glopped onto the grass.

He glanced back at his daughter, still balled up beneath the air exchanger.

She's not a killer...

Tavo panned across the Jeeps through the scope. He could see five of the six vehicles, one dead against the tilting tree. Another held the eviscerated gunman hanging over the side. The remaining three Jeeps parked nose-to-nose in a hasty stockade. Two of those had MG3s in the back dangling from pintle mounts, but no one had stepped up to man them. Tavo could see legs and helmets sticking out from around corners and edges of the vehicles—all men he could kill through the light metal skin. Almost nothing in the Jeeps would stop his .50 caliber round.

He spotted a soldier peeking around the corner of a building, probably from a Jeep he hadn't located. The man dropped back and disappeared.

Tavo preferred to let his men on the ground work the problem of the soldiers. He'd done his part to stop the vehicles, and he was in no hurry to draw rounds by sending another cone of flame from the Barrett. Beto could handle the grunts on the ground.

Tavo checked on his daughter and switched from the riflescope to his binoculars. With the binos, he could take in the whole battlefield in a single scan.

He didn't like what he saw.

Both Beto's team and Bravo Team had ducked inside a parking garage next door to the state office building. The soldiers pinned under and around the Jeeps were trading rounds with Beto's crew. As Tavo had seen before, men tended to settle into these fifty-fifty gunfights, which made no sense at all in the calculus of battle, but to them seemed the right thing to do at the time. Once a man got behind something thick and hard, he would be slow to leave it.

"Actual, Roadrunner." Tavo keyed his radio.

"Go for Roadrunner."

"Keep moving west. Exfil that parking garage. A squad of Mex Army is moving around the backside of your position."

"Roadrunner Two took a round to the throat. We're leaving him. On the move. Roadrunner out."

BRRRRRRR!

Tavo ducked below the wall, but the string of 5.56 went somewhere other than his perch atop the OXXO. Sofia crept up beside him at the wall, probably feeling safer next to another human being.

Tavo left her and jumped up behind the Barrett and quickly located the dart of flame that marked the MG3.

KA-WHOOMP!

The round fired before Tavo meant to send it, but it silenced the MG. Sometimes, when he accidentally fired, things worked out—surprise trigger break and all. He re-centered the scope on the belt-fed and found the soldier falling slowly backwards, gripping a severed hand. Tavo had impacted the machine gun body itself, and the twisted metal and red-hot frag had done its deadly work.

Fire from the soldiers beneath the Jeeps peppered the rooftop. Tavo crouched down and turned his head to avoid taking frag in the face. He came eyeball-to-eyeball with Sofía. Her panic seemed to have subsided.

"This is war, *mi amor*. This is what it takes to keep people safe," Tavo shouted over the *pop-pop-pop* of rifle fire down in the plaza. Killing a bunch of Mexican Army in order to kill gangsters in order to free priests? He couldn't tell if he'd convinced her of anything or not. Even to him it wasn't particularly clear. In combat, it rarely was. He'd shot and killed the guys trying to shoot and kill him. End of story.

"Roadrunner to Actual."

Tavo looked down at his radio. "Go for Actual."

"We're clear of the AO. Minus one VIP. Minus four blue team. Five mikes out from the ORP."

"We'll see you there in ten." Tavo reached up with one hand and slid the Barrett off the wall and into his arms. He faced Sofía.

"We saved the archbishop and all but one of his priests. Los Negros won't be a problem anymore. We've done what we came here to do. Let's go home."

She looked at him with wide, wet eyes and nodded.

CHAPTER 11

TAVO CASTILLO
RANCHO SANTIAGUITO, 65 MILES OUTSIDE OF
HERMOSILLO, SONORA, MEXICO

The ironwood mountainside chewed the sun as it sank toward the horizon, ending another day in the northern desert of Mexico.

Tavo sensed the opportunity escaping him, and he resented the daylight hours he'd spent sleeping.

America floundered in its death throes, the weakened shadow of a once dazzling empire. While the greatest opportunity he'd ever seen lay vulnerable, Tavo had been forced to catch up on the sleep he'd missed the night before. Given the opportunities, and the stakes if he failed, he couldn't afford to make decisions with a woolly mind. So, he'd slept eight hours after the night raid. He'd also run a 5k in the late afternoon cool-down, a highland desert circuit on the dirt roads that cut through the chaparral. He wanted to ensure that his physical and mental machine were in peak, working order. Over the next three days, he would lock in his destiny, either as a little-known criminal genius or as an emperor the likes of which hadn't been seen in a thousand years.

As he let his hot sweat cool in the setting sun, Tavo noticed a dead woodpecker chick curled on the desert floor. He sat on a chunk of crumbling granite and let his mind wander.

The baby woodpecker must've died leaving the nest, its plumage nearly, but not quite, full. A big ironwood and a mesquite tree overhung the rock pile, and Tavo felt certain he'd find a nest if he searched one branch at a time.

A caravan of tiny, black ants streamed toward the carcass and a parallel caravan of black ants streamed away, each ant with a minuscule grain of woodpecker flesh. Tavo followed the ant trail from the kill. The jurassic head of a horned toad lizard bobbed out from beneath the shade of a rock and slurped up a tongue full of ants along with the woodpecker carrion.

Twofer, Tavo mused.

Someone would absorb the carcass of America, just like the Spanish absorbed the Aztecs and the Turks absorbed the Roman Empire. Tavo sat on a rock, a mere hundred miles from the U.S. border, with thousands of men awaiting his order.

Somebody would be the ant, and somebody would be the horned toad, but in a short while, there would be but feathers and bones.

Tavo looked up from the small kill when he heard the squeak of bouncing suspension and the low hum of an engine.

His lieutenants had purchased twenty brand new Ford Ranger four door trucks and welded machine gun mounts in the bed of each. With the U.S. on the skids, they'd instructed the ranch hands to arm the trucks with the 240 SAWs and .50 caliber "Ma Deuce" machine guns that'd been tucked away in the ranch's massive gun vault.

Tavo shook his head as he watched the white Ranger lurch over the road. One of their street soldiers from Tucson jangled around in the back behind the SAW, trying to keep from being thrown from the vehicle. The driver must've seen Tavo because the truck veered off the road and cut a beeline in his direction across the grainy waves of the desert floor. The truck eventually ground to a halt, a cloud of dust enveloping both the truck and Tavo.

He waited, thinking about how nobody ever raced across a desert with good news.

Sofia jumped from the passenger seat as the dust cloud settled. "You've got a problem, Papi."

The worry in her voice sounded real, though Tavo had to wonder.

"The twenty-fourth infantry battalion out of *Zona Cuatro* has orders to arrest everyone on this ranch. They're preparing to come against you tomorrow or the next day. General Bautista called me from Pozo Rica to make sure I wouldn't get caught up in it."

If his daughter had wanted him arrested, why warn him?

"Why us?" Tavo began with the obvious question.

"They found two dead Special Forces men in full kit in the state building last night, and the archbishop said that American soldiers freed them from the gangsters. The army knew that wasn't true, but the town's bursting with rumors about a narco ranch with helicopters, tanks and machine guns, so the Mexican army put two and two together and, *surprise*—you win a military seizure." Sofia held out her hands, her worry cutting lines across her forehead.

One of the first things Tavo had done after arriving at the ranch had been to send two men to surveil the army bases in Hermosillo. He already knew that he wouldn't have to face "Mexico's finest." The real troops—the mechanized guys with light armor—were all based in Mexico City, 2,000 kilometers away. The local air base—more of a corner of the airport actually— had three Bell 212 helicopters and two prop planes, none of them with heavy ordnance. The local army base boasted about two hundred career soldiers and several hundred local conscripts who came in on weekends. They maintained a dozen Jeeps with machine guns. The Hermosillo base existed to give local conscripts something to do. When the Mexican government fielded troops against Sonoran narcos, they sent soldiers from Mexico City, not Hermosillo.

Tavo pictured the twenty-forth infantry battalion of the Mexican Army in their dusty corner of Hermosillo. It was really more of a company than a battalion, but Mexicans were nothing if not grandiose about their armed forces. He pictured the helicopters and the Jeeps. He pictured the other weapons *Zona Cuatro* might have mothballed on their base: heavy machine guns, rocket-propelled grenades, MG3s, Ma Deuces, M29 mortars, and maybe even some anti-tank rockets. They'd have a warehouse full of cast-off weapons from the U.S.; it was one of America's favorite ways to pat Mexico on the head. The U.S. handed down old weapons, like a big brother giving a little brother his old slingshot.

Only these old weapons weren't child's play. Infantry technology hadn't made major leaps since World War Two. The Browning M2, for example, was still fielded by the U.S. even though it'd been invented at the end of World War One. The U.S. handed these weapons off to Mexico, not because the weapons lacked power and lethality, but because the U.S. preferred more efficient, computerized killing machines. In this new, collapsing world, that fixation on complex systems would probably hit them right in the *culo*. The old weapons would likely turn out to be the best weapons in a collapse scenario.

Sofia rocked back and forth from foot to foot in the sand. "Papi. What are you waiting for? We need to leave."

Like a bullet sliding into battery, the new world jacked into place for Tavo. He'd been lost in thought, but his future clicked: he needed those old weapons, and he needed those Mexican soldiers.

He stepped back to the rock and picked up his iPhone, speed dialing Beto. He didn't bother to step away from Sofía. *Let her hear what she would hear.*

"Beto. The Mexican army is coming for us. We will ambush them en route. First, we need to take down the base at the Hermosillo airport. We can't let those helicopters off the ground. Have your men ready to go in two hours." Tavo had never given Beto an order before, but Beto accepted it without hesitation.

"*Si, Canoso.* Let's do it."

"What are you talking about?" Sofía exclaimed. "You can't ambush troops. We're cooperating with the Mexican army. They're our partners. They're our country!"

"No, *mi hija*. They're *your* partners," Tavo's hard eyes probably betrayed more distrust than he wanted to reveal, but the time for maneuvering had passed. Now was the time for action.

"Papi. Don't do this."

"Sofi. Things have changed. Without the American government, there is no Mexican government. Our economy will follow their economy right down a corpse-filled hole. But it doesn't have to be that way in Hermosillo. Or in Sonora. We grow the food for thousands of miles. We have our own gasoline. We aren't going to fall to pieces when the internet stops working. But we can't stand around, waiting to see if democracy survives to save us all. The Mexican democracy barely existed here in Sonora in the first place."

Sofía shook her head "no" over and over again, like when she was an eight-year-old girl; a stubborn, beautiful creature, her chestnut locks dancing around her head. If the stakes weren't so high, Tavo might've smiled.

"No, Papi. They are trying. They want to help. That's why they sent troops to rescue the archbishop, and that's why they're coming for the ranch: they want to preserve order."

Tavo snorted. "Those are perfect examples of why we can't

wait on government. The army showed up at the cathedral with just six Jeeps, hours late, and now they're mounting an assault against the *wrong guys*. They should be putting down the Zeta cartel in Hermosillo. Instead, they're coming after the men who actually got the job done. Some fat officer is angry that someone else saved the Catholic priests. We saved them, not the army. We have proven ourselves. We are the good guys here."

She continued shaking her head. "You can bury me in words, but men will die and their blood will be *on my hands*. I warned you that they were coming. General Bautista trusted me with that information."

Tavo understood the words, but couldn't fathom her endgame. Why would she pretend to care so much about a few half-baked soldiers?

"We don't have time for idealism, Sofi. By the time you figure out that your Ivy League world has crashed, it'll be too late for us to salvage our means of production and self-defense."

Her hands gesticulated wildly, as though chopping onions in the air. "*Bullshit!* You don't care about saving 'our means of production.' You only care about control. *You want weapons.* They intoxicate you. Well, you can have your weapons or you can have my help. Pick one!"

Sofía turned on her heels and stormed off across the rolling hills of the ranch, abandoning her ride back in the truck.

Nobody had spoken to Tavo like that in a long time. *Why hadn't he married a woman like that?*

She could be forgiven her innocence. She hadn't arrived at this moment with Tavo's fifty years of experience with the evil lurking in every man, woman and child. Often, all it took to release the demons was a tiny shot of liquid in the arm. He could forgive her for being ignorant of that reality. She had never tasted of the contamination that hung just below the rippled surface of life.

She would taste it soon. Everyone would.

How could he channel his daughter's raw horsepower? How would he make her useful in this new world?

The answer would come with time.

Tavo climbed into the truck. The driver had been sitting behind the wheel, pretending not to hear their argument. Tavo didn't care what he'd heard.

CHAPTER 12
NOAH MILLER
MCCALLISTER RANCH, FIFTEEN MILES OUTSIDE
PATAGONIA, ARIZONA

Noah knew his father was dead from the moment he saw the tire tracks going south into Mexico. Nobody could steal his dad's Land Cruiser unless they killed him first.

A fifty foot section of the border fence had been laid down in the bottom of Geezer Wash, and a dozen tire tracks had crossed over around eleven in the morning. One of those sets of tires had been Yokohama B97s, with all-season tread, set apart sixty-one-point-three inches.

Noah found the laid down section of fence, and the tire tracks, around one o'clock in the afternoon and he could tell from the slight crumble on the upper lip of the tracks that they'd been imprinted about three hours prior—eleven o'clock in the morning.

Bill McCallister had once trained the Border Patrol in man tracking, along with search and rescue crews in neighboring New Mexico. But that hadn't lasted. It didn't take long for the stink of federal government to ruin it for Bill. After one particularly bad run-in with a Border Patrol bureaucrat, Bill refused to train anyone but Noah. Noah had received double-measure of the old war scout's intensity; half instruction in man tracking and half bitching about pencil pushers and "robo cops" in law enforcement.

Bill's overarching rule of tracking had been *take your time and observe small.* Bill insisted Noah master both foot and tire tracking and be able to identify the age of the sign up to forty-eight hours after the print. So when Noah spotted the old Land Cruiser's track, he knew exactly what it looked like fresh and how long the track had been on this dirt road. He'd trained on tracking this exact vehicle.

As Noah paced off the spread between the Yokohama tire tracks, a pit hardened in his stomach. The other tracks intermingled with Bill's Land Cruiser had been low profile, front-wheel drive passenger vehicles. They were probably small Hondas and Mazdas from the city; gangbangers with lowered chassis and loud mufflers. Noah vaguely remembered hearing the deep, bass hum of modified exhaust late that morning. It'd been strange, but he couldn't see the road from his ranch house, so Noah had written it off as something he couldn't do anything about.

Along the outer edge of Noah's boot, he'd drawn inch marks with a Sharpie marker—an old tracker's trick passed down from Bill's military unit. The Land Cruiser sat wider and heavier than the rice burners and Noah knew the exact wheelbase of the Land Cruiser because he owned the same rig as his dad—both 1980s model FJ40s. Even though he was ninety-nine percent sure already, he paced off the tread width, not skipping any steps, just like his old man had taught him.

See everything. Ignore nothing.

The tracks were the right width to be his dad's vehicle. Noah packed himself into his own Cruiser and drove back along the tire tracks away from the border fence, fifteen miles north until he arrived at Bill's place. As he drove up to the gate of his dad's ranch, the chunk of wood in Noah's stomach hardened into a lump of granite. Stretched across Bill's yard, Noah beheld his first battlefield.

Bill didn't come out of the house at sound of his engine, which he did almost every time Noah drove up to the ranch. Then the smell hit Noah—a stench like when you light a barbecue and the harrumphing little gas explosion burns off the hair on your arm. Only this smell was a hundred times worse.

A pile of blackened bodies smoldered admist the gravel and weeds in the front yard. There were at least a dozen, maybe more than twenty. They'd been burned beyond recognition. It wasn't something Bill would do in his own yard. The smell and the rot would make his ranch house unliveable.

Noah gathered his emotions like a hen gathers her chicks. He'd need to think straight—not go off half-cocked and contaminate the scene hunting for his dad's body. The best way to find him would be to do this right.

A black Honda hatchback lay flipped upside down on the dirt driveway like a dead cockroach. The crater bore witness to the buried shaped charge Bill must have triggered as the gangbangers crashed his yard.

Noah would give his old man the funeral he would want—the only funeral an old military scout would care about enough to turn back from beyond the grave and smile. From his first step down from his vehicle, Noah would pick through each bit of sign, winnow out facts and divine the story of the battle in his mind's eye.

He knew the heart and mind of his father. Winning the battle would've been less important to Bill than fighting it well. And fighting the battle well would've been less important than his son *knowing* that he had fought it well. Noah's search of the battlefield might end with a burial or it might not, but the search would be a testament to the grizzled, old professional, and his nuts and bolts love for his son. Noah had become that professional too, and he would read his father's death in the dust and detritus.

Noah took a shuddering inhale, let go of his iron grip on the steering wheel, reached for his tracking pole, opened his car door and stepped down. He hefted his pole and scratched his head with the grip, taking a dispassionate view of the ground. His every cell wanted to rush in and find his dad, but somehow he knew it would be wrong. Like every other manhunt, the best chance at a good outcome was to go slow.

"Dad?" Noah shouted. "Are you here?" The bodies on the burn pile crackled and popped, but otherwise there was only silence. He weighed possible outcomes. His dad could've been left wounded and bleeding in the barn or the ranch house. He could be dead and thrown on the funeral pyre. Or, he could've been taken.

The aggressors had left with Bill's Land Cruiser and they had time to pile up the dead. It seemed extremely unlikely that they would've left Bill alive and wounded, particularly given the number of gangbanger bodies on the burn heap. Likewise, there was almost no chance they would've taken the old man with them. He'd killed well over a dozen of them and there was no way they would have let him live.

"BILL!" Noah yelled at the top of his lungs. Still nothing.

On the outside chance that Bill was still alive, Noah decided to stick with his plan—to pick the scene apart one bit at a time and to do it right. The most professional thing to do was to hunt down every bit of sign and to track the killers. Indeed, Bill would want it that way.

The scene spoke of supreme violence, but the blasts had settled and the clatter of bullets had died. Noah didn't even draw the Glock 17 hanging on his hip. He could feel it: the Grim Reaper had already left this place, and Noah could taste the stale gunpowder and drying blood of the fight on his tongue.

He took careful steps to the gate—the obvious chokepoint and "sign trap" that would force man sign into a narrow piece of ground. The gate was burst inward by the dead Honda. Blue paint, matching the Honda's fender, had scraped off on the galvanized pipe.

Bill must have heard the gangbangers coming, since he would've had to trigger the blast under the Honda as it busted into the yard. Bill had long ago buried a blast plate just inside his driveway. It was an upright two-foot length of cast iron sewer pipe, loaded with twenty pounds of ANFO in an old gas can and capped with a five pound disc of AR550 steel. The booby trap probably could've killed an armored personnel carrier. It must've thrown the Honda fifty feet into the air.

Hiding what amounted to a massive directional pipe bomb under his gravel driveway wasn't even the kookiest thing Bill had done to prepare for the end of the world. Between foreign wars and endless disputes with the Border Patrol, obeying the law wasn't a big concern of Bill McCallister. He didn't mind planting a huge bomb in his yard even if it was illegal as shit. But the directional charge under the driveway had been the subject of endless ribbing from Noah. He frequently relied upon the buried plate charge as his final piece of evidence when he argued that Bill might be a lunatic.

Now a gangbanger's car lay on its back and Noah knew that Bill-up-in-heaven was laughing his ass off. Even standing at the threshold of Saint Peter and the Pearly Gates, the old bastard would do a happy dance and brag about winning one last argument with his son.

Once Noah stepped inside the gate, he found a fan of footprints. He crouched down and spent ten minutes categorizing them. He didn't have his pad and pen or he would've taken another twenty minutes to draw them too. He counted seventeen distinct sets of prints.

Most of the prints looked like tennis shoes—some with the Nike logo in the tread. Noah imagined they were black low-top sneakers, but he reminded himself not to jump to conclusions. Assumptions and wild guesses were kryptonite to a professional tracker. Emotional conclusions tended to blind a man to more sensible options later. Given the low profile tires and the complete lack of boot prints, Noah strongly suspected these were city boys on the rampage—and that they'd come a long way to sneak into Mexico. The nearest city was Phoenix and that was over two hours north.

He glanced up at the dead Honda and noted the Illinois license plate, confirming his suspicion. These guys didn't drive all this way to rob an old hard case living in a dust and gravel ranch. They were heading somewhere specific. Somewhere south of the border.

But they'd stopped at the McCallister ranch for a reason that still eluded Noah, and that feeling generally came when he'd skipped a step. Even though he still hadn't penetrated the actual scene of the battle, Noah retraced his steps back to his Land Cruiser, conscious of each footprint he added to the tableau. When he got there, he took in the bigger picture.

That's when he noticed the sparkling nuggets of glass on the road. There were too many to have been made by bullet impact alone. Noah followed the tennis shoe prints backwards. They disappeared when they hit a band of shimmering gravel. He stood up straight and looked around.

He saw the cable.

Anchored to a huge boulder on the far side of the road, a three-eighths inch thick length of aircraft cable lay partially buried in the dust. The scattered and granular remains of automotive glass spread across the dirt road beneath it.

The first car hit the cable...

Bill picked this fight. Noah smiled. The old idiot had taken on at least twenty gangbangers by himself. Not a bad way for an old Green Beret to die.

He pictured it: when the cars came barreling down the country lane, Bill had pulled the cable tight with his tractor and clotheslined the whole caravan of rice burners. No doubt he knew what he was doing, and he knew he'd probably die in the process. But for some reason, the dumbfuck had yanked that cable and kicked off a losing battle.

At first, Noah blamed it on the *preps*. That's what Bill McCallister called his massive store of apocalyptic supplies and preparations: his "preps." His old man loved nothing more than to blather on about his end-of-the-world strategies; two-thirds of the time it had been Bill's default topic of conversation. Noah had heard, *ad nauseam,* for most of his life, how Bill was "ready for bear" when "the shit hit the proverbial fan." The old man must've been laughing like a schoolgirl at recess when all his planning actually came down to a gunfight with a pack of evildoers.

Noah crouched down and looked more closely at the roadway. Several blood trails extended from where the vehicles had been stopped by the cable. He almost missed them because the dry dust had sucked up the moisture and formed dirty, little cocoons around the blood trails. It didn't look like blood as much as dark brown caterpillars in the dirt.

Bill must've laid into the gangbangers with his rifle the moment he'd hopped down from his tractor. Noah scanned the surface of the road and discovered a constellation of dust clumps, laced with drying blood. He picked up one of the clumps and rubbed it between his fingers. A gelatinous grey slime squeezed out of the dirt clod. It was some dude's brains, more than likely. It smelled like a combination of pig fat and sunscreen. The disgusting goop on his fingers made Noah reconsider.

Bill hadn't brought this level of hate just to try out his preps.

Noah stood up and stretched his legs. The town of Patagonia sat just two miles down the road from Bill's ranch. Bill hated government and he hated most people, but he would do anything to protect that parched, one-horse town. Drinking coffee and telling lies every morning at the corner gas station made even a hard man love a place.

Noah pursed his lips and looked in the direction of Patagonia. The town hid behind a mountain, but it was dead south from Bill's ranch. It made sense that Bill would stop them here at any cost.

Now that he knew to look for blood clumps, Noah noticed a massive, congealed puddle in between the tire tracks of the rice burners. Bill had drained a man's heart with his big gun and that man had fallen dead on the spot. Noah circled the deathbed and found another two sets of sneakers running away from the battle and toward the rock where the cable had been anchored. They'd been the cowards—or maybe the smart ones.

Noah moved from the LKP, "Last Known Point," to where the men had rushed the gate. It happened after the Honda burst through the chain-link. Two of the 'bangers seemed to have died from fatal bullet wounds when they got out of their cars, and maybe more had died in the vehicle that got clotheslined by the cable. Noah didn't imagine that a modern airbag would save a dude from taking a three-eighths cable to the face.

Inside the gate, a bunch of new blood trails appeared on the gravel and in the dust. Noah counted six of them. Two of those looked like they stalled out behind the belly-up Honda. Those were probably wounded men who had taken cover.

The ground between the gate and the Honda was heavily sprinkled with Berdan-primed, steel casing 7.62 x 39. The gangbangers had been shooting AK-47s. There were a few nine millimeter rounds thrown in, but it struck Noah as odd that all twenty guys were shooting the same rifle.

Gangbangers usually shot whatever they could steal or buy on the black market. Why would they all shoot the same caliber and manufacture of bullet? And why would they pile up the bodies of the dead? These weren't the behaviors of random thugs.

Noah plucked up one of the AK rounds and smelled it. The smell told him nothing, but it gave him a second to ponder.

Maybe not gangbangers per se. Maybe cartel soldiers. Maybe they're heading back south across the border.

Why? Why cross over into Mexico?

The pockmarks in the dead Honda told Noah a piece that he'd already assumed: Bill shot most of these guys with his big FN SCAR rifle. The old man kept the massive thunder stick by the door, hanging from the coat rack like most people hang their keys.

If Bill had had more time, he probably would've come at them with his belt-fed M60 instead of the SCAR. He actually owned the M60 machine gun legally—having done months of paperwork with the BATF and having paid more for the belt-fed than he'd paid for his pickup truck. He might've won the battle if he'd had time to get the M60. He might've won the battle if his son had been here to fight by his side.

He should've been by Bill's side. He shouldn't have given Bill shit for talking during the movie. He should've been a better friend and a better son.

Funerals were no place for personal regrets, Noah reminded himself as he wiped away a tear. With the world shutting down, he couldn't imagine anyone taking time to honor their dead. This was all the funeral Bill would likely get, and Noah wasn't about to screw it up. He sucked in a breath and spent a minute watching a lazy cloud drift behind a hill. Then he went back to work understanding his father's killers.

After an hour creeping around the scene, examining the sign left by the gangbangers, Noah arrived at Bill's first shooting nest. Glittering brass danced in the midday sun where Bill had fired at least six mags of 7.62 x 51 out of the SCAR. The SCAR had probably been stolen by the 'bangers, but Noah could see the clear outline of the rifle in the dust where Bill had dropped it after it went dry.

In the middle of the field of brass, a hundred boot prints were stamped into the ground. Noah could picture Bill in his cowboy boots, pouring rifle fire into the small army of criminals while he turned to engage one group, then another.

A handful of spent cartridges had been mashed into the dry dirt by heel prints as Bill launched himself toward the farmhouse. Noah pictured him running his big rifle out of bullets, dropping it and hightailing it toward the house under a barrage of AK rounds.

With the sun now directly overhead, spotting sign would be difficult, but Noah was in no hurry. With a four hour head start, the cartel soldiers would've already hit paved road in Mexico and vanished into the Sonora. Tracking them would be long and difficult—probably futile. Another hour or two here at the ranch could yield information that might help Noah cut their track farther down the line.

In truth, Noah wasn't worried about taking revenge. Bill had already exacted a hefty price, taking his vengeance in advance with absurd interest. The old man had found the death he'd always wanted, and he'd dragged a passel of shitbags with him to Valhalla.

Noah realized that he'd drifted off for a moment, brooding over Bill's boot print in the field of cartridges. If he was going to find Bill's body at the end of the track, he damned-well was going to track it properly.

Noah bobbled his tracking pole and crouched down, scanning until he found the next cowboy boot-heel in the dust. He poked the pointy end of the tracking pole into the back of Bill's heel print and slid an orange rubber band up the pole until it marked the back of the first heel print—giving him the precise measurement between the left boot and the right boot. The stride measured almost seventy-five inches. That meant Bill had been running like his ass was on fire.

Noah's tracking pole was an old ski pole he'd found at a garage sale years before. He scratched inch marks in the aluminum and added the orange rubber band for this purpose —to act as a gauge between footprints.

He duck-walked to the next print, and again, held the orange rubber band at the back of the heel depression. He swept the pointy end of the pole forward in the direction of travel and followed it with his eyes. The human eye tended to wander unless specifically directed to do otherwise. The stick made focusing on a small area of ground much easier. He would've missed the next print if not for the tracking pole. Dust had partially obscured it.

With the help of the pole, Noah moved forward, one-print-at-a-time. After fifteen minutes of crouching on the ground and working the track, he reached the porch of the farmhouse.

He carefully scanned in and around the track and found no blood. Bill had apparently made it this far without any major holes in his rawhide.

The next boot track had been partially hidden by sneaker tracks in the dust on the porch. Those were probably from the surviving soldiers plundering the house.

His dad had definitely gone inside, then reappeared on the

threshold. Noah assumed he'd grabbed another weapon. Bill kept guns around the house like some old women kept cats.

Based on the doorframe being splintered all to hell, Noah assumed Bill had used the jamb as cover for his next attack. The new shell casings scattered on the floor were also easily-identifiable. Bill had grabbed his old Marlin .45-70. Noah hoped he'd blasted at least one city boy with the cowboy gun. It would have a symmetry to it.

Noah finally turned to the piece that'd been bugging him from the beginning: the blast mark in the dirt, just thirty yards off the porch. It wasn't another plate charge. It wouldn't have made sense to plant one so near the house and Bill had never bragged about a second booby trap. Plus, the blast scar was nowhere near as big as the hole under the Honda.

Noah had never tracked sign on a battle scene before. In fact, he had never shot at a man, much less killed one. He'd seen plenty of blood on the ground while tracking—mostly from whitetail deer and javelina. But he'd never seen a blast scar like this one. The old man had taught him about explosives, and the two of them had even lit off pipe bombs together just to get some field practice. But Noah didn't know enough to say for sure what caused the explosive scar on the hardpack dirt. Either the old man had hidden another explosive trap in his yard, or the gangbangers had brought grenades from Illinois.

If the old man had hidden another trap or had stashed grenades, Noah felt positive he would've told him about it. There was no way Bill would keep his mouth shut about a prep that dramatic, at least not from Noah.

A wave of emotion rolled over him. He needed to know for sure if his father was dead.

On the outside chance that Bill's body was in the house, Noah carefully piloted his own footprints around the porch and ducked through the shattered door. The house was blown all to hell. Thousands of bullets had torn through the walls and the furniture and had dismembered the place in a maelstrom of floating duff. There were few footprints, and all of them were city-bought sneakers, now mostly filled in with dust. He saw no cowboy boot prints, but he picked through the small ranch house anyway, checking the two bedrooms, the kitchen and the single bathroom. His father's body was nowhere to be found.

Still exercising meticulous care to walk around the sign in the house, Noah worked his way back to the front door. When he again saw the shattered door frame, he searched the floor for blood spatter and saw nothing beneath the transparent layer of dust and sofa stuffing.

Noah stopped and took a deep breath that reached all the way down to his balls. He fought back a sob that rattled its way into his throat. The backlog of so much loss felt like it'd accumulated in his chest and now it wanted out. Noah heard his father's words in his mind, uttered god-knew-how-many times as he'd grown up on the ranch.

Walk it off, son.

He wiped his face, put his hands on his hips and resumed.

The boot prints in the porch dust had been completely hashed by sneaker prints, but Noah walked a circle around the porch and cut across what might be a partial cowboy boot print. He rotated around to get the sun in front of him, and the shadows revealed it to be a clear print from the forefoot of Bill's boot. But when Noah went to measure from the heel of that print, the point of the tracking pole totally overshot another print. Bill had stopped running and started walking. Noah slid the orange band to the new stride—now about twenty inches. The new track hit the blast scar then suddenly vanished. Noah stood and looked in a slow circle.

Then he saw the top of a boot, tipped on its side, ten feet from the blast scar.

Bill's cowboy boots—the same boots he'd worn for almost ten years—had "pull-up loops" on the tops, making it easier to insert fingers and pull them on--particularly helpful for an old man with beat-up knees.

Noah saw the unmistakable shape of a pull-up loop. He picked his way to the boot, each step becoming more convinced it was Bill's. With his tracking stick, Noah speared the loop and lifted the boot off the ground. Inside, he found a ragged bone and a mass of red flesh.

Bill's foot.

Noah looked up to check on the lazy cloud, but his eyes swam beneath a flux of tears. He couldn't bring himself to look inside the boot again, so he turned it around in his hand and examined the outside. There was no question it was Bill's.

Noah held the boot in one hand and pinched the bridge of his nose with the other. The sob rattled from up inside him and Noah choked it down again, this time mashing it into a billet of steel in the back of his throat.

Bill had taken him in and poured everything a crusty, old commando could pour into a boy. Noah felt his grief and his gratitude comingle. He remembered Bill's words a few days earlier.

When you have something beautiful then you lose it, only a fool would waste time regretting it.

Noah ran his shirtsleeve across his eyes and argued with Bill for the last time.

Damn you, Bill. I need you. How the hell am I supposed to find true north without you around, yanging in my ear?

He had known his father was dead since he saw the tracks at the border fence. Now with his dad's boot heavy in his hand, he knew it in a different way. In an ultimate way.

Noah looked around at the violence and chaos Bill had left in the wake of his passing. He smiled away his tears, and laughed wet and loud at the extravagant manner Bill had chosen to go out. What a melodramatic old fart. He couldn't just grow old and vanish. He had to take down a pile of thugs and blow up his ranch in the process. Valhalla would be a better place for him. At very least, there would be more conversation around the feast table. Old Bill never knew when to keep his yap shut.

Noah walked over to the porch and dumped the dust out of his own boots. He no longer cared about disturbing track. This funeral was over. It was time to get back to work. Noah got as close as he could to the smoking pyre of bodies and tossed Bill's boot on top. With the body undoubtedly somewhere in the mix, he would keep it as whole as he could.

Noah wanted to get on the track left by the gangbangers, but first his old man would want him to pack up whatever preps he could and take them with him.

They'd always joked around, calling Bill's prep bunker Noah's "golden parachute," the only inheritance Bill would likely leave his son. The ranch was mostly owned by the bank, and Bill had spent what little cash he had on beans, bullets and bandaids for his "prep bunker." He never even talked about paying the land off.

"You working on my *golden parachute*, Dad?" Noah remembered joking a couple weeks before when he found Bill hidden away in his bunker.

"Yep, son. I got your inheritance waiting right here in my hand." Bill had held up his middle finger. Noah smiled at the memory.

With the sun going down and the funeral over, Noah wasn't going to piss off the old man's ghost. If he didn't load up the preps, Bill would find a way to come back from the grave and kick his ass.

Noah backed his Land Cruiser up to the barn, pretty sure that he would need to make a dozen trips to get the whole load. To his surprise, the bunker door was open and the stairs were exposed to the world. Noah climbed down the stairs and regarded the mess. The cartel soldiers had clearly raided the preps, but it didn't seem like they'd taken much of the food or sundry supplies. However, they'd obliterated Bill's stock of firearms and ammunition.

The "Doomsday Cache" had been hidden underneath the old man's "office" in the barn. That office had been where he'd stored his old army pictures, memorabilia, and where he drank that nasty mescal he got from his buddies across the border. But the bunker under the office was virtually impossible to find. Noah had lived there for two years as a boy without ever discovering its existence, and he'd scoured the damn ranch looking for cigarettes and porno magazines—anything the old man might be hiding from him. Even so, he hadn't seen the "prep bunker" until after Bill had given him a stack of hints. It'd turned into a two week scavenger hunt for young Noah.

As a boy, Noah noticed that there were two toilet plungers hanging next to one of the horse stalls—not particularly interesting except that there wasn't a toilet in the barn and the plungers were in mint condition.

Looking into one of the plungers young Noah saw a steel reinforcing pin from the connection point where the handle screwed into the rubber cup. The interior lip that normally formed the seal had been trimmed away so that the plunger was in effect just a big suction cup. Noah had confirmed that the second plunger was modified in the same way. Taking the plungers into the office, Noah sat at the desk and scanned from floor-to-ceiling, looking for concealed hatches.

He stepped around the room tapping the walls and floor with the butt of a plunger. He'd done this before, but the room had been stick-framed, so the alternating solid and hollow knocks raised no suspicion in the boy's mind.

In the corner of the room behind the coat stand, Noah had noticed a weird thunk. He compressed the plunger dead center of the polished wood and pulled. A three-foot section of wall moved. The plunger hadn't been strong enough by itself, but by adding the second plunger he was able to pull out a chunk of the wall. Once that section popped free, hinges allowed it to swing to the side. A section of the floor could be lifted in the same manner and hinged out of the way, giving access to a stairwell leading down. Noah had felt like the cleverest boy alive when he'd finally cracked his dad's secret.

But, somehow, the gangbangers had found this clever storeroom too. Noah concluded that Bill had left it open in his haste to go to war. Maybe he'd been putting a shine on his preps when the rice burners barreled down the county road.

Even with the guns gone, it'd take Noah all night to pack the remaining supplies up, and there was no possible way it'd all fit in his Land Cruiser, not in twenty trips. The sheer magnitude of the job robbed Noah of his impulse to move on and get drinking. He'd have to work at least two hours to do right by Bill, and he couldn't hardly do it wasted.

What was it about the borderlands that murder was so commonplace? Soulless criminals drifted in these hills like wayward coyotes and killing them made about as much sense. Noah could pick them off like mongrels and they'd just come back in packs, hardly noticing their dead.

Revenge killing wouldn't fill the holes in his heart, but something, somewhere might. He didn't think murder would do it, but following those dogs might lead to an answer. Without anyone to keep him in the borderlands, what would it hurt to go looking?

Noah put a finer point on his plan. He could load up what he could, button up Bill's prep bunker, and scout what the cartel was planning down in Old Mexico. If nothing else, the rice burners heading into Mexico made him curious.

Why the hell were drug dealers going south?

In any case, Noah could just as easily get shit-faced wandering around the Sonoran desert as he could at his kitchen table. Might as well get some questions answered while he did it.

CHAPTER 13
TAVO CASTILLO
EL VAQUERO GRIEGO RESTAURANT,
HERMOSILLO, SONORA, MEXICO

Tavo nursed a brown-bottled beer while he waited for Commander Prieto Ruíz to show up for his unexpected appointment. Beto's recon element had identified this little restaurant as the place where Prieto Ruíz met his girlfriend for lunch most days. From there, the *comandante* and his lady friend would disappear for an hour or two. Tavo hadn't bothered to find out where they went, though it wouldn't be hard to guess.

The commander's woman sat across the rickety table from Tavo—beside the waxy, floral tablecloth ubiquitous throughout Mexico. Her tears cut rivulets down her heavy makeup. Tavo couldn't avoid the cloying, chemical reek of her cosmetics. Occasionally, a whiff of barbecue from inside the restaurant covered up her stink, giving him a window to enjoy another taste of beer.

Between her sobs and his sips of beer, Tavo pondered the Persian Empire. The romantic warriors of the world celebrated the Spartans. But Tavo celebrated Xerxes.

The Persians, starting with King Cyrus, built one of the largest superpowers the world had ever seen, and they did so by surgically applying both courtesy and brutality. Xerxes was the last in a line of Persian masters. Like Xerxes, Tavo had come to ask the air force commander for "earth and water;" tokens of submission. It was always better to have unconditional subordination than to destroy a potential asset.

Forced submission would be easy, if it came to that. Tavo's man, Beto, lay on a rooftop a hundred meters away, ready to put a 7.62 x 51 bullet through the woman. Beto would then put one through the base commander. With that, one could say "problem solved," if one were so inclined.

But Tavo preferred the Persian way. There was a certain art to subordination. It required achieving a particular state of mind in one's adversary.

The *comandante* came trotting into the restaurant patio like a lovesick beagle. Waves of confusion passed over his face when he saw his mistress sitting with another man.

Husband? Another lover? Police? Cartel?

Tavo could track each expression crossing the man's face. It was like watching a kaleidoscope lit by the human brain. In truth, Tavo didn't respect men who cheated on their wives. It seemed unnecessarily vulnerable to him. Why spend so much energy, and incur so much risk, over something as impermanent as sex?

Tavo waved the base commander over to the table with his beer bottle.

"I'm a friend," Tavo explained. "Enrique Reyes." Tavo held out his hand and rose half-way from his chair. The man shook hands with a question mark lingering in his grip.

"Please don't be alarmed." Tavo sat back down. "I have a sniper watching across the street." The commander whipped around, searching into the sun. "He's not going to shoot anyone. He's here as an assurance," Tavo explained as though talking about a legal formality.

"What do you want from me?" the air force commander

asked, trying to sound like a "serious man," but not quite pulling it off.

"In America, most air base commanders have no contact with their commanding officers right now." Tavo had no idea if it were true. "Very shortly, neither will you. Who will you take orders from when that happens?" Tavo took a sip and could see in the man's eyes that he had never thought about that possibility—never considered what he would do if command broke down.

After a pause, he answered, "I would lock down my base until I received word from command."

"Okay, and what if you never received word from command?"

"Then I would order all air assets returned to Mexico City."

"And what if Mexico City and all its military bases were burning when the planes and helicopters arrived?"

The commander marshaled his courage. His back straightened and his voice hardened.

"I'd land them in the courtyard of the presidential palace before I'd allow them into the hands of an enemy."

Tavo launched himself across the table and punched the woman in the face, rocking her head back in the chair. Her body slid onto the concrete below the table in a tangle of limbs. Her head hit the floor with a wet *thunk*.

The commander looked up and glared at him. Tavo pretended to point a rifle at the man. "Bang, bang, *comandante*." Tavo smiled. "Help her back into her seat and let's not be enemies. America is falling and as you know—wherever America goes, so goes Mexico."

Tavo explained what would happen next as the man gathered his paramour up off the ground. He plotted each twitch and sag as the commander's face flicked from anger to resistance to inevitable surrender.

General Ignacio L. Pesqueira International Airport, Hermosillo, Sonora, Mexico

Before they reached the air base gate, Tavo considered reminding Commander Prieto Ruíz about the snipers. Tavo had positioned them at high points around the little base even before his lunch meeting. Given the conversation of the last half hour, and considering the truckload of Tavo's trained operators pulling in behind them, he wasn't worried about the commander. Upon seeing the operators—kitted up like American commandos—Tavo sensed that the commander's reliance on Tavo's good word, and the consequences of deviation, had gone up significantly.

"Commander Prieto Ruíz, which of your staff is going to object to your new chain of command?"

"Gonzales and probably Martín. The rest aren't going to care where orders come from." The commander rolled down his window and waved at the gate guard, motioning that he should let the small caravan pass. The guard stepped back and saluted.

Tavo had taken Prieto Ruíz's cell phone at the beginning of the car ride, after they dropped the woman off at her concrete house a few blocks from the air base. A handmade sign hung on a trash can on the street that said *"Manicura Cristy"* or "Christy's Nails." Tavo marveled at the power of culture—it'd taken only a couple generations of runaway consumerism and Mexican parents were naming their children after American glamour models instead of traditional Catholic saints. Tavo might have to do something to reverse that trend.

He handed the commander his cell phone. "Call Gonzales and Martín and have them meet us somewhere out of the way."

Tavo marveled at the wood crates stacked to the ceiling in the dim and musty warehouse. While they waited, he made a game figuring out what the stencil-painted letters and numbers meant. Like a monument to the stupidity of the military, the crates had all been marked differently and none of them were marked in a way that made their contents obvious.

Why wouldn't American quartermasters just mark their crates "Mortar Rounds for the M29 Mortar" instead of "RIAFB H.E.I. M97 M3 BRHS Tetryl?" Tavo had studied arms and combat for most of his adult life and still could only figure out what two-thirds of the crates contained. Regardless, ten minutes walking around the musty warehouse had been a revelation: he now knew that the air base contained a lot more weaponry than he had first thought.

Tavo's men shuffled into a defensive posture without being ordered to do so, probably sensing the danger in the transfer of power of a military installation. Noticing his fascination with the crates, Commander Prieto Ruíz broke the uncomfortable silence.

"There are three other warehouses loaded with American junk like this one."

Tavo didn't see any junk. He saw the mill that would grind up any resistance to a new empire in the region—an empire he would lead.

"And what about the army base?" Tavo asked, waving at the crates.

The base commander snorted. "Maybe ten times this much. Why should the Americans build storehouses in America when they can ship their garbage here and make us store it for them?"

Natural light suddenly pierced the warehouse as Gonzales

and Martín marched through the door together, slowing as they noticed the twenty armed commandos.

"¿*Comandante?*" one of them asked, worry creeping into his tone.

Tavo had prepared his operators for this moment, so no words were necessary. One of them took out his cell phone and began recording the interaction.

"I'm your new Aviator Pilot General, Enrique Reyes" Tavo said, assuming the military title without offering a handshake. He wore tan 5.11 jeans and a black polo shirt, with his Glock holstered on his belt. Nothing about Tavo's appearance, except maybe his physical fitness, bespoke a Mexican air force general.

"*No es cierto,*" Martín blurted. "That's not true."

Tavo drew his Glock, like pouring water from a pitcher, and shot Capitán Martín through the bridge of his nose. Even Tavo's own operators startled at the sudden violence.

Major Gonzales maintained remarkable calm considering the smoking Glock now centered on his face.

The major spoke with an air of resignation. "I see, commander. The Americans are falling apart, so now this." Gonzales motioned at the gunmen standing around the dim warehouse. "You are the men who killed the gangsters in the city and freed the archbishop two nights ago, am I correct?"

Tavo nodded, tracking the man's eyes through the tiny window of his Trijicon RMR pistol sight. "Yes. We saved him from the Negros gang."

The officer's eyes defied the barrel of the handgun. "You're not an officer. Anyone can see that. But I would be willing to fly under orders of the archbishop." Gonzales reached slowly into his camouflage jacket and withdrew a silver chain and a small, silver cross.

Tavo prided himself in taking good ideas from wherever they came. "What makes you think we need you to fly for us?"

The pilot smoothed his hair. "Why else would you kill only one of us?"

Tavo ignored the question. "You'll fly for the archbishop, but you'd rather die than fly for me. You don't even know who I am."

"I know enough. There's only one type of man in Mexico who would shoot Capitán Martín like that...*Narco criminal.*"

Tavo wasn't clear how many pilots were on base, so he hesitated. He could always have him killed later. The lie cost him nothing.

"You'll be flying for the church, so you can relax." He holstered his pistol.

Tavo turned to the base commander, who stared down at his dead pilot, splayed on the ground, the room filling with the stench of his bowels. "Are we good, *Comandante*?"

"*Si, Señor Reyes,*" the commander muttered, not taking his eyes off the dead man.

"*Comandante.* Look at me," Tavo ordered.

The base commander looked up and met Tavo's glare with eyes of surrender.

"Are we good?" Tavo asked again.

"We're good," the commander replied.

Tavo held his gaze for a moment and then pointed to the soldier filming with his cell phone. Tavo hoped the message was obvious—he had film of the commander's complicity. He would never be able to deny it. The base commander nodded and returned his attention to the dead man on the concrete.

"Flex cuff this man and put him in the passenger seat of my car," Tavo lifted his head in the direction of the pilot, Major Gonzales. "The rest of you stay with the *comandante* at all times. No personnel or aircraft are to leave this base without my orders. No communications in or out. Collect all cell phones and radios and cut the land lines. This facility goes dark for the next forty-eight hours."

Six commandos peeled off and herded the base commander out of the warehouse and toward the office. The rest took control of Gonzales and led him into the sunlight.

The last man left the warehouse, leaving Tavo alone with the corpse. His thoughts returned to Xerxes of the Persian Empire. Using the specter of violence, he'd taken a Mexican military airbase with the loss of only one life. Was there any limit to what could be accomplished with dispassionate intellect?

The young pilot had unwittingly offered him another chess piece in the game he'd set in motion—perhaps even a knight or a rook.

Tavo had been in danger of forgetting: people were ethereal creatures and not even fear of the most dire violence would motivate them for long. As time and distance increased, terror would wear thin. Authority would dilute. The Persians knew this well, and they spread their priests and their religion with their dominion. Though they were idol worshippers of the blackest rank, the principle had withstood the test of time: fear of God would motivate men much further and deeper than fear of death.

So much the better with the true god presiding.

CHAPTER 14

NOAH MILLER

HERMOSILLO-GUAYMAS HIGHWAY, 50 MILES
NORTH OF BENJAMIN HILL, SONORA, MEXICO

Noah had followed the sign of the gangbangers and their low-slung Hotwheels, over thirty miles of dirt two-track through the night until they hit pavement and disappeared. Without credible sign to follow, he decided to commit the cardinal sin of tracking and "jump track" forward to Hermosillo. Given that pavement rarely yielded trackable sign and given that he'd already pounded half a bottle of Jack Daniels, Noah figured Bill would forgive him for being a little sloppy.

The sun poked its accusing head over the horizon just when Noah reached pavement about twenty miles south of Nogales. The voice of Bill in his mind insisted that he backtrack to a bivouac position with good cover and concealment before getting a few hours of badly-needed shuteye. Rather than take his chances alongside the Mexican blacktop, Noah did as his old mentor's voice instructed and he doubled back a few miles on the dirt road.

Come to think of it, Noah would need to stop worrying what a dead man's ghost might think. Superstitious hand-wringing was unbecoming of a cattleman.

He found a good spot for his bivouac and fell asleep almost immediately. He woke with the sun beating down on the Land Cruiser and a stifling headache. With the midday heat and a stomach full of whiskey, Noah felt like an oven-baked shit pie. He let out a rank belch, spilled out of the driver's side door and went to find a place to relieve himself; Numbers One and Two and maybe a good, old fashioned puke—the Grand Trifecta of a night of hard drinking.

When he returned to the Land Cruiser, he actually felt much better. He hadn't forgotten that he'd lost his dad the day before, but it was hard to anguish with the sun shining like a holiday and his guts feeling like they'd been given a new lease on life.

Autumn had finally begun its work on the pecan trees along the road between Nogales and Hermosillo. A slight breeze jangled the glowing leaves as if to herald the coming of a new year and a fresh start. His Cruiser pointed south into the Great Unknown, and something told him that the road before him held promise. Maybe not "win the lottery and buy a house next to Jay Leno" kind of promise, but it definitely felt possible that he wouldn't drink himself into oblivion that night. Noah chalked that up as a win.

He drove off the dirt track and down the highway to the bellowing of his Land Cruiser's chunky tires on the blacktop. Noah rolled down his window and enjoyed the fecund breeze as it whispered through the pecan orchards.

He'd heard news reports of American highways jammed with cars—urbanites fleeing the big cities. Here, in the two-hour stretch of road between Nogales and Hermosillo, the exact opposite was true. Everyone seemed to be holding tight in their square, cinderblock houses. He'd only passed a few dozen cars in as many miles. Nobody appeared to be escaping the city of Hermosillo, at least not to the north. Why would Americans run and Mexicans stay put?

Noah literally scratched his head, vexed by the question. The thought of running from his ranch because of the collapse had never crossed his mind. He wasn't entirely sure if he was more American or Mexican. Living a few miles from the border muddied those waters.

It made him think about the big, wide world as it ate itself, tail-first. The strangely-quiet roads implied a coming apocalypse, but the wind carried no such menace.

Noah turned on the Land Cruiser's radio—something he hadn't done in years. Truth be told, he only liked music when he was drinking. Plus, all his favorite music was on an iPod Leah had given him many Christmases ago. The Land Cruiser didn't have a CD player, much less a USB port. The '94 FJ40 scarcely had a cassette deck, and even then, the old speakers barely overcame the road noise.

Leah had pre-loaded the iPod with music before she gave it to him, otherwise Noah would've never waded through the bullshit required to get it set up. Leah knew her man and she'd taken the time to upload every song recorded by Johnny Cash onto the little, plastic brick of music. The next year, Leah had given him a speaker box for Christmas so he could stick the iPod into the speaker and play classic country while he sat at the kitchen table. It was a good thing, too, because by the next Christmas, Leah was six feet underground and Noah was doing a LOT of drinking at that kitchen table.

But the sun on the Mexican pavement and the fall leaves glinting on the pecan trees shouted against all that sadness. It challenged Noah to get his ass back to the real world where people mattered to other people. As of yesterday, his list of people who mattered to him had dropped by one hundred percent. Rather than dwell on it, he turned on the radio, hoping for a little news.

What he got was nothing. The radio didn't make a sound. Not even static.

Noah pounded the dashboard—his go-to response for trouble with electronic devices. Still the radio sulked, the howling of his tires against the road his only companion.

He stared at the radio, trying to figure out the inscrutable black buttons, four on one side of the cassette and four on the other. He twisted the left knob and stabbed his finger at the buttons in random sequence.

The radio yelped to life and the cabin of the old Land Cruiser roared with music. A gravelly-voiced man belted out half-a-verse and continued into a chorus.

> When I am worn and I've been unmade,
> your love is like a fire that will light my way.
> When darkness comes and dreamland fades,
> your love is like a fire that will light my way.
> It's always burning and warming my soul;
> calling me forward, fanning the coal.
> I may be lost, but never betrayed,
> your love is like a fire that will light my way.

Like warm water pouring down the inside of his skin, tenderness overtook Noah. Vast oceans of tears sprang from his eyes. Endless waves of warmth flooded down his throat and into his hardened heart. He gasped for air, choked on a massive sob and broke into a cry he had never before heard himself make, not even after Leah and Katya were killed.

He swerved to the side of the road but couldn't find a shoulder wide enough for the Cruiser, so he stopped in the middle of the blacktop, weeping and swimming in such a profound sense of grace that he could hardly locate himself on the planet. The tsunami of emotion had come from nowhere, unlike anything he'd ever felt.

Startled, afraid and oh-so-hopeful, Noah, bawled into his T-shirt. Maybe for ten seconds. Maybe for ten minutes. The next thing he knew, a semi-truck was behind him honking it's earth-shaking horn.

Flooded in emotional molasses and half out of his mind, Noah laughed like an idiot. He put the Land Cruiser in gear and crept along the highway until he found a place to pull over, barely able to see the road through his tears. The semi truck roared past.

Noah remained there on the shoulder of the Hermosillo-Guaymas Highway for a long time, sniffling and running his fingers through his hair. *He had no fucking clue what had just happened.*

The wind jostled the Cruiser and a white grocery sack sailed past his windshield, caught a draft, and lifted straight into the air. It danced in front of Noah's wet gaze for a full three seconds before another gust inflated the sack and spun it away off toward the horizon.

The music was still playing, filling the Land Cruiser with God-breathed honey. The gravelly-voiced crooner had begun another song while Noah had been losing his shit.

> Don't give up hope.
> Don't give up now.
> There's always something noble,
> Waiting around the corner.

As Noah returned to Planet Earth, the sense of well-being abided. It was as though the world had refilled with hope and purpose in the space of one song. One damn song. And with that one song, the very color of the air had changed.

Noah shook his head and laughed, squinting at the radio. He found the eject button and the old stereo spat out the cassette tape—but not a store-bought tape. It was a homemade mix tape, like girls used to make in high school of Journey, Chicago and Bon Jovi. This homemade cassette tape had two words on the sticker in the handwriting of his dead wife.

It read, "The Crusader."

Noah slid the tape back into the player, fearful that it had all been an illusion—a standard-issue break in sanity, entirely explainable due to the fact that he'd just lost his father.

The music resumed, and Noah found that he didn't care if it was insane or even a break in sanity. He could feast on this feeling for the remainder of a lifetime. It felt like Leah and Katya and Bill were right there in his Cruiser, laughing and enjoying some soft-serve ice cream, together again, the world profoundly right. The day excruciatingly perfect.

He had never heard any of these songs before. He had no idea what "The Crusader" even was. Leah had gone through a born-again Christian phase back in the year she was pregnant with Katya—the third year after they were married. Maybe it was that. Or, maybe the band was an artifact from Leah's grunge music phase her senior year of high school.

How an ancient cassette tape had ended up in his car would forever be a mystery. He couldn't even look the band up on Google now that the internet was hashed.

All Noah could say for sure was that his heart—an internal organ long-forgotten—had been frayed, splayed and filleted.

Noah pounded on his dashboard with a fist, flush with joy, attempting to sing along to words he didn't know. Instead, he yowled with the music, making himself laugh. Being the fool had never felt so right.

Well I've been fighting the long fight,

swinging hard for the big prize,
Doing all that I can
just to stay alive.
But I'm never gonna let go,
even if I'm alone.
And you'll find me fighting,
until the Lord takes me home.

Maybe he had heard these songs before. Yes, maybe during Leah's Christian phase. She'd never pushed her religion on him and, now that he thought about it, maybe she'd never moved on from it. His wildflower wife had probably died as the girl who would belt out the cheesy, Jesus-freaking lyrics of "The Crusader" in her husband's car.

Noah had just tuned it all out.

He laughed out loud thinking about how big of an dipshit he'd been. In that softened moment, tilting half on and half off a Mexican highway, Noah knew three things, and he knew them like he knew the sun shone in the autumn sky.

One.

He was okay. The truth had always been there—this *okayness* despite his many failings—but he'd never been willing to accept it. He was a dirty-assed, good-for-nothing drunken gunslinger but something out in the blanched-blue sky loved him. Down to the marrow of his bones, Noah knew that life, death and the whole-damn-shooting-match was all right. More than all right.

Two.

He would be with Leah, Katya and old man Bill soon enough, and it would be entirely okay when he rejoined them.

Three.

He had something important to do first.

If he had to describe it, he would say that Leah had reached out to him across time and space and slipped a cassette tape into the radio in his Cruiser to call him out of his self-involved funk to do something that mattered—something that Noah had been born to do. It was something that his birth father—that closed-minded, polygamist bastard—would never have understood, but that his real father—Bill McCallister—understood through gut instinct. This whole fucking life of Noah's had been a giant setup. It'd been a play perfectly orchestrated and timed to reach this place at this moment.

Even as he thought it, Noah felt a lurch in his gut.

(Yes!)

With that, he drew his Glock, press-checked the chamber, saw brass and slid it back into its holster.

"I'm ready," Noah said, to whatever ghosts were listening.

CHAPTER 15

TAVO CASTILLO
HERMOSILLO-GUAYMAS HIGHWAY, KM 247,
SONORA, MEXICO

The column of Jeeps, trucks and buses drove into the ambush like cattle toward a water trough. Tavo clacked off the IED himself, bursting one of the dark green buses nearly in half like a fat caterpillar in the midday sun. The surviving men spilled out onto the sizzling asphalt.

Tavo didn't really want to kill them. On the contrary, he wanted the same thing that they did: peace in Hermosillo and a reliable supply of food and water. He just wanted the soldiers in that bus to need him for a moment. It would allow him to talk with the officers without having to overcome their egos. Nothing humbles a man quite like being blown up.

Two days prior, Tavo and his three lieutenants had planned this operation down to the minute. The only surprise had been the extra day it'd taken the base commander to gather the nerve to attack them. He assumed the army had taken the extra day to get over the confusion caused by their air base going offline. His commandos at the airbase had knabbed three messengers from the army base trying to make contact.

Tavo had gunmen surrounding the ambush site, but he didn't think they'd be necessary. With the single IED, the company of soldiers had been thrown into total confusion. Their initial reaction demonstrated at least some training; the troops formed a sloppy, defensive cordon around the damaged column. Once it became clear that a follow-on attack wasn't imminent, the screams of the injured overwhelmed discipline and nearly everyone in the column fell into rendering aid to the wounded and dying. The Mexican army hadn't had much experience with IEDs.

While Tavo waited for the "mass casualty event" to settle down, he counted the soldiers that'd been sent to assault his own commandos and their base of operations. As Tavo had suspected, General Parras—the commander of the Hermosillo army base—had sent pretty much everyone.

Hey Diddle Diddle. Everybody up the middle.

Mexican fighting forces had never been accused of being overly-nuanced when it came to battlefield strategy. In the coming days, Tavo would change that.

At this moment, his lieutenant, Alejandro, would be hitting the near-empty Zona Cuatro army base with a team of commandos who'd arrived the night before from San Diego. Another team under Beto would roll up the television and radio stations in Hermosillo. Saúl would assault and kill off the last pockets of Zeta cartel in Hermosillo with fifty drug soldiers from Texas and the American Midwest.

If everything went as planned, Tavo would control the City of Hermosillo by nightfall. After that, he'd complete the roll-up of the Catholic archdiocese.

Throughout history, killing people had always been an inefficient means of owning battle space. The hardiest empires *bought* their way into a position of control, then they used culture and faith to consolidate gains.

Tavo wanted these two hundred Mexican army infantrymen alive and willing. Saúl would lose trained commandos taking down the remnants of the Zetas in Hermosillo and each of his commandos fought like the equivalent of a hundred infantrymen. They would be mourned as expensive losses, indeed.

Tavo's three lieutenants had spent the last few years carefully and secretly training their best foot soldiers in the U.S., turning them into top-notch commandos, and leaders of their *Templario* units. Through layered holding companies, they'd paid cash for discrete land, out of sight of the public. Then they'd sent their top twenty most intelligent and credible drug runners to U.S. shooting schools run by former special operations forces veterans. Those twenty were then trained and vetted by Beto, Alejandro and Saúl themselves—forging their own hybrid operating style. Those twenty trained men went on to train thousands more in their home regions and inculcated all of them in the *Caballero Templario* creed.

By some miracle, Beto, Alejandro and Saúl had worked up this training package without ever being penetrated by U.S. state or federal law enforcement. Lucky for them, the hubbub about "militia groups" had died in the U.S. with the election of a Republican to the presidency. Federal surveillance of militia activity had dropped away to nothing, and Tavo's organization had slipped through that crack.

Every beating heart in his commando teams cost Tavo and his partners around fifty thousand dollars. When one of those guys died, that investment vanished into dust: fifty grand in prelaundered dollars. It represented an irreplaceable asset, especially given the end of the United States and its appetite for drugs. If Tavo could get these Mexican infantrymen out in front of his trained commandos—absorbing most of the losses—the only thing in the region that could stop them would be the American military.

Through his binos, Tavo watched the last of the Mexican army perimeter melt back into the wailing caravan of drab green trucks and buses. He gave a nod to his communications guy who then sent out a call.

Tavo stood and stretched, giving the area of operation a once-over. He'd placed his tactical operations center on top of a mini-mart at the foot of the Cerro de la Virgen. Red and green painted stairs climbed the mountainside to a thirty-foot tall image of the Mother of Jesus painted on the cliff face. He had no idea how the giant altar had come to be. Undoubtedly, someone had seen Mother Mary appear on that spot, but Tavo didn't know the story. Divine appearances by the Mother of Jesus were common in Mexico.

He made the sign of the cross and continued his scan of the AO. He'd placed the ambush in the narrowest canyon he could find, which happened to be a location with religious significance.

A plume of dust rose from a side road five miles south of the ambush, then vanished in the wind as a string of vehicles climbed onto the highway. Those would be Tavo's pre-positioned ambulances coming to save the day.

The communications man stepped up to Tavo and saluted. "General Castillo. Colonel Alejandro called to say they've taken the army base. No word yet from Colonels Saúl or Beto."

Tavo and his lieutenants had awarded themselves military rank just to keep things clear for the subordinates.

"*Bueno.* Let's go talk to the fat man." Tavo slung his HK416 and climbed down the ladder on the side of the mini-mart. He drove down the dirt road, parked a couple hundred yards back, then walked into the broken army caravan. He timed his arrival to coincide with the ambulances. Tavo waved them toward the twisted bus, as though he was part of the medical team. Tavo's men poured out of the ambulances, rifles slung and in full combat kit, each man carrying a medical kit.

Tavo cut a beeline for the commander, who had stopped

giving orders to the men around him and now gaped at the twenty medics rendering aid.

"Who are these men?" the heavyset army major asked, holding his hands palms up.

"I can explain, Major," Tavo called out as he walked toward the officer. "We were just down the road when we heard the bomb. We were sent from Tucson by the diocese to help the Hermosillo archdiocese. We heard they had problems with local gangs, so we came as fast as we could." Tavo leaned over and rested his hands on his thighs, pretending to be winded.

"But why are you in Mexican ambulances? And why are your men armed with rifles?"

Tavo ignored the questions and pulled a small radio from his plate carrier vest. The cell phones in Hermosillo had stopped working the night before. "Commander Prieto Ruíz can explain." He handed the radio to the army major.

Tavo leaned back on the fender of a truck and let his rifle slip around to the front, pulling the slide on his sling loose to give him more room to work with his rifle, if need be. His men, now rendering aid to the wounded, monitored the interaction out of the corner of their eyes. They sat down their med kits on the asphalt and inconspicuously prepared their rifles for battle.

As the major turned away with the radio to talk to the air force commander, Tavo rehearsed in his mind what he'd do next if things went sideways. Tavo and his men had done a physical rehearsal the night before at the ranch, but there had been little they could do to predict the size of the force and the precise disposition of the vehicles.

If things went apeshit, Tavo would shoot the major and all other officers or senior NCOs standing nearby, then he'd get behind the giant tire of the truck and kill anyone in Mexican army uniform who picked up his rifle. It wasn't much of a plan, but he and his twenty men had the element of surprise. Plus, they had another twenty riflemen in the surrounding hills with FN/FAL scoped rifles providing cover fire. They would prevail one way or the other. Unfortunately, Tavo would be at the center of the chaos.

Maybe it would've been better if he'd just ripped the army column to pieces with IEDs. Tavo had plenty of anfo—the diesel fuel explosive they'd used for the bomb. He could've brought the mountain down on the column, gigantic Virgin Mary and all. But he wanted the soldiers. He needed them.

Tavo waited while the air force commander explained over the radio to his army counterpart how screwed they were if they didn't cooperate with this so-and-so *narcotraficante*. Hopefully that was the gist of the conversation.

Without looking at Tavo, the army officer handed him back the radio. The major's hand dropped to his side and his back straightened. Based on his body language, the officer knew that his next words could end his life. The man stood, looking to the hills, the morning sun now angling down into the canyon.

The major's shoulders slumped, and he turned to Tavo. He didn't seem surprised to find the business end of Tavo's suppressor pointed at his feet.

"Commander?" Tavo asked with an expression of extreme confidence.

"What would you like me to do? Will you render aid to my men, at least?"

"Of course, commander. They're both of our soldiers now." Tavo reached out his hand. The major was smart enough to hesitate only for a second.

CHAPTER 16

NOAH MILLER
HERMOSILLO-GUAYMAS HIGHWAY, KM 247,
SONORA, MEXICO

> "I see all those lost souls,
> Burning up their time.
> Making all their big plans,
> To have a life divine."
>
> — *The Crusader*

"What the hell..."

Noah had been shadowing the Mexican army convoy since they left their base that morning. With hundreds of narco ranches surrounding Hermosillo, he could search for a year and never find the drug soldiers who'd killed Bill.

So, instead, he posted across the boulevard from the army base on the outskirts of Hermosillo and waited for them to come out. It was fifty-fifty odds that the army would either go challenge the narcos or link up with them. Fifty-fifty odds seemed better than wandering around the desert looking for trouble.

Early that morning, the army hauled ass out of their base looking for all the world like they meant to kick some ass. Instead, forty miles down the road, they'd been taken down in an ambush. Then, the same enemy that'd blown them up, came in with medics and went to work on the wounded. The convoy packed up and everyone drove back north toward Hermosillo.

It was the damnedest thing he'd ever seen.

Noah had stashed the Land Cruiser around the bend on a dirt road, so the army convoy limped past on the highway without noticing him. But not everybody went north. A few trucks headed south.

Noah leaned against a huge boulder, smeared a rivulet of sweat across his forehead and ran through his options. His job was simple: *don't lose them.* But he didn't actually know who *they* were. Nothing he'd just seen proved that any of them were connected to the cartel soldiers who hit Bill's ranch. Even so, Noah had a feeling in his gut that they were. How many narco gangs could operate in one region without either joining up or exterminating one another?

His father, Bill, hadn't been a big fan of "following your gut" when tracking. He'd apparently seen a lot of pet theories turn into boondoggles on the trail of soldiers, murderers and illegal aliens. Evidence and reason were Bill's favorite tools, and they'd served him well as a tracker.

Bill would not have been a big fan of Noah's roadside revival the day before. Big emotions were like curdled milk to Bill and making decisions from big emotions was Bill's definition of foolishness.

"The *Libtards* got themselves in another crying jag!" Bill had shouted two weeks before at the ranch. "They've gone all weepy-eyed about keeping the illegal immigrants in tents and cages. Those tents are twenty times better than the shanties they're living in down in Honduras! Them Liberals need to wipe away their tears and get an eyeball full of what life's really like." It was Bill's typical rant.

Every time the liberals did something Bill considered stupid, he'd blame it on their *pot-smoking drum circles* or *New Age feelie-fests*. Noah had sometimes wondered if Bill lived up against the Mexican border because that put his ranch as far from Seattle as possible without crossing the Mississippi. He waved a curse every time he went into the "big city" and passed a Starbucks.

Bill McCallister ran a one-man, up-at-dawn war against the feel-good proclivities of the human race. He would not have approved of his son snotting up his Carhartt T-shirt alongside the highway because of a love song, or grunge song or even Christian rock song. Bill probably would've called it "defiling the cockpit of the supremely functional FJ40 with snowflake antics."

Noah hid behind the boulder as the army convoy trundled by on the blacktop. He missed his dad, the old fool.

In about thirty seconds, Noah would need to make a decision: either head south after the six trucks that had turned right on the Hermosillo-Guaymas highway, or hang a left and follow the army convoy back toward Hermosillo. Nothing he'd observed provided a clear direction. His best guess was that the cartel soldiers had jacked the column of Mexican army, and they were heading back to the base to consolidate gains. That'd mean the other six vehicles were returning to a cartel base—and probably to wherever Bill's murderers called home.

Following the killers in the rice burners—that'd just been something to do while Noah got squared away. He'd never really set his heart on revenge-killing those assholes, and the idea hadn't grown any muscle overnight, either. If they popped up in his gunsights, he might take the shot, but chasing men around Indian Country just to kill a few former drug dealers sounded like succumbing to what his dad would've called "emotional nonsense." So then, what was he doing in Mexico, anyway?

His mission was a work-in-progress and Noah had to admit that he'd turned himself over to some inner oracle—half John McClane in *Die Hard* and half Morpheus in *The Matrix*. He didn't know what he was going to do next.

Surprisingly, the thought didn't bother him much.

So, Noah followed his feet to the Land Cruiser, climbed in, and drove down the dirt road. He turned left toward Hermosillo and back to the army base.

CHAPTER 17

TAVO CASTILLO
RANCHO SANTIAGUITO, 65 MILES OUTSIDE OF
HERMOSILLO, SONORA, MEXICO

"Good morning, Papi." Sofía kissed her father on the head as he ate a breakfast of refried beans, eggs and jalapeño at the kitchen bar, but the kiss carried a perfunctory air.

Tavo's wife, Isabel, worked silently at the sink, sorting and washing beans for the evening meal. "Buenas dias, Mama." Sofía graced her mother with a deep hug from behind. Her mother patted her arm, still looking out the window at the courtyard.

Tavo had been wondering why his wife washed, sorted and cooked her own beans. She had all the house help she could ever want, especially here at the ranch. Then again, Tavo didn't know what else she'd do with her time if not sort beans.

One thing he was sure of: asking her would be a bad idea. These days, when it came to his wife, he had a hard-and-fast rule. *Don't ask unless you already know the answer.*

Sofía poured herself an *agua de papaya*, stepped around the bar and sat down beside her father. "So, how many did we kill yesterday?" She asked like she was asking him to pass the jalapeños.

"Don't speak to me like you're an American princess. It

cheapens you," Tavo shamed her. He'd woken up in a foul mood, and the bile in his stomach turned him, once again, toward suspicion.

"I'm not for sale, Papi. So don't play me. Please answer my question. I saw the men get ready yesterday. I know you acted on my information from General Bautista. If I'm going to be part of the killing, then I should know how many died." Sofia drilled her father with angry eyes. "I've seen the killing myself and I think I deserve to know the truth."

The fact that she had brought this up with her mother in the room represented a tectonic disrespect in their family—a naked aggression. This was shaping up to be their first serious argument, ever.

Isabel didn't even turn around at the mention of killing. She sorted the beans like an act of penance, picking through them like rosary beads.

Tavo's counter-strike, an outright lie, returned the moment to his control. "The archbishop has asked to meet with us today about the protection of Hermosillo and the archdiocese. I take it that you're not interested in being part of that conversation?"

He saw the wheels turning in Sofia's head as she stalled, sipping her *licuado*.

A liar will always assume a lie.

He had lied, more than anything, to see if she would call him on it. Even unprepared, he played two gambits at once, the one nested inside the other. This lie about the archdiocese would either bring his daughter along or reveal her as a player in the big game.

Had she ordered the Kaibil strike on him or not? Was she a sociopath or not?

Sofia looked up at her mother's back, as if seeking her approval. "Okay. I'll go to your meeting with the archbishop. What time?"

Tavo punted, "I'll let you know. Phones are dead. Where will you be today?"

"I'll be here waiting for word, sorting *frijoles* with mama."

Tavo walked toward the archbishop painted in his most-dazzling smile and an outstretched hand.

"Good afternoon, Your Excellency." Tavo blocked his daughter's view of the archbishop's confused face, his eyes darting between the four strange people who had ambushed him in the anteroom to his office. "My name's Gustavo Castillo from the diocese of Culiacán. I was with the group of paramilitaries who rescued you and the other fathers from *Los Negros*."

They stood in the antechamber to the archbishop's office in a three-story wing off of the cathedral. Seemingly without a secretary—likely due to the domino collapse that had finally hit Hermosillo—the archbishop appeared adrift. Their unannounced visit did nothing to reduce the elderly man's befuddlement.

"Really?" A light dawned in the priest's eyes. "I thought the soldiers were American."

"No, Your Excellency. They were faithful Catholics." Tavo laughed and gently steered the man toward his office.

Tavo's party filed behind the archbishop and arranged themselves in the heavy wood chairs arrayed around the desk. The cleric took the seat with a cushion nearest the desk and folded his hands, glancing from one guest to the other. After a moment of silence, he spoke. "I already know our two commanders from the army and air force." The archbishop smiled at Commander Prieto and Commander Salinas. "But I don't believe we've met." He gestured toward Tavo and Sofía.

"I'm a patrón from the Los Mochis diocese. We organized a

paramilitary group to help protect the farms from criminals. We came north when we heard of your troubles here in Hermosillo. The gentlemen from the army and air force offered to help us maintain order in the region until a new government, outside the influence of the Zeta cartel, can be formed."

The archbishop had seemed dubious at the mention of a paramilitary group, but his expression hardened with mention of the Zetas.

"So you are against the cartels?" He asked, clarifying.

"Yes, Your Excellency. We would like to form a peacekeeping force under the church to maintain order until the trouble passes."

The archbishop must've been remembering his captivity, high-centered in his own trauma. "The cartels behave like demons. The mayor and the police do nothing to stop them. Money is more powerful than faith here." The archbishop stared at Tavo intently.

Tavo began to wonder if the archbishop didn't know precisely who he was. "We can handle the Zetas." Tavo moved to a more practical line of reasoning. "But the Zetas are the least of our concerns today. Have you seen the supermarkets? They're ransacked. Regular people are hoarding anything they can. Some Catholics are looting and stealing and leaving the rest with nothing. They know that this power and water problem isn't like the normal stoppages. This one may last months, if not years."

The priest blanched. "Because of the terrorist attacks and problems in America?"

"Yes, Your Excellency. I'm afraid we may have turned back the clock two hundred years. Northern Sonora is without electricity and transportation for the foreseeable future, and we have to find food and water for hundreds of thousands of people. Together with my esteemed army commanders, we've posted guards on all the storehouses, box stores, the hospital and the gas stations, but the small stores have been looted out. As soon as the roof cisterns empty, the entire city will be forced to relocate to the reservoir just to have water."

"But why are you talking to an old priest about it? These are municipal issues."

"The municipal government has vanished," Tavo lied, holding out his hands. If it weren't true, Tavo would make sure that it was within the hour.

"You want the church to take over civil affairs," the archbishop concluded. "I'm afraid you're wasting your time, gentlemen. We are prohibited by the constitution of Mexico from involving ourselves in government. We are not allowed, nor are we prepared for those responsibilities."

Tavo didn't have time to convince an old man of plain facts. The opportunity to preserve the assets of northern Sonora would evaporate in the next forty-eight hours, long before this old priest caught up to reality.

"Of course you can't, Your Excellency. We're only asking that you provide a liaison with the archdiocese to help us maintain calm among the people. The military can enforce order, as is our job." Tavo blended his "paramilitary" command with the commanders sitting beside him in the archbishop's office. "We need a priest to speak to the people—let them know that the government may be gone for a time, but God hasn't forgotten them."

Tavo wondered if he had overshot his appeal to faith. The archbishop said nothing, slumped in his chair, either contemplating the situation or drifting into a stupor. Tavo couldn't tell.

"I'll assign my abbot to help you. He's still young enough to understand these issues."

Tavo decided to remove the archbishop at his earliest opportunity—make him vanish into another archdiocese. The abbot would do nicely. If Tavo recalled correctly, the man was in his forties and probably much more ambitious—and subject to influence—than this ancient creature. "Thank you, Your Excellency. If you would please allow us a meeting with the abbot, we will serve the church however we can."

―――

"The archbishop didn't ask for that meeting," Sofía accused her father as soon as they cleared the steps of the cathedral.

Tavo felt himself running out of patience. "Do you want these people to live?" he waved at Hermosillo from the steps. "Whether you approve or not, I'm their best hope. That dirty water in the reservoir will kill a third of the children within two weeks and many of the adults. Even if I hadn't eradicated *Los Negros*, these people were going to tear each other apart over scraps of food in the next two weeks. Men with guns are the solution, Sofía. If you want to help, pick up a gun and point it at someone looting a store. Otherwise, you're another useless mouth to feed. With all that expensive education, are you still blind to what's happening here?"

Sofía stomped her foot but held back argument. She fired back with a question instead. "How will you get food to them?"

"What do you mean?" Tavo asked.

"How are you going to transport food from the fields in Sinaloa to these people in Hermosillo?"

"Trucks." He hadn't spared much thought for anything beyond military matters.

"Trucks require gasoline... I will arrange for gasoline. I'm no 'useless mouth.' Do you have a satellite phone?" Sofía reached out her hand.

"Who do you want to call?" Tavo's suspicion stepped into high gear.

"General Bautista and my people in Monterrey," Sofía answered. "If it's bad here, it's worse there. We need to secure those refineries today. I'm not going to point a gun at anyone, Father, but I can get the gas and the trucks to transport food, and maybe distribute clean water. Can I borrow your phone? Now, if you please."

Tavo handed her his satellite phone.

CHAPTER 18

NOAH MILLER
HIGHWAY 15, KM 144, SONORA, MEXICO

> "Well, I've been fleeing, just like an outlaw,
> But I am willing and I am able
> To stop and stand, on the rock.
> It's been a long time comin'."
>
> — *The Crusader*

Noah watched up close as a fly walked across a dead man's pupil. God only knew what nourishment the fly was gathering from a dried-up, human eyeball.

The bodies of four men were arranged in a circle, heads toward the center, feet pointing out. Little gusts of wind blew sand across the altar and into the dead mens' eyes.

So this is what death looks like without makeup.

Noah had never seen a dead human body outside a mortuary, except for Leah and Katya. Within minutes, his wife and daughter had been rushed away in an ambulance. It was as though modern society needed to protect him from the sight of his own dead. The next time Noah saw them, all the holes had been filled and color restored by the morticians.

Apparently, in this new world, nobody protected anybody from the sight of the dead. On the contrary, death had become the new entertainment.

Dried candle wax mingled with dust and blood to form clumps in the colorless sand. The candles had burned down to nothing, but the arrangement implied a cross. If he didn't know better, he'd think it was a Catholic death ritual—but that kind of thing hadn't been done since the Crusades.

Noah regarded the stone altar in the center of the heads, not much more than a pile of rocks, drenched in the blood of the victims. By the look of the trampled ground, at least twenty people had watched as they'd been carved up and sacrificed. Based on the blood trails and disturbances in the sand, the killers had held each man over the stone altar while someone carved a cross in their torso, piercing the heart and jetting blood over the stone. Then, as the bodies quieted, they'd arranged them in a circle, heads in and feet out.

Noah reminded himself that this wasn't archaeology. It was criminal psychology. Some sick bastards returning from the U.S. had committed this atrocity on their way to join with some other sick bastards. The cartels were clearly consolidating and that could only mean one thing: suffering for the innocent.

The days of whisking away death to protect the gentle sensibilities of the living were officially over. With the now-permanent arrival of what they were calling the "Black Autumn collapse," death would be *the Main Event*. Nothing stood between human predator and prey now that the gears of society had ground themselves into metal sand.

Noah checked his six—taking a slow look around the deserted cartel campsite—wary of lingering danger. Then, he panned over the site again, this time searching for potential scavenge.

Focusing on the constellations of human activity printed in

the dirt, he looked for anything that might have been forgotten or lost. The band of murderers appeared to be a small team of cartel soldiers moving south, just like the team that hit his dad's ranch three days before.

He found a mostly-full bottle of water, a dusty can of black beans, and then a small pile of dried out corn tortillas. The tortillas had turned into dry frisbees, but he chomped one anyway. Scavenge always tasted better than an MRE. Found food was the best food.

Noah stepped carefully to where the cartel vehicles would have been parked, mindful of his footfalls. Things often fell off vehicles in the rush to leave. Laying on its side in the dust, he spotted a partially-buried plastic milk jug.

"Jackpot," he said out loud. He'd discovered a quarter gallon of gasoline, the bangers must've been carting around in the back of their cars, probably using any container they could find. He took a good look at the plastic jug.

"Roundtree Family Dairy, Des Moines, Iowa. *We love our cows and you love our milk."*

Noah wondered if the cows loved the arrangement half as much as the Roundtrees. The rolling hills and idyllic cows on the label got him thinking about dairies. He was a cattleman, not a dairy farmer, however he knew that milk markets were regional. Nobody shipped milk more than a few hundred miles. These 'bangers must've come from Des Moines, Iowa or close by. He couldn't do the math in his head, but he figured it to be around 1,500 miles from Arizona. If they'd come that far, it made sense that they'd be stockpiling gas along the way.

They were under orders, that much seemed clear to Noah. Why would they bother to build an altar? He didn't know many drug dealers, but he did know a lot of Catholics. This wasn't something learned in catechism. This was an atrocity someone had cooked up for another reason.

Strangely, the two factors seemed companionable in Noah's mind: following orders, as implied by the 1,500 mile trek south, and religious fanaticism. Adding a dash of the supernatural would definitely help unite an army. It seemed like it'd been done before in religious history, though Noah didn't know enough about history to say precisely when.

He expanded his search circle around the camp, his interest piqued. Far outside the circle of human activity, he found where someone had taken a shit behind a big clump of sage brush. They'd taken their dump on the ground without digging a hole first. Old Man Bill would've curled his lip and labeled the offender a "Surface Shitter," which was one of Bill's most rueful maledictions. Noah assumed his adoptive father had stepped in someone's surface shit "over in the sandbox," since the insult had a darker spin on it than the practice probably deserved. A father's shame had magical powers, and even as an adult, Noah would never think of shitting outdoors without digging a hole first. So when he saw the barely-drying human turds curling on the sand, scorn swamped him. He hadn't felt nearly as much disgust with the gangbangers when he'd examined the corpses.

The realization made him smile. His father would always be with him, buried in a thousand lessons, habits and deep predispositions. The old man had big opinions, and most of those had become his own. As a young man, Noah had rebelled against many of them. Now as a man with wounds of his own, in a way, he treasured them.

The scorn at the sight of the shit subsided and Noah's practiced eye caught a piece of paper wobbling in the breeze, snagged in the twigs of a nearby sage. He knew it'd be covered in shit—recently used to wipe a gangbanger's ass—but he plucked the paper out of the bush anyway. Holding it by two corners, he stretched the little page out and read the print beneath the yellow smears.

"*El Codigo de los Caballeros Templarios,*" the top of the page read. "The Code of the Knights Templar."

Noah didn't know anything about the Knights Templar, except what little he could recall from *The Davinci Code*. His wife had made him watch the movie with her. He remembered it having something to do with crusaders and a secret society. But the movie couldn't hold his interest. He had preferred Westerns.

"We shall help the poor, fight against materialism, not kill for money, and not use drugs. To do otherwise, we shall offer ourselves up to the order of Knights for execution."

Noah raised his eyebrows. What a crock of shit. But it made sense. A narcotics organization would have a serious issue with soldiers and dealers using its product. Making sobriety part of a larger "code of ethics" would serve to limit waste. The other stuff —materialism and helping the poor—would just be ancillary crap meant to paint the enterprise in the colors of Robin Hood and Zorro. These drug soldiers would cast themselves as the golden-hearted outlaws who only committed acts of violence to further the will of God. Whoever created this cartel wasn't an average idiot. The man had spent some time thinking about how to extend power from Sinaloa to the farthest reaches of America. The realization brought Noah a new understanding of his enemy—and he began to see the breadth of his own crusade. He hadn't been sent on a mission to pick off a few bad guys and die in a blaze of glory. He'd been pulled up short by something from the Great Beyond and set on a path to resist an immense evil. With that realization came a sense of responsibility. People were counting on him.

Noah let the wind re-take the shit-paper, twisting and tumbling until another sage bush grabbed it.

He retraced his steps to his own camp, about a mile away over the rolling hills. Once atop the rise above his camp, Noah lingered, watching his back trail and observing his own camp with a small set of binoculars. If anyone had moved in to ambush him, he would leave his beloved Land Cruiser behind. Nothing was more important, now, than fighting this bunch of sickos. Not even his Cruiser.

Nobody had followed him and nobody had taken up bushwacking positions in his camp. Noah made his way down the hill and checked the trip lines around his rig. From now on, he'd cover the Cruiser in camouflage netting before moving out to cut track. He'd also do a better job setting up his base camp with "sign traps"—cleared areas in the sand that'd make it easy to see from a distance if anyone had come in. He was one man against a smart, organized enemy. They had many lives to give and he had but one.

Noah walked a hundred yards from the Cruiser to his hidden cache: a full backpack and a scoped, lever action 30-30. The cache had been placed away from any line of approach, so if he had to bug out, his supplies would be ready.

Satisfied that his camp remained secure, he climbed just short of the top of a hill to rest and eat his scavenged food. He had plenty of Bill's MREs in the Cruiser, but he preferred the way of the scavenger. He'd eat what he'd found and conserve resources against an uncertain future.

His vantage point allowed him to see the surrounding area and would give him time to react in case anyone approached. He poured water into a canteen cup, crushed the tortillas, and dribbled them into the water. They slowly turned to mush. He built a tiny fire from dried sage twigs and warmed the mush over the licking flame.

The sun sagged to the west and the little fire crackled its wistful song. He took a deep, cleansing breath and settled back onto a hillock of sand. It felt like settling into a new life. Like a man just emerging from winter, Noah regarded his mission fresh, through open eyes and an unfettered heart.

Without a care for the future, he would ply all he had learned from Bill against the darkness rolling across the desert. He'd been tracking a few lapping waves heading south, but he suspected that a great swell would turn and pour northward in the days to come. He would go out in front of that flood, and he would know what to do when the moment was ripe.

Old Bill had harped endlessly about ignoring intuition and obeying the sign on the ground. But Old Bill hadn't known the ghosts Noah knew, and Bill hadn't ever been brought into the counsels of the souls who drifted in the desert stars.

The signs of man's passing would be heeded by Noah, with every bit of skill he could bring to bear. But the greater signs in the sky—the light that cast shadows onto his heart—would be his masters. Noah would be vigilant, but grace-filled. He would be keen in his craft, but surrendered to the warm winds.

He could feel the bands of murdering coyotes coalescing across the desert sands, becoming one force focused in one malignant will. Noah had no idea who that might be, but he knew his place in the universe: to stand against that man and against all who would follow him.

With the warm evening breeze consenting to his mission, Noah drifted into the arms of sleep.

CHAPTER 19

TAVO CASTILLO
US HIGHWAY 19, AEROSPACE PARKWAY EXIT,
TUCSON, ARIZONA

They were too late, and Tavo knew it when they crossed the abandoned border station at Nogales. The inky haze of smoke had been visible for almost seventy miles, and smoke that black could only come from burning oil—a lot of burning oil.

There was no good reason to set fire to a refinery, but it took only one vandal or one pyromaniac with a blowtorch to set off eight and a half trillion BTUs of dazzling fuel. With every minute, Tavo could feel the psychotics inching closer to every refinery in the western United States. His plan of empire could rise or fall based on the whims of sickos who liked to whack themselves off to the flames of a burning structure.

For the moment, he had gasoline in the tanks of his Jeeps and trucks. Between the gas he'd managed to place under guard at the Pemex stations in Hermosillo and the fuel Sofía had shipped from Monterrey, Tavo launched his foray into the United States.

He had planned on seizing a fuel refinery in Tucson, but now that idea had likely gone up in smoke. Ten miles outside of the city, Beto jogged back to Tavo's Humvee from his command position at the front of the convoy.

"*Canoso*. Check it out. We're in America, *carnal*." Beto put his hand on Tavo's shoulder and beamed.

His lieutenant spoke truth. Despite the probable loss of the refinery, they had successfully invaded America. Tavo's recollection of the Mexican-American war was rusty, but he thought that he might be the first Mexican to invade America since Santa Anna crushed the Alamo.

"*Viva Mexico.*" Beto whispered.

Loyalty is a strange and fickle creature, Tavo thought. The man beside him had been born in Mexico, raised in America and had undoubtedly sworn allegiance to the American flag as a Navy SEAL. But faced with the idea of his adoptive country in flames, Beto's true loyalty revealed itself. The dust of Mexico had worked its way into his soul, displacing the gleaming steel of America. Yet Tavo's own daughter, when she discovered his invasion into America, would probably repudiate him. *Loyalty was indeed fickle.*

What did she care if America fell into Tavo's hands instead of falling into ruin?

He suspected she would care very much. Or she might pretend to care while working another angle. He hadn't witnessed his daughter commit a single devious act in her life, but he juggled her motives in his mind, never climbing out from underneath his suspicions.

He needed to put his mind at ease. This day was worthy of celebration—of leaving behind the gadflies of family and treachery. Not three hours ago, Tavo's four hundred and fifty-man army rolled through the American City of Nogales without firing a shot. The scant border town—a soulless cluster of dirty, stucco buildings and a Denny's restaurant—could barely be called a city. Even so, it was an *American* city, and that meant he was the first military force to invade America in a long, long time.

It was a victory, but Tavo wasn't sure how much to celebrate. If anything, America was collapsing too fast; devolving into chaos before he could get his arms around their assets. The whole point of taking down America would be to accumulate and protect key resources, all of which dangled in the wind, vulnerable to scavengers.

Gasoline was at the top of his list of resources, and the burning refinery in Tucson spoke to the ticking clock that had already begun to erode his plan. Like a sandcastle chewed by the surf, Tavo's future empire would not wait long. Perhaps a week. Maybe less.

Nobody in modern times had seen such an immense civilization collapse. Would it dwindle like a socialist third world country or implode overnight like America during the Great Depression? By the look of the Nogales border station, America had already broken all records for historical collapse. In just one week, the nation had crumbled inward like a tower of ash.

"Bravo One, Charlie One, this is Actual." Tavo keyed his radio. "Converge on me. We need to talk."

———

Between Nogales and Tucson, as they passed the Blue Skies Indian Casino, a tattered banner hung between the pillars of a dead electronic sign announcing a law enforcement expo. But all the police must've left because they encountered no resistance.

As they rolled closer to Tucson, the southbound side of the freeway filled with stumbling Americans, walking or driving south with their families. Saúl stopped one of the walkers and learned that the water had shut off in Tucson four days earlier, not long after the electricity. Anyone without water storage—which was almost everyone—was being forced to relocate their families to the water treatment facility south of the city.

Like hikers passing a bear cave, Tavo's four-hundred and fifty men were painfully aware of the massive U.S. airbase looming to their east. Even a single A-10 Warthog or attack helicopter could destroy their military expedition in the blink of an eye.

But Tavo had a fair understanding of the American military. A fighter jock couldn't just hop in an A-10 and come blow them up. There were logistics, support and authorizations that had to be satisfied before American government released hellfire. His grab bag of Mexican soldiers and highly trained gangbangers hadn't fired a shot on American soil. So far as America was concerned, they were undocumented immigrants. America's first impulse might be to give them a hot meal and shelter, not grind them up with the Avenger cannons of their ground attack planes.

Tavo was betting that American National Guard command, communications and support had become unstable in the last week, especially around National Guard bases where soldiers could walk home to their families. How many soldiers would maintain readiness, no enemy in sight, while their families suffered without water?

Even if he was wrong, and if the American military was alive and well, they would certainly give Mexicans—their neighbors and allies—a generous opportunity to head home. He half expected to see a mayor drive up in a car and ask them "can I help you with something." There would be a first-mover advantage in any fight, and Tavo had that advantage in spades. The man who came primed for violence usually won.

They'd passed thousands of pairs of eyeballs on the freeway, and Tavo's column appeared to be exactly what it was: an invasion force. But nobody would believe it. In retrospect, he should've ordered his men to invade in passenger vehicles instead of green-painted trucks bristling with machine guns. But even in army vehicles, Americans would have a hard time believing they'd been invaded by their insignificant neighbor to the south.

Given the speed of their probe into America—it'd only been four hours since they'd crossed the border—Tavo frankly didn't know what to expect. The Americans he'd seen so far seemed defeated, if only by their circumstance. But he'd spent countless hours attending American firearm trainings, and he knew full well that Tucson was no New York City, full of hapless Millennials and gender-confused urbanites. Tavo had shared sack lunch sandwiches with the *other kind* of American—the kind who fantasized about Mexican narcos streaming across their border after a collapse. Somewhere in the city of Tucson, men and women carried AR-15 rifles and vests bursting with loaded magazines. Even if the military was dead, not everyone would be dragging themselves, hapless, toward the last remaining water in southern Arizona. Some citizens might actually be revved up to protect their city, and he knew that kind well enough to know they wouldn't wait for government permission before shooting.

In any case, speed would be Tavo's greatest ally. Passing quickly through Tucson would give him a straight shot at the National Guard armory to the southwest of Phoenix, and that armory would deliver a mountain fortress and fifty Humvees, some of them up-armored.

Every day his force grew by a couple hundred men, and many of them were *Templario* commandos. His lieutenants had arranged for emergency communications with their organization via pre-arranged sat phone call-ins. Even as the cell networks fell apart, the satellite phones remained solid. His cartel had ordered thousands of fighters to rendezvous in Hermosillo, promising food, work and plunder. When Tavo returned to the ranch in the next day or two, he expected to greet another wave of thousands of men, ready to join his expedition. If he could capture and arm a National Guard garrison *inside* the U.S., he could re-route reinforcements to that garrison and speed the process of force consolidation.

He stopped his army outside the city of Tucson and scanned ahead to confirm the source of the massive column of smoke. As expected, the Chevron Sunset Fuels refinery burned like Iraqi oil fields on CNN. Given the loss of the easy refueling point, Tavo would need to move even faster, lest he be cut off from five or six gas refineries that would be easy pickings—the few lonely storage facilities strung between Tucson, Arizona and Boise, Idaho. California would be crawling with dangerous refugees, and the refineries of the Midwest would require that he cross the Rockies. Tavo would do everything he could to avoid the oilfields of Texas. It was one thing to invade Arizona, but it was another thing entirely to invade Texas. History could cut both ways. Passing through dozens of Texas towns with a lightly-armed military force would be like daring the townsfolk to "remember the Alamo." Tavo preferred to move directly up the center of the American west, taking advantage of the wide open spaces. By the time he took the flatlands between the High Sierras and the Rocky Mountains, he'd have the food and fuel he'd need to seize anything else he desired.

Tavo's lieutenants considered the maps he spread out on the hood of his Humvee and looked at one another with eyebrows raised.

"We needed that refinery." He pointed to the mile-thick column of smoke, twisting skyward like a dancer on a pole. "If we are forced to run this op on Mexican fuel, our supply chain will spread across hundreds of miles. This area will be crawling with starving lunatics in a week. A long supply chain will require us to leave troops along the way, and it'll whittle down the tip of our spear. The Tucson refinery would've allowed us to range out from here instead of from Hermosillo. Now we have a problem."

"How far are we going?" Beto asked.

"We need to reach Salt Lake City. It's a nexus for fuel out of Wyoming and Northern Utah." Tavo traced the lines of several pipelines that terminated in Salt Lake City, Utah. "As long as the psychos don't set fire to the refineries, we can push into Idaho and even eastern Washington. We'll capture trillions of dollars of American infrastructure and the farm belt of the west."

Tavo could tell this was a lot of information, probably coming at them too fast.

"Look at it this way," he tried to simplify. "If we bring guns, we bring order. If we bring order, we are kings. Without us, these people will tear each other apart like starving dogs. Why not enforce order, bring back the church and set ourselves up like emperors all at the same time? Everyone wins."

"Okay, Boss." Alejandro shook off the grandiosity of Tavo's vision. "Just tell us what you need us to do. We're soldiers. We know how to take ground. You're saying that we need to take *a lot* of ground, right?"

"Yes. I think this corridor north will be uncontested, minus a couple small, military holdouts and a couple pockets of citizen militia. But we need forward operating bases to protect our fuel supply. Tucson refinery looks like a total loss, so my contingency plan is this town." Tavo poked a finger at the map in the middle of New Mexico.

"Alejandro, take Bravo Company and hightail it directly to this town, Artesia. Don't stop. Don't engage opposition. There's a big refinery, and with that fuel we can leapfrog straight to Salt Lake City."

"Are you sure, *Jefe?*" Alejandro gave Tavo a sideways look. "We're in the United States, now. This ain't Mexico. There are weapons here that can waste this little army in one shot." Alejandro held up a finger. "And that's not counting the millions of guns owned by American rednecks. Are you sure we shouldn't sit tight until we have a better idea, *Ese?*"

Tavo hated it when his lieutenants talked like street people. "No, *ese*. I don't think we should sit tight. There are only two logical possibilities: if they launch a cruise missile, we have nothing to worry about because we'll be dead before we know it. If they can't launch their million dollar bullets because they don't know how to leave the house in the morning when the coffee maker doesn't work, then we're going to roll through here before they know what happened—unless we wring our hands until the gas gets burned up by psychos. In that case, we won't be going anywhere. You know as well as I do, the first guy to throw a punch in a street fight usually wins. That black sky up ahead; yesterday, that was once our ticket to more money and power than you ever imagined and it's going up in smoke. We will have one, maybe two more chances to secure the fuel we need. Can I trust you to get this done, Alejandro?"

"Yeah. I'll get it done. But you guys be careful. Any time I start thinking there's only a couple ways something can go down, some *puta madre* comes up with a third option that hadn't occurred to me."

Tavo had always allowed, even encouraged, debate between him and his three lieutenants. He reminded himself that Alejandro wasn't being belligerent. He just hadn't figured out the new reality. They were at war, and in war, debating earned a subordinate a bullet in the face. Tavo couldn't think of a good way to threaten a man that he was about to send off on a mission, so he took another tack.

"Obviously, we're doing something right or we wouldn't have made it this far. We have been at the right place at the right time, every step of the way. So far it certainly appears like we're on the path...of God."

Alejandro huffed despite Tavo's hard eyes boring into him. "We're drug runners, *carnal*. I make it a personal policy not to count on God for anything."

Tavo held up his hand instead of putting it on his Glock, which he desperately wanted to do. "And yet here we are. In America. Unopposed. We have the northern Mexican army backing our play. If I'd told you two weeks ago that we'd be standing here today, you would've never believed me. The people of Hermosillo have food and water on its way instead of being raped by the Zetas. Is it so hard to believe that God is using us to save lives?"

Alejandro shook his head, then nodded. "Yes. It's hard to believe."

Tavo glanced from Alejandro to Saúl then to Beto. Saúl seemed ready to roll with the group's consensus. Beto's face had something else going on—an inner eagerness that could be either battle lust or faith. In either case, he was good-to-go. Alejandro saw it too.

"You are some crazy *pendejos*." Alejandro smiled and nodded his surrender. "Okay. I guess we conquer America. Let me know if Saint Michael shows up in front of you guys with a flaming sword or some shit like that. I may need a little faith-booster when shit gets real over here." He said the last word like a gang-banger. *Over he-ya.*

Tavo smiled and put his hands on his hips, one resting lightly on his pistol. Nobody seemed to notice.

"We've got the abbot with us, and the blessing of the archbishop of Hermosillo. Plus, we have twenty belt-fed machine guns and fifty rocket-propelled grenades. If that isn't Saint Michael with a flaming sword, it's pretty damn close."

"Maybe so, *hermano*. Maybe so." Alejandro bro-hugged each of the men, then left to lead his unit east toward New Mexico.

CHAPTER 20

NOAH MILLER

US HIGHWAY 19, NEAR DREXEL HEIGHTS,
TUCSON, ARIZONA

> "And, yes, the Man, He is a consuming fire
> the flames burn away the chaff.
> Yes our Man, He is a consuming fire
> He bears the wind, and grips the staff,
> and heats this heart of stone."
>
> — *The Crusader*

As soon as the cartel pushed through the border crossing station at Nogales, Noah lit out for Tucson. He'd encountered an encampment of law enforcement officers milling around the Indian casino at Blue Skies. He convinced them that the cartels were indeed invading—LEOs were forever skeptical. But after telling them about the human sacrifice he'd found in the desert, the majority of the cops pulled up stakes and headed for Tucson. They'd agreed that it'd be the best place to make their stand, especially if they could enlist air support from the National Guard airbase.

When he reached the airbase in Tucson, he'd been sorely disappointed. The place had been locked down as though the

U.S. government was saving it for a rainy day. Noah drove twice around the entire facility without seeing a living soul inside the perimeter fence. He prayed the security force was monitoring the video feeds, but if they were, nobody came out to investigate, even when he rammed his Land Cruiser into the north gate. The gate held and Noah failed to attract attention. After almost an hour of trying to raise the alarm at the airfield, he gave up.

After that failed attempt, he raced up and down residential streets, honking his horn. Not a single person came out of their house, if they were even there.

While driving a grid pattern, looking for volunteers, Noah heard a spat of gunfire. He raced to the sound to find three cops firing their guns into the asphalt. They holstered as he approached.

One of the cops leaned in his window as he rolled to a stop. Noah recognized him from the Blue Skies casino. "We figured knocking on doors would get us shot. Shooting into the dirt brings out the right kind of survivor." Two minutes later, four armed men and a woman crept out of their homes. The cops waved them over with a white flag.

"We've probably sent a hundred men to Drexel Heights so far," the cop explained.

He let Noah know that ten groups of cops were working the streets, rallying the residents of Tucson and sending them to the meet up. Noah figured he couldn't do any better so he flipped a U-turn and headed toward Drexel Heights to see if he could help organize the ambush.

He found hundreds of armed men, mulling around the massive parking lot that served the Santa Cruz Outlet Stores. Other than the fact that they were all in the same place, Noah couldn't discern any organization whatsoever. The tableau raised visions of the American Revolution. He didn't know where those images originated—movies, probably. He could picture this same scene playing out two-hundred and fifty years before; men running around with hunting rifles, rushing to prepare themselves for the British Army as it cut a swath across the colonies. It made him think about their unlikely victory, and the creation of a nation where "bearing arms" would forever be a part of the national culture.

Those original American revolutionaries had envisioned fighting off kings and tyrants with their guns. What would they think if they saw this—an army of foreign drug dealers, paid for by America's hunger for narcotics? Would they even find this nation worthy of saving?

Whatever they might think, Noah knew his calling. The biggest, brightest thing in the parking lot was a fire truck, so he angled the Cruiser toward it.

"Is your chief here?" he asked the oldest-looking man. Everyone was in street clothes, so Noah didn't know for sure they were even firemen.

The man hesitated. "I'm Chief Blanchard." He reached out his hand and the two men shook.

Noah took a deep breath. Just from the man's tentative body language, he surmised the chief had arrived at his position as chief more from being a "team player" than being a man of action. Noah reasoned, these days, a city fire chief probably had to be a political operator over a two-fisted man of action.

"The cartel army is coming. They'll be here in under an hour. You need to organize these men," Noah said, getting right to the point.

The chief shielded his eyes from the sun and sized up a knot of men fifty yards away. "The guys from the PD are never going to follow a fire chief."

Noah shook his head. "I don't give a shit who leads, but someone needs to take charge, and it needs to happen fast. Fire up your sirens and get everyone over here. Make a plan, any plan—just so long as when those narco bastards drive past that hill, they get pasted."

"I know what needs to happen. I'm just not sure how to coordinate it without anyone from city government to set up lines of authority." Chief Blanchard held out his hands.

"Fuck those city guys. They're not here. You are. Make some noise and get these men all pointed in the same direction. I've got to go get eyes on the cartel convoy. Make it happen, Chief. Light up your siren. You'll know what to do from there."

Noah jumped in his vehicle and sped away south down the highway. As soon as he was on the road with his tires howling, his worry ramped into high gear. The entire southbound shoulder of the 19 was filled with Tucson refugees stumbling south, probably toward the water treatment plant out in the desert. These were the least-prepared of the Tucsonites, and they were also, probably, the easiest to lead. The men in the parking lot he'd just left were better prepared for hard times, but they were a bunch of prickly individualists—men who bucked the system enough to own guns, even when owning guns meant you weren't "woke." It also meant they were a pain in the ass.

This wasn't a game. Soldiers were coming up the highway with machine guns and rocket-propelled grenades. If the locals hit that convoy like a bunch of confused girl scouts, it'd be a massacre. Luckily, Noah still couldn't see the convoy from his Cruiser, even after driving fifteen miles south. Maybe the Mexicans had turned away from their attack on Tucson. Maybe they'd taken surface streets and cut over toward Interstate 10 and headed east. After what Noah had just seen at the parking lot, he would welcome the reprieve. He desperately wanted to hit the Mexican convoy, but not if his volunteers were going to get ground into hamburger. Without air support, this fight could go really bad, really fast. He'd seen it happen before in his own front yard. When the guns come out, what should happen and what does happen part company, fast.

Noah swerved off the highway and onto an overpass that would give him some elevation. As he scanned the road ahead, he could see that—one way or another—there would be bloodshed. The cartel convoy had stopped to surveil the approach to Tucson not three miles south of Noah's position. They were stacked on the off-ramp, mirroring Noah's own surveillance. He could see them and they could probably see him.

As Noah watched, a sizable portion of the convoy broke east at the off-ramp and turned down surface streets. Either they were heading for Interstate 10, or they had seen the ambush and were setting up a massive flanking maneuver on his citizen militia. A few minutes after the force split, the main convoy began rolling, continuing its move northward up the northbound lanes of Highway 19. The southbound lanes were filled with zombies streaming out of Tucson, oblivious to the coming slaughter.

Noah couldn't stick around to figure out if they were being flanked. He'd be overrun by the convoy within minutes if he didn't get moving.

"Son of a bitch," he swore as he set his binoculars on the passenger seat. There was nothing he could do but pray the cartel wasn't flanking them. If they did, everyone who had come to Noah's call would be dead in the next two hours.

Noah threw the Land Cruiser in reverse and backed down the onramp. Once he'd cleared off the military crest of the rise, he flipped a backwards, three-point turn, raced down the off-ramp and crossed over the bar pit between the south and northbound lanes. Then he roared north, his hands kneading the steering wheel.

Standing to one side of the firetruck, a circle of six men raged at one another. Chief Blanchard stood two steps back from the fray, looking for all the world like a defeated parent.

"Just LISTEN TO ME! *LISTEN TO ME!*" one of the men shouted at the top of his lungs. "I am a former SWAT commander and you need to do what I'm telling you to do!"

"Are you joking?" Another man yelled. "I served in fucking *Ramadi* and I can promise that no SWAT cop knows shit about what's about to go down. You're going to get everyone killed. This isn't a fucking hostage negotiation!"

Noah wiped the sweat from his forehead. He knew literally *nothing* about leading men into battle, but he did know a clusterfuck when he saw one.

In the knot of arguing men, there was a former SWAT commander, and then some kind of vet—probably a Marine or Army infantry if he'd actually fought in Ramadi, Iraq. Noah knew enough from listening to Old Bill's war stories to put that much together. The next guy was probably a cop too. He had to be at least fifty and had a pretty good beer gut in contrast to his huge biceps.

One of the other guys standing in the circle was so loaded down with military kit that he couldn't actually be military. He was wearing old jungle cammies, Viet Nam-era combat boots, a fully-loaded plate-carrier vest and a boonie cap. Noah figured him for a militia leader.

"Stop! All of you stop!" a heavy-set man without a visible gun shouted. "Can't you see that this is exactly like the fight against the Philistines? If we don't harken to the Lord, RIGHT NOW, we will be defeated. I guarantee it."

The other five men looked at the man—obviously some sort of pastor—like he'd just told them he wore ladies' underwear.

The militia guy took advantage of the gap in the conversation to champion his own plan. "We need to hit them with chlorine gas. I'm telling you. We give them NO QUARTER! Our militiamen are bringing forward barrels of gas right now. This is just like the book *Lucifer's Hammer*. We hit them with chlorine gas and GAME OVER!"

"Are you crazy? We'll gas everyone, including our own guys and any locals still in the area. *Great idea, GI Joe.* Let's use chemical weapons! What could go wrong?" the Iraqi veteran shouted. "Let's start this thing out with war crimes! Great plan."

Noah drew his Glock and blasted a 9 millimeter crater in the asphalt. The six loudmouths froze in differing states of shock. One of them stood with one leg off the ground, his hands over his nuts. Two of them had drawn their handguns.

Noah spoke, their ears still ringing. "The cartel soldiers are coming. They'll be here in less than twenty minutes. They've stopped at the Pima Mine exit, but they're getting back in motion right now. They have belt-fed machine guns, rocket launchers, mortars and they have a leader, which puts them way, way ahead of us." Noah holstered his Glock. The pastor's mouth still hung open.

"You." Noah pointed at the SWAT commander. "Take Militia Guy, all the cops and all the men who will follow you and get to the top of that hill." He pointed to the big mountain beside the highway. "Do it now."

"Who the hell are you?" the SWAT commander fired back.

"I'm the guy telling you how it is. We need to be on top of that mountain in ten minutes. Please. Pretty please. Stop talking and do it... You, you and you." He pointed at three more men and the fire chief. "Get everyone else and hide in the river bottom on the opposite side of the highway. Don't shoot until you can look them in the eyes." Noah was ninety-percent sure he'd just pulled battle tactics from a Johnny Horton song.

"Let's go. We need to be set up before they enter the bit of road beneath that hill," he said firmly, and was astounded when the knot of men actually hustled away, apparently to follow his plan.

A school bus covered in steel plate rumbled into the parking lot, listing precariously on its overloaded leaf springs.

Oh Lord, please don't let this circus act end in tragedy, Noah prayed as he jumped in his Land Cruiser and raced toward the hill.

Noah had been on-the-run for ten hours straight, and he felt so tired he could barely force his eyes to focus, which would've been fine if not for the fact that he would be in combat for the first time in about ten minutes.

He'd taken a position at the top of the hill overlooking Highway 19. It wasn't the best location for his Winchester 30-30, with an effective range of only a couple hundred yards, but it was more important to see the enemy's order of battle for himself. The green snake of trucks and jeeps extended at least a mile up the northbound side of Highway 19. Noah was no military genius, but he seriously doubted his raggedy-ass band of Tucson fighters could beat the column in a fair fight. The narcos had more numbers, more guns and certainly better command and control. The only thing the Arizonans had going for them was this bit of high ground.

Noah agitated as the men and vehicles scurried around below the hill like cockroaches when the lights flick on. There was no way this force would maintain the element of surprise, and that was their only advantage. Getting them to stay put in a coordinated ambush had proven impossible without strong leadership, reliable communications and military discipline. They had none of those things. Men rushed back and forth across the freeway below Noah, doing God-knows-what and blowing their element of surprise.

Noah swore under his breath at the inanity of man.

Dammit to hell. Please stop moving. You're going to get us all killed.

The last four hours had been an emotional rollercoaster. Not only had Noah run a one-man surveillance operation from in-front of the enemy, but he had become a Southwestern Paul Revere—rallying whatever opposition he could ahead of an invading army. Luckily, there was only a single travel corridor up the center of Arizona. Otherwise, it would've been impossible to stay ahead of the cartel forces. He couldn't say for sure if he'd been operating on good guesswork or divine inspiration. Either way, he'd correctly guessed that the Mexican cartel intended on pillaging American cities—and that they'd start with Tucson.

As predicted, the leading edge of the convoy rolled up along-side the alfalfa fields following the Santa Cruz River. In this season, the Santa Cruz was nothing more than a dry wash. The convoy had been running with a scout element a half-mile out front, but since they'd just started rolling again from the Pima Mine offramp, the scout element hadn't been able to gain much distance from the column. Apparently, the cartel commander had told everyone to move out at the same time, and the scouts were hurrying to re-establish a lead on the main group. Maybe, like against the Philistines that the pastor had mentioned, God was with them too.

His ambushers were never going to get a shot at anything more than the leading element of the convoy, which was over a mile long. The ambush zone was only a few hundred yards deep—but the more soldiers they could bottle up in the ambush, the more pain they could cause the cartel. Inflicting pain, then running like hell, was the most the Arizonans could hope to accomplish.

If the cartel army committed itself to a protracted fight, Tucson would fall and the patriots would die. If the string of trucks that had split off a half-hour before was indeed flanking them, they would all be trapped and exterminated. But, if the patriots could deliver a bloody nose, they might turn the cartel aside from Tucson. They might even turn them back to Mexico, at least for the moment.

What do they want from us? Noah wondered for the first time. Conquering territory meant holding territory, and history had proven that to be a devilishly-difficult proposition. Did the cartel boss actually think that he could take and hold territory in America? Why would he want that?

Plunder.

The idea came to Noah like a revelation—so crisp and clear that he didn't doubt it for a second. He suddenly knew: the most-common reason throughout history for invasion was to steal: food, luxuries, women, weapons, fuel...

Fuel.

The thought hung in Noah's mind like a stick bobbing downstream then pinning itself against the rocks.

The Tucson oil refinery had been destroyed. Why attack Tucson?

Maybe *they're just passing through. Maybe they aren't attacking.*

Noah's thoughts were swept away in a surge of adrenaline. The scout element was entering the ambush zone. Amazingly, nobody scurried across the road and the army rolled forward as though nothing was amiss. Noah's ambushers had settled down and maybe—just maybe—the convoy of soldiers hadn't seen them dicking around like a bunch of rednecks at a gun show.

"Come on. Hold. Hold..." Noah coaxed the Arizonans to hold their fire and, miraculously, they did. The first three, army-green Jeeps rolled deeper into the ambush zone as the front-end of the convoy entered as well.

"Hold on, boys. Hang on just another minute..." Noah would rather the scout element pass all the way out of the trap before it sprung, but that would be asking a lot of the men. He looked around, suddenly terrified of a possible flank. Things seemed to be going perfectly—too perfectly, in fact.

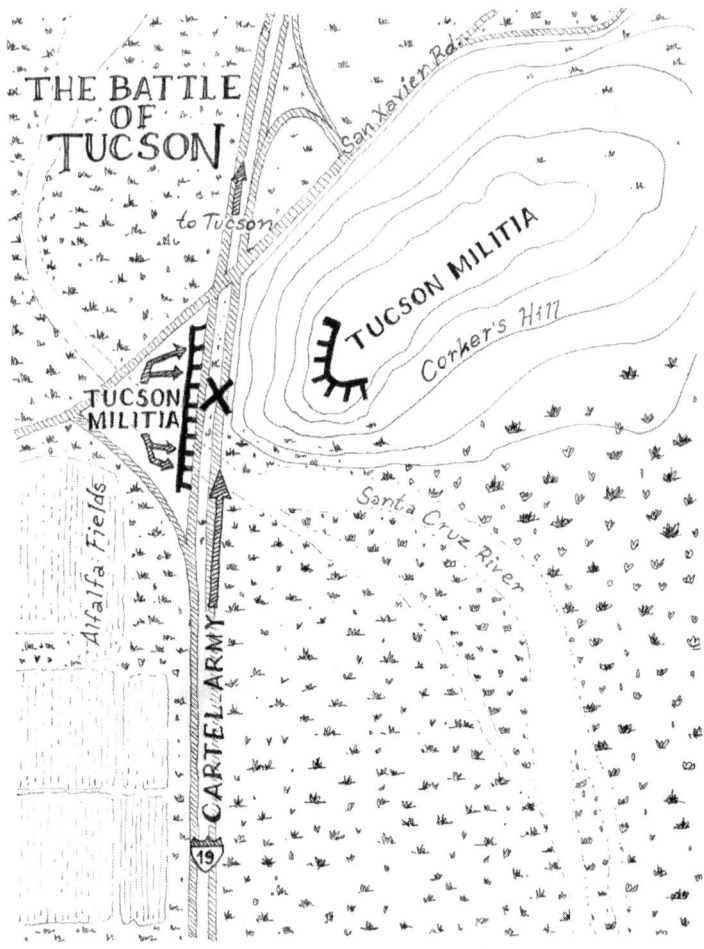

CHAPTER 21

TAVO CASTILLO
US HIGHWAY 19, NEAR DREXEL HEIGHTS, TUCSON, ARIZONA

"Estas seguro?" Tavo barked into the satellite phone. "Are you certain?"

While they'd been on the road, heading toward Tucson, his satellite phone chirped, a scheduled call that'd slipped his mind with rat-face Ortiz, the assassin.

"We found a post-it note in her apartment with the name 'Salazar' and a phone number in Guatemala City."

Tavo had ordered the *sicario* to search his daughter's apartment in Mexico City. They'd also hacked her phone the week before. He could picture his daughter talking to someone on the phone in her apartment at the capital and jotting down the contact information of the man who had set him up for capture in Guatemala—Agusto Salazar, his half-brother and quite possibly, an agent of his criminal father.

It was strangely difficult to write something in a cell phone if it was being used for a call at the same time. That'd been her mistake. She'd gone analog with her treachery by writing on a post-it note.

"Did she call the number?" Tavo asked, remembering the phone hack.

"Yes. Twice. Once, three months ago and again just two days before the target date." He'd used the words "the target date." That meant that the assassin realized that he knew too much. The rat face must've reached the conclusion that he was swimming in shark infested waters. He'd probably figured out who Tavo was, and that the subjects of his investigation were family. The assassin must've sensed the danger of knowing too much information about the kind of man who paid him in diamonds. "The day of the Kaibil assault in Antigua" had become "the target date."

He's right, Tavo mused. He had planned to have them both killed: the *sicario* and the handler.

What a difference a week makes, Tavo thought as his Humvee rumbled down the freeway. Now, with federal police fighting for their lives in the streets like everyone else, Tavo wouldn't bother having the sicario and his handler eliminated. The assassins were far enough away that they might as well be in Borneo, for all the exposure they represented to Tavo.

He watched the fields and desert south of Tucson roll past his window as he thought about his daughter. A steady stream of refugees dragged themselves south, heading toward groundwater like desperate animals. He had been lost in thought for a moment, the satellite phone up against his ear.

Something buzzed in the back of his mind, and he felt like he should get off the phone and come back to the here-and-now. "I'll talk to you again at the appointed time."

"Of course, *Mister Juarez,*" the contract killer emphasized his false name. It was a futile attempt at denying that Ortiz knew his daughter's name and would know Tavo's name as well. Once Tavo's DNA had been used in the investigation, any chance of maintaining anonymity had vanished. The assassin knew his half-brother's name, his father's name and now his daughter's. That knowledge would've been a death sentence a week before.

Now Tavo didn't give a shit. He had bigger fish to fry. He needed to get off the phone. He needed to set his daughter's obvious treachery aside.

"Goodbye." He hung up the sat phone and stared at the column of black smoke that'd become a massive pillar as they'd entered the outskirts of Tucson. A metallic glint up on a hill instantly abolished his reverie and Tavo's nerves stood straight up.

"Stop!" he shouted to his driver. He reached for the radio, but before he could key the mic, violence enveloped Beto's lead unit. Wedged between a muddy river and a blackened, cut back cliff, the front half of his motorized column fell into a bristling trap.

Tavo jumped out of the rolling Humvee and brought his gun to bear, much too far away to be any good.

"Move, move, move!" he shouted into his radio. "Push through!" The shouting was unnecessary. Beto had trained him in response to ambush in the first place. If it was possible to assault through, Beto would do it. Tavo stopped shouting, calmed himself and did what he did best. He worked the problem.

He looked at the laminated frequency card taped to the pocket in his plate carrier vest and called Alejandro, now probably fifteen miles away, heading east toward New Mexico.

"Coyote Actual to Kit Fox, over."

"Go for Kit Fox," the radio squawked.

"Return immediately. Contact with enemy at the south edge of Tucson."

"Good copy, Actual. Returning to Tucson, maximum speed. Estimate two-five mics. Over."

"Copy, Kit Fox. Standby in five mics for more. Coyote Actual out."

It wasn't lost on Tavo that Alejandro had been right when he'd urged sticking together. He'd be rushing back to save Tavo from a mistake—one that Alejandro had predicted. Tavo knew he should appreciate his man's insightfulness, but the acid churning in his stomach yearned to kill him instead.

All he knew from his position at the rear of the column was that the front third of his force—everything below the shadow of the hill, had come under massive fire, probably from positions on the cliff and maybe from the riverbank as well. He waited for radio contact from Beto. The bass thunder of his belt-fed machine guns joined the fight, hopefully carving out hot flesh from the opposition.

Finally his command radio crackled to life. "Coyote, this is Roadrunner. Standby for contact report."

"Go for Actual," Tavo responded, dropping his rifle into its sling and clamping his Peltors tight around his ears.

"Estimated six-zero riflemen on the hill to the east...Standby." The radio went silent and a new sound, a deep thumping, added to the chorus of battle. Explosions carried on the wind.

"Roadrunner for Actual. Armored elements—police APCs and what appears to be a steel-armored school bus have come alongside our position on the southbound leg of the freeway. We're taking heavy fire from both sides of the highway. Advise withdrawing to your position. We're down thirty men and two technicals."

"This is Actual. Good copy. Withdraw to my position." Tavo grabbed his binoculars from the front seat of the Humvee and used the doorframe to steady himself.

"*Dios mio,*" he whispered as he scanned the hillside above his retreating men. Not only had his men failed to destroy the elevated ambush positions, but he watched in horror as trucks on the ridge unloaded blue, fifty-five gallon drums. He could only imagine what those drums contained. Maybe gasoline. Maybe oil. Perhaps poison gas. At least the American military waited for permission before committing atrocities. Apparently, American citizens were capable of anything.

The front third of his column had been nearly enveloped—the high ridge to the east, a blocking force to the north and ambush elements popping up along the dry wash to the west of the freeway. The belt-feds in the center and rear of his column opened up on the ambushers dotting the hill crest and Tavo watched as machine gun fire raked one of the trucks unloading the blue barrels. From a distance of over eight hundred meters, he couldn't tell if the men on the ridge were convulsing from the 7.62 rounds or if something more ominous had escaped from the drums, striking men down like a viper in the grass.

He tried to picture the chain of events that might lead to such a vicious attack inside of such a tight timeframe. They'd only been in U.S. territory for four hours. Perhaps police at the convention, or even the people of Nogales, had raced north to Tucson, marshaling what weapons they could from the National Guard armories and airbase. Maybe the police had rallied residents, going street-by-street, calling up American gun owners to protect the city.

Tavo's imagination flowered, and in it bloodthirsty American "preppers" mustered their perverse creativity to slaughter Mexican invaders—weapons, explosives, booby traps, even chemical weapons.

WHOOMP! WHOOMP! WHOOMP, WHOOMP!

Something big exploded on both sides of the freeway, showering the front third of his column with burning gasoline and something that appeared to be flaming gel. A mushroom cloud rolled skyward, pregnant with flame. Another bomb launched gouts of flame a hundred yards onto the highway, cutting off the front third of his column from retreat.

"Get out of there, Beto!" Tavo screamed into his radio. The

flaming tarmac blocked his view of the battlefield, and he could only listen as the firefight kicked into high gear.

"Focus on the ambushers to the west side of the freeway!" Tavo spoke into his command radio. "Shift left. Shift fire left."

He climbed on top of his Humvee to see over the flames. Like hungry flesh beetles, the American partisans swarmed the west side of the freeway. They leapfrogged alongside Beto's retreating men, using a drainage culvert and the fleeing refugees to cover their attack.

"Actual to Saúl. Flank to the west and cut off that ambush element. Roadrunner needs breathing room."

"Copy. Already on it," Saúl replied.

A bullet whizzed past Tavo, but he ignored it. He watched as Saúl led a group of assaulters in a sprint to the west, charging over the sand and dropping over the far side of the southbound highway. A parallel dry riverbed swallowed the team below the raised bed of the roadway. They disappeared for two minutes, then three.

Suddenly, rifle fire crackled from a berm five hundred meters north. Saúl opened up his flank against the ragtag Americans in the wash. As the ambushers became the ambushed and as the flames on the asphalt burned themselves out, the front wounded half of the column fled back toward Tavo and the safety of numbers.

At first it was only clusters of running men. Then a Jeep. Then two technicals. Tavo saw someone who appeared to be Beto, giving orders as he ran. Tavo looked again through his binoculars and blew out a breath he'd unconsciously been holding.

Beto had survived. Saúl and Alejandro would've become a problem if their brother-in-arms had been killed this soon after crossing over into the U.S. They might've second-guessed Tavo's judgment and that meant friction. Tavo couldn't afford friction at the moment.

Tavo watched Beto through his binoculars, now clear of the worst of the fighting. Beto reached for his radio. There was a split-second delay as the radio waves covered the distance between them.

"Roadrunner to Actual."

"Go ahead, Roadrunner."

"We're out of the hot zone. We lost maybe a quarter of my company and half our vehicles."

"Good copy. Sending corpsmen. Actual out." Tavo switched to his command frequency.

"Saúl."

"Go for Saúl."

"Bring me American survivors. I need two. Kill all the rest."

"Copy."

With the battle for Tucson past its apogee, Tavo sat on the hood of his Humvee. The smoldering asphalt commingled with the oil fires at the Tucson refinery, creating a layer of black haze that flattened over the valley. The sun sulked orange, dropping toward the hills, oblivious to the petty squabbles of man.

Tavo's column had retreated before discovering what else the preppers of Tucson had dreamed up. God only knew what entrapment awaited them in the urban canyon lands of the city. The front third of his column had been mauled, and they hadn't even intended on capturing Tucson. They were just passing through.

Tavo reflected on the savagery of the fight against the Arizonan irregulars. The American army wouldn't be his only concern. Not by a long shot. He hadn't seen a single military vehicle other than the two police armored personnel carriers. All the fight had come from hundreds of irregular forces, and they'd been enough to seriously damage his column.

Population centers and organized knots of police could be even more unpredictable than organized infantry, at least here in the desert. Cities, and even large towns, were to be avoided at all costs, he decided. Not a single aircraft had joined the fight, and still his losses were sobering. Texas wouldn't be the only region infected with angry Americans. He'd have to start thinking of the entire southwest as hostile territory.

"All stations. Withdraw to West Campus Road," he ordered into his radio. He scanned his map for a way around Tucson. "Go around the city on side roads and take Alternate Route C to Objective Rally Point Charlie. Shift to Route C, copy all stations."

"Good copy, Actual. Shifting to Route C. Rally at West Campus Road, acknowledged."

Tavo searched his vest and dug out the sat phone that'd sunken to the bottom of his binocular pouch. He called Alejandro and filled him in about the ambush and got him turned back on his original mission to the refinery in New Mexico. There was nothing Alejandro could do now that Tavo's column would skirt Tucson. There was nothing in Alejandro's reply that even remotely implied "I told you so."

Smart man, Tavo glared at the map while he considered the human element to his conquest. Alejandro had known when to shut his fucking mouth. *Finally.*

At the end of another wasted day, Tavo wondered if this military adventure into the United States was even possible. Could he and a small force of men take down the shuddering corpse of the mighty U.S.?

If the stragglers defending Tucson could put even one Warthog or one Apache gunship in the air, he and his men would be cooked into the asphalt before morning, like so many jihadis in the Middle East. After what he'd seen this afternoon, he was certain that the Arizonans were moving heaven and earth to field planes, helicopters and maybe even tanks. Tavo looked up at the setting sun with gratitude for the cover of night.

A group of forty men appeared like djinn from the dry riverbed on the far side of the highway. The road shimmered with mirage in Tavo's binoculars. By the way the men walked, he guessed that it was Saúl returning with prisoners.

The men crossed the two southbound lanes of the Arizona highway and cut a beeline toward Tavo's Humvee.

"How is Beto? Did he make it?" Saúl queried Tavo as he approached.

"*Vivo.* He's alive," Tavo said as he looked the prisoners up and down. He was eager to see his new adversaries close up. The captured men hardly resembled the wealthy American gun owners he'd met at expensive shooting schools. These three Americans looked like trailer trash.

One of them curled his lip as Tavo looked him up and down. The bravado made him smile. He remembered being twenty-five, just off the streets of Guadalajara and making his way in the world of criminals. He'd curled his lip many times in the face of older men with higher standing.

It was obvious that the man hadn't had a good meal in a while. Tavo slid his Boker Magnum from its sheath on his chest rig, gripped it like an ice pick, stepped forward and buried the knife to the hilt in the soft side of the young man's temple. The sneer vanished—along with every other expression. The young American piled on the ground at Tavo's feet.

"I asked for *two* prisoners," he said as he bent over to wipe the blade on the dead man's rat-chewed army jacket.

Why would anyone wear a jacket when it was eighty degrees outside?

Saúl shrugged, staring at the dead man. The glaze in Saúl's eyes belied the harsh adrenaline come-down from combat. To put the counter-flank on the Americans, Saúl had run the equivalent of a 5k footrace and bookended the run with ferocious combat. He could be forgiven a little lassitude.

Of the two remaining men, one appeared resigned to his fate. The other looked like he was quietly plotting.

Tavo started with Mister Surrender.

"What unit are you with?" he began with a simple question, but even that seemed to confuse him.

"Unit?"

"Yes. Who do you fight for?" Tavo tried to explain, wondering if he'd chosen the right word in English for *unit*.

"I fight for the United States," the man replied as though it should've been obvious to anyone.

"Yes, but you're clearly not in the army. You're too old and fat. Who called you to fight in this…battle?"

"A policeman shot his gun. When I came out to check on it, he sent me here. He said that the Mexicans had invaded Arizona and that we were going to attack them at Corker's Hill alongside the I-19. I had a shotgun and had done some quail hunting, so I joined up."

"You shot quail before with a shotgun, so you figured you could kill Mexican soldiers? What about your family?"

Mister Surrender hesitated and choked on a sob. "I'm protecting my wife and girls. That's why I came."

"And you fought with a shotgun?"

"Well, someone loaned me a better gun when I got to the outlet mall."

"So, you fought with a borrowed gun," Tavo summed it up. The man wore blue jeans and a triple-extra-large T-shirt. The shirt said, "Coffee or Die," and it looked like it'd been worn for days.

Tavo turned to the other captive, Mister Plotter. "What's your story, hardcase?"

"I'm just a regular cop," the man answered with a looseness in his voice that worried Tavo a little. "There's a few million just like me waiting for you north of here. You'll get to meet 'em soon enough, narco motherfucker."

Tavo assumed he meant "north of here" as in "north of here across America." There weren't even a million people in Tucson, much less a few million cops.

"And you think that a bunch of thrown-together insurgents are going to defeat my army, even given my machine guns and my organized troops?" He stepped closer, looking the man straight in the eye.

Mister Plotter flicked a glance back toward the battlefield. A mile of freeway smoldered like a barbecue pit that'd flamed out of control. "Yep. There's not a question in my mind. You'll all die here."

American arrogance; Tavo had watched it with curiosity his entire adult life. He'd always wondered why, with all their comfort, America still produced such implacable defiance. Even in the best of times, Americans were angrier than any country he'd ever visited.

On closer inspection, Tavo believed that the man had been a police officer. He wore camouflage BDU pants and a filthy, black polo shirt. He looked a little soft around the middle, but his arms bulged inside the tight sleeves of the polo. He'd probably played high school football in the distant past. And here he was, still trying to beat the rival school and impress the cheerleaders.

"Yet you stand in handcuffs," Tavo argued.

The man smiled and held Tavo's gaze. "There's lots more where I came from."

Tavo saw the blow coming, but a split-second too late. A blinding flash blotted out his world as Mister High School Quarterback head-butted him with tremendous force. The strike missed Tavo's nose, catching him instead on the forehead. He staggered back, flailing his arms. He recovered his backwards pinwheel, but the man was already on him, scrabbling for Tavo's Glock.

He felt the Glock ripped from his battle belt. His consciousness returned enough for him to react. Drawing on what little Jiu Jitsu he could remember, Tavo lunged toward Mister Football, fighting to get inside the working range of his own gun.

BOOM!

The Glock went off in the gap between the grappling men. The bullet flew into one of Saúl's men. Tavo drove desperately into the big American, his only play to use his body to foul the action of the handgun. As they fell backwards, Tavo pawed at the man's hands, fighting to regain control of his pistol. The man's huge, cuffed hands gripped the Glock like a vice.

They hit the ground hard, Tavo on top. He fought for the gun and to retard the slide, praying that it hadn't cycled after the last shot.

BOOM!

The American's hands went limp and Tavo dug the Glock out of the ball of muscle and bone. Saúl stood over them both with his M4. He had shot the American in the head, point-blank.

The Glock's slide had indeed tangled with the dead man's polo shirt, and the gun had stove-piped, a chunk of brass poking up out of the breach. Tavo ripped the gun free of the polo shirt, rocked back on his knees, and gasped for air.

He struggled to his feet and swiped away the blood stinging his eyes. He looked at his Glock as though the gun had betrayed him. Saúl's wounded soldier lay moaning on the ground, shot through the gut.

If one defeated, angry American could wreak this much havoc...

Tavo wiped his bloody face again, ran the slide of the Glock, cleared the malfunction, stood up and shot Mister Surrender in the face. The man dropped instantly to the road beside his dead comrade.

Twenty men stood around Tavo slack-jawed—all stunned at the intensity of the violence. He took another big gasp of air, dropped the partially-used Glock magazine to the ground and reloaded with a fresh magazine from his battle belt.

He looked up at Saúl through a curtain of blood on his face. "Next time, cuff the fucking prisoners in *BACK*, not in *FRONT*."

The column of Mexican soldiers and narco commandos had retreated a couple miles from the maw of the ambush site, and Tavo had accepted a few stitches on his forehead from the corpsman. He would carry a nice scar to remind him of the time he'd underestimated a fat American.

Still looking at his map of the southwest, he weighed what he'd learned. His campaign for America would have to thread the needle of timing, force and surprise in order to avoid the bottled violence of this culture.

Even given the most recent cartel violence—mostly driven by the feral Zetas—Tavo knew that Mexico would endure a collapse with far less ferocity than America. His home country would dig in the ground, plant what they could and starve to death if they must. There would be plenty of theft, of course, but there would be little violence.

America, on the other hand, would burn itself out in a rage. Like a sweet wine gone bad, America had burst its cork. Millions of guns, coupled with pent-up social resentment, would send America back to the days when Texans and frontiersmen ruled these deserts with heavy-bulleted rifles and hulking revolvers.

Tavo would have to pick his battles very carefully, as each

bullet loosed by his men would draw down a riptide of fury. Even starving Americans might abandon their families to come fight, if on principle alone. Just one rifle shot from his men could bring a reckless army of American irregulars down upon them at any hill, bridge, or narrow pass. He would be wise to concentrate his forces on the assets, rather than trying to conquer territory. Like the Persians, he could come back later and buy up survivors with food and promises of peace.

Sow the wind, reap the whirlwind, Tavo remembered from the Bible. His damaged head—probably a concussion—thundered like the drums of war, and he felt no desire to bring down any more pain upon himself than this mission required.

He couldn't remember all the details of the ancient war between the Persians and the Spartans, but he remembered that Xerxes had ultimately defeated the Spartans and had Leonidas' body beheaded and crucified. He remembered from the movie that the Spartans had come to fight with only three hundred men. It made Tavo think of the cop's last words: that there were millions more just like him.

He looked northward and gently ran his finger across the stitches on his forehead. All around the burning ink pot of Tucson, featureless desert ran to the four corners of the compass. There were no narrow passes like Thermopylae he would be forced to navigate. He had a half-million square miles of open desert where his men could maneuver.

But he would need better, more devastating weapons. Like Xerxes, he would need his Immortals.

CHAPTER 22

NOAH MILLER
US HIGHWAY 19, NEAR DREXEL HEIGHTS,
TUCSON, ARIZONA

> "When I leave this world,
> Don't you cry for me.
> When I leave this world,
> 'Cause I'll be doing fine.
> When I leave this world,
> When I leave this world behind
> Don't you miss me,
> 'Cause I'll be doing fine."
>
> — *The Crusader*

Luckily, someone had shot the dude before he cut loose the barrels of chlorine gas. Noah wiped his face and shook his head. The truth came unbidden: he didn't know any of these guys. What kind of maniac would dump chlorine gas onto the highway? More than half of the Tucson fighters were down in the riverbed, exactly where the heavier-than-air chlorine would end up.

His kind of maniac, Noah realized. These were his men. Undisciplined, rebellious, cantankerous. It was his fight now, and first blood had been drawn on the narco convoy. Noah's ghosts had drawn him to this moment and he could feel their favor—not just with the outcome, but with the vindication of America. Though bloodied and weary, they stood, backs straight and dauntless.

The highway below Corker's Hill—as Noah had learned it was called—was littered with dead cartel soldiers, as well as a half-dozen trucks and two Jeeps. Other than a couple dozen casualties on his own side, the ambush had worked like a cast-iron sonofabitch. They'd done a lot worse than bloody the cartel's nose; they'd chopped off their nose and half their face.

He had no idea if he'd killed anyone. He'd rained gunfire down on the road like everyone else—working the lever-action of his 30-30 and falling into the same shoot-shoot-shoot-load routine he used hunting javelina. At well over two hundred yards, it was altogether possible that he'd been shooting under his targets. He hadn't had time to range the distance and figure out the dope on the big bullets of the 30-30. In the chaos of battle, he'd taken his best guess and held over half a head high in his scope.

Noah hadn't been in a gunfight before today. He'd always wondered how he'd do facing incoming fire. Now he knew: he simply ignored it. At one point in the battle, one of the big machine guns mounted to a truck had raked his position on the hilltop. Bullets impacted to his right and to his left. One of those bullets had killed the guy about to release the barrels of chlorine gas. Noah just kept firing, regardless.

Shoot-shoot-shoot-load.

He didn't know if that made him brave or stupid. Maybe he was protected by angels.

Noah laughed out loud at the thought. He was pretty sure the angels had their hands full helping hungry babies and frightened mamas survive the apocalypse. Standing on top of

Corker's Hill, surveying the death he'd brought to the cartel army, he felt a bit like an avenging angel himself, if not for his loved ones, then certainly for America.

Bill would've been proud, Noah thought. He would've fist pumped and slapped Noah hard on the back. This world—where the good guys shot the shit out of the bad guys—would've been perfect for Old Bill. He'd enjoyed it once, as an overseas freedom fighter for the United States. He would've loved protecting his homeland with blood and bullets. Dudes like Bill were born for battle. As Noah breathed in the smell of burning asphalt and blackened bodies, he felt a bit ashamed of the truth: so was he.

It was as though his life up to this point had been missing a key element—something he hadn't even known existed. He'd been like a German Shepherd that had never been taken off the leash. A corner of Noah's soul unfolded. This was his calling and if he died in pursuit of his prey, all would be well. At long last, a full understanding of his adoptive dad descended on him. A warrior's heart, once unlocked, would never quite be satisfied with anything short of the fight.

But Noah also knew that his heart and his father's heart were not the same. He'd come to Corker's Hill to fight and kill, yes. But the same dark storm did not roil in Noah as his father. Noah had his ghosts to move him. Even in the shadow of hundreds of dead invaders, hate had no place in him.

Men's voices, raised in argument, rose above the din of men celebrating their victory. Noah walked across the barren ridge and found the SWAT guy and the militia guy arguing about what to do next. He stopped. These men were no longer useful to his mission. They'd served their purpose, now they could argue all they wanted as far as Noah was concerned.

He turned aside and shuffled down the steep hill toward where he'd parked his Land Cruiser.

Fuel.

Noah heard the word again, carried on the breeze.

They need fuel.

Why would the cartel want to plunder Tucson? Besides women, what could they want from Tucson that hadn't already been hoarded, wasted or consumed up by the residents? It seemed like cities would be the worst places to pillage. The city people were like a plague of locust—consuming everything in their path as soon as panic set in. Surely, the cartel knew that everything worth taking in Tucson had already been used up. So, why attack Tucson?

They were passing through—heading north. Looking for gasoline to fuel their invasion.

A light winked on in Noah's mind. The group of cartel who had turned east; could they be heading toward the oilfields in eastern New Mexico and Texas? They hadn't flanked his ambush, thank God. Where had that group gone?

He dug his keys out of his jeans pocket and looked southeast, in the direction of the splintered convoy. He saw nothing moving except the huge column of black smoke spiraling into the sky from the Tucson refinery. The refinery had already been on fire when Noah arrived that morning—likely set ablaze by vandals.

He had already "jumped track" once in the last couple days, and he was disinclined to commit the same professional *faux pas* again. If he leapt ahead into New Mexico, in an attempt to prove a pet theory, Old Bill would turn over in his grave. The sacred rule among trackers was simple: go step-by-step. But something told Noah that he'd need to trust his gut once again. The road east—Interstate 10—called to him.

He'd need to let go of the main column of the cartel. He had seen them withdraw to the south after the ambush and then peel off to the west, probably looping around Tucson to make a stab toward Phoenix. Noah's obvious choice would be to latch onto the main convoy's back trail and somehow rally a defense of Phoenix. Maybe he could secure another victory like this one and send the cartel back to Mexico. Of course, he'd need to get around them in the night, and then guess correctly at their destination. Just because it'd worked this time didn't mean it would work again. In war, the enemy always got a vote.

From his balls to his gut, jumping track to Phoenix felt like more of a *Hail Mary* than jumping track to the east. Heading east left a broader swath of options for Noah to pursue. Phoenix was a single point on the map. Going to Phoenix meant reducing his target down to a single guess: that the cartel would hit Phoenix just like they'd hit Tucson. And maybe they hadn't meant to hit Tucson at all. Maybe they'd come through Tucson because the main highway went through there.

Noah had been standing beside his Land Cruiser with his keys in his hand for several minutes, the Arizonans arguing and celebrating in the background of his thoughts. If he stood there long enough, somebody would come along and drag him into whatever drama the Tucson hotheads were cooking up. He needed to get the hell out of there, if only to avoid another moment where he'd feel compelled to lead. Once he went down that rabbit hole, he knew he'd get high-centered—and the cartel would move away into the night, committing whatever obscenities they had planned.

Noah stepped up into the driver's seat and turned the key. The blaring radio cut through the adrenaline aftermath of the Battle of Corker's Hill.

> "You fought the demon every day,
> And it's dragged you to your knees.
> But facing dawn, you'll come to find,
> 'Fore me, that demon flees."

Noah turned the music down.

"Sounds good to me. We'll head east, then." He cranked the key and smiled.

Some people were given guardian angels. He'd been given ghosts in his cassette deck. That sounded about right to him. So long as he wasn't expected to babysit a bunch of post-apocalyptic mall ninjas, he was good with the arrangement. Subject to that one condition, the ghosts could point him wherever they liked.

CHAPTER 23
TAVO CASTILLO
PHOENIX BYPASS ROUTE, GILA RIVER, BUCKEYE, ARIZONA

The town of Buckeye, Arizona glinted in the cool, dawn light. The clay-colored homes and white-painted industrial buildings nestled in the Gila River Valley, preparing to soak up any bit of cool air coming off the river. The day would be a scorcher, especially with air conditioning gone forever.

Tavo wondered if these residents would make a go of it—remaining in their clustered, suburban neighborhoods while the civilized world collapsed around them. Buckeye, Arizona could pull water from the river and even irrigate from the canal that carved a straight line through town, doling out water to a patchwork of a hundred fields. From up on the ridge and a mile away, it looked like the perfect place to sit out the apocalypse.

With the coming light, rifle fire crackled on the valley floor. Tavo's heartbeat quickened despite knowing that the shooting had nothing to do with his invasion force. Hours before dawn, he had sent a recon element across the valley to gather intel on the Arizona National Guard base wedged in the sunbaked mountains on the opposite side. If his recon element engaged, he wouldn't hear them five miles away. This was something else.

Still, he checked in with Beto to make sure. "Roadrunner, this is Actual."

"Go for Roadrunner," Beto replied.

"SitRep."

"We're golden. I count twenty OpFor and at least forty turreted Humvees. Only three of them are ready to fight. The rest are moth-balled. The target has a shit-ton of solar panels, so they must have AC. They're pulling water from a bowser in the courtyard. I think we're looking at what's left of the professional staff. Advise green light on Assault Plan Alpha. This place is perfect."

"Acknowledged. Standby." Tavo returned to glassing the valley, searching for the source of the shooting. The distances caused the crack and whine of the rifle shots to bounce around, echoing from several directions. Finally, Tavo caught movement in a field on the near edge of town. A small group of civilians fought with another small group of civilians, maneuvering around a field of what appeared to be kale.

Somebody was defending crops, and somebody was challenging ownership. The majority of the fields appeared to be alfalfa and cotton, and maybe late-season wheat. Very few of the fields looked to be growing anything immediately helpful to humans. Lettuces, kale, pumpkins. People would have to eat massive amounts of those vegetables to survive, especially considering the many suburban subdivisions of Buckeye. A lot of people lived here—fifty thousand, he guessed. It'd take a shit-load of kale and pumpkin to feed fifty thousand people. And things would get much worse once the Phoenix ghettos began their inevitable exodus toward water and farmland. Maybe he was witnessing that exodus right now, as farmers battled desperate urbanites.

No matter. The National Guard Armory would be the ideal garrison and rally point for Tavo's push north. His men would eventually dominate Buckeye and put down any armed resistance. They would have to collect all the civilian firearms, but that could be accomplished with checkpoints and by infiltrating the local, civilian leadership. Given enough time for the lowlifes of Phoenix to make their way into Buckeye, the citizens would probably welcome some law and order, even if it mostly spoke Spanish.

He caught this town and the National Guard Armory at the perfect moment; hanging between modern civilization and the apocalypse. The power was out, but the danger not yet known. Cataclysm had not come to rural towns yet, and it would naturally take longer before terror would overtake them. Hypothetically, Tavo could work his way up a string of such towns, all the way to Salt Lake City. His army would be their first and last hint that things had changed forever.

"Actual to Roadrunner. En route to your position. Assault Plan Alpha. Set go-time for ninety mics. Eight-hundred and thirty hours."

"Acknowledged. We're go on Assault Alpha at eight-hundred and thirty hours. Roadrunner out."

Three dirt roads led to the National Guard Armory tucked into the Goldwater Mountain. Somebody, at some point in time, had chosen this location because it would be difficult to assault. Maybe it'd been an old waypoint for U.S. Army or local frontiersmen fearing the Navajo because it was a natural fortress.

Apparently, the Army National Guard soldiers hadn't gotten the memo. To them, it was an inconveniently-located office where they came to work. Even with the collapse of military communications and the meltdown of order, the national guardsmen hadn't bothered to place LP/OPs on the mountain-tops that ringed the armory. As soon as he took possession, Tavo would remedy that oversight.

Before first light, he sent two teams up onto the Barry Goldwater mountain range to find and disable any cell towers. One team had found a tower, broke in and destroyed the electronics. On the opposite site of the valley, Tavo's cell service dropped from five bars to one. His men on the mountain couldn't get a signal at all. The armory wouldn't be able to call for help on their cell phones.

Tavo had split his force into three equal companies of a hundred men each, with the technicals equally divided between them. Main Road, Mountain Road East and Mountain Road North. They'd collapse on the armory simultaneously, concentrating fire on the three turreted Humvees that appeared positioned for defense. Then they would rush the perimeter. North Company would take down the communications array at the back of the compound. The only obstacle would be the chainlink fence, and Tavo made sure each company had men with bolt-cutters or technicals to run the fence down.

The sun rose over the mountain, carving back the last of the shade in the huge, manicured-gravel courtyard of the armory. Men and women strolled about the grounds in ACU camo, chatting and joking. Meanwhile, three hundred enemy combatants silently prepared to kill them all.

Five, one-story offices buildings and one, massive storage building ringed the gravel yard in an esthetic nod to fortresses of the Old West. Tavo marveled at the intellectual failing of the design—really the same intellectual failing of the entire nation. Nobody had imagined America could possibly go back in time. Except for a few tinfoil hat-wearing whackos, an entire nation believed that modern civilization came with a lifetime guarantee. If modern convenience was all they had ever known, how could the future be any different?

Tavo reached for his radio and paused. Something rumbled in his gut. A sudden roar consumed the Gila River Valley and fear shot through him like ice through his veins. Two screeching A-10 Warthogs tore down the valley at four hundred miles per hour, nearly level with their position on the mountainside.

They're hunting us, Tavo realized. *They figured out how to get an air platform off the ground. Now, two pilots want us dead.*

"Take the armory now. All companies execute, execute, execute." Tavo exhaled. He clipped his rifle into the single-point configuration and climbed into the passenger seat of the command Humvee. The warthogs hadn't seen them or else it'd be over already. Tavo's window of safety had just begun, since the warplanes would be unlikely to return immediately to an area they had already searched. Apparently, the warthogs had no comms with the town of Buckeye, or the locals would've blown the whistle on the column.

"All commanders, minimize smoke signatures. Good hunting. Actual out."

From his position on the road, racing toward the main gate, Tavo watched his column plunge down the dirt road to the east, pouring belt-fed fire onto the two National Guard Humvees on that side of the perimeter. The Humvees weren't returning fire, so the gunners were either dead or cowering inside.

As Tavo approached, men and women poured out of the concrete buildings, seeking fighting cover, but the armory hadn't been built for that. Either they stayed inside blind, where Tavo's men could maneuver around them, or they went outside and fought in the open. Tavo had to give them credit; though outnumbered ten-to-one and fighting from a modern joke of a fort, the guardsmen didn't hesitate.

"No parlay. Kill them all," Tavo barked into the radio. With the warthogs somewhere over Arizona, there would be no time for games. A white mushroom cloud billowed from the back corner of the compound, probably an RPG hitting the communications array. It'd been a primary objective for the company coming down Mountain Road North, still the smoke made Tavo cringe.

He jumped out of his vehicle and searched the sky. He saw nothing but fresh sunlight and blue-on-blue firmament. The warthogs had flown from Tucson, halfway across the state. Even with the smoke, hunting Tavo's fighting force would be like hunting a rat in a boulder field. Half of Phoenix and most of Tucson had been aflame, with fifteen dozen smoke columns rising over the cities and handfuls of fires in the suburbs. Unless the pilots could get on-the-ground intel, the warplanes would buzz around like flies in an outhouse—they'd have plenty of targets but no idea where to attack.

The fighting inside the armory built toward a crescendo, tens of thousands of bullets filling the air. Eight bodies of American guardsmen lay in the courtyard, and the rest had retreated to the buildings, fighting through doors and windows.

To the neophyte, concrete buildings seemed like a good defensive fortification. In truth, once inside, defenders couldn't see much. Enemy forces could maneuver at will, surrounding every angle and lining up shooters on every window and doorway. This was no Alamo, where riflemen could take cover on elevated walls and shower death on anyone attempting to cross no-man's-land. These buildings were more like coffins with windows.

The shooting died down as the defenders barricaded themselves inside, probably clinging to the hope that someone would come to their rescue. The nearest neighboring national guard armory was thirty miles away in downtown Phoenix, and those guardsmen were probably locked down against the threat of civil disorder. Tavo had killed any chance of the guardsmen calling out. Tucked in a lonely mountain canyon, not even the local farmers would bear witness to their deaths.

"Actual to Roadrunner."

"Go for Roadrunner."

Tavo considered his next steps. "Try a call out, Roadrunner. I don't want to risk breaking the solar components. Let's see if we can get them to trust us." The world had become a very unkind place, very quickly. To a group of national guardsmen tucked away in the mountains, the collapse still probably seemed like a camping adventure. Among the civilized, violence took time to become one's bedfellow.

"We are the Buckeye City Defense League," Beto blared over a megaphone. "We're here to take possession of the solar panels and the Humvees for the defense of our city. Please surrender them and we'll let you return to your families. The equipment in this armory belongs to the people."

Tavo admired Beto's lie. It had the ring of truth. Any alternative probably sounded better than dying behind a barricade of government issued furniture. Someone shouted from inside the main building, but Tavo was too far away to understand the words.

Beto replied on the megaphone. "We give you our word. We don't want anyone else to get hurt."

Tavo grinned. It was just the kind of thing an American would say.

Bedraggled men and women in camouflage trickled out of the buildings, their hands in the air. They formed up in the courtyard, probably in the same order they did every morning. Some of them gawked at their fallen comrades. A few burst into tears.

Three commando teams from Beto's company coalesced and they began to search the armory. Shots rang out. Several small firefights blended into one another in the desert air as assaulters cleared holdouts in the buildings. The men and women lined up in the courtyard shuddered helplessly and more weeping ensued as they listened to their brave brothers dying inside the buildings.

The last of the shooting stopped and the three teams of commandos drifted back into the courtyard. Tavo couldn't get a count, but he saw at least one wounded and maybe a couple missing from his own men.

"Roadrunner. Good copy?" Tavo radioed.

"Go for Roadrunner."

"Shoot them," Tavo ordered.

The crackle and pop of gunfire resumed and the men and women standing in the courtyard dropped. A few tried to run, but they didn't get far.

"Get those fires out, *prontisimo*," Tavo commanded as soon as the shooting stopped.

Tavo, Beto and Saúl took stock. They had only lost four men in the assault, and three of those had been killed clearing the buildings. They had caught the armory completely unprepared, other than the three Humvees at the entrances, which was probably nothing more than SOP during heightened security.

Now that they could get inside the buildings, they counted forty-nine functional Humvees, thirty-two of which had armored turrets with 7.62 machine guns. Strangely, the base only had ten thousand rounds of 7.62 and another ten thousand rounds of 5.56 for the rifles. Tavo figured that the National Guard must have had a policy of storing ammunition somewhere beside where their guns were kept. Adding weight to that suspicion, they found a dozen pintle-mounted Mk 19 grenade launchers for the Humvees but not a single grenade.

How was the National Guard supposed to guard the nation without ammunition?

Tavo scratched his head. He'd spent enough time in America to know that it probably had something to do with lawyers or budgets or both. Every time he saw something nonsensical in America, it usually came down to something like that.

"Where's all the bang-bang?" Tavo asked his lieutenants, frustrated. He felt like this expedition was turning into a game of two steps forward and one step back.

"Maybe the National Guard doesn't keep ammunition in armories. The stuff we found looks like it's for base security," Beto guessed. "The explosive stuff might be stored in army depots. The closest ammo could be at the Navajo Depot outside of Flagstaff. I did some training with the Teams there twenty years ago. If memory serves, those guys had Humvees and even some light armor. There's another depot in northern New Mexico and I think there's one outside Salt Lake City."

"If they have armor, then they might be a lot harder to kill than this armory." Tavo waved his arms around them, already moving on to bigger and better things.

Beto rubbed the stubble on his chin. "Let me work on that problem. I'll send a couple teams to target gun stores and then roll up the gun local owners who filed 4473 forms with the ATF. I should be able to pull together enough 7.62 ammo for an assault on the Navajo Depot." Beto seemed to assume that he'd be in command once Tavo headed back to Hermosillo, which made sense since he was the senior man among the lieutenants.

It was closing in on noon and all the air conditioners at the armory were humming. Amazingly, the battle hadn't resulted in the destruction of any of the solar components, though bullets had almost certainly damaged some panels.

At noon Tavo scheduled call-in via satellite phone with Alejandro to see if he had secured the refinery in New Mexico.

Trucking fuel from eastern New Mexico would work a lot better than trucking fuel from Monterrey, Mexico—cutting the distance to one-third—but it was still almost six hundred miles to Alejandro's new refinery. Deposits of oil lived wherever God had planted them, so they would have to make do.

Scavenging local fuel might be easier, but every desperate survivor would be thinking the same thing, and probably getting there first. Rather than run around trying to scramble each gas station, Tavo would control the source.

"Go ahead Kit Fox," Tavo defaulted to radiospeak even though he and Alejandro were on a satellite phone. Alejandro chuckled on the other end of the line.

"You want the good news, the bad news or the really good news," Alejandro teased.

"As you please," Tavo replied like ice, barely willing to tolerate the soldier's humor. He had a nation to conquer.

"Right. We have the refinery under control and there's a shit-ton of gasoline and diesel fuel here. The bad news is that the locals think this is fucking Red Dawn and they're the Wolverines."

"What's that mean?"

"It means they're going to be a problem. The locals are surrounding us like we're an invading army of Cubans. We're taking rifle fire from the perimeter of the facility, and they've already punched holes in several of the storage tanks. We're patching them, but you can't just bust out a welder and fix a leak on a gas storage tank. It requires a big plate that we have to epoxy onto the sidewall. Luckily, the guy who knows how to do the repairs is still on-site. For now, we have the problem contained, but this refinery will have to be secured 24/7 and even then, we will eventually run out of steel patches. I think rednecks are coming over from Roswell too, just to fuck with us."

Tavo thought about the supply chain again. If they were

already having problems at the refinery, the roads between there and Buckeye would be vulnerable to ambush as well.

"What's the other good news?" Tavo hated that Alejandro made him ask.

"I sent a team north to check Cannon Air Force Base—just to make sure we weren't going to get our asses shot off by F-16s, you know. The base didn't have any airplanes, anywhere. It was like they'd pulled up stakes and moved the whole operation somewhere else."

"How's that really good news?"

"Check this out; almost a hundred M1 Abrams tanks are sitting on the runway, *at an airbase*. There are soldiers meandering around, but they look like they're waiting for something."

Tavo rubbed his face. "Explain to me how having a hundred main battle tanks near your position is good news."

"These guys aren't here to fight and they're not close to the refinery—it's over a hundred miles. We captured an American soldier who was AWOL—trying to sneak away from the base at night. He told us that they were ordered to wait at Cannon AFB for some muckety-muck from Washington to land with his family. The VIP was supposed to arrive three days ago and he's still a no-show. The armored brigade combat team has been sliced up and most of the armored personnel carriers and Strykers have been reassigned to Colorado Springs to wait for the VIP there. They left the tanks and a few guys because they didn't need them in Colorado Springs and because the Abrams burns too much gasoline to make the drive. I'll bet you a case of the good stuff that those tanks are going to be up for grabs."

"Don't they require jet fuel?" Tavo remembered something to that effect.

"Nope. They'll run on cat piss if the cat got into the tequila the night before."

"Are they armed?" Tavo had his fill of finding weapons but no ammunition.

"They each have a full, combat load-out of XM1028 Canister rounds according to the guy we caught. All we need are the ignition codes."

Finally, the world clicked for Tavo. With a hundred M1 Abrams tanks, no citizen militia, or even an army base, could withstand him. The only thing that would stop tanks would be more tanks or the kind of air assets that only an organized nation could muster.

"Take the tanks as soon as possible," Tavo ordered.

"Hang on, Hoss." Alejandro chuckled.

Tavo didn't like his tone. The other two lieutenants had accepted Tavo as their commanding officer and their whole demeanor toward him had shifted. Alejandro was shaping up to be a problem.

"*Canoso*, we can't hit these tanks until they stand down. If we go rolling in there with trucks and machine guns, if even just one of those tank crews jock up, we're going to wake a dragon that we won't be able to put back to sleep. We need to let declining morale do its job. Let the cancer fester. When enough soldiers give up on the mission, we'll have our operational window. Until then, we'd be giving them a reason to go hard."

Tavo didn't like the pushback, but he sensed Alejandro was playing it smart.

"Agreed. Stand fast. Secure the refinery. Let's set next comms for twelve hundred hours tomorrow. I'm returning to the ranch to send another company of commandos your way. We secured a national guard garrison outside of Phoenix, complete with up-armored Humvees, so now we have two hard points within America."

With two fortified locations inside the U.S., they could have their U.S. gangland soldiers meet their main forces without crossing into Mexico, shaving off hundreds of miles of travel. Beto's business territory had been west of the Rocky Mountains. Saúl had owned the Midwest and Alejandro had been working the growing markets on the east coast. Their mission would pick up speed now that their street soldiers and commandos didn't have to travel into Mexico to join up.

For sure there would be attrition. Tavo couldn't expect more than about twenty percent of the fighters to follow orders all the way to Hermosillo—not with their families being left behind in urban hellholes. It'd help that their rendezvous had been moved a few hundred miles closer, but he could expect at least the same level of desertion as the American military. The promise of plunder would help keep his army together. With the tanks, anything seemed possible. Armor seemed almost too good to be true.

It all hinged on the tanks, Tavo concluded. The refinery, the army depot, Salt Lake City. If he got his hands on those tanks—and the gas to maneuver them—he would rule everything from the California High Sierras to the Rocky Mountains.

A hundred M1 Abrams main battle tanks waited in the desert; low-slung and compact like a prizefighter. He'd gawked at the M1 Abrams when they rolled over the top of Saddam Hussein's forces during the Gulf War. He remembered grainy video of the M1 Abrams plowing through fields of smoldering, Russian T-72s. If memory served, each Abrams carried forty 120mm rounds. His tanks had hopefully been loaded with anti-personnel rounds rather than anti-tank sabots. Those hundred tanks would hand Tavo 4,000 shots from the main guns and hundreds of thousands of bullets from the secondary machine guns—either .50 caliber or 7.62 mm. He could exterminate whole groups of insurgents like they'd faced in Tucson, blowing through them like Gulliver stomping Lilliputians. Just one M1

Abrams would've sent that ambush in an entirely different direction.

Tavo needed to get back to Hermosillo, consolidate forces and take command from Alejandro at the refinery in New Mexico. Fate awaited him, like a queen at the altar.

One hundred tanks. Undefeatable armor. Hundreds of thousands of rounds. In a world without technology, he would be god. He could see the path of conquest, perhaps all the way to the Pacific Ocean.

He hung up the satellite phone and returned it to the pocket in his vest. Tavo gazed down the creosote-speckled canyon descending from the National Guard armory. In the distance, a wedge of green showed between the mountains—the Gila river bottom glowing in the midday sun.

So much life force energy had been thrown to the wind in the American collapse. American prosperity had required incredible organization, tremendous control. The Americans believed that democracy would blindly drive that life force forward, as though it was a birthright.

Tavo knew better. Everything in his life had demonstrated the opposite—that nature naturally tended toward chaos and destruction. No birthright stood the test of time. He had the scars to prove it.

The Americans' miscalculation would be his window of opportunity. He had prepared for this moment, not quite seeing the details, but sensing the opening for years. Those tanks, that refinery, and his fate as emperor. He would have them all in his hands within the next seventy-two hours, and there was nothing he wouldn't sacrifice to make it so.

CHAPTER 24
NOAH MILLER
HIGHWAY 82, EAST OF HOPE, NEW MEXICO

> "I wasn't searching for more,
> Than what I had yesterday, every day.
> I wasn't searching for the door,
> To find a way from all the gray.
> Then you appeared—a brown-eyed wonder."
>
> — *The Crusader*

Noah drove through the night. The 10 freeway became Highway 70, which then became Highway 82. East of Hope, New Mexico, his headlights picked up the telltales of oil and gas drilling. Pumps and holding tanks dotted the rolling expanse of scrub, like mechanical mosquitos, sucking the corpse of an ancient, rotted forest buried under ten trillion tons of sand.

He had used up the last of the fuel canisters he'd lifted from Bill's barn. From that point forward, scavenging gas would need to become a priority.

He'd stolen a few hours from the night to hide the Cruiser on a side road and grab some sleep. The rest had done him good, but over the last hour, the monotony of the road had lulled him into a hypnotic state.

Suddenly, a pickup truck materialized like a ghost at the edge of his headlights, parked across both lanes. Noah stood up on the brakes and the Cruiser howled in protest. The vehicle fishtailed from side-to-side, slipped onto the sandy shoulder and slid into the sagebrush. Remarkably, it didn't flip.

Noah leapt out of the cab and hit the ground, his Glock drawn. He stared into the black desert, seeing only the vague outline of the pickup truck in the halo of the Cruiser's headlamps.

"Are you going to make me kill you?" a baritone voice shouted from somewhere in the dark. "I've got the shot and I know you don't, so just walk away now and save me one more ding in my banged up conscience."

That seemed like a lot of talk from a road bandit, Noah thought. He squirmed deeper under the carriage of the Land Cruiser, though he knew it was futile. He'd been ambushed and that usually ended just one way for the guy on the wrong side of the surprise. The music in the Cruiser kept playing and it added a surreal dimension to highway robbery. It was like a soundtrack that gave the scene an epic feel, as though a screenwriter had thought this moment up to prove the hand of God. Noah shook his head to cast off the cobwebs. He was being robbed, that much was certain. His best bet was to play for time.

> "I wasn't searching for more,
> Than what I had yesterday, every day."

"I'm going to set my gun on the tire," Noah shouted over the music and squirmed out from underneath the Cruiser. He slowly got to his feet and placed the Glock on the tire. His Winchester was still inside, shoved between the seat and the console, but he had little hope of reaching it. In any case, the guy was still buried in the night.

"Thank you, fine sir. Now, please walk backward toward my headlights with your hands up." The truck lights flipped on, making it even harder to penetrate the dark.

Noah backed up, as instructed. He heard a shuffle on the roadway, then the bandit grabbed his right hand with a ferocious grip, folded it behind Noah's back and cuffed him with flex cuffs. The man patted him down, found his folding knife and removed it. The whole operation screamed "law enforcement" to Noah.

The man turned Noah around by his elbow. Noah stared into the face of the biggest Mexican he had ever seen. The guy had to be six foot tall and well over two-hundred and fifty pounds of solid muscle with a chin so strong he could be mistaken for a cartoon character. He wore a chest rig full of AR-15 mags and other assorted gear, a gray-and-black American flag velcroed to the strap.

Definitely not cartel, Noah concluded. Definitely law enforcement.

"Hot damn. I always wanted a Land Cruiser. What's it? An Eighty-two?" The music kept playing and Noah caught himself feeling an upwelling of good will that contrasted with the fact that he was about to lose everything he owned.

"Eighty-four," Noah answered reflexively. There was never a wrong time to talk about his Land Cruiser, he reasoned.

"I knew a guy once with an Eighty-two. Looked exactly the same. The guy was an asshole, but I did love his Jeep."

Noah bristled visibly in the light splashing off the headlights.

The big Mexican let his AR-15 dangle on its strap and waved a hand. "Yeah, yeah, yeah. I know you guys hate it when people call it a 'Jeep.'"

"If you're going to steal it from me, at least don't disrespect it," Noah chuffed.

"I'm sorry about that. I got no choice. I need your stuff. What can I say? I've got a shit-load of kids. I'll leave you enough water and you can walk back to the town."

Noah decided to press the angle. "Why would a cop be out here in the middle of the desert robbing travelers? Don't you have people? Don't you have a home?"

The big guy exhaled and slumped a bit. Noah wondered if the music wasn't doing a job on the guy's mind too. "I'm not a cop and I need to get my kids back to Phoenix. Their mother is going to be losing her mind, and I don't have shit out here in the middle-of-nowhere. I was instructing a course and it was my weekend to have them. I got caught with my balls hanging out. But, hey. Enough about me. You should start walking." He pointed west. "Town's that way."

"Take me with you. I'll help with the kids," Noah blurted out, not sure where he was going with it. The music swelled on an emotional tidal wave, as though he and the big Mexican thief would now go on to conquer the world together.

"The fuck you will…" the big Mexican stroked his bushy, black mustache. "You'll cut my throat the moment you get the chance, and then where will my kids end up?" But his tone of voice belied the truth: he'd considered the idea.

"Plus," Noah pushed his advantage. "You don't want to take them to Phoenix. A column of Mexican cartel is taking down cities along the I-19. Your kids are safer out here."

The big guy stroked his mustache again. "You just came from Phoenix?" he cocked his head as though he doubted it. Noah decided to tell the truth.

"No. I just came from Tucson and a group of a few hundred of us ambushed the cartel outside of town. After that, they went around the city instead of through it, and kept heading northwest. I'm guessing they'll hit Phoenix tomorrow morning."

The big guy nodded, still lost in thought. "I should never have opened my big mouth. I'm not very good at robbing people, turns out." He laughed at himself. "Rule Number One: don't start a conversation with the asshole you're trying to rob... And what the hell is this music?"

"Rule Number One should be 'Don't Rob People.'" Noah said, pushing his luck.

"I take it you don't have children." The big Mexican turned Noah around to face away from him. There was a flick of a knife and Noah felt the flex cuffs cut away. "Don't make me regret not robbing you better."

Noah turned around to face the man. He consciously refrained from rubbing his wrists.

"So, what now, big guy?" Noah asked, standing nose-to-nose.

"Now you help me with my kids, right?" The big man offered Noah a wry smile, inviting him to either throw down or get along. Noah thought about hitting that big jawbone with a right hook. He rubbed the hand, knowing from past experience that he'd probably break it in the process. He knew the look on the big Mexican's face from past experience too—the look that said, *this wouldn't be my first rodeo, either, and I can handle myself just fine in a fistfight.*

With the help of the ridiculous music, Noah contemplated his own mission. He didn't have any "people" anymore, with his family gone and his dad now dead. That sad truth left him free to help anyone he pleased, even a highwayman and his kids.

"By cutting me loose, you're missing out on owning one of the finest vehicles ever to grace the highways of America," Noah warned, and smiled.

"True. But I can only drive one vehicle at a time and all my shit's already in the back of my truck. My name's Rocco." The big man held out an oversized hand.

"Noah Miller." They shook hands.

"Follow me." Rocco turned and walked toward his truck, barely looking over his shoulder as he did. Noah noticed the man's right hand drifting to the pistol grip of his AR. He was trusting Noah, but he wasn't an idiot.

Noah picked up his Glock from the tire and holstered it. At this point, there was no advantage in trading bullets with the guy. If he was what he said he was—a desperate father—Noah would know soon enough. If not, Noah could drive away across the desert. Plus, given the switch-up of songs that'd happened during their conversation, Noah had gotten it in his head that the ghosts that inhabited his cassette deck liked this guy.

And, as he'd reminded himself earlier, he didn't have "people" of his own anymore. Sooner or later, he'd probably have to find some. Despite the fact that he'd planned on robbing Noah, the big Mexican was, more or less, part of Noah's tribe: a man who talked straight and could handle a shooting iron. If the man had kids, then Noah wasn't going to blast him.

True to his word, the big Mexican did have a shit-load of kids. Five dusty-faced children slept around the campfire in sleeping bags. Rocco's oldest son must've been fourteen, which explained why the man didn't really need Noah's Land Cruiser. He didn't have anyone who could drive it.

Rocco dug around in his cab and came out with a bottle of Leadslinger's whiskey.

"Want a nip?" Rocco held up the bottle like an apology.

"You are forgiven, my son." Noah made the sign of the cross and reached for the bottle. They both dropped into camp chairs.

Rocco stirred up the glowing sage branches and added a few more.

"We're coming from the town of Artesia," Rocco explained. He took the bottle back and sucked the whiskey through his teeth. "A cartel seized the refinery there. That's why we left. I can't go to war while I've got my kids with me, much as I'd like to."

"What the hell were you doing in the middle of New Mexico?" Noah asked, taking the bottle back.

"Instructing pistol/carbine at the Border Patrol training facility. I brought the kids up for the week. I wanted to show 'em around the campus and maybe take my oldest out on the driving course—give him a little off-road, evasive driving experience. Then everything went to shit."

"What now?"

Rocco shook his head. "Man, I'll be honest: I'm high-centered. If we were back in Phoenix, at least then I'd have my shit. I have food in the pantry back home—sacks of beans and rice. I even have a big barrel of water out back. I never thought about being stuck on a training rotation when I laid that stuff up at home. The only reason I've got my gat with me is because I was instructing. If not for that, I'd have a whole bunch of nothing. That's why I set up the roadblock. We're about to run out of food and I need to turn bullets into eats. Know what I mean?"

Noah heard the regret in the man's voice, and he didn't envy him the position he was in. "I've got plenty of food in the Cruiser. You can have some of it. It should be enough to get you home."

Rocco tilted the bottle toward Noah. "Much obliged. You don't have to do that, but I appreciate it all the same. Where are you headed?"

"I need to see that refinery. I'm tracking the cartel and rallying the locals ahead of them."

Rocco's eyebrows shot up in the light of the campfire. "You're a tracker? Search and rescue?"

"No. It's just something my old man taught me. He used to be an instructor for the Border Patrol too."

"Bill McCallister?" Rocco threw out the name.

"That's him...er. That *was* him. The cartels blew him up at his ranch."

Rocco shook his head. After a time, he spoke. "Oh man, I'm sorry to hear that. Bill was a piece of work, for sure, but he deserved a warrior's death."

Noah nodded. "Oh, he got his warrior's death. There was more blood on the ground than a slaughterhouse. Those gangbangers paid in gallons to kill Old Bill."

Rocco poured a splash in Noah's red, plastic cup and raised his bottle of Leadslingers. "To Bill McCallister. May his pecker work in heaven."

Noah raised his Solo cup to the stars. "Amen. That we should all be so lucky."

"What do you plan to do at the refinery?" Rocco asked after a quiet moment. "There's at least a hundred cartel soldiers encamped there. It's no soft target."

"I'm not sure what I'll do. I do know this: we can't let them have that gas. I've got a feeling they have plans for it. Big plans. The kind where a lot of people die. One way or another, we need to set that place on fire."

Rocco sat in silence for a minute. The sage in the fire crackled.

"I know where the Border Patrol guys are camped in the desert. They pulled up stakes and moved out of town so the cartel couldn't find them so easy. They've been running harassment raids with a few locals. You might like their way of thinking."

"Nah. You don't need to take me. Just give me directions and get your kids out of here."

Rocco shook his head. "It'll only take a couple hours to take you there and for me to get back here. It's the least I can do for... running you off the road and all."

Noah nodded. "I'd appreciate it."

"Bill wasn't the most popular guy with the brass, if you know what I mean. He left Artesia on less than stellar terms. Don't expect that being his son will buy you much say-so with the super troopers."

"I didn't think so. I don't need to trade on his name, anyway. I can carry my own water. Thank you for the heads up, though."

"Daddy, I'm thirsty." A little girl, maybe ten years old, sat up in her sleeping bag. Noah picked his water bottle up off the ground, stood and walked over to her. He flicked a look at Rocco. "Do you mind?" Rocco nodded.

"Here you go, princess."

The girl stared at the blond man hovering over her sleeping bag with her big, brown eyes. The eyes swam with doubt. The man definitely wasn't her daddy.

"It's okay, *cariña*, he's a friend."

She reached up for the water, unscrewed the cap and drank —keeping one eye on Noah. His own ten-year-old daughter had dishwater blonde hair instead of brown hair and her eyes had a bit of hazel instead of deep brown. Otherwise, the two ten-year-old girls could've been sisters. The girl made a tiny smacking sound as she finished drinking. Noah remembered Katya making the same delicate noises when she ate and drank.

Is anything in this world more-worthy of giving one's life than a little girl?

She handed the water bottle back to Noah and gazed at him with a face as open as Sunday morning. She brushed the hair that'd drifted over her eyes.

"He's not one of the bad men, right Daddy?"

"No, darling…lay down and go back to sleep."

She remained, looking up at Noah.

"Can you make them go home?" Noah knew exactly who she meant.

"I surely can try, little one. Sometimes I can be pretty convincing." Noah smiled at her and she smiled back. Then, she lay down and closed her eyes.

Noah walked back to the fire and lowered himself into the camp chair.

"In the morning, I'll draw you a map to my ranch and my dad's ranch and you can take the kids there to sit this thing out. The wife too."

"Ex-wife," Rocco corrected. "And thank you. That's beyond gracious, particularly given how we met."

Noah took another sip of whiskey. "Don't worry about it. I'd do the same. I mean, I *would've* done the same. My family's gone now. You're a lucky man… Do me a favor and mind the cows back at my ranch. I left them a half-dozen round bales and they'll need a new bale every week. The hay's in the old barn and the key to the tractor is in the scissor drawer in the kitchen." Noah had blasted right past the part about his family being gone. After looking the little girl in the eyes, he definitely didn't want to talk about it.

Rocco seemed to notice the hiccup, but he didn't pry. "I don't know nothing about cows, but I can sing them a pretty tune now and again." Rocco admired the stars for a few moments, and a companionable silence fell over the desert camp.

"You know," Rocco said. "I don't think you have to set the refinery on fire. Seems like with the right rifle you could poke holes in the fuel tanks without closing to contact with the enemy. In Iraq, when we didn't feel like assaulting a compound, we'd have our snipers shoot a couple holes in their rooftop water tanks with the big Barrett fifties. After a day without water, ain't nobody gonna stick around a dry compound. They'd always sneak out after a day or two. Seems like the same principal applies here: if you want to make the refinery at Artesia inhospitable, put holes in all the tanks. With a .50 BMG, you should be able to do that from a couple miles away. Maybe more."

Noah considered the idea. It had the aura of destiny, and he'd come to trust that gooey halo as much as his own horse sense. "Do you have fifties at the Border Patrol training facility?" he asked.

Rocco laughed. "I wish. There's no use for Light Fifties in the Border Patrol. We call in the DEA when things get hot with the cartels. Lots of locals around here shoot long-range, particularly over the border in Texas. Their precision shooting club holds its annual shoot in Brownfield. It's one of the few natural resources this godforsaken place has in abundance—long ranges for shooting. I don't know how you'd reach out to those guys, but I'm sure they'd love to practice on the cartel. It'd probably make their year."

CHAPTER 25

TAVO CASTILLO
RANCHO SANTIAGITO, 65 MILES OUTSIDE OF
HERMOSILLO, SONORA, MEXICO

He had strategized this conversation on the road back from Phoenix—seven hours of role playing and predicting his daughter's reaction to each argument. He worked the conversation out in his mind, handled her objections and then started the process over again, each time improving his talking points and delivery. With each iteration, Tavo realized that he didn't want so much to be king as he wanted his daughter to be queen.

But she had likely betrayed him. Her own father...

He decided that it didn't matter. In fact, if that was the case, he should feel proud of her. He *needed* her to be canny and headstrong. The last thing he wanted was another version of her mother. There were enough women in the world to sort beans. The world needed kings and queens. If Sofía had chosen to have her father imprisoned in order to assume command, maybe it was good news. It would mean she hadn't waited for him to grow old and retire, but instead had attempted to take his place at the time of her choosing.

In retrospect, he could see how, for decades, she had ingratiated herself to his lieutenants—carefully building emotional ties to her "uncles" stronger than anything Tavo could, even as their brother in arms—ties even stronger than money. She had played her beauty and her innocence like a virtuoso, even drawing Tavo into forgetting himself.

If he couldn't be proud of her skill, her artistry in pulling others into her orbit, then Tavo had no business calling himself a father.

He couldn't be sure that she had done any of this, but he was doing his best to see it from a dispassionate perspective. His mind was working overtime to engineer a frame for her treachery that allowed him to love her still. Like a carpenter building a bathtub beneath a roof that would not stop leaking, Tavo needed a proper container for his anger. Most of the time, when people intruded on his personal peace, he vanished them. Perhaps, this time, God was teaching him about the inevitable progression of fatherhood—that we create our children to surpass us.

He knew for a fact: she had spoken to his half brother in Guatemala and hadn't told him. Tavo had only recently discovered the man through a chance revelation in his five-year investigation into his father.

Locating Tavo, for a savvy criminal like his father, wouldn't have presented a problem. Looking at it from his father's perspective—from the eyes of a shot-caller for MS-13—he would be easy to find. He'd done nothing to erase his connection to his mother or her parents. Tavo had even kept the family name: Castillo. Finding Tavo and then manipulating his daughter into mounting a coup, would fall squarely within his father's likely skillset. Tavo had educated Sofía for the world of business, not to absorb punches from the likes of his diabolical father. If he'd gotten his hooks into Sofía, Tavo's father would undoubtedly make the most of the opportunity.

Regardless of her motives, he knew this: Sofía was the only

person who knew he would be in Antigua during their meeting. Tavo followed the chain of events: she had called his half-brother, then his half-brother went to Antigua. That same day, the Kaibiles showed up to arrest him.

Tavo wasn't in the business of lying to himself, so he wouldn't start now. The thought of Sofía setting him up had wounded him and angered him, as much as that was possible. But after spending hours on the road, the hot, sticky blacktop rolling past, contemplating the betrayal, Tavo had gathered himself. He wasn't Pablo Escobar and he wasn't Chapo-fucking-Guzmán. He had more intelligence than both those men combined, and he wasn't a man to have family murdered because they hurt his feelings.

Sofía brought a lot to the table. She had co-opted the Mexican army into Tavo's petroleum scheme and had manipulated them into protecting fuel assets in Mexico. She had won the hearts of his lieutenants by batting her eyes and calling them "uncle." She had even blinded her own father to the fact that she had inherited every ounce of his ruthless ambition.

Sofía had become a formidable woman, and Tavo was not a man to cast talent aside. Her betrayal meant only one thing: that she was ready.

―――

Tavo asked Sofía to take a walk in the desert. The ranch overflowed with street soldiers and commandos recently arrived from the smoking embers of urban America. The ranch's paramilitary intentions could no longer be concealed, and the flatlands were now divided into firing ranges, force-on-force combat training grounds and outdoor classrooms where the men were being indoctrinated in a fusion of Special Forces combat and *Caballero Templario* doctrine. Since the assault to rescue the priests, Tavo had been adding more and more quasi-Catholic dogma into their command routine. Something told him that a religious backbone would be needed in the days to come.

They walked along rolling hills that rose toward a jutting mountain of iron-grey basalt. Their walk skirted the base of the mountain, and it would take them at least two hours to circumnavigate the one peak on the ranch. He needed those two hours to recalibrate his sense of his daughter. Now that he had concluded she had made a move on him, he needed to know what had motivated her.

What did she want? Once he knew, he could maneuver her.

For certain, confronting her about Antigua was off the table. He would never reveal a piece of inside information unless he had no other choice, particularly to an adversary. She couldn't know that he knew.

"Papi, when are we going to talk about all these soldiers? When are you going to tell me what you plan to do with them?"

"Did you study the Roman conquest of the ancient world?"

"Yes... Western Civilizations. Sophomore year at Vanderbilt."

"The people that the Romans conquered experienced an increase in birth rate and a decrease in infant mortality. The Roman Legions brought war, and after that populations flourished." Tavo didn't know if it was entirely true, but it sounded like it should be.

Sofía refused the bait. "So then tell me how you're planning to conquer because I'm worried. I'm worried about your soul. I'm worried that you'll be killed."

Such a masterful answer, Tavo thought in a flash before picking up the thread of her new argument.

"Julius Caesar didn't go to hell for building the Roman Empire, Sofía." The counter-argument sounded weak even to Tavo, so he shifted to a more direct, emotional appeal. "I hope you understand that I'm doing all of this for you. I'm building this for your benefit."

Sofia stopped at the top of a rise in the sand and looked her father in the eyes.

"You don't really believe that, do you? That you're doing this for me?"

"Why else would I build a legacy? Why would I do this except for you?"

She searched his eyes, looking for something. For a moment, he felt like a child who had wandered into a laboratory. He had no idea what she hoped to find in his eyes.

"Papi… you do it because you can't stop yourself."

Tavo marveled. People could live together their whole lives and not know one another at all. How could she be so totally wrong about him? Tavo was aware of his every feeling and thought. He'd built his world on faultless control, achieving life-or-death leverage over thousands of people. His results couldn't lie: he'd created the biggest, most-secretive cartel the world had ever known. For his daughter to picture him as some kind of obsessive-compulsive who built sprawling empires because he "couldn't stop himself" … the suggestion was ludicrous and insulting.

"Why would I want to stop myself? We're on the verge of achieving everything we ever wanted. I realize that you're restless and ready to take my place, but please just wait while I settle this new opportunity. Let me pacify this region and get it under control. It'll only take a few months and then I'll hand you the reins. I'll step back and you can manage the landholdings. Isn't that how our partnership works? I conquer new territory and you build a fence around it? I make gains and you make those gains permanent? You are the Augustus to my Julius Caesar. I am a conqueror, Sofi. The people need a conqueror now more than ever. After I'm done, the people will need you."

It had been the big speech he'd practiced on the drive back to Hermosillo. But, as his words trailed off and he watched his daughter's cheeks go slack, he felt like they were two swimmers on a black ocean, paddling past one another in the night without hearing the slightest splash.

How could she not know him? Not know her own father?

"Papi..." She touched his arm. "I don't want to control anything. I don't want to conquer anyone. We can help people without stripping away their self-determination. I'm no Augustus Caesar. That was two thousand years ago, and people are different today. People...know better than to conquer one another."

She talked to him like an idiot, like Tavo used to talk to his senile father-in-law. Fresh-faced out of college, his daughter now regarded him as the fool. He was a man that millions feared. They feared him like they feared the *Chupacabra* or *El Sacomán*, a dark specter who could snatch away their lives and their families' lives on a whim. Yet this girl felt like she could touch his arm and patronize him like a decrepit, defanged wolf.

She hadn't seen what he'd seen in Tucson. She hadn't seen men blow each other up with roadside bombs. She hadn't watched as some maniac tried to drop barrels of poison gas on their countrymen. She hadn't watched Americans shoot at each other for a bite of kale. She might be ready to have him arrested or killed, but she wasn't ready to face the new reality. Like all the other castaways wandering in this broken civilization, her mind was still marooned on an island of modern dreams, even after a hurricane had swept that island down to naked sand. Without a doubt, she was the fool. Not him.

What did he really need her for anyway? The gasoline she and her pet general guarded in Monterrey was a backup plan to his backup plan. This girl who had her hand on his arm—she wouldn't dare stand in his way if he decided to take the Mexican refineries. What harm was there in allowing her delusions of prissy humanity? Let her think that people were somehow different now than they were when Genghis Khan rolled over endless fields of the dead, or when Mao Zedong culled tens of millions from his own country. Eventually she would see the truth.

Tavo brushed her hand off his arm and her liquid, brown eyes reflected the sting of it.

"You will see. People aren't any less brutal now than they were in the Roman Empire." Tavo hadn't meant to imply that *he* was the brutal one, but brushing her hand away had unwittingly sealed that impression. At this point, he didn't really care.

Sofia reached up and gently pulled his face around to look at hers. "Even if that's true—and I understand that you've seen more evil than me in this life. I know that terrible things have happened to you. But even if people are just as brutal now as they always were, I won't be part of it. *People* may be the same, but I'm not. And neither are you."

She said the last sentence with more hope than conviction in her voice.

"You might as well know it," Tavo gave up attempting to convince his daughter, "I'm going to pacify the borderlands. You'll see: the people will be better off."

They'd stopped walking. Sofia looked away from her father and turned toward the horizon. "For every Julius Caesar or Ghengis Khan, there were hundreds who died trying to be conquerors. I don't want you to die," Sofia said, her eyes swimming with concern. She turned back, and again touched his arm.

Tavo hardened, but didn't bother removing her hand. "The Spanish had the weapons and they had the moment. They took down America, from Mexico City to Canada. The Conquistadors erased the brutality of the Aztecs and the Apaches and replaced it with order and progress. If I don't do the same now, nobody will. If I don't succeed, this region will descend into violence that you could never imagine."

For the first time—her eyes framed in both sorrow and resolve—Tavo couldn't see his daughter. For the first time, he saw only his enemy.

CHAPTER 26

NOAH MILLER
THE PECOS RIVER REFINERY, ARTESIA, NEW MEXICO

> "Sin and shame
> Remorse and pain
> Your damned credibility.
> Here and now,
> Lay them down,
> At the Big Man's feet."
>
> — *The Crusader*

In the middle of the night, cartel patrols had tapered off to nothing. They'd been playing cat and mouse all day. His men—Border Patrol agents and hard fighters from the town of Artesia—would fire a volley of rifle rounds at the refinery from over a mile away. Then, they'd displace another mile back and wait for the cartel to send a squad of *narcos* to hunt them.

That's what the American partisan fighters had begun calling them... "*Narcos*." Not "Mexicans" or "Cartels" but "*Narcos*." Noah hadn't been to war prior to this moment, but Bill had filled his nights with stories about Iraq, Afghanistan, Africa* and every other dank corner of misery on the planet. For each enemy, they'd had a name.

Hajjis, T-men, Ali Babas, Skinnies, Daeshbags, Talis, Savages, Camel Jockeys, Towel Heads. Jihadis...

In the war between the Southwest and the cartel, *"narcos"* rose as the preferred nomenclature. In the cultural collapse of post-America, the term threaded the gap between a burning hatred of the invaders and a still-percolating fear of racism. Plus, half the guys fighting the cartel looked like ethnic Mexicans. Even roughneck American fighters couldn't use a racial slur when the guy next to him in the foxhole might have skin as brown as suede shoes. So, *"narcos"* it'd be.

When a squad of narcos came out to strike their last position, his teams would lob a few rounds at the men themselves then scatter into the desert. An hour or two later, they'd rejoin at a rally point and do it all over again. But the cartel squads had either learned their lesson—that assaulting little knots of snipers wasn't buying them anything—or they'd turned their attention to other matters. That gave Noah and his men freedom to plink away at the refinery for as long as their ammunition held out.

Noah hoped the plan was working. The sniper teams had only dug up a single .50 caliber rifle in town—a bolt action beast with a huge scope that'd run out of ammo sometime during the night. With the big fifty down, they'd been hitting the storage tanks with .308s, 30-06s, .338s or whatever big hunting rifles they could find. Most of the hunting in this region had focused on javelinas and small Coues deer, so large caliber hunting rifles were rare. Noah's men hadn't confirmed if the large caliber rifles were perforating the double-skinned fuel storage tanks. He wondered if maybe the narcos had stopped sending out assault squads because his snipers weren't doing any damage.

His team of snipers had just sent a volley into a tank inside of the facility. It was so far away that Noah could barely see the big white cylinder through his 10x Nikons. There was no way he'd be able to confirm a fuel leak through even the most powerful binoculars.

Noah turned to check with the four other guys and they all shrugged. Nobody had optics that could see a .308-inch stream of gas from over a mile away. Noah wasn't sure such an optic even existed.

The five men hunkered behind a big bitterbrush. Two of the guys had the close-cropped hair of Border Patrol trainees and the other three wore mis-matched camouflage and carried hunting rifles—obviously guys from town.

"I'm out of here," Noah whispered. "You guys keep up the good work." He wasn't sure why they all whispered, except that it felt like the thing to do when hunting men. They were over a mile from the nearest enemy. "I'm going to boogie back to my Cruiser and drive over to Brownfield across the Texas border. I heard they have some fifty caliber rifles over there. Maybe I can get some ammo and a few more blasters. Let Rankin know that I'll be back in twelve hours, give-or-take." The men nodded. Captain Rankin was the ranking officer at the Border Patrol facility, and he had become their de facto leader. Noah couldn't even guess how many men they had in the command. They'd been running around in the desert raising hell, so it was impossible to get a head count.

As far as Noah could tell, they were winning. At very least, they were shooting at the narcos and not all getting killed for their effort. The best thing he could do at this point was to rally more guns and gather more ass-kickers.

Noah slapped the guy next to him on the back, exchanged a silent nod, and took off at a trot toward his Cruiser.

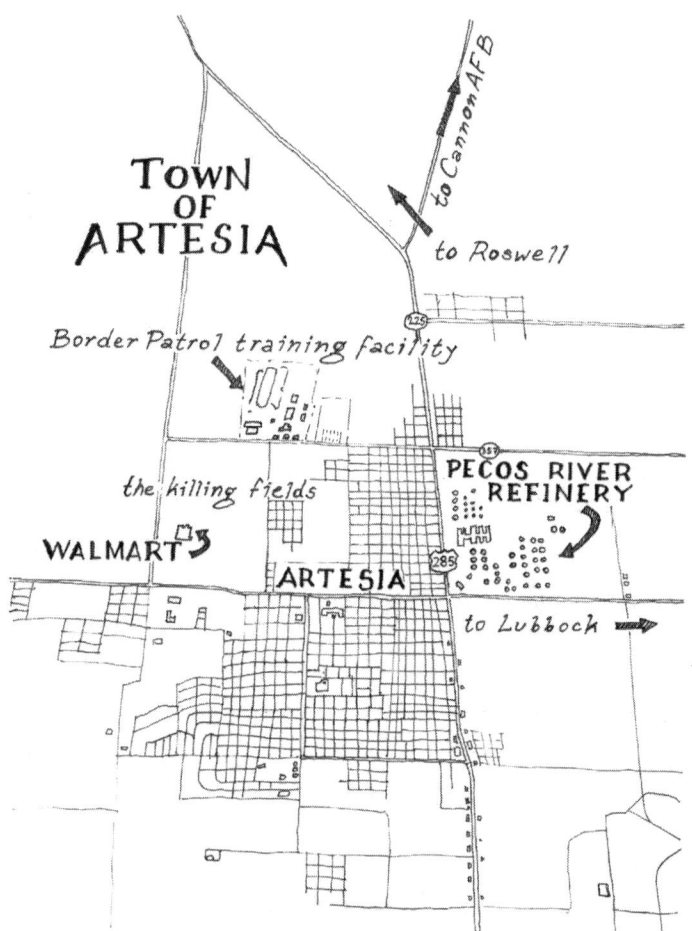

CHAPTER 27

TAVO CASTILLO
THE PECOS RIVER REFINERY, ARTESIA, NEW MEXICO

Tavo glowered as he watched gasoline pour onto the desert sand in a stream as thick as a garden hose. He thought about finding a stick and shoving it into the hole, but the godforsaken desert didn't grow anything big enough to do the job. This had been the sixth bullet-size leak he'd been shown. He didn't know much about hydrodynamics, but a storage tank this large must be generating enormous pressures—more than a stick could defeat.

"I hope you killed the motherfuckers who did this," Tavo seethed.

Alejandro shrugged, looking for all the world like a hapless idiot. Tavo felt like shooting him in the face.

"We've shot a dozen desert rednecks, but they're firing from ridiculous distances. It's almost impossible to hold a perimeter when the enemy shoots from over two miles away and lobs bullets onto the target. It's hard to miss a fuel tank that's three hundred feet wide and sixty feet tall. They can just about shoot from the Texas border." Alejandro guffawed and Tavo again suppressed the urge to kill him.

"You say we're out of patches?" Tavo already knew the answer. Alejandro nodded.

"What's the status on the Abrams tanks?" Tavo asked.

"A group of tank crew left last night. There must've been some kind of pact, because all but twenty or thirty holdouts scrounged up vehicles and headed back in a caravan toward El Paso."

"Then we hit them tonight." Tavo started to walk away—he needed a drink of water—but he couldn't turn his back on the wasted gas. "Find wood posts. Have them whittled down and pound them into these holes. If we don't slow the loss of the fuel, we'll end up stranded here."

THWACK! Something struck the tank and reverberated like a bass drum. A full five seconds later, a rifle shot sounded on the horizon.

Whumpf.

Tavo searched the storage tank for another leak, but the bullet must've impacted above the fuel level since there was still only one amber fountain.

"The first thing we're going to do once we get those Abrams fueled up and moved here is to level this shitty town," Tavo said, indulging his rage. "I want the mayor and I'm going to make him bleed."

"I don't think the mayor is responsible for the organized resistance. Weirdly, this little town not only has the biggest refinery in the state, but they also have a huge Border Patrol training facility. It's built on the old community college campus. You can bet your balls that the dudes we smoked out on the perimeter yesterday were from there. They looked military to me, or former military at least."

"Have you taken it down?"

"Taken what down?" Alejandro asked too quickly.

"The fucking training facility," Tavo shouted.

"No. You said we should hold the refinery. Other than checking on the air base with the tanks, I haven't allowed anyone to go outside the wire for the last day. I didn't want to get men wasted for no good reason."

Tavo reminded himself that Alejandro had been to war enough to play it smart. No reason to roll up on a federal paramilitary training camp without overwhelming force. Now that Tavo had brought another five hundred men from the ranch, Alejandro's list of options had expanded.

With this latest outpouring of local resistance, Tavo sprouted a new hatred for Americans. These assholes weren't willing to do a damn thing to save their country when it could still be saved. Now that the absurd American circus had collapsed, they were lately fighting and dying like real patriots. Where was their patriotism before, as they squabbled on Facebook about transvestite bathrooms or beat each other up in the streets while burning their own flag? In Tavo's mind, they had already forfeited the right to bitch. The time for taking personal responsibility for their homeland had passed while they were posting memes about cats.

THWACK!...whumpf. Another shot echoed across the desert.

He hated to admit it, but this whole, rural America fight did, in fact, remind him of the movie Red Dawn. He had watched it at least a dozen times as a kid, and he remembered the Spanish voiceover of Jed Eckert played by Patrick Swayze. He had even dreamed about dying heroically someday, on a park bench with the little brother he never had, sacrificing himself to help innocent children live.

How far the years had carried him from that silly dream. How much he'd learned in later years in orphanages about abuse and terror. He'd learned that he'd much rather be the victor than a defeated hero.

He couldn't quite cast himself as Colonel Bella—the Cuban

insurgent invader in the movie—but he couldn't avoid the relentless truth: if he pushed long and far enough, he would run into American partisans flying the banner of the "Wolverines." He might not see himself as Colonel Bella, but they certainly would. As they were defeated and died, they would cast him as the bad guy in their own war drama.

Tavo's thoughts turned to Sofía—always back to Sofía. He hoped she had inherited his efficiency of intellect, but today he doubted it. Of all the people he had been able to read like open books and to bend around his will, his daughter eluded him. Would she cast him as the bad guy in the end too?

Tavo turned to grab a bottle of water from his Humvee and Alejandro followed.

"We take the tanks tonight," Tavo repeated. "Organize the men now, or it'll be hell in the dark. We will hit the American soldiers at 0400 hours when they're foggy."

Cannon AFB, Clovis, New Mexico

They laid down the chain-link fence along a fifty-yard section of the Whispering Winds golf course, tucked inside the north boundary of Cannon Air Force Base. Tavo led his men across the third fairway, winding through the sand bunkers and rolling grass hills. Their recon detail had found no roving patrol around the base and only a night watch over the two-dozen remaining tank drivers, posted around eight, tidy rows of M1 Abrams tanks lined up in front of a massive airplane hangar. Most of the soldiers slept inside the hangar, oblivious to the two hundred men surrounding their position.

Tavo approached a sleeping American guard, his head

nodding against his chest, gray and grainy through Tavo's white phosphor night vision goggles. He stepped behind the man, clamped his hand over his mouth and slid his razor-sharp Cold Steel Vaquero across his throat. The movement was so smooth that the man might have died in his dreams.

Tavo turned to make sure the squad of operators had seen him draw first blood. It didn't hurt to build his personal legend as a warrior. He had hoped to see the men wide-eyed and impressed, but the soulless oculi of their NVGs stared back at him, waiting for his orders.

He held up two fingers and stabbed a knife-hand to the left, sending a fire team to check for guards around the south edge of the tanks.

Boom-boom-boom!

The small hours of night came alive with the crack of M4 rifle fire, probably a dying American's last act.

He ran across the tarmac toward the open door of the airplane hangar, weaving between the Abrams tanks and the sleeping men. They couldn't afford for even one of the tanks to join the fight.

Before he could make the hangar door, the dark erupted in a mass of gunfire. Tavo reached the last row of tanks and a round pinged off the edge he was using for cover. He ducked back, but not before seeing muzzle flashes coming down the line, pouring fire into the hangar. His men had overrun the tanks and were fighting in the no-man's-land between the tanks and the hangar.

"Cease fire. Cease fire. All units hold fire." Tavo hunkered down and spoke into his command radio, "Take and hold cover behind the tanks. We need some of the Americans alive." Rounds pinged and wizzed as they impacted the ceramic armor, caterwauling into the dark before dawn.

As the American soldiers set up defensive positions inside the hangar, the gunfire dwindled. The dark gave the Americans no target so long as Tavo's own men refused to provide muzzle flashes to focus their fire. He suspected the Americans had neither night vision nor electronic sights, which meant they'd be shooting blindly through their open sights.

His men, on the other hand, had NVGs, electronic sights and IR lasers. Tavo didn't ask, but he doubted he'd lost anyone to the barrage. Given another few minutes of fighting, his men would go through the tankers like a badger through a henhouse. Tavo hoped enough of the Americans had survived the first exchange of fire to give him what he needed.

He shouted in a Texan drawl, "Send out your CO for a parlay. We're all Americans here and we don't want to shoot anyone else. Nobody needs to get hurt. We're on the same side." Nobody here had been around to see Beto use the same ruse on the National Guard, so Tavo saw no reason not to borrow it.

A minute later, someone yelled back from the shadows of the dark airplane hangar. "I'm coming out."

Tavo popped the suppressed Glock out of his Crye GunClip and called the officer over. The man stepped around the corner of the tank and Tavo pressed the end of the suppressor into the officer's chest.

Pfft. Pfft.

He injected two rounds into the man's heart and dropped him without a whimper.

There was no point in negotiating with officers. They would only present hurdles. It was the NCOs and enlisted men Tavo wanted to talk to.

He waited five minutes before doing anything. Confusion, at this point, would work in his favor.

"Tankers!" Tavo yelled in his best mimic of the tone of the officer's voice. "Form up on me. Bring your weapons." Tavo's multicam fatigues matched the tankers' multicam fatigues, so when Tavo waved his tallest man forward to stand in the gap, facing away from the hangar, the Americans didn't know if they were looking at the backside of their officer or the backside of an enemy combatant. In any case, the sun had only begun to show the slightest color on the eastern skyline and any disorientation would add to Tavo's advantage.

A half-dozen flashlights flicked out of the dark corners of the hangar and the bewildered soldiers saw their commanding officer standing erect in front of their tanks at parade rest, as though forming up.

If you show people what they expect to see, they will usually believe it. It wasn't the first time Tavo had used that trick.

Men rambled out of the hangar, their M4s in a variety of postures of self-defense, but all moving toward the parade area. Tavo flicked his tac light on and blinded the soldiers, waving for his men to do likewise. His men rotated their NVGs up on their helmets and followed Tavo's lead. One-by-one, they drifted to the parade area and lined up, stopping short of their CO out of habit. When one NCO finally moved up to address the officer, Tavo came out from behind the Abrams and headed him off.

In the dim light of morning, wearing a bump helmet and tactical gear, Tavo looked nothing like a Mexican national. Plus, he had almost no accent.

"Son," Tavo put his hand on the man's chest and held him back. "We all want the same thing here. We want to get America back on its feet. We need your help and there are foreigners crossing the border even as we speak. They need to be stopped, so I'd appreciate it if you ordered your men to lay down their weapons and help us get a couple of these tanks moving toward Tucson. They're going to need the help."

The man looked Tavo over in the dark and nodded. The NCO didn't use his flashlight to get a better look at Tavo, probably because it'd be rude to shine a flashlight in another man's face two paces away. Tavo smiled; people were so awesomely predictable. The NCO had just sacrificed his entire unit over a question of good manners.

"Form up, men," the Sergeant shouted. More men filtered out of the hangar and joined them. Tavo counted twenty-six.

"Surround them," Tavo ordered into his radio. All two hundred of his men converged from the dark and pointed in at the twenty-six Americans, most of whom were just recovering their night vision from having looked into the flashlights.

"What's this?" the NCO finally realized his mistake.

Tavo drew his suppressed Glock and pointed it at the man's face. "Shut up and put your rifles on the ground or we'll execute you all." The cartel soldiers followed his lead, stepped closer, and tightened the noose.

"Who are you?" the NCO stalled for time.

Pfft—snap! Tavo shot him through the bridge of his nose. With his left hand, he grabbed the collar on the man's jacket and pulled the sagging body close as cover from any incoming fire.

Another American in the line stumbled—the bullet had over penetrated and hit him in the throat. The wounded man folded sideways and slumped into the man beside him. Half the Americans had been in the process of laying down their weapons when the suppressed shot had killed their NCO. Since it hadn't sounded like a true gunshot, their reaction had been mixed.

Tavo yanked the dead man close and shouted to the group. "If you lift your rifle you die."

A volley of fire from his men ripped through the Americans standing in front of the hangar. More men keeled over onto the asphalt. The shooting died off again.

"Get your hands off the guns. It's the only way you live to see the morning sun." Tavo had lowered the man to his knees and he'd gone down with him, still using the dead NCO as a human shield. He congratulated himself for the bit of poetic flair. Fully half of the soldiers had looked toward the sunrise. Then they dropped their rifles. Never seeing another sunrise just seemed more tragic than simply dying.

The vagaries of human emotion...such a delightful puzzle, Tavo mused.

A handful of Tavo's men collected the weapons and laid them on the front apron of the closest tank.

"Flex cuff them," Tavo ordered.

As he watched the American tank crews being restrained, Tavo marveled at his new power, bestowed on him by the United States Army. Throughout history, the largest force almost always won. In just a few, famed battles, boldness, connivance and good luck rushed into the gap and handed off-center victories to the brave and the clever.

As Tavo stood before his prize—a hundred of the deadliest ground machines in history—he gave himself the credit he was due. He'd successfully invaded the United States, overrun an armory, and forced the surrender of the most-potent fighting force in the southwest. And he'd done it all with the loss of just a few "borrowed" men from the Mexican army.

He touched the wound on his forehead and remembered that it hadn't been without challenges and setbacks, but he had achieved something utterly remarkable. Now that God had seen fit to provide him with these weapons of war, he would be invincible.

The first sliver of sun broke the plane of the desertscape. Tavo imagined he could feel the warmth of it speeding across a hundred million kilometers—a bolt of incandescence sent from a God who sometimes looked up from his labors to notice men of focus and power.

History was the Hand of God written in the annals of man, and Tavo had placed his handprint on history this morning. He felt a solid conviction that even this conquest would shrink against a backdrop of what he would soon accomplish. History was on the move with Tavo, and God with it.

His daughter's words sounded in his ears—about Tavo's soul being in danger of hell. Given the sun at his front and the behemoths of war at his back, her warning rang petty and false. How could she understand God, given the slightness of her own works? How could she understand her father when all she'd ever done was enjoy the scraps from his table?

The small people in the audience would never understand the greatness of the playwright. They would be carried by the play, and deposited neatly outside the door after the denouement, taken on a journey they could never comprehend.

But Tavo didn't require their understanding—or his daughter's admiration. God's approving glance, and history's assent, would be enough.

CHAPTER 28

TAVO CASTILLO
US 285, 75 MILES NORTH OF ROSWELL, NEW MEXICO

Tavo hammered the console of his Humvee with the ball of his hand like a jackhammer trying to kill a mosquito. The driver stared straight ahead, as though searching for something in the distance. The Humvee stood in the middle of a lonely highway in the middle of nowhere. Tavo had just gotten off the radio and had ordered the convoy to stop.

There were few other places in the southwest where, horizon-to-horizon, not a single mountain could be seen. The convoy of Abrams tanks, trucks, Jeeps and Humvees had stopped on the dirty, orange moonscape while Tavo figured out what to do next.

Go forward or go back.

Alejandro had just radioed to tell him that the Pecos River Refinery was under steady attack. Tavo felt like an Olympic sprinter with paracord tied around his waist. He could run as fast as he like, but at some point the rope would go taut. If he was running full-tilt in that moment, he could be torn in half. If he ran out of fuel, and lost tanks, he would never be able to return. The tanks would become an impossible defense for the cowboys and townsfolk of the Southwest. Gasoline was the rope, and Tavo was the runner. He needed that rope to free spool all the way to the Great Salt Lake. Salt Lake City held billions of gallons of gasoline, and once he seized it, anything would be possible.

Tavo exhaled and released his irritation with Alejandro. The locals had magically agreed—in the middle of starvation—that their top priority would be to harass Tavo's little army. Two days before, only a couple dozen shooters had been sniping at the refinery. Since he left with all hundred Abrams tanks and most of the men, the vultures had descended upon the refinery in force. Somehow those dirty-ass rednecks knew that the refinery mattered to him. Or maybe, like yipping hyenas, they just attacked targets wherever they seemed weakest. He had no idea who or what had raised such a deliberate defense of the town of Artesia. Why would they shoot the refinery? It was as though some malignant son of a bitch was reading his mind.

Tavo had a decision to make: keep driving toward the Navajo Army Depot and then move on to Salt Lake City, or go back to the refinery in Artesia to destroy the insurgents. At the army depot, he would pick up dozens more Humvees, a few Bradley Fighting Vehicles and a lifetime supply of ammunition and top-notch bang-bang. But he wouldn't get much farther north than the depot without more gas—a lot more gas. The next big refinery wasn't until Salt Lake City.

Tavo had learned a few things about tanks, and they weren't good things. For starters, even after using every drop of fuel from the fleet of 20 HEMTT fuel trucks that'd accompanied the tanks from Fort Bliss, the Abrams barely reached the refinery in Artesia. These juggernauts of land battle only had a 200 mile operating range, which explained why he'd seen so many tanks loaded on rail cars in the past. It was stupid to drive them anywhere. Moving overland was a logistical nightmare. Since Tavo hoped to eventually ride them to victory all the way to the

Pacific Ocean and the Canadian border, this shortcoming mattered *a hell of a lot.*

The tanks were like heavyweight prize fighters only capable of going two rounds before having dizzy spells and fainting in the ring. Tavo would have to consider a new layer of strategy into his plans of conquest. Fuel and supply lines would become his primary focus. He couldn't just pillage his way to Salt Lake City. The gaps between refineries were two and three times the operating range of his armor, and the small gas stations and regional suppliers wouldn't have enough fuel to do the trick, even assuming they hadn't been drained by local scavengers.

His tanks could defeat any insurgent force. The millions of weapons in the hands of American gun owners would fold like wet sawdust before the mighty Abrams. But the tanks required an ironclad supply chain. Tavo had been born to grasp complex networks of logistics and to build elegant solutions for entropic problems. *This was his jam,* he reminded himself, quoting something Alejandro had said to him earlier on the sat phone.

"This is your jam, Canoso. You make the plan and I'll kick some ass,"

Tavo had terminated the call with Alejandro in order to think through the web of logistics. He needed his big map, but he didn't want to dig through the back of the Humvee to find it. The logistical problem was clear enough in his head, anyway.

At least learning to operate the tanks hadn't been a problem. Three of the American tank drivers had given his men instruction on how to drive, running them through the ignition sequence, the controls and the idiosyncrasies of the machine. Surprisingly, not one soldier would teach his men how to operate the weapon systems even after executing a few of them in front of the others. Apparently, it was less unpatriotic to teach tank *driving* than to teach tank *shooting*. In the end, he'd kept the five tank crew who'd been most cooperative and shot the rest.

Two dozen dead, zip-tied soldiers lay on the tarmac at Cannon Air Force Base, a feast for the flies. The last thing Tavo wanted was more American partisans plinking at his oil refinery.

What really hung Tavo up was a leadership shortage. He had four assets: Alejandro, Beto, Saúl and himself. Beto had the most maturity and experience; five years older than the other men and a former Navy SEAL, so his training went deeper than anyone. He knew America, and the American military. His English was perfect. But Beto was never more than halfway to grasping the big picture.

If he could trust Beto to be competent, Tavo could split his force of tanks, send fifty of them to the National Guard armory in Phoenix and order Beto to capture the ammunition depot in northern Arizona. Beto would have to take a serpentine path around Phoenix, Flagstaff and any city bigger than a watering hole. Southwestern Americans were like dogs that'd been hit by a car. If you tried to handle them, you would end up with stitches for your trouble.

As much as he hated trusting Beto with his new weapons, Tavo would have to send him with half the tanks to take the munitions depot. He would go back to the refinery himself. Saúl was with Beto, and that made Tavo feel a little better. At least Beto, would have someone looking over his shoulder. He didn't think much of Saúl's ability to lead, or even to think, but at least Tavo trusted him to help Beto avoid the biggest mistakes.

In the end, he still didn't trust Alejandro to protect the big asset. The ammunition depot was a luxury. The refinery was a necessity. He would personally see to the pacification of the town of Artesia and delegate the munitions depot to Beto and Saúl.

Tavo went to work splitting his company of tanks in half. Even that would take hours.

After sending half the tanks and all the fuel trucks ahead to Beto, Tavo and his half-column rumbled east. They arrived at the Pecos River Refinery after nightfall. A vicious night battle raged across a twenty-mile front around the facility.

Rounds pinged off Tavo's Humvee as the column passed through the refinery gates. Gunfire sparkled from every direction at the edge of the night. Other than the sparkle of headlights and muzzle flashes, the desert closed in like a shroud.

Tavo did the math in his head as he climbed out of his Humvee: the refinery was a square about a half-kilometer across. The partisans were able to hit the storage tanks from about two miles out from the fence. That made a diameter of about seven-point-two kilometers…times pi—three-and-change…It penciled out to a circular perimeter of over twenty-two kilometers.

With fifty tanks, he would be able to place one tank every half kilometer. Even with fifty tanks, partisans were going to slip between them and take shots. He could set up intermediate LP/OPs between the tanks, but even then, his men would be stretched thin and would be easy to kill in the night. If the insurgents found a way to shoot the storage tanks from farther—Tavo didn't think the 7.62 x 51 round could fly more than two or two and a half miles—then his whole perimeter would have to be moved out even farther still, and the size of the gaps would make perimeter defense untenable. To make matters worse, the refinery was tucked-up against Artesia, putting almost the whole town inside the two mile perimeter. Tavo could see the occasional muzzle flash from snipers on the roofs of buildings. He'd have to fight street-by-street.

If he didn't want a protracted battle, there would be only one way: he would eradicate the town and go "scorched earth" against the insurgents. It was either that or give up the refinery, and he hadn't returned hundreds of miles to give up the refinery. Like rats in the corn, he'd burn it all down and drive them into the open.

"What's the status of the fuel?" Tavo barked at Alejandro the moment he saw him.

"We have seventy-two storage tanks. Half hold unleaded. Fifteen of them hold crude. Ten are kerosene, which must be a byproduct or something. Twelve of the tanks are empty or mostly empty. All of the storage tanks on the outside of the facility are full of holes—they're a lost cause. We're out of proper patches and we're pounding wood pegs into the holes with sledgehammers as you suggested, which cuts the leakage down, but they still leak."

"Bottom line it for me, Alejandro," Tavo ordered.

"We have fifteen storage tanks, of various sizes, that still hold unleaded."

"Ammunition and men?"

"We're still good on ammunition. We've lost eleven men on patrols to round up snipers. One guy took an unlucky bullet to the melon just walking around the refinery." Alejandro chuckled until he noticed Tavo glaring at him in the light of his red headlamp. "We're good, Boss. We need to counter-attack in the morning at the latest."

"Quit fucking around and kill them all," Tavo said. "Without this refinery, we'll be forced to haul fuel from Monterrey and every American gun-toting asshole between here and there will be winging bullets at us as we drive by. You think this is bad? Imagine a supply chain a thousand kilometers long that passes through scores of Texan towns. I told you to level the Artesia, you didn't, and now we're getting our asses kicked. What did you think would happen?"

Alejandro shuffled his feet. Even in the dark, Tavo could tell his harsh words had stung. He and Alejandro had been friends for many years, and he had tended his ego like a tulip farmer. Now the gloves were off. This fight was not for slightly-larger drug territories or healthier margins on crack cocaine. This fight was for conquest. Real world, history-making, ruling-with-an-iron-fist conquest. They didn't have time for egos. They needed results. They needed fuel for the Abrams tanks.

"Alejandro." Tavo's voice softened, "This is for all the marbles, *hermano*. We'll never fight for profit again. We fight for conquest—for Mexico and the church. For every one of these cowboys we kill, we save a thousand lives. This is Big War and it all comes down to this refinery. Every moment we spend dicking around with pissed off hillbillies, Utah gets farther and farther away—gas reserves are being burned up by crazies. I shouldn't be here talking to you. I should be taking down an ammunition depot, so that day after tomorrow, we roll into Salt Lake City and nail down the refineries there. So let's quit prancing around and let's make war. They are bringing the fight and they won't stop until we crush them. Do you understand me, hermano?" Tavo couldn't keep the knife-edge out of his tone. "We must make war on these assholes with hatred. We must murder them without mercy. We need to stop fighting like *indios* and start fighting like *conquistadors*. We do that or we die here… *you* die here."

Tavo couldn't read Alejandro's face in the dark, but his next words sealed their mad brotherhood, and forged together their deathless sin.

"*Si*, Canoso. I get it. Tomorrow, we burn them all."

CHAPTER 29

NOAH MILLER
TEXAS PRECISION RIFLE CLUB, WEST RANGE, BROWNFIELD, TEXAS

> "Sin and shame
> Remorse and pain
> Your damned credibility.
> Here and now,
> Lay them down,
> At the Big Man's feet."
>
> — *The Crusader*

Noah had been staring at the mural, painted on the side of the big barn, for probably ten minutes. He felt a kinship with the mural—as though the bizarre scene depicted in brushstrokes had a lot in common with his own mission. Both seemed like acts of insanity in a world turned upside down.

He leaned up against the fender of his Cruiser while five men drew down on him with AR-15 rifles, silent as stone. He was being held at the entrance to the Texas Precision Rifle Club while the "brass" figured out what to do with him. Apparently, this part of Texas didn't cotton much to strangers.

The title of the mural made sense. The painting made sense. But the action in the mural—and why anyone would paint it in the first place—eluded Noah entirely.

Ranchers of the Panhandle Fighting Prairie Fire with Skinned Steer.

The mural showed two ranchers dragging a half-skinned steer behind their horses trying to put out a prairie fire on the ground with its blood and body. Apparently, at some point in history, dragging a half-dead cow behind a horse had been the most effective method of putting out a fire. Noah scratched his head.

I'll be damned.

Three older men stepped out of a ranch house down the dirt driveway, and walked toward Noah, red puffs of dust curling up behind them. Each man carried a revolver on his hip and a rifle over his shoulder.

These are the sons of the sons of the sons of the men who put out brush fires with bloody steer carcasses, Noah reminded himself. These were the very definition of men "not to be fucked with."

The thought sat well with Noah. In fact, it made him feel at home.

"What's your name and who are your kin?" one man barked as they drew near. He carried a huge octagon-barreled rifle over his shoulder. Given the man's age, Noah wondered if he could still shoot it. The gun had to weigh fifteen pounds.

"I'm Noah Miller was raised by Bill McCallister over in the borderlands of Arizona, but my kin are the Millers of Santa Cruz County." Noah didn't make a move to shake hands yet. He knew better than to jump the gun on a handshake in Texas.

Another of the old men, this one with fancy AR-15 slung over his shoulder, spoke. "I knew Joel Miller down around Ciudad Juarez back in the seventies. Any relation?"

"Joel Miller was my uncle, but I left Ciudad Juarez as a young man."

The three men nodded, knowing what it meant to leave the Mormon settlement in Juarez "as a young man." It meant Noah wasn't a Mormon, which was a mark in Noah's favor. These men would be old school Protestants, without much affection for Mormons.

The three old men stood quiet for a moment, apparently working on a judgment of the "young man" before them.

On his way into Brownfield that morning, Noah had been stopped at a roadblock on Highway 380, disarmed, interrogated and finally allowed to drive on to the Texas Precision Rifle Club. A Terry County deputy had followed him and blocked him in with his police cruiser. The deputy now waited patiently, leaning across the cab of his cruiser with a shotgun pointed in Noah's general direction.

Noah sincerely hoped he'd get his 30-30 Winchester back from the deputy. It hadn't proven to be a very good battle rifle, given the eternal deserts and tremendous distances of southern Arizona and New Mexico. But he loved that gun. Old Bill had given it to him on his seventeenth birthday.

The five men at the gate lowered their rifles as the three older men stepped forward and offered their hands. Noah went the rounds, shaking hands with the three men and the other five men who had covered him with their rifles not moments before. Each handshake was a minor contest of strength; one man cranking down on the other man's hand just enough to let him know "I work for a living too."

"Are we to understand that you're fighting Mexicans over in Artesia?" the oldest of the three started off the conversation. Noah didn't love the implied racism of the comment. While they all called the Southwest home, Noah was the only man who actually lived in the borderlands. He considered himself part

Mexican and more than half the people he knew were Mexicans.

"Sir, we're fighting a force made up of Mexican cartel and some Mexican army that they captured last week." Noah emphasized the word "cartel," but he doubted anything he said at this point would change their perception: as far as the Texans were concerned, the Mexicans had invaded America.

"And you want us to come kill those Mexicans at the big refinery over in Artesia?"

"Yessir." Noah left it at that.

"We're not much good for combat operations. Most of us served, but war is a young man's game," the oldest guy said, sharing his thoughts out loud. "But I understand that long-shooters are doing most of the work against the Mexicans. Is that right?"

"Correct," Noah replied. "We need to destroy the fuel storage at Artesia. We believe the cartel took the refinery because they need gas. If we cut off their gas supply, we hope they'll go home."

The three old men nodded, taking their time. Thinking it through.

"We'll talk about it amongst ourselves. We might be able to do a bit better than rifles. Wait here."

The three turned and ambled back toward the farmhouse. The five went back to pointing their rifles at Noah.

Damned Texans. Noah smiled.

CHAPTER 30
TAVO CASTILLO
WALMART SUPERCENTER, W CLARK DRIVE AND
26TH STREET, ARTESIA, NEW MEXICO

Tavo picked out the guy running with the Texas flag and steadied his breathing.
Boom!
The blast of his SCAR Heavy rippled through Tavo's gut. The sound was muted by his earmuffs and a dozen other gunshots erupting around him, but the concussion shared a tiny fraction of the death being dealt. The Texan instantly disappeared into the grass.

Like rats in the corn, the people fled the town of Artesia, New Mexico.

Tavo didn't see the man fall, his sight picture through the 3x ACOG scope bobbed with the recoil. But he no longer saw the Texas flag, just a panic-stricken, helter-skelter mass of men, women and children fleeing across a mile-wide field between the edge of Artesia and the WalMart Supercenter. Tavo had positioned his men on the roof with large caliber rifles and he joined them in order to make sure it was done properly.

If he was going to keep the refinery, the town would have to be erased, and he couldn't let the people bleed off into the desert. The townsfolk of Artesia had already proven they would persecute his soldiers to the last man. There'd been something undeniably vengeful about the attacks from the townspeople. They hadn't been shooting at the refinery just to get the troops to leave—they were projecting *hatred* toward him and his men.

Hatred begets hatred, Tavo thought as he lined up on another man in the killing field.

Why would a man choose to carry a Texas state flag as he fled his home? These Americans were taking this fight personally, finding some strange vindication in the sacrifice of their petty lives.

So be it...

Alejandro had organized a six truck, ten tank detail to raze the town. The tanks mowed down any resistance with their M240 machine guns. Enemy snipers were obliterated with either the Ma Deuce or the main gun on the Abrams, depending on their cover. The refinery trucks came behind the armor and sprayed the homes and buildings with kerosene. Once the phalanx cleared each block, a team set it all on fire.

Luckily for Tavo, the wind blew from the south that morning so the smell of burning bodies drifted toward Roswell instead of doubling back on the refinery. A hundred years of Western settlers' dreams were being incinerated like so many stalks of dried corn.

Boom!

Tavo took the top off a brown-haired woman's head and her inertia carried her forward flat on her face into a hillock of dried grass. Her body actually bounced before coming to a final rest. There was no way Tavo could let the women disappear into the desert to support the men. This was no Red Dawn, where he hoped to occupy and pacify the town. Tavo needed that refinery, secure and unopposed. For two miles around the Pecos River Refinery, he would let no man or woman step without being cut down. His fields of fire had to be absolutely clear. He'd even ordered a bulldozer to go in behind the wall of flame that consumed the town and knock anything down higher than a meter.

Boom!

Tavo's SCAR Heavy ripped a young mother away from her daughter, leaving the little girl running in circles, wailing. Tavo didn't shoot the child. He'd ordered his men to let the children go. The more children that wandered the desert, the better. Most of them would die of thirst in a day or two anyway, but hopefully, some of the insurgents would put down their guns and care for them instead of putting holes in his refinery.

The bodies had begun to add up in the field. No one had even the slightest chance of crossing the no-man's-land between the town of Artesia and the open desert unless Tavo's men permitted it. Every adult pouring out of the sixteen block section of town would be killed. Tavo figured there were four hundred dead townspeople and another fifty or sixty kids mulling around. Tavo guessed the town of Artesia had a population of around 10,000 people. Seeing the four hundred or so dead in this field, Tavo wondered what 10,000 bodies actually looked like, scattered on the ground, with their possessions blowing in the stubble.

From what he could see from atop the WalMart Supercenter, it didn't seem like something that confession might cover. Yes, he had heard a thousand times before how the cleansing blood of Christ would remove even the darkest sin.

"Though your sins be as scarlet, they shall be as white as snow..." or something to that effect.

A voice deep in his soul rumbled, inchoate. But Tavo thought maybe he understood the gist of the rumbling: *don't believe it, asshole.*

It'd been a long, long day—reducing a small town to rubble and its residents to corpses. Men and women had sweated and toiled in the New Mexican sun for over a hundred years to raise up the town of Artesia, and it had required some effort to raze it from the surface of the earth.

It seemed fitting. Even with bullets and flame, obliterating a billion hours of human energy should require at least a bit of toil. It made Tavo think of Hiroshima and Nagasaki. With a single bomb, Americans had flattened those cities. It seemed like a sacrilege to Tavo—to put to death so much life force with so little effort. At least he and his men were completely exhausted after a day of mass murder. The night now came and wrapped around them, inviting unwanted reflection.

Ka-whump! The storage tank beside Tavo boomed with a deep *thunk*, followed by the sound of oil sluicing into the sand at high pressure. A full fifteen seconds later, the sound of a gunshot reached him, a *woof* in the wind.

"*Hijo de puta!*" Tavo screamed at the stars. Alejandro came running out of the dark.

"*Estas bien*, Tavo?"

"Where did that come from?" Tavo levered the headlamp around his neck and located the hole in the side of the massive storage tank. The edges of torn steel splayed outward instead of inward.

"*Madre*," Alejandro swore. "That's a .50 BMG round—and it must've tumbled because it impacted sideways. This bullet came a long, long way, Tavo. Maybe three miles or more. The hole's big enough that the pressure inside the tank bent the sheeting back. I don't think we can pound a stake into this one, *Canoso*," Alejandro stated the obvious. The hole was as big as a baseball and the stream of gas shot out six feet from the tank before curving down to earth.

Woof. Woof...Woof. Woof.

The big gun—or guns—thrummed from the edges of the night, like meteors sent by an angry god.

"Order your stupid *hijos de putas* to turn off their flashlights. *Now!*" he hissed at Alejandro. "We're giving them targets. Do it now!"

Tavo hoped that was the problem. He hoped those men, lying on the desert floor with revenge storming in their guts didn't have night vision goggles. If they did, they could shoot all night at the refinery, no matter how blacked-out.

Woof, woof, woof, woof, woof, woof...

Tavo closed his eyes in grief. The perfect percussion of the fire could mean only one thing: some malignant son of a bitch was shooting at them with a large caliber machine gun. Probably the M2 Browning.

Even with only the vaguest idea where the refinery was on the horizon, a good M2 gunner could plunge hundreds of rounds into the facility. Fifty-caliber hunks of lead and copper would rain down upon them until the sons of bitches ran out of ammunition or until his men found the muzzle flashes and exterminated the gunner. Of course, the insurgents could stop shooting when Tavo's soldiers got within a mile or so and displace. Then they would start all over again. Hypothetically, the insurgents could do this forever. They could shoot with their machine guns for three miles away until the refinery had so many gushing holes that Tavo's men would struggle to sponge up even a bucket of gas.

Sow the wind, reap the whirlwind, Tavo heard the words on the dry wind, punctuated by the Ma Deuce machine gun.

You kill an American town, you set a different kind of monster in motion—the kind of monster whose hunger can never be satisfied. The kind of monster that feeds on rage.

A new beast roamed the desert, Tavo realized, and that beast licked up the brain matter of the heads Tavo had split in half.

The beast fed upon the anguish of children, wandering and tear-streaked. That beast would hunt Tavo anywhere within two hundred miles of this place of fire and death. He had awakened the spirit of the filthy men who long ago settled this blighted land.

The tortured, solitary souls who dragged their hapless women into this desert a hundred years ago had also brought an anger so acrid that it nested into their cells and passed itself down from generation to generation. While polite American society enjoyed their modern luxuries, the beast had hidden, barely below the surface, like a demon not-dead but almost forgotten.

Now with civility blowing away like ash, and with corpses festering in the thousands, the beast had stirred, and now it would feed.

The kind of man shooting at Tavo had waited for dark to bring vengeance. This kind of man would rather die a million gruesome deaths than to allow the murder of women to go unanswered. Even as their flashlights blacked out around the refinery, Tavo knew in his heart that it was lost, if not tomorrow, then the next day.

They would be forced to abandon hundreds of thousands of gallons of fuel, glistening like amber promise in the bowels of the storage tanks. The land of eastern New Mexico and West Texas had been poisoned, as if someone had dropped a sarin gas on the region. *Hate* permeated the soil and clung to Tavo's clothing like a toxin.

In the dark of the New Mexico night, the stars blazing overhead, Tavo was forced to admit it: he had misjudged the Americans. He'd accepted a modern caricature of them as spoiled children. He'd forgotten that the blood of their forefathers would rise up in them and take hold.

The children of this land would revert to who they had been

born to be. Old ways would spring up in the gaps left behind by Facebook and *Fox & Friends*. These were the children of the children of the great-great grandfathers who had been driven out of Europe because they couldn't get along with other people. They were the prisoners, the bondservants, the religious zealots. They were the rebels and the Protestants. They were the cast-offs as Europe gentrified—the broken pieces in the assemblage of human machinery that would become modern England and France, Ireland and Denmark. These were the great, great, great grandchildren of people who *could not get with the fucking program.*

Tavo had thought to conquer them; and as fifty-caliber projectiles hammered into the iron skins of his fuel storage tanks from farther away than the human eye could even see, Gustavo Castillo felt the coming storm, the wages of his iniquity.

"Actual to Alejandro," Tavo spoke into the radio in the top pocket of his six hundred dollar plate carrier vest. Not a single drop of blood or bit of dirt marred the multi-cam. He'd killed scores, maybe hundreds of people, and his clothing was still spotless.

"Go for Alejandro."

"We leave tomorrow morning. Fill every tanker truck with gas. Do it tonight, before they dump it all on the ground."

The radio went silent for a moment. Alejandro, undoubtedly needed a moment to absorb the implications of their defeat. "Good copy, Actual. Fill all tankers with gas and be ready to exfil in the morning. Alejandro out."

The gas from the Artesia refinery would get them as far as Northern Arizona. To reach any farther, Tavo would have to unleash another kind of war. In truth, he'd probably already done so the moment he'd taken off the brown-haired woman's head with his SCAR.

Twenty HEMTT tanker trucks and fifty Abrams tanks lined up for fuel in the dark. Even blacked-out, Tavo could see the twinkling of dash lights and the red glow of low-viz lights stretching over a kilometer.

The shimmering lights of the column reminded Tavo of a massive, rumbling snake—a modern incarnation of Quetzalcoatl, the plumed serpent god of the Aztecs. Being Catholic, Tavo hadn't taken much stock in native Mexican mythology, but the immortal serpent god took up a home in his troubled thoughts.

While the tanks and tanker trucks lined up, clouds devoured the nighttime canopy of stars. The black night echoed Tavo's mood. He felt like the head of the Aztec serpent, ever hunting and ever famished. He held limitless power in his hands, but he possessed a great weakness—a hunger that never slept.

He lost himself in the macabre image: the winding snake, the black night, the endless desert; the bursts of rifle fire as insurgents pierced his refinery with lead. The plumed serpent tensed its muscles and fortified its resolve. It would stop at nothing, consuming anyone and anything in its path.

This wasn't the first appearance of the serpent in Tavo's life. With it, he had clawed his way off of the streets of Guadalajara. It had wolfed down the bodies of the drug dealers whose territories Tavo had consumed. It had bled his wife's family to attain social cover and anonymity. But for the last decade, the serpent had slept while Tavo digested his prey. He had slowly forgotten the single-minded appetite for supremacy that hibernated within him.

Now, on this soulless night, the serpent awoke in him. Like the monster within the Americans, the serpent would stop at nothing. It would feed and never capitulate. The mighty Quetzalcoatl would consume this land until the snows of the distant north marked the edge of its domain.

The mantle of brute fate descended on Tavo and all else fell away. The insurgents, like biting fleas, would be swept away by his tail. The hunger for gas, like a birthright granted, would be satisfied by his ruthless will. His daughter, like a wayward demigod, would be brought to heel.

Now fortified by the power of his dark will and the hunger of the serpent inside him, Tavo stormed toward his Humvee. "South, toward the fuel," the serpent demanded.

In Mexico—in the shadow of fate—his daughter would meet her father for the first time.

CHAPTER 31

NOAH MILLER

NEAR THE WALMART SUPERCENTER, W CLARK DRIVE AND 26TH STREET, ARTESIA, NEW MEXICO

> "All the promises that I've broken,
> All the times I've let them down,
> You know them, like yesterday.
> Still I hold the pain that makes me drown,
> Still I cradle the guilt wove in the crown."
>
> — *The Crusader*

The reek of cooked flesh poisoned the midday heat. Not a breath of wind stirred, yet Noah smelled the bodies of women and children, turned under and consumed by the flames that had reduced the town of Artesia into concrete rubble and black, human paste. Like a plate of eggs cooked on high heat for hours, thousands of human beings had been rendered into oily char—their dreams, their passions, their love, scorched from the earth by the sister-evil that had erased his family.

And Noah was to blame for both.

He looked out over the field of the dead, the colorless sun beating down from directly above. He resisted the urge to count them. He let go of that all-too-human compulsion to count the cost and regain control over his crushing remorse.

So-and-so many lives sacrificed in exchange for so-and-so many lives saved in the coming war. They died for a cause...

Bullshit. He would not diminish them—these people who were massacred—to satisfy his mental masturbation.

He had no idea how many dead lay across the weed-choked fields around the WalMart Supercenter. He only knew that they were men, women and children. Hundreds of them. Their beloved belongings swirled around them in the wind, like fragments of their past lives still flitting around their souls, unsure where to go next.

Noah despised himself. He hated how easy it was for him to bend the world to his will. He wallowed in the truth: how little thought he had given to the cost others would pay. This wasn't the first time he had strolled in with his glowing blonde hair and ruddy good looks, and sprinkled perfumed confidence into a scheme that, at best, should've warranted grave consideration.

He literally hadn't spared a single thought for what the cartel would do to the town of Artesia if the Texans and their fifty caliber rifles destroyed the refinery. It simply hadn't crossed his mind.

Instead, Noah had plucked a patriotic, holy war from a forgotten cassette tape, had electrified it with his dashing smile, and had rallied hundreds of simple people to their deaths. Now their children's bodies baked in the noonday sun like carp in a dried-up pond.

Noah had tried to avoid seeing this. He'd been told about the massacre of Artesia by one of the fighters from the Border Patrol school. Despite himself, he pulled over along Highway 82 to stop and see the killing fields with his own eyes. He'd resolved to drive west and hopefully die in a hail of bullets somewhere before he reached the end of the road. Before leaving the area for good, he'd pulled over to drink in the full price of his victory.

Noah leaned across the hood of the Land Cruiser, his face in his hands. He began counting the bodies. Again, he stopped himself.

More than he could count.

That's all he would ever know. He'd made decisions and got people pumped up to fight and now the dead numbered more-than-he-could-count. When he'd destroyed his own family by screwing with the cartels, that'd been just two dead. Now, he'd killed hundreds—probably thousands—based on a whim, set in motion by his crying jag on the road to Hermosillo.

More than four years ago, his personal Armageddon began on a whim too. Noah had grown tired of his dogs barking their fool heads off at night when cartel pack trains crossed his land, loaded down with drugs. He had already alerted the Border Patrol to the cartel point of crossing, but it became apparent that the Border Patrol monitored hundreds, maybe thousands, of crossings just like the one at the south end of his ranch. The Super Troopers, as locals called them, did nothing.

So, Noah got clever. He waited for winter and painstakingly dug up a patch of western poison ivy at the far end of Bill's ranch. Then he transplanted the poison ivy in clumps all along the fence where the smugglers liked to cross. Every day, when he ran water out to the stock tanks, he passed by the poison ivy in his four-wheeler and gave it a sprinkle. To his delight, the transplants exploded, and by late summer the border fence, the wash and the riverbanks were crawling with poison ivy. He sniggered every time he rumbled past the fence line. He knew from first-hand experience the living hell it was to endure poison ivy and he delighted in the knowledge that his biological weapon had cartel tough guys scratching their balls and scouring for home remedies. Nothing took a hard man down quite like a burning rash over his entire body.

Noah's dogs quit barking at night, and Noah bragged to his wife over his triumph.

Clever-ass Rancher: One. Cartels: Zero.

Then they came for his family. Somehow, the cartel deduced that the poison ivy was intentional. Noah would never know how.

He did everything he could to wall out memories of that evening when they came to kill his wife and daughter, but one bit of it stuck in his mind. The one scene jumped straight up like a startled cat every time he thought of that afternoon.

He remembered one of the filthy smugglers putting his hand on his daughter's perfect throat. The smuggler hadn't strangled her. Instead, a few minutes later as the sun worked its way down to the west mountains, he shot both his wife and daughter in the head.

Seeing their beautiful brains turn to mist in his front yard wasn't really the scene that stuck in Noah's mind. It was the look in his two year-old daughter's eyes when the smuggler put his dirty hand all the way around her throat—her eyes went wide and her cheeks quivered. Those eyes and those cheeks revealed her sudden awakening into the real world. That brutal world that had nothing whatsoever in common with her Disney princess movies or her mother's relentless love.

Noah watched as that man erased her innocence moments before he ended her life. What stuck in Noah's memory, like a long-dead tick buried too deep to remove, was the look in her eyes, not just of fear, but of betrayal. He had violated the pact between a father and a daughter. He saw in her eyes the sum total of all the ways his manhood had been an utter joke.

Noah drowned that look in his daughter's eyes beneath countless bottles of Jack Daniels, and the guilt that'd once stunned him like a steer taking a hammer to the head had abated over the years.

In the fog of that forgetfulness, he'd once again fallen for his own sham; that listening to his warrior father talk about war somehow made him a warrior himself. Noah could sell it all day long and twice on Sunday: he could regurgitate warrior-speak and military acronyms that lit up the battle-lust in other men.

"We'll set a two-click perimeter around the AO and drop plunging fire on top of the fuel storage tanks from here, here and here."

Those were the precise words Noah had used, over a map, to finally assure the Texans that he knew what the hell he was talking about. His well-honed warrior-talk had convinced those wind-burned old men that defeating cartel would be a clean, surgical affair. They'd all rolled into Artesia believing that their huge bullets would fall only on inanimate objects and those bullets would blast fear into the hearts of smaller men. They'd been led to believe that they could destroy things without being dirtied by real war.

Better than anyone on earth, Noah should've known: he could choose when and how to attack, but his adversary would then get his own turn.

Maybe the Texans headed back east without seeing the fields of the dead and without smelling the cooked flesh of women and children.

Guilt poured down his back. Noah actually fucking cared what the Texans thought of him, and that realization drove his self-hatred deep. Even as he stood over the rotting victims of his recklessness, he weighed what other men might think of him. He dishonored the dead with his vanity. How different was he, really, from the monsters that had massacred this town? What possible penance could scratch the surface of what he'd done in his galactic arrogance?

He should stay and bury the dead. He should face the cost of his personal crusade against the cartel. But he knew he wouldn't. He would move on, tracking the narcos like a dog, driven by raw instinct. He would leave these killing fields behind to mix with his road dust, and when the opportunity presented itself, he would bury this too, under a mountain of whiskey.

Noah climbed into the driver seat of his Land Cruiser and turned the key in the ignition. The radio blared to life.

> "You are still the potter and I am the clay,
> And though I know I am too proud…"

Noah mashed the eject button and the tape spat out. He snatched it out of the cassette deck and threw the tape out the window. The tape spun across the road and landed in a bitterbrush. He slammed the Cruiser in gear and stomped on the gas pedal. The Cruiser lurched onto the road and roared west down Highway 82, slipping in behind the cross-hatched track left in the asphalt by the Abrams tanks. He didn't know how the cartel had gotten their hands on tanks and it probably didn't matter at this point. The specter of fifty tanks added to his realization that he'd drastically underestimated them: he'd underestimated their brutality and he'd underestimated their ability to wage war. He was nothing in comparison to this level of violence and power. These were no petty, Mexican criminals. These were men of iron will and sobering resourcefulness.

Capturing even one American tank would've been an accomplishment. Capturing fifty main battle tanks put this cartel on the path to dominion over the region, and maybe more.

All that was left for him was to follow the churned up furrows left by the tanks in the hot blacktop. Noah could follow, but he would no longer pretend to wage war on the invading army. Not ever again. He wouldn't wager his secondhand warfighter act against these men of power and violence. He wouldn't rally men and their families to die for his personal fantasies.

The best he could hope for now was to throw his own life on the pyre of those who had already died. If he could contribute some small thing with his death, it would be the best he could do for them, impersonator that he was.

Noah slammed the brakes and the Cruiser chirped to a stop. A blue puff of smoke curled around the vehicle and whipped away in the wind.

Up ahead, a white grocery sack danced on a gentle updraft from the desert floor. It bobbled and looped toward the road. Then it whipped out across the rolling hills. Noah squinted and followed as the trash bird lilted into the distance, taunting gravity and denying the earth's hold.

Noah exhaled and kneaded the steering wheel. Emotions flushed through his gut, crossing like the mad currents before a tsunami. He closed his eyes and sighed.

He worked the Cruiser into a three point turn across the deserted highway and pointed back the way he had come. He doubled back on Highway 82 and stopped at the bitterbrush. He climbed down from the Cruiser and picked the cassette tape out of the branches. He returned to the Cruiser and made another laborious turn, resuming his shadow, ten miles behind the cartel convoy. The cassette tape dangled between two fingers as Noah shifted the Cruiser and regained highway speed.

After he hit fourth gear and the Cruiser settled into highway speeds, he tossed the cassette tape, side-arm, into the back of the Land Cruiser. It cracked against the window and dropped into the rear compartment.

CHAPTER 32
TAVO CASTILLO
PEMEX REFINERY, LA CADEREYTA, OUTSIDE
MONTERREY, NUEVO LEON MEXICO

Somewhere between San Antonio and Laredo, Tavo had a very bad phone conversation with his daughter. He had sent Alejandro west with half the company of M1 Abrams tanks with strict instructions to avoid cities and to join up with Beto at the Navajo Army Depot. It would consume all the gas just to get there, but it would consolidate his army in one place, halfway to Salt Lake City.

Without firing a shot, Beto swept into the Navajo Army Depot that morning; fifty tanks against an Army security team. Base security had surrendered at the gate. Last they spoke, Beto had been inventorying the underground ammunition bunkers.

But that victory was in the past, a vanishing sunrise against a rising storm. Tavo churned with frustration while his Humvee weaved between Texas towns, avoiding the worst of the apocalypse like a cutter navigating reef-choked waters. In the distance, he could see the twisting, black snakes of Texas oilfields and refineries burning off their lode of fuel.

Tavo had called Sofía on the satellite phone, and the conversation cranked his resolve to Level Ten. His decision to leave the tanks in Arizona and travel to Monterrey had been prescient. His daughter was digging in her feet, refusing to give him any gasoline from the Monterrey refinery. He'd been wise to get on the road, even before he knew for sure she'd resist him.

As he pulled up to the gate at the Pemex Refinery, Tavo took a deep breath, then a long exhale. Arrayed at the gate and inside the fence, stood the second largest military force between Mexico City and his own company of tanks at the Navajo Depot.

Thousands of Mexican soldiers occupied the Monterrey refinery, transforming the industrial site into an ad hoc Mexican military base. General Bautista must've consolidated army units from the entire region to this one location, even scrounging a few light armored vehicles to top it off.

Tavo very much disliked the setup. He never negotiated from a posture of weakness, but his daughter had drawn battle lines during their sat phone call: she would not allow Mexican gas to cross the American border. He would make his stand here, and one way or another, he would leave with the fuel.

Tavo concluded that this was her big play—her backup plan to having him arrested in Guatemala. She would face him down with troops while his own forces starved for fuel, surrounded by hostiles. Part of him wanted to shoot her in the chest. The other part wanted to destroy her army first, then force her to bow to him as her benefactor and father. Either way, General Bautista, her lackey, would die a gruesome death. That much, Tavo had already decided.

The gate guard let the Humvee through, and Tavo's driver pulled into a parking lot, now filled with temporary offices, military tents and communications antennas. Sofía and her general climbed down the steps of an office trailer as Tavo's Humvee pulled to a stop.

Her beauty in the waning light of afternoon gave him pause. The oblique sunshine drew out the red tones in her cheeks and lit up the green-on-green glint in her eyes. Despite their earlier argument on the phone, she smiled, the same smile she always wore when she reunited with her father after time apart. She didn't seem surprised to see him. Tavo's iron resolve flagged, his red-hot anger cooled.

Then the general stepped through the doorway behind her, stoney-faced and resolute. The old bureaucrat was fat around the middle, Tavo noted with disdain. True fighting men never grow soft. He wondered if the fat general and his daughter were sleeping together.

"Papi!" She ran across the parking lot and kissed him on the cheek. He couldn't blame the general for falling into her trap. Her beauty and feigned innocence had been tailored to captivate men.

"You didn't drive all this way to continue our little debate, did you?" She looked at him askance, a smile in her voice.

"Sofía, don't be difficult. The gas I need won't even put a dent in Mexico's reserve. And you're still producing oil in the Gulf. Mexico is at no risk of running out of gas." Tavo found himself arguing with her instead of killing people.

"Thanks to your daughter, Mexico *is* at no risk of running out of gas." The general interrupted and reached out a hand to Tavo. "Otherwise, this refinery would be on fire just like every refinery in Texas. She convinced me to protect critical fuel assets. Now our gasoline production has launched us ahead of the rest of the world. She's a Mexican patriot. You should be very proud."

Tavo brushed aside the compliment. "I just came from America and they're in total chaos. They need our help, especially in the southwest."

The general grunted. "Is that what you're doing across the border? Helping Americans?"

The general didn't realize that he'd just signed his death warrant.

Tavo countered for the sake of argument with his daughter, not really caring what the General thought. "We're stabilizing the region. Northern Sonora cannot survive if Americans are pouring across the border with military-capable weapons, stealing our food and water. I'm pacifying the border region for our self-preservation."

"How can you pacify millions of armed Americans?" the general raised his eyebrows. "Even their police have better weapons than the army of northern Mexico."

"I have a hundred M1 Abrams tanks under my command."

The general shuffled his feet, obviously shaken by the revelation. Just two of those tanks could destroy his entire army.

"Regardless," Sofía interrupted. "We don't have enough gas for adventures into America. We only have enough gas to get Mexico back on its feet. We can transport the winter harvest and hold back starvation in Mexico with this gas, right here in Monterrey. We don't have enough to pacify the United States, or whatever it is you're doing, *Papi*."

"Sofía, I'm not talking about fighting a war. I need enough gas to protect the border. My tanks need enough fuel to return to Phoenix and then reposition across the frontier. We only need maybe a hundred thousand gallons—not even ten percent of just one of these tanks," Tavo waved at the refinery. "We can defend the border with so little gas that it'd be a mathematical rounding error to you."

In strict terms, Tavo only needed enough gas to come back to this refinery with a handful of tanks and wipe these idiots off the map. If this little army refused to concede the fuel he needed, he would attack. This pompous prick and his make-believe soldiers would be dead and smoking like charcoal by this time next week. Of course, if he could leave here with the fuel he wanted, perhaps he might let them survive another week. Maybe two.

"We've done the math," Sofía shot back, fire in her eyes. "We know the amount of fuel it'll require to feed Mexico. We know *down to the gallon* what it'll take, and that doesn't account for fuel theft. We don't expect your deal with the Zeta cartel to hold."

Tavo checked the general's face to see if he had known about Tavo's treaty with the Zetas. The general's eyebrows shot up. He apparently hadn't known that Tavo engineered the end of the Zeta's fuel thievery. General Bautista was probably just now realizing that Tavo had much more power than he had originally assumed. His daughter hadn't told him that Tavo was a major *narcotraficante*. The general's eyes shifted back and forth, weighing the new realization.

He must be thinking a great many new things. Tavo smiled.

If Tavo were the kind of man to rein in the Zetas, what did that make him? The Zetas were the most-feared cartel in Northern Mexico. Bautista must be concluding that Tavo wasn't the kind of person he should jerk around.

The implications played across the general's face—the new danger to his life must have dawned on him like an icicle down his back. The only thing more frightening than a cartel boss who could shut down the Zetas would be a cartel boss with a hundred M1 Abrams tanks. The general cleared his throat.

"Miss Castillo. I think we can make this accommodation. We have over a hundred fuel trucks parked in the back lot and several hundred more on their way. I think we should send a hundred trucks with gas enough for your father and his men to protect the border. We can replace the gas in two days. I think we should do it." The general looked to Tavo for approval.

Sofía's face churned, frustration knit into her eyebrows. Once again, her father had out-weighed her. "No farther north than Tucson. That's all the buffer we need and that's all the fuel you're going to get. A hundred thousand gallons has to last your army forever, so they best stay close." Sofía jammed her hands on top of her hips. Tavo felt the urge to slap her but he forced himself to relax instead.

Does she forget who she's talking to?

He had funded her every move in school and then in business. Tavo had deftly engineered the largest drug cartel the world had ever seen, and he had done it without anyone knowing his name. He had killed many men and had assaulted a dozen hard targets personally. He was probably one of the top five combat firearm masters in Mexico, and he had tested that ability against the finest fighting men in Mexico and abroad, all of whom now rested forever in wooden boxes. What *girl* would stand before him with her hands on her hips and tell him the rules of the game *he had contrived?*

Tavo inhaled and forced his shoulders to relax. His daughter's arrogance would be a fight for another day. Today, he had everything he needed. He never allowed himself to act on principal or pride. He acted on cold, hard reason—considering the implications and calculating the ramifications. He would return to Arizona with a hundred thousand gallons of fuel. It wasn't enough to reach Salt Lake City, but it was enough to make his next play. Whether he would return to Monterrey and obliterate these pretenders or continue north and gobble up the Americans, he could decide in the coming days.

"Very well. General, if you would be so kind as to order the trucks filled. The longer we wait, the more the American refugees move south. They were already walking en masse from Tucson toward the border," he lied. "Also, we could use a protective detail for our convoy, preferably one of your LAVs to head the column."

"Of course, Señor Castillo," the general replied.

Perhaps this man wouldn't need to be killed. The general had read the new reality quickly enough and had adapted without hesitation. His daughter might actually have handed him someone useful.

Sofía, though, was another matter. Even with the issue of the gas settled, she remained erect, her hands still on her hips, apparently seething over the general's capitulation.

Tavo had done the math very quickly, not pausing to double-check his fuel consumption and range calculations. He would certainly need more than these hundred thousand gallons of gas, but one way or another, he would get all the gas he needed. One petulant girl stood before his serpent, which wasn't much considering all he had overcome.

Flagstaff to Salt Lake City was about five hundred miles. His tanks burned a gallon of gas every one-half mile. He would require at least a thousand gallons per Abrams to reach Salt Lake City, times a hundred tanks plus the fuel for his Humvees and technicals. The math seemed easy enough—mostly round numbers. What the math didn't take into consideration was maneuvering in a fight, something Tavo hoped to avoid given the overwhelming power of the M1 Abrams. The "X Factor" would be the grimy Americans themselves. Tavo couldn't afford even the slightest weak link in his supply chain or the insurgents would exploit that weakness with hunting rifles and Molotov cocktails. They were nothing if not resourceful, and they had a hound dog's nose for vulnerability.

When Sofía finally discovered that he had taken the Pemex tanker trucks all the way to Flagstaff, she would rally against him. But that hardly mattered. Tavo could do what he pleased once the tanker trucks left this refinery.

Several days prior, he had sent a recon element forward on motorcycles to check the refineries in Salt Lake City, and yesterday they'd called in. At least two of the refineries north of

Salt Lake were intact. He ordered his recon men to burrow in and observe. They had seen some coordinated military action against one refinery, which corporate security forces repelled.

Just that report put Tavo's stomach on edge. If men were already assaulting the Salt Lake refineries, how much time would he have before they were taken or destroyed? The Salt Lake refineries would not stay safe forever. Those stockpiles of gasoline were like crystal stemware on a picnic table near a pack of dogs tearing one another to shreds. If that gasoline hadn't been torched inside of a week, it'd be a miracle. According to his recon team, Salt Lake City and the surrounding suburbs had been seized by chaos just like everywhere else. A Latino gang, one of the Zeta allies, had rolled up most of the city and had raided out most of the rich neighborhoods. The gangbanger captain styled himself the next Pancho Villa. Tavo would bring him to heel as soon as he could, but in the meantime, Salt Lake City was a flaming war zone. A thousand fires burned in the valley, and if just one of those fires wormed its way into his refineries, all would be lost.

Tavo had dispatched another recon team to check out the refinery north of Las Vegas, and their report didn't make him feel much better: Vegas had totally succumbed to depravity. It wasn't anything his tanks couldn't crush, but Tavo considered that second refinery in Las Vegas his Plan B. The Vegas refinery was safe for the time being, but violence was spreading out from the Las Vegas Strip like a plague that jumped between the weak. It'd follow the freeways, where refugees awaited the predations of the strong and the violent.

He had no desire to pacify more desert. He wanted farmlands—potato crops and corn harvests. Livestock and alfalfa. Rich carbohydrates and animal fats would be his weapons of pacification once the anti-personnel shells and machine guns of his Abrams tanks softened the insurgency.

Conquering more blighted desert would buy him no joy. Salt Lake City, and the rich band of farmland extending through Idaho and eastern Washington would be his vein of human gold. God willing, he would follow that vein up to the snowfields of Canada.

CHAPTER 33
TAVO CASTILLO
CAMP NAVAJO, OUTSIDE BELLEMONT, ARIZONA

For almost two miles before he reached Camp Navajo, Tavo passed his one hundred main battle tanks, technicals and tanker trucks sitting in the westbound lane, spanning the American highway like a conquering army at parade rest.

Beto met him in the parking lot in front of Camp Navajo. The day waned and their Humvees were parked nose-to-nose. Tavo had just arrived from Monterrey and Beto greeted his boss at the gate. He immediately delivered the bad news.

"There's nothing here. We've searched all seven hundred and seventy-seven concrete bunkers and they're mostly empty. We did find a couple million rounds of 5.56, a hundred hand grenades and several dozen 40 millimeter grenades for the vehicle-mounted grenade launchers, but most of our guys shoot AK-47s and the 5.56 ammunition isn't going to help us. We need to switch the men over to AR-15 rifles, or we're going to run out of ammo after one or two engagements."

Tavo flushed with anger. In the last twenty-four hours, he'd come face-to-face with four gross miscalculations—and he had been the one to make them. He couldn't remember ever feeling this way before. His calculations had always been accurate, so prescient. Now, with the stakes sky-high, he was screwing up. Before the stock market crash, he hadn't really thought that society could collapse until he saw it actually collapsing. His preparations had been a bit ambiguous—like planning a child's life before she was born. Now, with the collapse a deadly reality, he was relying on decisions his past-self had made while living in an entirely different universe.

Failure One: he hadn't prepared to take and hold refineries. He could've ordered his street soldiers to capture the refineries in Tucson and Salt Lake City ahead of an invasion. That one bit of planning would've smoothed penetration of the intermountain region. He would be sitting pretty in Salt Lake right now if he'd secured the Tucson refinery as soon as the stock market tanked. Tavo had suspected a collapse might happen and that fuel reserves would be the stepping-stones of conquest. He hadn't properly weighed the crucial role fuel would play, not until he saw a hundred M1 Abrams tanks slamming gasoline like a vaquero slams Sunday *cerveza*. All of this chasing gasoline around the American Southwest could've been avoided with one phone call to his lieutenants, one day prior to the collapse.

"Secure both the Salt Lake and Tucson refineries if the stock market closes."

But he hadn't seen the problem in all its horrific dimensions until the riots began. He had been prepared, but he hadn't been prepared *enough*.

Failure Two: he hadn't planned to acquire the weapons he'd need.

Case in point: they now stood inside the wire of the region's largest munitions depot. But it had been emptied of major munitions by bureaucrats, for some godforsaken reason, sometime in the hazy past. He had known the depot existed, but he hadn't known *what was inside*. He had assumed that a munitions depot would contain actual munitions.

The Arizona National Guard would keep their munitions *somewhere*. Tavo never considered the possibility that they would keep them *outside of Arizona*. This information had probably been on the internet, but Tavo hadn't dug deep enough to find out. He'd assumed that Americans would keep bullets near their weapons. For some unfathomable reason, they had decided to keep their bullets fuck-all faraway from the weapons that fired them.

Failure Three: he compounded Failure Two by ordering that all his soldiers train with the AK-47. No matter how many munitions depots they knocked over, he would never find stockpiles of 7.62 x 39 ammunition in America. He remembered clearly why he had decided to use the AK-47: it'd been because his street soldiers were idiots. He knew the AK to be the perfect weapon for idiots—easy to learn and easy to employ. The rifle functioned even when poorly maintained. He didn't plan on training marksmen, so the differences in accuracy between the AK and the AR-15 meant nothing to him. The AK seemed the perfect fit, *unless one hoped to collect ammunition from the dying body of the United States Army.* In that case, the 7.62 x 39 cartridge would indeed become a problem. Soon, he would have no choice but to issue the M4 carbine—the rifles they had found by the hundreds at the Arizona National Guard armory—and he would have to re-issue that rifle in the middle of a war in the middle of a foreign land infested with insurgents.

Failure Four, and this was a failure he could barely face: he had misjudged his own daughter. Tavo's Plan B for fuel now became Plan A because the damned Navajo Weapons Depot had turned out to actually be the Navajo Summer Camp for

Girls. Tavo would now have to seek more ammunition before they could move to Salt Lake City, and that would force a detour into Nevada. Detours required fuel.

He would be forced to attack the Hawthorne Army Depot, three hundred miles northwest of Las Vegas, and that shift would add a massive dogleg to his route. He would be forced to turn west, capture the Dry River refinery north of Las Vegas, then capture the Hawthorne Munitions Depot. He couldn't push straight through to Salt Lake City with the Abrams tanks—they simply didn't have enough gas to do it. Tavo could send a few tanks, tanker trucks and the forty Humvees to take and hold the refineries in Salt Lake ahead of his main force, but there were tremendous risks going into Utah at partial strength, particularly with insufficient ammunition of the wrong caliber. If they came up against any kind of organized resistance, like the resistance that had appeared out of the smoke in Tucson or the desert rats who had hit him in Artesia, he would have a divided force relying on a long, vulnerable supply chain stretched out over five hundred miles—under-fueled, under-manned and under-supplied with ammunition. He'd studied World War Two enough to know that Adolf Hitler had placed a similar bet against Russia and had eaten a bullet as a result.

The one source of gasoline Tavo could absolutely count on was Monterrey, Mexico and that refinery had been rendered uncertain by his daughter and her bureaucrat boyfriend. Tavo would've dearly loved to send tanks to seize that refinery, but it would burn at least three days and would force him to roll through Texas with an armored column. God only knew what the Texans would have in store for him when he returned north after that.

More importantly, based on reports from his recon element in Utah, the Salt Lake refineries there were still under siege. He could lose them at any moment. As he'd learned in Tucson, a single match could make the difference between millions of gallons of glittering fuel and a charred heap of slag.

The entire enterprise seemed hung on the whimsy of a college girl. Not only had his daughter set him up to take a fall in Guatemala, but she stood between him and the conquest of the Western United States. Thousands of men, a hundred thousand metric tons of armament and the fate of a starving nation—all waited with a Sword of Damocles dangling over it. And that sword had a name: *Sofía Castillo.*

Tavo felt reasonably certain that he could manage General Bautista with Sofía out of the way. He had no idea who else in the Mexican army she had swayed, but Tavo had seen it in the general's eyes; he was a man who could be managed. But the removal of Sofía from the equation would have to be swift and complete.

Tavo had tremendous military power north of the border, with thousands of 105 millimeter explosive rounds and unbeatable armor, but in Sonora and Sinaloa, he'd held nothing in reserve. The Monterrey refinery was his ace in the hole, his fallback position. Sofía might already know that he had advanced beyond Tucson, and she could be hard at work turning the Mexican army against him. He needed to get home and settle this issue as soon as possible, but he needed an intact refinery in the United States even more.

Tavo walked to his command Humvee, reached in the window and pulled out a map. He spread it on the still-warm hood and motioned for Beto to join him. The dark inched in around them in the parking lot and Tavo flicked on the headlamp he'd been wearing around his neck since crossing the border into the United States.

"How many men do we have?" he asked. Foot soldiers from

his drug operation had continued to filter in from the four corners of dying America.

"With Alejandro's group, the Mexican army guys and the last of the guys from Hermosillo that showed up today, we're at a little over three thousand men."

"Out of the 250,000 street soldiers before the collapse, only three thousand followed orders and showed up?" Tavo had hoped for ten times that number.

"Most of our guys were only *affiliated*—we didn't have much of a hold on the affiliated gangbangers. Their loyalty was to their original colors. We had 20,000 men combat trained. Those guys should've made it. I figure the situation in the cities is far worse than here in the desert and that our commandos got stuck. Their initial orders were to soften the cities by fighting cops and national guardsmen. Once they engaged, maybe they had trouble cutting loose from those fights. I don't know, Tavo. Whatever killed the U.S. military definitely took a toll on us too."

Tavo waved away the issue. Three thousand men would be plenty now that they had the Abrams. Alejandro's crew had figured out how to run the M1 Abrams, which turned out to be easier than he had expected. They'd even fired a few shots from the big guns. Turns out, the M1 Abrams main gun wasn't that different from a regular gun.

Tavo angled his flashlight down on the map. "Nevermind the number of men. The three thousand will do fine. We will leave ten tanks here at the Navajo Depot, along with a half-dozen Humvees, and we'll move west toward Las Vegas tomorrow with everything else. We cross the river south of Lake Mead at Hoover Dam. Then we secure the refinery north of Las Vegas and send a contingent to take Hawthorne."

Beto went wide-eyed. "We're going to Hawthorne, as in Hawthorne Army Depot? That's a long, damn way from here."

"It's six hundred miles, give or take," Tavo guessed.

"Two or three tanks of gas..." Beto pointed out, apparently hesitant to weigh in too heavily.

"We'll move on the refinery north of Las Vegas first. That's only one tank of gas from here and we can go with the entire column; everything except a small force to hold the forward operating base here at Navajo Depot."

"Are you sure we shouldn't just head straight for Salt Lake City with half our tanks and all the gas?" Beto studied the map.

"If we get into a fight in Salt Lake like we did at the Artesia refinery, we could run out of gas maneuvering. We could lose tanks. We would definitely run out of AK-47 ammo. Also, the tanks can't make the return trip to Arizona unless we send tanker trucks with them, and the tanker trucks are easy to kill. If we run out of gas and have to walk away from fifty Abrams tanks in the middle of the I-15 corridor, we would be handing those fifty tanks to any Utahn who can figure out how to fuel them. Utah and Wyoming are full of gas. Right now, we're the only kids on the block with baseball bats. We'll win any fight so long as we don't lose any of our Abrams. If we climb out on a limb without the gas to get back, and we're forced to leave the tanks behind, we can expect a much harder fight when we return. We might as well go back to Mexico if that happens. The Utahns have an army depot outside of Salt Lake. They have everything they need to make war, except these tanks."

Beto stood quietly, leaning on the warm hood. He seemed to struggle to take it all in, a former SEAL now planning set piece battle strategy.

"So we don't want to split our force because the halves would be vulnerable? Even fifty of these tanks don't seem vulnerable to me," Beto said without conviction.

"The tanks aren't vulnerable. The gasoline is vulnerable. We could run fifty or a hundred tanks up to Salt Lake City, but then we wouldn't have the gas to get back if the refineries are destroyed. Las Vegas is half as far, and the refinery is located in the middle of nowhere. There are no population centers anywhere nearby. We have the gas to hit that refinery and return," Tavo took the time to explain. Whether he liked it or not, he might eventually have to leave Beto in command of his army while he went home to handle his daughter.

Beto nodded, still trying to do the math in his head. Tavo forced himself to be patient. Not everyone was a genius.

Tavo interrupted Beto's mental struggle. "Put it this way: if we capture the Dry Lake refinery north of Vegas, then we're set to launch straight up the middle of Utah with a limitless source of gasoline at our back and all the ammo we'll ever need from Hawthorne. We'd also be a hundred and fifty miles closer to Salt Lake City. If we fail to take the Dry Lake refinery for some reason, we can still come back here and refuel from Monterrey."

"Okay, *Canoso*. I think I get it. We get two bites at the apple going for Vegas where we only get one bite at the apple going for Salt Lake City." The haze in Beto's eyes made it clear that he didn't really get it.

Tavo didn't feel like belaboring the point. Pretty much everything he had said was bullshit anyway. In truth, he no longer had access to the refinery at Monterrey unless he took the refinery by force, quite possibly burning it down in the process. Tavo needed to take the Dry Lake refinery north of Las Vegas so that he wouldn't have to negotiate with his daughter for Mexican gas. But that wasn't information Beto needed to know. There was no reason to make himself look weak in his lieutenant's eyes by bringing up his problems with Sofía.

He turned back to the map, running through the plan again, looking for anything he might have missed. Complicated plans usually failed. This one had the smell of a complicated plan, but he saw no simple alternatives.

Why did these tanks consume so damned much gasoline?

He felt like a crack addict scouring the countryside for his next fix. He hadn't even bothered to search for smaller fuel sources—gas stations and fuel trucks. The metal beasts at his command burned gas at the rate of fifty thousand gallons a day. He needed quantities of fuel found only on an enormous scale. A single major refinery would provide enough fuel for a year's worth of combat operations ranging into the American west, but the western U.S. wasn't littered with refineries. There were surprisingly few.

"We'll move through the night and roll directly into the Dry River refinery tomorrow morning. It should take us about twelve hours to cross north of North Las Vegas, assuming we don't run into problems."

Beto smiled, probably thinking about how many potential problems the M1 Abrams tank could solve. "Tavo, we have a newcomer," Beto added before Tavo could end the conversation. "He came in with the last of our soldiers rendezvousing with us from the ranch in Sonora. He's another American Special Forces guy, but this dude is really and truly old—like old as you." Beto grinned, probably trying to reawaken some of the camaraderie between them. "I think you should meet him. He's proven useful already."

Tavo raised his eyebrows.

Beto continued. "I think you're going to like this guy. He's a *Norte Americano*, but he's lived on the border of Mexico for twenty years. Our soldiers promised not to hit his local village and that was pretty much all it took for him to come along. He's a broken down, old *cabron* looking for a war to fight."

Beto was rambling and Tavo grew impatient. "I'm sure if you're good with him, I'm good with him," Tavo said, trying to end the conversation. He had problems of his own. He didn't need to vet Beto's new employees.

"Yeah. Okay. He's running a hunter/killer team if you need them. I just thought you'd like to know."

"Great...Let's move out in four hours." Tavo shifted the conversation back to what mattered: namely, gasoline and getting more of it.

"Roger that. I'll get ready to roll." Beto hurried back to his Humvee and went to work mobilizing the armored column.

CHAPTER 34

TAVO CASTILLO
ROUTE 66, TWENTY-FIVE MILES EAST OF KINGMAN, ARIZONA

A hundred gas trucks, ninety tanks, fifty Humvees and fifteen pickups with machine guns drove east on Route 66, lit up like a five kilometer circus train. For the tenth time, Tavo asked himself why he'd brought the whole army for this one, straightforward mission.

Because you don't trust them anymore.

The thought came unbidden, but on some level Tavo already knew it. He'd changed the rules. He'd dropped the charade with his lieutenants and they no longer thought of themselves as the Big Swinging Dicks, with Tavo as their gray-haired mentor. Now they knew exactly who called the shots and nothing would be the same again. War is not the same as business.

Particularly in the drug game, people needed their egos fed. They needed layers of motivation to stay loyal. They needed their heads patted and their bellies filled. Tavo had worked overtime to keep Beto, Alejandro and Saúl thinking they were brothers-in-arms. Now that they were actually at war, he needed subordinates. Otherwise, they would lose the war, plain and simple. The fact that he was tired of pandering to their egos had nothing to do with it.

They never meant anything to you, anyway.

Sadly, it was true. The brotherhood had been a meticulously-crafted strategy meant to keep his lieutenants out front where they would take the bullets when the FBI or CIA kicked in the doors.

That made him think of the attack on the Hotel Filidelfia which reminded him of Sofia. He wondered if she had colluded with his lieutenants in the same way she appeared to have colluded with his father and his half-brother. She and her cohorts had meant to have Tavo captured and to steal his empire. Somehow, in the desert night, with his window down and the hot air carrying the stink of creosote, it was easier to see the corruption his daughter kept so perfectly hidden. Nobody else could see it, but he could, if only around the edges—if only in the wee hours of the morning, with the oily smell of desert chaparral lubricating his paranoia.

The road clicked by. The broken yellow lines flashed in the headlamps at a maddeningly-slow pace.

Tick...Tick...Tick... Tick.

There was no reason to run dark; they were an indomitable force, bristling with machine guns and cannon, driving across the night-blackened sands of the badlands. So the column ran with headlights blazing. Besides, if he ordered them to drive without lights, his moronic foot soldiers would certainly collide with each other and the whole column would end up delayed. Better to run the lights and avoid complications. They hadn't seen an aircraft of any kind in seven days—not since the pair of warthogs shot past over Buckeye. They hadn't even seen the contrails of a passenger jet.

Dead vehicles littered Route 66 like desiccated beetles, their guts spilled on the shoulder and strung out across the road. Strangely, Tavo hadn't seen a single dead body, though he was certain that the passengers of the cars had wandered off somewhere to die. It wasn't as though they'd found salvation in the desert. There was no food or water. He wondered where people went to finally die, when all other options for survival shriveled in the sun. Did they crawl under a bush? Tavo scanned beneath the rare, desultory shrub as they rolled past, finding nothing but rocks.

A flicker of red light caught his eye, two kilometers distant. The only thing he could imagine that would make such a light would be another vehicle.

Maybe a rancher fleeing his convoy?

Tavo leaned forward onto the dashboard, causing the Humvee driver to sit up straight. Tavo saw the red light again.

"Break formation and run ahead," Tavo ordered the driver. Their Humvee swung into the left lane and sped ahead, easily passing the other Humvees and trucks. The column could only sustain forty-five kilometers per hour. The Abrams tank could go faster, but they'd suck even more gas if they pushed it.

Tavo waved the driver forward, urging him into the desert night out from under cover of the guns of the column. The driver gave him a darting glance and Tavo urged him on again. The red light had disappeared, but Tavo thought he saw where the vehicle had been. A slight haze of dust hung over a turnout on the left side of the highway.

The Hummer pulled into the turnout. The dusty haze was unmistakable in the Humvee's headlamps. He ordered the driver to stop and stepped out. His hand drifted to his handgun. He found himself on an elevated rise, the highest point for miles. He didn't see any indication of a ranch house anywhere in the black folds of the nighttime wasteland and the red lights had disappeared.

What he'd seen had been a vehicle out ahead of their column—probably someone tracking their movement. Seeing the red light in the distance had been sheer luck.

"Actual to Roadrunner."

"Go for Roadrunner," Beto replied on the radio.

"Someone's shadowing our column from in front," Tavo said. "Looks like one vehicle based on the tracks. Probably a Jeep." Tavo kicked the dusty ground.

"Don't see what good it'll do them," Beto remarked. "Not unless they have a mechanized infantry unit or an air wing. And if that were the case, they wouldn't be shadowing us. They would've hit us and we'd be hamburger."

Tavo thought through the implications. He thought about the ambush in Tucson and the devastating sniper fire in Artesia. He couldn't envision how starving American refugees could screw with a column of tanks and fifty armed Humvees. But then again, he'd underestimated them before.

"Roadrunner. Send your hunter/killer team ahead to my position at the top of the rise. Actual out."

They finally arrived at Hoover Dam. As dawn colored the eastern sky milky grey, Tavo took in the massive, two-prong traffic jam that blocked their way across the Colorado River. Thousands of vehicles packed the roads and the shoulder as far as the eye could see, trailing back toward Las Vegas.

Even with the light barely coloring the dam, the scale of it astounded Tavo. The cool morning air mixed with the booming mist more than two hundred meters down on the bottom of the canyon, churned up by relentless gravity and giant turbines. He considered the millions of man hours and billions of dollars in material that had been consumed to build such a concrete monster.

In this moment, Tavo owned it. For the sheer fact that he stood over it with a hundred Abrams tanks, he possessed this hulking wonder and every watt of electricity it produced. In so many ways, military conquest was the most productive endeavor of man. Tavo's net worth had doubled just by standing on this spot with the tanks to his back. No wonder war had been so common throughout history.

"Push the cars out of the way," Tavo ordered Beto, standing beside him.

"Roger. A few of the tanks have plows for this situation. I've already sent them down to the bridge to clear a path. We should be mobile again within an hour or two." Beto's understanding of the American military had been useful in dozens of ways. He knew volumes that Alejandro and Saúl didn't, due to the fact that he'd been part of the greatest war machine on the planet. Just knowing that a company of tanks would also have mine-clearing attachments was proving a game-changer.

From their vantage high on the canyon wall, the rising light seemed to give up hope as it filtered its way into the maw of the gorge. The white face of Hoover Dam lightened by minuscule degrees. The churning waters at its base were now barely discernible in the dawn. Cars had lined up on the dam, blocked by an abandoned Humvee that the army must've positioned there when things collapsed. Another vehicle looked like it had busted through the rock wall and hung precariously over the Lake Mead side of the dam. The two lanes on top of the dam were hemmed in by stone walls and a fifty meter drop on one side, a two hundred meter drop on the other.

A bridge had been built just south of the dam, with two lanes and a robust shoulder on each side. Empty cars jammed every inch of the bridge, but Tavo watched as the plow-equipped tanks began to shovel the dead cars up and over the railing. The vehicles cartwheeled slowly in the air before smashing into the steep sides of the canyon or splashing into the Colorado River. Occasionally, a car would get hung up on the spiky protuberances on the plow edge, and the Abrams would have to shuffle back and forth until the vehicle un-impaled itself. The plows had been designed for mine clearing, not road clearing. In any case, the spikes on the plows were costing them time. The tanks would need every minute of two hours to get the road cleared, probably more.

"We found 'em," said an old white man, wearing a tactical vest trudging up the road toward Tavo and Beto. "We found their rig. They crossed the dam on foot," he reported. Three of Tavo's combat-trained commandos accompanied the old man.

"Tavo, this is Ben Madison. The American veteran I told you about last night," Beto introduced the old man to his boss.

"Thank you for joining us." Tavo slipped back into his habit of charming those who served him.

"I had no previous engagements," the man answered and accepted Tavo's outstretched hand. "That Toyota Land Cruiser back there is still warm, so that would be your shadow. Nobody in it, of course. The driver left on foot. His spoor points west across the dam. I estimate he's about forty-five minutes ahead of us."

"Thank you. He'll take up a position somewhere between here and Vegas to observe. We'll get another shot at him now that we know what we're looking for." Tavo stared into the distance, trying to spot the man through the haze of the early morning.

"Oh, we won't see him again, I'll wager. I know his type. I'm surprised we saw him in the first place." The aging warfighter smiled at Tavo, unafraid. The dusty veteran turned around and his gangbanger companions turned with him, walking back toward their place in the waiting column.

Tavo noticed a slight disharmony in the man's report and he considered the possibility that he was an infiltrator. The odds of that were hardly any greater than the odds that Beto, Saúl or

Alejandro were working cross-purpose against him too. At least the old man was a snake in-the-open. He was definitely holding something back. Tavo could keep him where he would do no harm. His thoughts turned to the harm his daughter might be doing back in Mexico in his absence.

None of that would matter after he captured this next refinery. The Vegas facility would be even better than Tucson or Artesia. It put them closer to the heart of the intermountain west. Between the snow-choked passes of the Rocky Mountains and the impenetrable California High Sierras, Tavo would have a full season to take territory before anyone could send troops or mechanized infantry into Utah, Nevada, Idaho, eastern Oregon and eastern Washington. Without snowplows clearing the roads, that vast tract of land would become a forty-five million square kilometer ice fortress. By spring, he'd own a country inside a country. Tavo smiled thinking about it. It would be a nice upgrade from owning a drug cartel. The land and the capital improvements alone were worth trillions of dollars.

Tavo pulled the satellite phone from his vest and stepped away for a moment's privacy.

"Report," he ordered as his recon team answered the satellite call from the other side of Las Vegas.

"The Dry Lake refinery is intact, *Señor*. Nobody coming or going. As far as we can tell, there aren't even security guards."

"Kill anyone—*and I mean anyone*—who comes within a thousand yards of that refinery. We'll join up with you in three hours. Acknowledge."

"Acknowledged. Aguila, out."

CHAPTER 35
NOAH MILLER
LAKESHORE ROAD, BOULDER CITY, NEVADA

Noah looked back for a last glance at Hoover Dam as he turned the corner in the canyon. The towering rock on both sides of the carved-out canyon glowed burgundy in the dawn. Two Abrams tanks lumbered down the bridge toward the traffic jam on the opposite side of the Colorado River canyon and began shoveling dead vehicles over the side.

Noah had left his Land Cruiser on the other side of the gorge and hoofed it across the bridge with just his rifle and his "get home bag." That'd been the easy part. He pushed himself to the limit as he marched up and out of the Colorado River Canyon, feeling every bit of Jack Daniels he'd drunk in the last two years. The roadway was choked with abandon cars, but he didn't see a soul. The owners of the vehicles must've fled toward water. Though the dam was surrounded by a glistening lake, it lay hundreds of feet below the edge and it was surrounded by cliffs for miles. Thirsty people would be forced to loop back toward the town of Boulder and cut north to get to the backside of Lake Mead. He commiserated with them, knowing the half-gallon of water in his backpack wouldn't last very long once the sun began its relentless toil.

When he was just out of high school, Noah and a few buddies—all of whom had abandoned the borderlands for the big city in the years that followed—had taken to making weekend "fun runs" to Las Vegas. As a result, he knew this road and knew the way into Las Vegas from the east. He also knew that winter, spring, summer or fall, when the sun hit the roadway, this area would be a cast iron bitch. He needed to get clear of the coming heat, but more than that, he needed to figure out where the cartel would go once it cleared the Hoover Dam Bridge. He deduced that they'd be looking for large stores of gasoline, since that had been their focus in New Mexico, but he didn't know where to find refineries in Las Vegas. He'd only ever gone straight from the dam to the casinos on the Strip. There weren't any refineries on that road that he could recall.

Weaving through the cars that jammed every inch of roadway, he climbed out of the Colorado River gorge and came upon the Hoover Dam Lodge at the lip. More a casino than a "lodge," the parking lot marked the upper edge of the traffic jam.

He didn't know much about traffic, but there had to be certain physics to the phenomenon. How did a bunch of cars, moving along at the same speed, become gridlocked?

In the case of the Hoover Dam Bridge, the answer had been obvious. Two cars had collided on the way up Highway 93 on the Arizona side. The wrecked cars had probably stopped in the narrow pass and waited for "the authorities" to come to sort out fault and insurance. Of course, no authorities were forthcoming, given the total collapse of civilization. A paralyzing fear of being denied by insurance, or charged with hit and run, had led to a ten thousand car traffic jam. Every car thereafter met the traffic jam unaware of its semi-permanent state and the concrete barrier between the east and westbound lanes offered them no options. By the time they figured out that the car in front of them wasn't moving at all, there were half-a-dozen cars behind them. When cars began running out of gas and when people began abandoning their cars for water, undoubtedly taking their keys with them, the traffic jam went from semi-permanent to set-in-stone.

But the Hoover Dam Lodge had been where urban idiocy met common sense. Almost two miles upstream from the initial wreck, anyone who stopped at the lodge could plainly see the serpentine traffic jam ahead of them. At the same time, the parking lot of the lodge expanded the two lanes of the interstate into a paved bulge. With the extra room to turn around, even the most foolish motorized moron could find a way out of the trap.

As he approached the parking lot, two latecomers pulled up to the traffic jam, figured out the futility of crossing the bridge, made messy turnabouts and zoomed away back up the hill toward Boulder, Nevada. Even more than two weeks after the crash of the stock market, people were still attempting to flee Las Vegas by car.

A sick feeling cooked in Noah's stomach, the combination of two years of shoddy fitness and the gut-burning climb up the hill from the bridge. Just then, the sun peaked over the far side of the Colorado River gorge and gave him his first taste of the coming heat. There and then, he decided he best not dick around.

As he walked up to the turnout to the lodge, a fancy, gleaming-black truck roared out of the parking lot. The bed was crammed with belongings and the cab held a small family. Noah caught the panicked expression of the rotund father behind the wheel, looking for all the world like a fat rabbit trying to escape a fox. Noah jumped into the bed of the pickup truck and held on to an antique desk the family had rescued from the apocalypse.

Rather than stomp on the gas, the driver froze. The big black

Dodge idled, and Noah waited while the man dithered. Finally, Noah leaned out and looked in the driver's side mirror. He could literally see the whites of the man's eyes and both of his hands clamped on the steering wheel. Noah gave him a wave and flashed his best shit-eating grin, as though nothing whatsoever was amiss. The man had certainly seen the 30-30 slung over his shoulder and combined with the friendly gesture, it must've fried a circuit in his brain. *What does one do when an armed man hops in the back of your pickup truck and waves at you?*

Noah smiled even bigger and waved the man forward, hoping to get the situation off high center with bullshit self-confidence. A second later, the truck went into gear and drove on, crossing the interstate back toward Vegas.

A mile later, the truck took a right onto Lakeshore Road—the most likely route back toward Lake Mead. The family was either looking for water or another way across the Colorado River. Noah still didn't know where he was going, but he felt good about the direction, even though they were leaving the interstate. Every turn away from a main road meant a greater chance of losing the column, but this turn jibed well with his mental map of the area.

From what little he knew about Las Vegas, he seemed to recall that there was nothing but desert and solar power plants to the west—on the blighted highway coming in from Los Angeles. He was fairly certain that there were no refineries between Hoover Dam and Sin City given his high school forays down that road. That left only the desert north of Vegas, heading toward Saint George, Utah. Noah would put his money on it—Las Vegas needed fuel storage of its own, given the distances to other population centers. Assuming that, the nastiest land where one might park an ugly refinery would probably be to the north of Vegas; just off Interstate 15 if memory served. He knew it was open, arid land, with an Air Force Base and a motor speedway; the perfect mix of industrial sites for a refinery. If his mental map was to be trusted, taking a clockwise turn around Lake Mead would shortcut the distance between the dam and the north fringes of Las Vegas.

Plus, it felt right.

The rush of feel goods was quickly followed by a rush of dread. The last time Noah followed his "inner child," thousands had died a gruesome death. He closed his eyes and took a deep breath—a breath full of guilt and shame. Once again, sitting atop a family's belongings in the back of their pickup truck, he'd used his homespun good looks and sparkling smile to bamboozle innocent people. Hopefully, he wouldn't get this family killed too.

He opened his eyes and saw a sign whip past with a white grocery sack hung up on the corner, flapping in the wind. He pounded the side of the pickup and the driver hit the brakes, probably as a reflex. When the truck whinnied to a stop, Noah hopped down and gave the family another bullshit wave. The driver stomped on the gas and roared away.

He backtracked to the sign and saw what his subconscious mind had likely noticed already. The sign read, "Kern River Gas Pipeline." The grocery bag still burbled in the breeze, alive but unable to take flight. He stepped back from the sign and took in the bigger picture. The sign had been posted in the middle of a fifty-foot wide disturbance in the desert floor. Some time in the not-too-distant past, Kern River Company had dug a gigantic trench around Lake Mead for their pipeline. Given that the pipeline ran north-south, and given that it lay on the west side of the Colorado River, he guessed that it probably carried fuel products from the oilfields in Wyoming to the fuel-users of Southern California. He didn't know much about oilfields or pipelines, but he guessed they would always carry fuel from the source to the market. In the case of the American West, the large markets hustled and bustled on the California coast--and may God have mercy on their souls.

If logic held, and if the map in his mind was correct, he thought he could probably track this pipeline easement back toward some kind of refinery in or around Vegas. In other words, he'd landed exactly where he'd need to be in order to get out ahead of the cartel—assuming they were, yet again, trying to score gasoline.

He watched the grocery sack flutter for a moment, pitting fact and superstition against one another in a mental struggle. So much had changed and so much had gone to shit over the last two weeks. If Bill had been there, he would've kicked Noah's ass. Noah had "jumped track" so many times, he'd lost count. He had ranged ahead, relying on brazen guesses and "gut reads" and, to his credit, he'd managed to stay out ahead of the column of Mexican cartel. But his method had been shoddy—half-steeped in grief, hope, and a fortune teller's fake science. Thousands had died on his watch, and he was pretty sure he was one hundred percent to blame. Without him bringing in the pissed-off Texans with their huge-ass rifles, the town of Artesia might still exist today. There was just no way around that fact. Noah had pulled the levers that had led to the flaming death of an entire town.

Yet, he wasn't ready to off himself. He wouldn't eat the end of his rifle, as alluring as that did sound. Not yet, at least. If he wasn't going to drown himself in sorrow, he needed a way forward and there were precious few facts to inform his decisions. Like the way his eye had caught the Kern River sign and marked it, in a split-second, as a critical waypoint—he would need more of those blurry talismans to guide his way. Otherwise, he'd be hunting around aimlessly in the desert like a man trying to find his car key in a pocket full of bolts. He was one man conducting surveillance from in front of a brutal, murderous invader with *fucking tanks*. If he didn't deserve a little gosh darn divine intervention, he didn't know who did. God could exact bloody penance on him for his arrogance later. For now, they had a column of narcos to kill. As much as he felt like a piece of shit, he also felt like God, or whomever, still looked over his shoulder like a stern father—flabbergasted at His son's foolishness, but not willing to turn His back.

Maybe it was just this all-fired beautiful sunrise that was making him feel optimistic. Noah sighed and rubbed his nose. He'd done so much second-guessing since Bill died that he wanted to punch himself in the face, if just to get his onboard computer working right.

But he didn't punch himself in the face. Instead, he looked around and took in the sunrise. The lake shimmered like the apocalypse never happened. As the sunlight hardened, he spied about a zillion people piled up on the shoreline like tiny mice. Their cars, trucks and campers littered the sand and overwhelmed what used to be an orderly campground. Noah had wondered where all of Las Vegas had gone, and now he knew. They'd gone to the lake.

It made sense: Vegas would've probably run out of water five minutes after the power died. Even stupid people from Las Vegas knew where the water waited when it wasn't in their pipes. It waited in Lake Mead.

Noah had no desire to mix it up with the desperate hordes from Las Vegas. He eyed the road warily, praying that it would cut around the shoreline, and avoid the teeming masses. Given the rise and fall of the lakeshore in dry years and wet years, he doubted the engineers had run the road close to the waterline. There was a good chance that the road circumnavigating the lake might be free of traffic and free of idiots. In any case, there was no chance he would be able to walk to North Las Vegas and still beat the cartel to the refinery, if there was one. He didn't know how far it would be, but he knew his water would run out by mid-afternoon if he attempted to beat the sun at its own game.

That meant stealing a car. By the looks of the mayhem down by the water, he didn't figure stealing a car to be overly difficult.

God would just have to add Grand Theft Auto to his growing bar tab of sin.

———

Noah didn't have to use his theoretical knowledge of hot-wiring in order to steal a ride. He picked out the closest thing to a Land Cruiser, an early model Jeep Cherokee, found the keys dangling from the ignition, and drove away. The owner must've been camped down by the shore, because there wasn't anything but trash inside the Cherokee. It even came with a half-tank of gas.

Thank you Sweet Baby Jesus for this stolen ride. Amen.

Noah wasn't much for praying, but he tended to talk to the sky when he felt cheery.

Ten miles later, he'd made his way around Lake Mead and was heading into the desert—every inch of shore had been packed with refugees. Lakeshore Drive gave way to Northshore Road and cut west away from the lake.

Kern River had unlimited desert options for its pipeline, so they'd laid it as close to paved road as they could. He tracked the yellow poles marking the pipeline every hundred yards. So far, so good. When Northshore Road split off from the lake, so did the pipeline. It headed north, exactly as Noah's "inner child" had predicted.

The road dipped down, crossed an emerald wash with a rivulet of water and continued north into the badlands. Again, the road split and so did the Kern River pipeline. Ten miles of uninterrupted, sun-scorched road later, Noah rolled to a stop.

The road had been bending west for five miles and he didn't want to go west. He wanted to go north. The Kern pipeline had abandoned the blacktop and had disappeared into the desert, heading toward where he imagined North Las Vegas to be; on the other side of a looming, brownstone mountain.

The split in the road didn't look like a public road. A large sign marked it as the "PABCO Gypsum Mine, which Noah didn't have any trouble believing since the desert sparkled a desolate white color off in that direction. If he wasn't mistaken, gypsum was the white, chalky crap they used to make drywall. He had no desire to drive down a private road that'd end in a mine, but the fork in the road headed north and the pipeline had gone north.

Huffing in frustration, he made the turn and rolled toward the mine. Miles later, a gigantic facility rose in the distance, tucked into a depression in the desert. He pulled over and scanned the mine with his binos. He immediately found a Humvee with a turret-mounted machine gun blocking the access road. Two men in camouflage sat on the ground on the shady side of the Hummer. Another truck, also military, was parked with its ass-end up against a warehouse loading dock on one of the big, white buildings. A guy in camo waited by the driver's side door of the truck with an AR-15 dangling from a sling.

Noah suppressed the urge to barrel down to the soldiers and start whooping about the invading Mexicans. Instead, he did another, careful, scan of the mine facility. The paved road led both into the mine and back out on the far side. A half-mile on the other side of the mine, the pipeline easement reconnected with the road. There, another Humvee stood guard. To the north of the mine, a massive solar field sparkled in the sun. Other than the Hummers and the truck, he saw no human activity.

His current mission already had a "Hail Mary" aspect to it, so he didn't hesitate to drive down the road and talk to the men behind the Humvee. He certainly wasn't going to drive back and head west into Vegas. If he had to go the long way around, he'd never beat the cartel. It was this or nothing. If they blasted him, so be it.

The soldiers jumped up and manned the belt-fed machine gun long before Noah's Jeep approached their roadblock. One man stood behind an open door while the other aimed the mounted machine gun at Noah.

Leaving his 30-30 and his go bag in the Jeep, Noah parked, stepped out and approached with hands held high.

"Turn around and go back the way you came," the soldier behind the door shouted.

"No can do, soldier," Noah yelled as he kept walking. "You've got bigger problems than me coming down this road. Not far behind me are a hundred M1 Abrams tanks and a couple thousand Mexican cartel."

The words didn't seem to penetrate. "Turn around, go back to your vehicle and leave."

Noah stopped within talking distance of the Hummer. "Son. Stop doing your job and just listen. I shit-you-not: there is an army of Mexican cartel coming across Hoover Dam right now and they have Abrams main battle tanks. I don't know how they got them, but I know they are just fine killing Americans. I watched them wipe an entire town off the map three days ago. Whatever you're doing here, you need to shift fire and focus on the bigger picture—or you will all be dead by sundown. Do you copy, soldier?"

It seemed to get their attention. The gunner and the negotiator conferred in hushed tones. The negotiator leaned his head toward his chest-mounted radio, probably getting orders.

"Follow us. Don't do anything stupid or we'll waste you." The negotiator boarded the Hummer and turned it around. The turret pivoted and the machine gun pointed directly at Noah as he climbed aboard his stolen vehicle. The Hummer and the Cherokee rolled down the road toward the mine.

When they reached the loading dock, an older gentleman in camouflage stepped out of the shadows of the warehouse where he'd been enjoying the shade. Noah parked and walked up to the dock while the soldier behind the big machine gun laboriously tracked him.

"Mister Cowboy. Would you mind repeating what you told my men?"

Noah had forgotten that he was wearing his Stetson. The military officer on the loading dock had ordered him to talk with only the slightest pretense of courtesy. Apparently, things were just as tense here as everywhere else. Noah could tell the man was a captain, but he wasn't clear if he was army or another branch of the military. Either way, there wasn't much to be said.

"Sir, there are at least two thousand drug cartel soldiers coming north over Hoover Dam and they have about a hundred M1 Abrams tanks. They're murdering sons of bitches and I can guarantee that they plan to ruin your weekend."

The officer wiped sweat from his mustache. "It's not that I don't believe you, Cowboy, but I happen to know for a fact that Mexico doesn't have Abrams tanks."

Noah stepped up to the edge of the loading dock to get out of the direct sunlight. The machine gun adjusted its point of aim.

"I don't know where they got them, but I've been running ahead of them all night from Flagstaff to the Colorado River. Unless I'm going blind, they've got a hundred tanks, half a hundred Humvees and a shitload of trucks with machine guns."

The officer waved away the barrel of the belt-fed and sat down on the edge of the loading dock. "Well, if what you're saying is true that's bad news. How do I know you're not full of shit?"

Noah tipped his hat back and read the man's name tag. "That's easy, Captain Sparks. Wait around with your dick in your hands for another few hours and those narcos will come by and blow the shit out of you and your boys. Then you'll know."

The officer smiled, but his eyes looked like they were working the problem. "I guess it doesn't much matter either way. We don't have anything at the base that'd stop an Abrams tank."

"Which base?" Noah asked.

"The only base around here: Nellis AFB. The powers that be scrambled all our aircraft and consolidated them in bases away from population centers. It's a good thing too, because the good people of North Las Vegas overran Nellis four days ago. They picked it clean."

"Then what are you doing here?"

Captain Sparks hardened his eyes and ignored the question. "We fell back to Lake Mead Base and tightened the security team around a smaller perimeter that we could defend."

Noah could tell he was withholding information, but there wasn't time to figure it out.

"Whatever you're defending, Captain, I think you're going to lose it. Once they refuel, the narcos will get back to what looks to be their primary mission: finding more bad ass weapons. So far, they're batting a thousand and we are out of time." Noah knew he was bullshitting to some degree. He didn't really know what the cartel's intention was, other than fueling their gun platforms. He just knew they'd targeted a refinery and a weapons depot in the last week. It was a fair bet they'd stick with the program. The best way to determine what a tracking target would do next was to look at what the target had done before.

The Air Force captain chewed hard on the information and kept his eyes locked with Noah's. He peppered Noah with questions about the cartel's activities, Noah's eyewitness observations and then drilled down relentlessly on Noah's background. Fifteen minutes later, Noah felt like he'd been interrogated.

"So you think they're going for the refinery?" Captain Sparks summed it up.

"That'd make sense. They didn't get much out of the refinery in Artesia. Not after we shot it up. I assume there's a refinery north of Vegas?" It was the one piece of the puzzle Noah didn't know for sure.

"Yup. Dry Lake." The captain hopped down from the loading dock. "I'm going to level with you, Mister Cowboy. We could line up all twenty of our base security Humvees against even one M1 Abrams and we wouldn't even slow it down. That tank would go through us faster than shit through a tin goose."

"You've got no aircraft. No tanks. No TOW missiles…Sounds like you've got nothing but dress up clothes," Noah pressed.

Captain Sparks laid back the green canvas tarp covering the Deuce and a Half truck that'd been sitting next to them. "I wouldn't *exactly say* we've got nothing."

Noah looked inside. At first, he didn't quite know what he was seeing.

He turned back to the Air Force captain. "If we're going to do anything, we have to do it now. How many men do you have?"

"Fifty base security men and another forty locals we're paying with MREs to work base security, but I can only send some of them."

Noah pointed in the bed of the truck. "Can I have all this and half the men?"

"I'm not going to place my men under the command of a civilian I barely met. You can have any of the civilians you can talk into it, and I'll send half my airmen under the command of my first lieutenant. And, Mister Cowboy, I can assure you that my lieutenant will shoot you dead if he finds out you're fucking with us to any degree. Is that clear?"

"My name is Noah Miller, by the way, and I hope I'm wrong about the armored column coming here, but I really don't think I am." He returned the hard stare. "I was there to see the genocide they committed in New Mexico. If you knew what I knew, you'd be sending *all* your men and commanding them yourself, Captain."

"No, I wouldn't, Mister Miller. I'm under orders you wouldn't understand."

Noah had no idea what he meant. But he did understand the sentiment. He'd spent the last two weeks under orders he didn't understand too.

―――

"They got a hundred Abrams tanks?" a man at the back of the room voiced everyone's incredulity. He wasn't wearing a uniform, but he didn't look like a stranger to firearms, either. He wore a cowboy's plaid shirt, cowboy boots, Wrangler jeans and he cradled an over-under shotgun across his lap.

"Affirmative," Noah answered.

The old cafeteria exploded in conversation. Without air conditioning, it had to be over a hundred degrees and Noah was sweating like two rats screwing in a wool sock.

At least this cafeteria had been built before air conditioning, Noah thought to himself. *Modern buildings were absolutely hotboxes now that HVAC had gone the way of the brontosaurus.* He glanced around for clues as to how they'd managed indoor circulation before modern refrigeration. He had no idea.

Noah stood on a small stage at the front of the cafeteria beside the base captain and he did his best to reign in the distractions that beset him. Standing in front of a room full of fighting men was literally the *last place* he wanted to be.

That damned grocery sack...

Captain Sparks had called everyone together in the base cafeteria the moment they'd arrived from the gypsum mine. An understanding of the situation evolved in Noah's mind.

This small force of a hundred men, give or take, had pulled back from the massive Nellis Air Force base back to the vintage, 1950s base at the north end of the property. It appeared to have been the air base when the Air Force still fielded prop fighters and bombers—the runways far too short for modern aircraft. It was a miniature version of the modern base, and because of the geography and the roads, it'd been much easier for base security to hold this piece of ground than the full footprint of Nellis. But why were they holding the base at all? Why hadn't everyone just gone home like Noah had seen at the Tucson National Guard airfield?

Captain Sparks shouted for order and the room quieted.

Noah continued. "I believe the narcos are trying for the Dry Lake Refinery. I'm ninety-nine percent sure that they need the gas. If we move fast, we can destroy the refinery right now and deprive them of their objective."

"Where are the tanks right now?" a young airman asked.

"I don't have eyes-on the tanks, but I believe they're about three hours out from Dry Lake, moving across Henderson and North Las Vegas. They're being forced to clear the roads ahead of themselves."

The desert rat at the back spoke again. "Yeah, but if we blow up the refinery, we'll still have an armored column and two thousand gangbangers on our doorstep—more pissed off than a kicked rattler. What about the nukes? We can't stop tanks, Captain."

Noah turned to the captain and gaped. He knew nothing about any nukes.

"Gentlemen," the captain interrupted, "please remember operational security." The captain sighed and turned to Noah.

"We're defending nuclear ordnance. That's our mission here. The Air Force didn't have time or assets to relocate the Level Six munitions stored at this base. They're underground in bunkers between our current position and the solar field we passed on our way here."

Another crusty-looking civilian interrupted. "If those *criminals* can get American tanks running and gunning, they can probably get the nukes working too. What's a drug cartel going to do with nukes? We got families here, Captain. They ain't dying in a nuclear fight. I ain't going to let that happen."

Captain Sparks shook his head. "Nuclear munitions don't work like that, Bobby. They require fire codes and technical expertise in order to arm them."

Even Noah could see that nobody in the room was entirely convinced. They were probably all thinking the same thing: *if narcos could figure out the M1 Abrams main battle tank, given enough time, they could almost certainly figure out the nuclear warheads.*

Reading the room, Captain Sparks sighed and put his hands on his hips. "Can we bring the refinery down on top of them, Mister Miller? You've seen this before. Can it be done?"

"It doesn't matter. We have to try," the man with the shotgun shouted from the back of the room. "We gotta do all the damage we can, even if we all die in the process. Fuck those dirty sons of whores. We're all walking dead men anyway. Let's burn 'em."

The room erupted in agreement. Captain Sparks raised a hand.

"Gentlemen. I hear you loud and clear. There's not a single coward in this room and we're all willing to sacrifice our lives to protect our families. But there's a smart way to do this and a dumb way to do this. If we're going to die, let's make it count... Mister Miller, how do we make it count?" The Air Force captain turned to Noah.

Noah felt way, way outside his pay grade. He was being

asked to risk lives again, and he'd promised himself he wouldn't get sucked into that. Not after what happened to Artesia. Still, it made sense. Of everyone in that room, he was the only man who had faced the *narcos* on the field of battle. Apparently, the captain felt the same. The men in that room were clear on the risks, and they had no illusions about the suicidal nature of their mission. No matter if Noah was a fresh-faced fraud or not, he had been here before, and that made him the smartest man in the room.

God help them all.

———

For better or for worse, the die was cast. Men poured out of the cafeteria, each one to the fight that would define his life.

"Sir. Hold on..." Noah pushed through the crowd and caught up with the cowboy. The man spun around when Noah put a hand on his shoulder. He looked lost in thought, which made sense given that he'd just volunteered to die.

"Brother," Noah handed the man his 30-30 rifle. "How about we swap guns, just for tonight? I'm guessing you know how to run one of these..."

The aging cowboy accepted the 30-30 and traded Noah his over-and-under shotgun. The cowboy ran the lever on the 30-30, ejected a live shell and caught it spinning in mid-air with his right hand.

"Yep. I hunted whitetail with one of these for thirty years back in Oklahoma. My dad hunted with one, and his dad before him. I wish that hunting rifle was here right now in Nevada, but this one will do. It'll do perfectly." The man ran the slide over an empty chamber and reloaded the loose round in the tubular magazine. The cowboy didn't smile, but the sun-worn, wrinkled skin around his eyes bespoke a long look down the hallway of eternity. "I'll buy you time, Mister. You make the time count. Got it?" The cowboy drilled Noah's eyes with his own and Noah nodded. "Is it sighted in?"

"It's dead on-the-nose, sir." Noah dug a box of 30-30 shells out of his pocket with the hand that wasn't holding the shotgun and passed it to the cowboy. The cowboy stuck the box of shells in his Wranglers.

"Hey, you should know that the last time I did this..." Noah waved to the crowd of men preparing for a gunfight, "a lot of good people got killed. I'm probably to blame." He didn't know why he'd just blurted that out. It wasn't the best idea, given they were heading into battle and low morale wouldn't help anyone.

The cowboy stared into Noah's eyes through wind-burned slits. "Good judgment comes from experience and a lotta that comes from bad judgment." The cowboy glanced at the 30-30 in his hands, nodded to Noah, turned and walked out into the merciless sun.

CHAPTER 36
TAVO CASTILLO
DRY LAKE REFINERY, INTERSTATE 15 AND
HIGHWAY 93, FIFTEEN MILES NORTH OF LAS
VEGAS, NEVADA

Tavo called his recon team for the sixth time with no answer. He'd ordered the column to stop at the offramp to the Dry River refinery. From a kilometer away, the refinery seemed intact.

The column had finally arrived at the freeway turnoff at five o'clock in the afternoon. The roads had been choked with dead vehicles from Hoover Dam into Las Vegas and then again, from Las Vegas north to the Dry River exit. At least half of the hulled-out cars had California license plates. In the light of day, Tavo saw plenty of dead people under bushes. A couple times, he saw entire families. The putrescence of death drifted ripe in the autumn heat, cupped by the Las Vegas valley and cooked to perfection by the blazing sun.

That smell filled all space between thought. There was no hiding from it. Not in a car, not in a building, not out in the desert breeze. Even the wind breathed sweet with the curse of it.

The plow tanks had gotten more adept at moving cars without skewering them, but it'd still taken eleven hours to travel the last forty-seven miles to reach the Dry Lake refinery. Based on the absence of smoke, the refinery wasn't on fire. But his men weren't answering Tavo's calls, and that couldn't be good.

Far to the south, Las Vegas smoldered. Like the smoking corpse of the demon of greed, it had been burned on the pyre of Western civilization. No new cars issued from the corpse of Vegas, but plenty had tried to escape this way before the desert claimed them. Tavo's column had come north of the city, but the endless parade of carcasses and sun-scorched vehicles persisted off into the horizon—off toward the gateway to Southern Utah. With all else vacant desert, the line of dead cars pulled Tavo's binoculars back to the only thing worth glassing—the I-15 freeway. It was chock-a-block full of abandoned cars, dead people and the scattered remnants of their lives, but he could detect no living threat on the roadway. The desert stretched blank and lonesome for scores of miles in every direction, eventually rising up into steel-gray mountains that marked the borders of Utah.

"What's up, *Jefe*?" Beto sauntered back to Tavo's Humvee. They'd been stopped there for five minutes. Tavo didn't quite know, so he didn't answer. He climbed on the hood, trying in vain to locate his recon team—or the threat that killed them.

"The recon team isn't answering."

"You think they got ambushed?" Beto jumped to the worst possible conclusion.

The refinery sat about a kilometer off the freeway, but over that kilometer, and for kilometers around the refinery, there was no cover; not a stone nor a bush bigger than a trashcan. The ground ran sandy and flat as far as the eye could see. Still, Tavo knew the desert, and he knew that water had to travel somewhere when it rained, no matter how rare. There would be washes and depressions. An ambush would be waiting in one of those, if there was any ambush at all.

"Maybe they let their batteries run out on the sat phone," Beto suggested.

Tavo dropped his binoculars around his neck. "Would you let your batteries run out if your life depended on it?"

"Me? Of course not... I agree. This doesn't smell right. Then again, nothing has smelled right since Hoover Dam."

Tavo ignored the joke. He needed to order his thoughts, so he spoke them out loud, not really caring if Beto was there to listen.

"The refinery looks intact. Our recon team is likely dead. We have an overwhelming force, but the refinery is sensitive to kinetics. If we hit it hard, we lose it. This refinery isn't nearly as large as Pecos River or Monterrey. We can't afford to shoot in or around it. Nellis Air Force Base is a ghost town, and we didn't take any fire from Nellis when we passed. Any resistance in the refinery would likely be locals. That means they'd be unorganized. But if they're here, they know we want gas. Otherwise, why would they be here?"

"How do we know they're here at all?" Beto wondered, interrupting Tavo's thought process.

Tavo answered out of habit. "We don't know they're here. All we know is that our recon element isn't answering their fucking radio." The thought made Tavo turn and look the way they'd come, south up the Interstate. The column of tanks and trucks stretched back toward Vegas for four kilometers, disappearing over a gentle rise in the freeway.

The front third of the column had been set up to serve as Tavo's war hammer. He'd mixed Humvees, technicals and six Abrams tanks into the lead element. The center section of the column protected the fuel trucks. The rear third held the bulk of the Abrams main battle tanks with a smattering of Humvees as a quick reaction rear guard. No amount of organization could have prepared them for an air attack if Nellis mounted one, but they hadn't seen a single aircraft on the runways. The gates dangled open, the base a dried-out corpse.

"Okay. So what's the play, coach?" Since Tavo had taken command, he noticed that Beto had stopped doing his own thinking, opting to pass all decision-making back to Tavo. With the stakes being so high—total domination or total defeat—Tavo couldn't afford it any other way. But he still didn't like it. Beto had recently led a massive criminal enterprise. He shook his head at how quickly Beto had fallen back to taking orders. The human race was nothing if not predictable. Without a compelling reason for excellence, most every man devolves into laziness. Even life-or-death peril does little to change that sad truth. Tavo hated other men for their obviousness, but he celebrated it too. All of that predictability elevated him to where he stood now: a god among lesser beings.

"Tonight, we clear the refinery with our best assaulters. Tomorrow morning, we send twenty tanks and two hundred men inside the fence to protect the fuel tanks. Then, we make a ring around the refinery about three kilometers across." Tavo painted a loop with his finger in the air around the refinery in the distance. "Once everyone's set, we close the loop and trap anyone hiding inside. If we kick up ambushers in the desert, they'll be surrounded. After that, the refinery will be secure, and we can build permanent defenses and set LP/OPs in a three-kilometer perimeter. This refinery will be much easier to protect than Pecos River. Here, we don't have a town full of refugees pressed up against us, thank God."

"What if they're already inside?" Beto asked. The only cover for kilometers was the refinery—a jumble of tanks and pipes contained by a chain-link fence.

"If they're inside, it's a suicide mission for them. Any fight would bring the refinery down on top of them, with us surrounding it, cutting off any escape. I'm betting nobody is willing to die a flaming death just to defend some gasoline. No matter how ruined up their country is right now, they're still

Americans. They're not Al Queda. They don't sacrifice their lives on faith."

Beto boiled Tavo's plan down to his own terms. "We send an assault force inside tonight to root out any ambushers. Then we surround the refinery with a three kilometer ring and shrink it down until we clear any sleepers in the desert. Right?"

"Correct."

"The guys on the inside ring and the guys on the outside ring will be shooting toward each other if this thing touches off. Are we cool with that?"

"Yes. It's the only way to protect the gas. The gas is worth a thousand men."

Beto turned and watched the sun droop over the mountains to the west, slicing through the pall of smoke coming up from Vegas. The smoke-soaked sun painted everything deep orange. "Should we set our perimeter now and execute at first light?"

Tavo sighed. Beto really had relegated all conscious thought to him. "No. The advantage of attacking at first light would be negatively offset by the disadvantages of having our forces spread out over a thirteen kilometer ring all night. Circle the wagons here at the offramp. Send out the warning order to your assaulters that they'll be assaulting the refinery at 3 a.m. The tanks will move into position at first light and then prosecute when everyone's set. There's no advantage to surprise at this point. The whole world knows we're here."

Beto nodded. "Roger that, Boss."

"Assemble a team of forty assaulters. I want you to lead the hunt. You'll go in under cover of darkness and surgically pick that facility apart with NVGs and thermal monoculars. I want every inch of that refinery eyeballed before we send in tanks. If there's anyone stupid enough to start a gunfight in the shadow of millions of gallons of gasoline, you kill them one-at-a-time with NVGs and precision gunfire."

Beto grinned. "You coming, Tavo? Just like the old days?"

"Not this time. You do it." Tavo didn't feel comfortable putting himself downrange of Beto's M4, particularly not under the cover of darkness. At the moment, Tavo didn't trust anyone, particularly not this grinning fool.

The weather in his head had gone from sunny with a chance of afternoon showers to a storm-laden tornado watch. Being entirely honest with himself, Tavo wondered if his self-imposed isolation and the stress of combat was mucking with the chemical soup in his brain. Maybe it was his suspicions about Sofía. Maybe it was the threat of an ambush. Maybe it was just this horrible, fucking smell. For whatever reason, Tavo's intensity had cranked up to Level Ten.

It'd taken the collapse of civilization for him to find the ways he and Pablo Escobar were actually quite alike. At the end of the day, maybe both men were utterly and truly alone. Maybe when the do-or-die moments arrived, when they stood on the precipice of empire, perhaps destiny demanded utter withdrawal from humankind as its price of passage. An immortal would deny himself his brothers-in-arms. His fellows in faith. Even his family.

Pablo Escobar had been cut down on the verge. He'd been laid low and revealed as another petty tyrant. He lacked the fortitude history demanded for a man to cross over to live forever in the memory of the human race.

Did Escobar know it when he stood at that moment, overlooking the final battlefield that would select him as a man or as a god? Or did he console himself with tales of how other men had failed him or how the Fates had slighted him?

Tavo would overcome whatever history put before him. He could feel it in his gut, and it rumbled and popped like tanks crushing mens' skulls under their treads.

Beto stood beside Tavo with a stupid, curious expression on his face.

"Are you waiting for me to tell you what to do next?" Tavo finally asked.

"No, *Canoso*. Is that all you wanted?"

"Yes."

Beto shifted from one foot to another, waiting for more. It felt like watching a confused, adolescent dog, wandering around the edges of the pack. Tavo understood that he hadn't provided the customary words or body language that would release the underling from this conversation. So, Beto hung on his next words, unsure.

He didn't care. He'd given all the orders necessary and he'd moved on to the next plane of thought. It was no longer his duty to massage the sensitivities of fools. He'd shrugged them off and moved on alone.

When he finished his thought, Tavo returned to his Humvee.

After midnight, the desert cooled slightly. Tavo listened to the mission brief, at the back of the group of commandos standing inside a circle of trucks. He paid close attention to the command frequencies and challenge codes. He would go in with the assault team and Beto wouldn't know it until it was all said and done. Tavo would operate as just another squad member in the dark.

He desperately needed the sleep, but he wouldn't be able to sleep during the assault on the refinery anyway. His plan was to stick himself onto the back of one of the squads and to let them know his identity after they rolled out. He'd join the mission without Beto finding out until later.

Truth was, he felt like getting his gun on. Even if there was no enemy contact, the professionalism and intensity of an assault would smooth his frayed ends. In a best case scenario, he'd get a chance to mix it up with some Americans—maybe deal a couple *Jed Eckerts* out of the deck. Lord knew, those assholes had taken their bites out of him over the last two weeks. He'd take pleasure in ending a few more lives.

———

When the assault finally kicked off at three a.m., Tavo ghosted in behind a team. All his top-tier commandos carried AR-15s and they all had strict instructions to check their backstops, though Tavo couldn't imagine a tiny 5.56 round penetrating the double skin of a fuel tank. The .308 rifles back in New Mexico had penetrated the tanks, but they were three times the bullet weight and twice the powder.

Since they'd crossed the U.S. border six days ago, Tavo had kept his personal assault gear with him in his command Humvee. He pimped himself out with the highest-quality, most-expensive tactical gear money could buy—kit favored by American SOF shooting instructors. As a result, everything he carried was a notch above his commandos. They ran Gen 3 night vision; Tavo carried the newest white phosphor NVGs. They used regular laser pointers; Tavo ran a $3,000 ATPIAL infra-red laser. They wore no armor; Tavo ran with the lightest ceramic armor plates made. Tavo wore or carried $17,000 worth of tactical gear on his person and he would've spent ten times that much if it'd been possible.

It didn't take long for the squad leader to notice the extra guy at the back of his string, particularly an extra guy decked out like *SEAL Team Six*. When the squad leader looped back to find out what the hell was going on, Tavo stopped him with a hand to the chest and lifted his NVGs to show his face.

"I'm Gustavo Castillo. My call sign's *Cascabel*. Tell no one I'm here. Do you copy, soldier?"

"Si, *Jefe*," the team leader instantly pivoted and went back to work toward the front of his team.

Professional and intense, Tavo exhaled his pleasure. Rolling into an assault, he let the freedom of training and instinct carry him.

Gravel crunched under their feet as they passed through the entrance gate and the teams flowed toward their assigned sectors of the refinery. As Tavo's squad turned north along the fence, working their search pattern, they came to a choke point and the squad leader motioned for the squad to stop.

Huge pipes crisscrossed the refinery, connecting a mysterious sequence of storage tanks: long horizontal tanks, tall, narrow tanks and the occasional fat cylindrical tank. From the air, the refinery must've look like a collection of Tupperware, stacked and arranged in orderly rows.

Clusters of pipes crossed the yard horizontally, one on top of the other. The set of pipes in front of the team of commandos ran parallel to the ground, turned down, dipped underground, then popped back up again, continuing toward some kind of junction building. The underground run allowed trucks to pass over to the other side of the refinery. The effect was to create a twelve foot-wide gap in the pipes—the perfect choke point for an ambush.

Tavo moved up to the team leader and rested a hand on his shoulder. Tavo signaled with his hands that he and one other man would cut back, slip through the pipe and circle around the choke point, setting up an "L" counter-ambush against anyone who might be waiting to hit the squad in the gap.

The squad leader nodded his understanding. Tavo motioned for a commando to come with him and Tavo led out, doubling back on their trail.

The stack of pipes wasn't an absolute barrier. A man could slip between the horizontal pipes. Tavo waved for his wingman to go through the pipes first. The man rolled through the gap and the magazines in his vest made the slightest clank as they tapped a pipe. He took up a defensive position behind a metal valve the size of a refrigerator while Tavo slid through the pipes himself.

On the other side, he resumed the lead and wormed his way around a jungle of pipes and tanks. A series of sixty-foot long, horizontal storage tanks forced him to go farther into "Indian country" than he wanted, placing he and his wingman downrange of their own squad. Even though the deeper penetration would force him to shoot toward his own men, and them toward him, it had the benefit of placing them where no ambusher would ever think to look—deep behind them. Tavo considered radioing the squad leader, but even a whisper could blow his deep flank. Each minuscule crunch of gravel thundered in his ears.

As he rounded the end of the last horizontal tank, he found himself so far downrange that the hair on the back of his neck stood straight up. He was far from certain that anyone had set an ambush. In all likelihood, the refinery was abandoned. But he knew for sure that the remaining five men in the team were pointing their rifles directly at him and his wingman. Tavo could see their lasers dancing in the space between him and the team. *Santa Muerte* had definitely joined the party.

Tavo pointed his rifle in the air and drew infra-red circles in the sky, using his ATPIAL laser to mark his position for the team. He didn't know if the men had been trained to know what the air-lasso meant. He'd seen it on American TV, and it seemed obvious, but he didn't have a lot of confidence in the team's level of intelligence. They were former drug dealers, after all.

Tavo waved his wingman forward, grabbed his head and

peeled the IR sticker off the back of his bump helmet. The wingman let him, like a toddler submitting to an angry parent.

The IR sticker could only be seen through NVGs, and the sticker was meant to identify friend from foe. Tavo slapped the man's IR sticker on his own chest.

The squad's laser beams danced around the yard, still hunting for targets despite Tavo's efforts. Unlike his expensive ATPIAL, their lasers could be seen by the naked eye. Anyone laying in ambush knew the team was about to enter the yard.

Still unsure whether he'd draw his own squad's fire, Tavo sucked tight to the big storage tank and shimmied around the bulbous end, slowly opening up "pie wedges" of the yard. Another forest of pipes choked the opposite side, traversing up, down and sideways.

Almost immediately, he saw the shape of a man crouched in the clusters of tubing just opposite him. The man had no IR sticker and appeared completely unaware of Tavo and his wingman. The enemy stared intently at the green laser beams from the far side of the gap.

Tavo keyed his radio three times—the pre-arranged signal for "enemy contact." The squad leader keyed back once, meaning "acknowledged."

The ambusher faced directly away from him, so Tavo hazarded another slice of the pie, side-stepping around the tank and searching even deeper within the tangle of pipes. He picked out another form—a second ambusher.

The blood pounded in his ears and the adrenaline washed over him like the instant after a snort of cocaine.

He held these two mens' lives in his hands, like paper-mâché dolls ripe for crushing. Getting the drop on another man dripped with sweet ecstasy. The gods of Olympus, alone, had enjoyed this dominion over man. Tavo lingered, allowing his adrenaline to ebb, toying with the men's lives. He could either continue "slicing the pie" and come out from behind the storage tank, giving himself a full view of the yard. Or he could start the death-dealing. Once Tavo pulled the trigger, his squad would open fire and the exquisiteness would end.

Should he take the two upon his plate, or search for more?

There hadn't been any shooting yet in the refinery. Nothing disturbed the pregnant pulsing of the moment. Tavo drew it out, like an orgasm held in abeyance, building but never peaking. He shuffled another half-step around the storage tank. He took in the whole of the yard.

Behind a giant wedge of concrete, he found another enemy, also fixated on the squad of assaulters still outside the kill zone. Tavo slipped back to cover and took several deep breaths. Each breath released a scrim of adrenaline. His hands shook and his face tingled, but he knew neither would interfere with the skill he'd honed over the last five years. He'd visited Mount Olympus many times before, and he knew his flesh would ultimately surrender to training.

Despite their professionalism, his squad would shoot at any muzzle flash, friend or foe. Some instincts training could not defeat. The adrenaline wasn't enough to make Tavo forget the truth about combat: men wouldn't concern themselves with downrange friendlies once the shooting started. They'd shoot at anything that moved.

Even inside his Helix suppressor, Tavo's muzzle flash would attract bullets like a corpse draws flies. He needed to hide his muzzle from the squad. Then he could release the hounds.

He slithered back away from the storage tank. He gave up the cover of the heavy metal, but moved deeper so the tank would block his squad's angle of view. He crabbed sideways and laid face-down in the gravel. The two enemies across the courtyard came into view again, and they remained oblivious to his executioner's axe.

It was the best he could do, given the battlefield geometry. His squad would have to fight the third man on their own. Tavo certainly wasn't going to step out into the yard and get his ass shot off for his trouble.

With his blood finally cooling, he eased his safety off. He steadied his IR laser, ignoring the electronic rifle sights. The IR laser would be his Destroying Angel, killing whomever it touched. In Tavo's NVGs, the laser sluiced across the dust of the courtyard, invisibly stroking the doomed men.

Chest, head, groin, head, the invisible laser teased.

Enough stroking...Time to feed.

Tavo exhaled and rocked the trigger.

PFFT. PFFT. PFFT, whip-SNAP, SNAP, SNAP!

Tavo didn't confirm the first three hits. He slid his laser over to the second man, who pivoted around in surprise at the strange snapping behind him.

PFFT. PFFT. PFFT. PFFT, whip-SNAP, SNAP, SNAP, SNAP!

Tavo dumped four rounds into the second man, he flipped backwards over a horizontal pipe and disappeared and shuffled sideways, still laying in the gravel, and hungry to gain a shot on the third man tucked up against the concrete pillar. But his world erupted in chaos before he could get a shot.

BOOM, BOOM-BOOM-BOOM-BOOM-BOOM-BOOM-BOOM...

Gravel leapt off the ground and hammered at his face. A vicious sting sprang up in his right ear. He scrambled for the cover of the storage tank. He felt something slap at his foot and then howling pain shot up from where his middle toe should've been. After an eternity of scrambling in the gravel, he reached the cover of the storage tank, jammed himself behind a concrete support, and peered back around, searching for new targets.

He found the problem. The first man he'd shot was still in the fight, maneuvering *deeper* into the pipe jungle, trying to make a killing shot on Tavo.

whip-SNAP, SNAP!

Tavo's wingman opened up and dropped the ambusher a second time.

Chastened, Tavo leaned out, looking for the second man he'd shot, but still not seeing him. He'd pitched out of view.

SNAP, SNAP, SNAP, BOOM-BOOM-BOOM, SNAP-SNAP-SNAP-SNAP-SNAP...

Tavo's squad must have pushed through the gap and engaged the third man. The pain in his foot had grown into a rip-roaring throb he could no longer ignore. He disconnected the pain from his conscious mind, stood and leaned around the tank into the courtyard, ducking back when a bullet pinged off the storage tank, his own men shooting at him.

"Shift fire, assholes. *Cascabel* is downrange. Acknowledge right now!" Tavo panted into the radio, his pain probably not as "disconnected from his consciousness" as he would've liked to believe.

"Bravo One, acknowledged. Shifting fire."

The shooting died off suddenly and Tavo inched out from behind the cover of the storage tank, dragging his maimed foot. His squad of commandos moved up the yard, several rifles swinging his way. He jerked his IR laser in the air, making desperate circles.

After a few moments of quiet, he felt relatively confident his own men wouldn't shoot him. He stepped into the yard and crossed in front of his advancing squad, casting a wary eye in their direction. Nobody fired. He stalked toward the man he'd killed, and his wingman went to secure the man who'd survived Tavo's first volley.

Tavo found the man sprawled across a pipe, his throat blown open. He wore standard multi-cam fatigues. The pant legs were tucked into his boots, which probably pegged him as a surviving airman from Nellis Air Force Base.

"Bravo *Cinco* for *Cascabel*," someone said in a thick Spanish accent over the radio. Tavo assumed it was his wingman. "Come to me, please, *Jefe*. This one is still alive."

Tavo hobbled toward where he'd seen the first man fall and found his wingman standing over a wheezing American draped against some white pipes, staining them with his blood.

Tavo flipped up his NVGs and switched on the red light attached to the rail on his AirFrame helmet. He wanted to see the man who had cost him a toe with his own eyes.

The red flashlight turned the man's blood black. The American bled from at least five places, any one of which would probably kill him eventually. Tavo's wingman had kicked the man's rifle to the side: a scoped, lever-action 30-30. The ambusher wore a blood-stained plaid shirt and denim pants. His cowboy hat had fallen to the side and the rim was splattered in blood. The American had come to war in leather-tooled cowboy boots.

"Howdy, *partner*," Tavo leered at the dying man.

"Yipee ki yay, drug-dealer," the American shot back. Apparently, not all of the fight had drained out of him yet.

"You know me?" Tavo raised an eyebrow.

"I know you well enough."

"How do you know I'm cartel?" The fact that he knew they were cartel raised interesting questions.

The man just harrumphed. "Heh, heh, heh," he ignored Tavo's question. "How's that ear and that foot feeling?" He nodded at Tavo's own wounds.

Tavo reached up and felt the side of his face. His hair, cheek and neck were covered in sticky blood. A chunk of his ear was missing. The thought of his appearance being altered by this piece-of-shit infuriated him.

"How's it feel to have your guts on the outside?" Tavo gloated. Even in the red light, the mass of shining offal hanging over the man's belt could only be one thing. "I think we'll take a few minutes to work you over a bit before you die. Maybe we can make your last shitty moments in this world even shittier."

"Do your worst, Mexicano." The man chuckled, then fell into a wet coughing fit. Tavo stabbed at the man's exposed guts with his suppressor, pushing the coughing fit into a deep moan.

When he caught his breath, the American spoke. "Hey. Narco Man. When I see you in hell, let's go another couple rounds."

"It's a date," Tavo said as he breach-checked his H&K 416 and clicked off the red light on his helmet. He pulled down his NVGs in order to see the infrared laser sight.

"Until then, suck a bag of dicks," the American spoke into the darkness.

Tavo shot him in the head twice, the spat of the suppressor the last sound the cowboy would ever hear.

CHAPTER 37
TAVO CASTILLO
DRY LAKE REFINERY, INTERSTATE 15 AND
HIGHWAY 93, FIFTEEN MILES NORTH OF LAS
VEGAS, NEVADA

Beto didn't ask why Tavo had joined the assault teams without telling him. In the flat light of late morning, the refinery seemed far less ominous than it had the night before. They'd killed eight insurgent fighters hidden within the refinery and they'd learned precious little for their effort.

Tavo, Beto and the squad leaders circled up in the middle of the refinery to conduct an after-action review.

"So, these dipshits were a mixed bag of airmen from the base and few locals?" Beto ran his fingers through his hair, drying it after wearing a bump helmet all night. "How'd they get organized so fast?"

"The guy in the Land Cruiser," Tavo guessed. "He got out ahead of us."

Tavo hadn't quite finished weighing the consequences of that mistake. He thought of Lexington and Concord at the beginning of the American Revolution. A couple revolutionaries had run out ahead of the British regulars and American partisans had mauled the British as a result. Tavo didn't like being on the shit side of history. Even so, they'd cleared the refinery without losing a single one of his commandos.

"At least that mistake's behind us," Beto said. "We own the refinery. Now all we've got to do is keep it."

Tavo wasn't so sure. "Let's stick to the plan," he contradicted his lieutenant. "We set a three kilometer perimeter, bring armor into the refinery, then close the circle. If anyone's skulking around the desert, I want them run under a tank. We do this one, careful step at a time."

Beto shrugged. "Yeah. Sure. Better safe than sorry." He used a patently American saying, which irked Tavo. Something about Beto seriously grated on him—something bone-deep. But with his ruined toe throbbing like an *hijo de puta*, everything grated on him.

One of the soldiers they'd trained in combat medicine had stitched Tavo's new toe stump closed and dressed it in gauze. Sliding his foot into a new boot had hurt even more than getting the toe blown off. Walking on it proved to be its own sort of hell. But walking on it with hardly a limp sent a message to his men: Tavo was not only smarter, he was tougher. He could see the legend growing in the eyes of the commandos. He was a leader who took the fight to the enemy *personally* and he was a leader who could take a bullet and walk it off like a stubbed toe.

I'd trade a toe for that, Tavo thought. Regardless of the training his lieutenants had received as SOF operators, Tavo had finally risen to their level. Having never served in the armed forces and even at fifty years-old, nobody could deny it: Tavo had become an operator—a gunfighter of the highest order.

"That's it then," Beto wrapped the after-action review. "Assaulters, set up your squads around the outer fence. We'll bring the armor in and spread it evenly around the perimeter. Make the spacing a hundred meters between tanks."

Beto finished the briefing. "Don't shoot until you triple-confirm targets. Any bullet you cut loose is going to rip through our own guys. Shoot only with a clear backstop or let the tanks run the peckerwoods down. Anyone who shoots is going to answer to me later. Got it?"

The men nodded in unison, but the slack expressions on their faces inspired little confidence. If anything touched off during this "Polish ambush," they'd lose men to friendly fire. The knowledge didn't bother Tavo overmuch.

―――

As the Abrams tanks growled through the refinery gate, the heartless sun burned directly overhead. The stink of the roadside dead had begun to blow the other way now that the sun beat down on the desert floor, reversing the winds toward the south. All Tavo could smell was the creosote that the tanks had smashed. It came as a welcome reprieve from the relentless smell of decay.

With the tanks occupying the refinery, optimism took root in his army. The scorching pain in Tavo's foot even retreated a little, subsiding to a dull thunder beneath the pain meds. So long as he kept standing upright, nothing but a bullet to the brain would entirely erase the discomfort. But even the pulsing of his blood in his foot made Tavo smile, a reminder of his invincibility.

"*Cuidado!*" someone shouted overhead. Tavo searched the refinery, shielding his eyes, and they came to rest on a man scurrying down one of the ladders attached to a big fuel storage tank. "There's something up here. ¡*Mira!*"

"What?" Tavo yelled and hobbled toward the fuel tank. A cold fear poured down his spine. "What the *chingada madre* is it?"

"I don't know, but it could be like…a bomb or something," the man dropped to the ground, garbling the last.

Tavo shoved him against the steel of the tank and put a hand to the man's throat. "Tell me, you useless *pendejo*..."

"I don't know what it is. Maybe a bomb," the man shrugged, but his eyes darted about, seeking escape. "I don't know anything about bombs. There are two bricks of clay and some wires..."

"*Dios mio!*" Tavo let the man drop and both of them lurched away from the gasoline storage tank, racing toward open ground. "Get out! Get the Abrams out! Get them outside!"

Tavo called Saúl on the radio as he ran. Saúl had been placed in charge of the armor. "Saúl," Tavo screamed into the radio. "Get the fucking tanks out of the refinery."

"The tanks? The gasoline?" Saúl replied in a panic.

"No, you idiot. The Abrams! Get them outside the fence. Go! *There's a bomb!*"

Tavo shambled clear of the pipes and storage tanks. The Abrams began the slow process of turning. Men sprinted toward the gates.

KA-WHUMP!

WHUMP...THUNK-WHUMP!!

Compression squeezed Tavo like a fist. His ears thundered. His brain reeled.

He looked up from the ground with no clue how he'd gotten there. The back of his head raged in jagged pain. He flipped onto his stomach and worked his knees under him. He heard only bass undertones, no treble. Someone grabbed his arm and tried to drag him upright. Then the man dropped him and kept running.

"Tavo. Tavo...Tavo." The radio broke through his deafness. "Tavo. Come in."

"Go for Actual," Tavo croaked as he lifted himself up and struggled to his feet.

"Are you alive?"

"Of course, *asshole*. What happened?"

"They blew the refinery. Get away!"

Tavo turned toward the wall of heat and took two steps backward. Three of the biggest storage tanks were ripped in half, their fuel dumping in flaming gouts into the trenches around their base. Millions of gallons had blown clear of the big tanks and almost everything burned, the flames worming into seams and cooking through valves, bolts, rivets...

"Get everyone out," Tavo screamed, not thinking to press the button on the radio.

KA-WHUMP!

Another blast threw Tavo to the ground on his back. The ground bucked and he kneed himself in the face. He crawled away from the thunder, scrambled to his knees and ran.

Pop-pop-pop, pop, pop, pop...

Gunfire opened up, but a million miles away. Tavo ran toward the gate as his mind hunted to find itself. The pain in his toe had vanished. His mouth swam with blood. His tongue dragged against the inside of his teeth.

As he passed through the gate, he rounded on the flames and took in the refinery. Hell had sprung up in place of the rust-speckled towers and whitewashed pipes. Lucifer stalked the ground where Tavo had killed two men the night before. Fire burned, unchecked, everywhere.

From where he stood, at least a dozen Abrams tanks were in flames. A charred form emerged from a hatch on the top of a tank, bent over at the waist and slid to the ground where the form went still; a knot of flaming meat.

"Tavo. Tavo. Answer me, Tavo."

"Go," Tavo answered his radio.

"The tanker trucks are being attacked. They're hitting our supply chain. We need armor over here now."

That's Alejandro, Tavo explained to himself. Alejandro had been left with the rear of the column. The gasoline trucks were under attack.

"Copy. Sending tanks."

Tavo hunted around in his chest rig, trying to remember how to switch to his command frequency. Somehow, his hands remembered on their own.

"Beto, come in." He couldn't remember Beto's callsign.

"Go for Fox," Beto answered.

"Get tanks over to the fuel trucks. Alejandro's under attack."

"Roger. Sending armor."

Tavo held his head in his hands, trying to stop the spinning world. He looked around, then forgot what he was looking for. He shuffled over to a concrete barrier by the gate and sat down. The shooting in the distance had elevated, the roaring of belt-fed machine guns rising *fortissimo* in the orchestral movement of a distant battle. As quickly as the belt-feds joined the percussion, they abated. The *decrescendo* tapered to an arrhythmic tinkling of small arms. The tanks hadn't had time to join the battle before the field went silent. The percussion hadn't had time to join the orchestra.

Guerrilla attack. Hit and run.

Tavo slumped on a concrete barrier, confused. Wounded. His head swam. His window to the world went dim. Then, it winked out.

CHAPTER 38

NOAH MILLER
NELLIS AFB, AREA 2, THIRTEEN MILES NORTH OF
LAS VEGAS, NEVADA

Noah's back burned like a sonofabitch. Something flaming hot had landed on him as he took cover from the blast that ripped the refinery to pieces. Still, he counted himself fortunate. Captain Sparks had been next to him in the dry wash, and whatever had hit Noah's back had splashed on Sparks head and chest. Within seconds, it'd cooked the airman's guts and brains. It'd happened so fast, the man was dead before Noah could tamp out the petroleum-fueled gouts of flame.

The inside of Noah's head sounded like a million sparrows chirping at once—like the big ficus tree at his dad's ranch in the summer, right at dusk. The massive overpressure of the explosions had jacked his brain and he couldn't string together two thoughts. While he prayed it'd get better, Noah still felt like the luckiest man alive. He'd just watched eight men die and another man get his brains fried inside his skull. The fact that he walked away from the explosion he'd just triggered seemed like a profound joke. If anyone should've had his head burned to a cinder, it should've been him. He'd been the man most ready to die in this whole fiasco.

Noah didn't know how many others had been killed in the blast and in the ambush on the cartel convoy, but as he neared the back forty of Nellis Air Force Base, he began to see other stragglers stumbling their way back to the base. They'd hit the cartel hard—even killed a few Abrams tanks—but the fight could be far from over. Pretty much every American on the field would fight to the death to keep the nukes out of the hands of the narcos. Blown up and torn up, it still wasn't Miller Time.

"Where's the captain," a fresh-faced lieutenant asked Noah as he passed through the Area Two gate of Nellis Air Force Base on foot.

"He's dead. Can I have some water?" Noah had just run/walked ten miles. What water he'd had in his assault pack had been burned through almost an hour before. The lieutenant handed him an old-school metal canteen.

"How'd he die?" the young officer asked.

Noah choked on a swig of water. "Doesn't matter. How many are left? Get ready for a counter-attack."

The lieutenant took a deep breath. "I guess I'm in command then...I think we're at about fifty men right now. More are coming from the convoy strike. I don't know how many. We lost comms an hour ago. Did you destroy the refinery?"

Noah grinned despite the horror of it all. Despite the man who had burned to blackened flesh before his eyes. Noah's blood rose as he dropped the canteen into the man's hands. A dark grin cut across his face and the lieutenant took a step back.

Never before had Noah personally killed a man. Now, he'd killed scores, if not hundreds. He'd sent the squad that'd killed the narco reconnaissance team. He'd planted the C4 plastic explosives from in back of the truck at the gypsum mine. He'd wired the detonators, just as his old man had taught him. He'd punched the detonator and blew the entire refinery down upon those evil motherfuckers' heads.

Conquistadors

He hadn't spared much thought about how it would feel to kill a man before. But he would've never guessed the jet black exhilaration he felt now in the shadow of the wholesale slaughter of his enemy.

"We murdered those assholes. Hard core. We paid them back for Artesia with interest. A bunch of Abrams went up in flames with them. I don't know how many. I have no idea how the other detachment did against their tanker trucks. I heard shooting but I haven't talked to anyone. We need to set up a perimeter defense the best we can and prepare for a full, armored assault." Noah reached again for the canteen.

The lieutenant's eyes went as wide as saucers. "Sir, there is no way to prepare for an armored assault. If they come at us, we're done."

"Well, then we better hope we fried their command, because what we just pulled off at the refinery was 'best case scenario' for us. God help us if it wasn't enough."

CHAPTER 39
TAVO CASTILLO
INTERSTATE 15 AND HIGHWAY 93, FIFTEEN
MILES NORTH OF LAS VEGAS, NEVADA

"Who were they?" Tavo asked. He struggled to his feet. He understood that he could only access a portion of his brain. Nobody ever explained what it felt like to be blown up. Turns out, it busted a man down to being a fraction of what he once was.

His three lieutenants stood around him in a circle near a shot-up fuel truck. The refinery burned in the distance, a second sun competing for glory with the hazy sun setting on the north horizon.

"Who gives a fuck?" Beto snapped. "They burned up fifteen Abrams, five Humvees, cooked more than fifty men and they *erased* the refinery. They were shit-eating American insurgents. Who do you *think* they were?"

Tavo would address the disrespect at some future moment. He made a note of it and put a fat, black star beside it in his addled mind.

You just killed yourself, Beto. Same as if you'd sucked on the barrel of your rifle...

Tavo's foot thundered—a sharp drum beat that radiated all the way up to his knee. The pain felt like it lived in his bones, as though termites had begun to work their way up the marrow, chewing on the sensitive, spongy part inside his shin. He wondered if infection might have already set in.

"Where did they get the Semtex to blow the refinery?"

Alejandro spoke, probably trying to stop Beto from saying another word. "I've been thinking about that. They either got the explosives from a local mine—there are mining operations all around here—or maybe there was some C4 at Nellis. Clearly, the base wasn't as dead as we thought. We killed eleven men and three women wearing air force cammies."

"How many men did we lose?" Tavo looked at Alejandro. He hoped Beto would cool down so he wouldn't have to shoot him here in front of the others.

"We lost a hundred and fifty men, give or take in the fire. We only lost a couple on column security. They didn't seem to be shooting at the men. They focused their fire on the tanker trucks."

"Are you going to tell me how much gasoline we lost or do I need to ask?" Tavo exhaled and tongued the back of his teeth for the thousandth time. He'd bitten through his tongue when he'd kneed himself in the face during the explosions.

"I don't have an exact inventory," Alejandro dodged. "Sixty-eight of the fuel trucks took rounds, but we don't know how much gas we lost. It depends on how high they struck the fuel tanks. But I don't think we have enough gas to get back to Camp Navajo. I won't know for sure until I top off the Abrams—until I fill up the ones that didn't get burned up, I mean."

"They meant to leave us stranded." Tavo turned and stumbled away without explanation and without leaving orders. In the back of his mind, he knew it diminished him in their eyes, but if he didn't sit down immediately, he was going to fall down.

The three men watched him go, glancing at one another. Tavo saw their body language out of the corner of his eye, but kept walking—angling toward a lonely, adobe shack where the dirt road met the paved road. He needed to sit down and elevate his foot. He needed to do whatever he could to get the cosmic starburst of pain to recede. He couldn't stand for another minute.

Tavo realized he was behaving strangely and that it compromised him. He didn't care. His hand groped absently for his satellite phone in his chest rig pocket. Wounded and dazed, only one part of him remained: the serpent. The feathered Aztec god who devoured men whole. He pressed forward despite his losses and the maiming of his body; the unstoppable force of will that even a thousand-foot-high pyre of fuel would not turn aside.

His satellite phone in his chest rig seemed perfectly intact.

―――

"I've pre-positioned *El Chucho* in Hermosillo," the assassin's handler repeated.

The voice over the satellite phone came through warbled and spackled, like a demon reaching across an ice-bound solar system.

"Sir," the man on the other end of the phone interrupted his fugue. "Please confirm. *El Chucho* to prosecute target Sofía Castillo Sausa in Hermosillo, Sonora."

The roaring ache in his severed toe rose like boiling water at the mention of her name. Tavo steadied himself with deep breaths and gripped the rotting lawn chair so tightly he feared the brittle armrests might shatter. After an eternity, the pain receded.

"Sir. I need you to confirm," the satellite phone chirped.

"Confirmed."

There was nothing else to say. The man on the other end of

the call disconnected, as though saying goodbye might be an inappropriate way to end the call.

The shack where Tavo rolled between pain, malice and regret must've been a guard shack in a previous life. The walls were decaying adobe, but someone had recently replaced the roof with gleaming, corrugated metal. It radiated the sun's relentless heat like a stone pulled from the fire. Whoever had replaced the roof hadn't bothered to pull down the 1980s porn calendar, hanging on a rust-chewed nail. A big-breasted Latina stared back at Tavo with a vacant smile, her visage yellowing from decades hanging there.

Such a strange room for an emperor, Tavo brooded. Again, his ruined foot throbbed so powerfully that it made his ears pulse with a dull thrum. Somewhere in Hermosillo, Mexico the daughter he had once lived to serve had now been marked for death. She was likely dressed in white today, like most days—a crisp breeze cutting through the desert heat. At that same moment, her father sweltered in a mud shack, wounded, swooning and spattered in his own blood.

Maybe all great men faced solitary moments in windowless rooms like this one. Maybe all great men committed deeds that only steadfast men could.

To move forward, the next step had been obvious, given the yellow holocaust burning on the horizon: the serpent required fuel. Sofía stood between the serpent and its fuel. Great victories required great sacrifices.

Tavo told himself that his decision had nothing to do with her betrayal.

An ear. A toe. A daughter.

He would continue to cut away parts of himself if that was what conquest required.

An arm. His family. His home.

He would deny the altar of the gods no sacrifice.

Tavo's mind submerged beneath the pain again.

Shadows lengthened. The heat from the corrugated ceiling abated. Sometime later, someone came for him and dragged him into the back of a Humvee.

He thought maybe it was Saúl.

CHAPTER 40
NOAH MILLER
BETWEEN O'BANNON AND ELLSWORTH, NELLIS AFB, AREA 2

Noah had squirreled away some instant coffee, but no matter how badly it cast doubt on his manhood, he could barely stand to drink it without creamer. And, he had a habit of forgetting to bring creamer.

Once again, he sat alone in the desert with his thoughts and his ghosts. If he ever had a home, this was it. By himself with his ass in the sand, enjoying the billion gleaming souls in the canopy of stars. His JetBoil stove hissed companionably on the ground, warming his next batch of creamer-less feel-good.

The night had entirely overcome the day and the stars finally reached their full dominion. They flickered, clumped and clotted like a floating miasma of tiny sea creatures adrift on the firmament.

Noah wondered, if the configuration of the stars changed from one night to the next, would he notice the difference? He thought he might. He'd spent so many nights staring at the glowing Milky Way that he felt sure he knew each speck of light by heart—two stars in particular, just to the north of Orion. Leah and Katya.

The desperate, young lieutenant had given Noah a radio and

asked him to set up an outer picket along the access road to provide advance warning of an assault. Neither Noah nor the lieutenant thought that advance warning would do them any good, but it seemed like the right thing to do. It made Noah chuckle. They were mouse-like men with their mouse-like plans.

The stars. The Abrams tanks. The massive refinery fire in the distance. The nukes. They all combined to make Noah feel insignificant. At the same time, he couldn't help but feel like there had been an invincible, guiding hand during the last fourteen days of his life.

--Had it only been fourteen days?--

In fact, he felt oddly certain that the armored column would never come down the road below his little observation post. He knew, on some mystical level that the Fates had been guiding this endeavor from the moment he'd left his ranch on the borderlands. Captain Spark's flaming death had been written in the Book of Life since then, as had Noah's undeserved survival. He sat with a cup of coffee in his undeserving hand; resting, alive and only slightly banged up while so many others had been peeled off into oblivion.

Most men felt like God paid more mind to them than the next man. It was part-and-parcel of the affliction of self-awareness. And yet, even knowing that, Noah couldn't deny his certainty that God's hand had, in fact, been tipped. He had revealed himself over the last two weeks as the Grand Architect of this jacked up, blood-soaked plot to follow the narcos into America. It rang strangely true to Noah—as though the Creator had fallen so deeply in love with the saga that thousands of lives could be consumed in the story's wake. Yet the author was so much more than a madman. So much grander than a simple storyteller.

A voice came unbidden from the black of night and Noah

sprang to his feet, the over-and-under shotgun hunting for a target.

"Well at least you don't drink your coffee like a pansy anymore."

Noah's mind raced to connect the voice with a face. When it came to him, his knees went watery.

Bill McCallister stepped into the slight, blue light of the JetBoil.

Noah gasped and lowered his shotgun.

"You…" he looked at his father, then looked at his father's legs. They were both whole. There was no blown-off foot. Bill wore a pair of light combat boots. "I held a funeral for you."

"My boy. You jumped track just like I knew you would." Bill chuckled. "You always tended toward the dramatic, and emotional trackers are easiest to fool."

Something ominous stopped Noah from embracing him, or even from laying down the shotgun.

"How did you find me here?" Noah asked as he side-eyed his adoptive father.

CHAPTER 41

BILL MCCALLISTER
MCCALLISTER RANCH, FIFTEEN MILES OUTSIDE OF PATAGONIA, ARIZONA

Two Weeks earlier...

"There are fifteen Japanese cars with loud-ass mufflers comin' down Hartley Road toward your place. They just passed my gate." Tom Bartley's place was five miles up the road. At thirty miles an hour, that would give Bill about ten minutes to prepare.

"Thanks, Tom. Gotta go." Bill hung up and ran toward the tractor in the back of the house. He stopped on the porch, turned, ducked back inside and grabbed his SCAR Heavy rifle and a chest rig with six magazines that'd been hanging on the coat rack for years gathering dust.

Never, in all his time living in Rio Rico County, had vehicles like these driven down Hartley Road. Given the collapse, Bill didn't even have to guess what they were up to. His good nature didn't extend far enough to let them head past and into the town of Patagonia without a fight. He could already hear the low rumble of their modified exhaust, miles away. He couldn't know for sure that they were criminals coming to rape and pillage, but he couldn't afford a conversation about it, either. His property would be the end-of-the-road for either them or him.

He slipped into the chest rig as he ran. Hardly pausing, he hauled himself up onto the old International Harvester tractor and fired the engine. He popped it into gear and roared around the house to where he'd recently anchored a big loop of aircraft cable, sticking out of the grass next to the cottonwood tree in his front yard. He backed the tractor in, jumped down, and looped the cable around the ball hitch. Then he climbed back onto the tractor and waited as the mufflers blared louder and louder out of the north. With his final seconds, he checked his mag and then breach-checked the SCAR. The old commando was ready to rock.

Moments later, the first of the low-slung street racers came roaring over the rise in the county road at the north edge of his ranch. Bill loosened the slider on the three-point shoulder sling and rested his hand on the gear shift of the tractor. A split second before the first vehicle passed Bill's gate, he slammed the tractor in gear and pulled the cable so taut that the front wheels of the tractor jumped off the ground.

The lead rice burner hit the brakes and slid into the cable going almost twenty miles an hour. Amazingly, the cable didn't decapitate the roof of the car. It did decapitate the driver, slicing through the airbag and into the headrest of the driver's seat. The next car in line slammed into the first, and so on, causing a six-car-collision.

While the passengers were still stunned, Bill slid down off the tractor and poured five or six rounds into each vehicle, aiming for where the drivers' head should be. The window tinting made it difficult to target ID, but Bill was fully committed to the ambush and he was definitely in it to win it.

Men poured out of the cars and, sure enough, they were all

saggy-pants gangbangers. The last time Bill had seen so many silver-plated handguns, it'd been in Saddam Hussein's palace in Iraq during the GWOT. But moments later, the ghetto boys began pulling legitimate assault rifles out of the vehicles.

Return fire thwacked into the tractor, but there wasn't much Bill could do about it. He tucked tight to the front of the engine block and shifted fire from target to target, dealing out three rounds each and knocking men to the ground like he'd hit them with a wrecking ball.

The first effective round pinged Bill in the scalp. He felt the smack and then the burn and his vision went a little blurry for a moment. When things came back into focus, five men were trying to climb over his gate. He put at least one bullet in each before a second round hit him in the shoulder. Again, the bullet felt like it'd gone through-and-through. He shook off the raging storm in his shoulder and hunted for more targets. He'd already burned through three mags and the gangbangers were rallying, seeking cover and making their shots count.

Bill had played this scene out in his mind many times—the battle for his yard. He hadn't imagined so many cars and so many enemy combatants, but the principles of the ambush remained the same. Except in this case, he'd certainly die against so many opponents. When the collapse went down in the big cities, he'd buried the blocking cable across the road and had moved the trigger to his detonator over by the cottonwood.

Some enterprising gangbanger read his mind, and Bill peeked out from behind the tractor to see a blue Honda Civic revving its engine and un-sticking itself from the row of smashed-together gangster-mobiles. Bill could've hammered the Honda with .308 rounds, but leaning out from behind the tractor to shoot had become perilous. He definitely didn't want to die before he got the chance to clap off his booby trap.

Sure enough, the blue Honda bellowed as the gangbanger went max-velocity toward Bill's gate, hurtling through the chain. A millisecond later, just as the Honda catapulted into his yard, Bill touched off the plate charge he'd planted under his driveway.

Nobody really understood an explosion unless he'd been near one. Even from behind the tractor and the tree, the overpressure of twenty pounds of ANFO rattled Bill's melon to the point where he forgot for a moment where he was. He'd been blown up before, but it wasn't something a man got good at. It was like Jesus had pressed the reset button in his brain and his hard drive had been shut down.

Bill got up off the ground and current events came back, bit by bit. The hard drive whirred and the onboard RAM clicked and hummed. He searched about for his battle rifle and found it on the other side of the cottonwood. He breached checked it, but couldn't remember how many rounds had been in the mag before the blast. He did a tac-reload while the "warrior program" reloaded in his brain.

A few rounds of gunfire rattled off from across the county road, but nobody on the battlefield could aim for shit. The entire yard was choked with a dust cloud as thick as Grandma's honey. Bill could barely see the blown-up Honda, not a hundred feet away, laying on its back.

As the dust cleared, he began identifying targets and picking them off one-by-one. The gangbangers were taking a bit longer to recover than he was, so maybe a man did get better at being blown up. Eventually, though, the city boys recovered fully, and the full measure of return fire resumed. Bill's cottonwood was getting picked apart chunk by chunk by hard-hitting AK rounds. He returned fire from both sides of the tree—from high and then from low. He scored hits on the gangbangers, but the inside of his head began to buzz in a way that couldn't be good for his long-term health. Not that his long-term health was a huge consideration.

The battle rebounded back to full tilt when Bill discovered that he'd come to his last mag. He could've hunted around in his pockets for the partial mag that he'd kicked out during the tac-reload, but counting bullets in a partial mag wasn't going to happen given the intensity of incoming fire. He needed a full mag for his next move.

When he noticed a slowdown, Bill popped over the saddle of the tractor and dumped the entire mag into the gangbangers. They had all scurried behind their rice wagons after the big explosion, so his barrage probably wasn't dealing much death. He succeeded in getting the gangsters to put their heads down, so he broke and ran for the porch, dropping his empty rifle in the dust as he charged as fast as his old legs would carry him.

He hit the porch in a hail of gunfire, but nothing connected. He crashed through the screen and rounded on the door jamb. There against the wall, he'd stashed two special weapons: a lever-action .45-70 and a single, baseball hand grenade. He'd put them around the door jamb that very morning imagining they would be his last stand in the zombie apocalypse. If he was going to die holding steel, he'd want it to be the big, cowboy lever action and a hand grenade. Bill smiled big as he picked them up and made his peace.

He wasn't a fool. He knew that the .45-70 couldn't hold a candle to the SCAR in a gunfight, or even the AK-47s, but if he was going to die, he wanted to die fighting with a man's gun.

Twenty years before, he'd taken a huge risk bringing the hand grenade back from the Iraqi war. He'd stowed it in his footlocker inside a heavy, copper incense lamp. He'd carefully cut the lamp open, wedged the grenade inside, then soldered it closed. He still had the lamp in his barn office, a trophy that said "fuck you" to military regulation. He valued it more than his bronze star.

As the front wall of the farmhouse absorbed hundreds of AK rounds, little pock-marks of light winked around the door jamb and the wall. Splinters and dust blew inward. The room grew brighter by degrees.

Bill made himself small behind the jamb as he breach-checked the .45-70 and slid the grenade into a mag pouch on his vest. He kicked the door open and took a quick look.

The gangbangers had moved through the gate and had taken cover behind the Honda, the tractor and the cottonwood. He slid back inside just as he caught movement around the tree. He aimed for the gap and caught a gangbanger in the open, running for the corner of his house.

BOOM!

The .45-70 swept the man's feet out from under him and he hit the ground face-first. Bill ran the lever and hammered two more rounds into the cottonwood. A man lurched out from behind the tree screaming and holding his eyes. Bill put a slug in the man's chest. He gasped and crumpled like he'd been stomped by the Jolly Green Giant.

Bill ducked back inside as AK-47s ripped his house apart. The sunlight illuminated millions of bits of floating insulation and couch stuffing. He felt a sting across his back—whether from splinters or a bullet, he didn't know.

He snapped a peek and caught two more men in the open. The doorway again exploded in splinters and he returned to cover. He fished the grenade out of the mag pouch and underhand tossed it where he'd seen the men running.

KA-WHUMP!

The grenade blew and someone screamed an unholy screech, like two live cats in a sausage grinder.

"*¡Cese el fuego!* Cease fire!" someone shouted from the front yard. Bill considered rolling around the doorframe and shooting whoever had yelled, but truth was, he was getting tired. He'd pretty much accomplished everything he'd hoped for after he'd taken the phone call from Tom Bartley just fifteen minutes before. He hurt all over, almost more than he could stand. But it'd been a good fifteen minutes. As far as Bill was concerned, he was already dead. But bravery and exhaustion were two different animals.

"*Viejito*. Are you done yet?"

"Are you all dead yet?" Bill fired back.

The gangbanger in the yard chuckled. "Pretty fucking close, *Viejito*...tell you what we're going to do. We're going to back away from here and leave you inside your busted-up house to live out the rest of your short-ass, busted up life. Then, we're going to head down the road and fuck the shit out of your town. How's that sound?"

Bill curled his lip and thought about it.

"What the hell do you want from me, then? Why the threats, *puta madre*?"

The gangbanger replied. "Because this is what I do. I'm a talent scout, *ese*. When I see fifteen of our soldiers shot up and two blowed-up craters in the ground, I think you maybe know how to fuck shit up for real. Navy SEAL-shit right here, *Viejito*. How about you come with us? If you do, maybe we'll just drive by your town and keep going. How's that sound, *Viejito*? Hey. It's the end of the world. Who gives a shit, right?"

"I step out and you're going to shoot me. You think I'm stupid?"

The big-mouth gangbanger laughed. "*Ese*, if we wanted to kill you, we'd just set your shitty house on fire, bro. We wouldn't need you to come out. We're giving you a shot at breathing, at least for another day or two. How's that sound?"

"How do I know you'll keep your mongrel hands off the town?"

"We have places to be. If I bring you in, maybe the bosses want you, maybe they don't. I ain't going to lie: I really don't know what the bosses think about shit. But I promise we won't jack your town. That I will guarantee if you come with us and show us how to blow shit up. I mean, *hijo de la chingada.* You jacked some *vatos* up out here, homeboy."

Bill could either die in the next few minutes, or he could help the town and maybe die later. Dying later pretty much always seemed like the better option. At this point in his life, he didn't care about anyone except his son and that town. The rest of the world could go to hell. It wasn't as though it bothered him to join up with Mexicans. War was war. He had never fought for anyone he didn't come to despise later. They were all pieces of shit as far as he was concerned.

He reached around the ruined door jamb and leaned the .45-70 up against the wall.

"All right. I'm coming out," Bill announced.

A big, tatted-up gangbanger stepped out from behind the cottonwood and crossed the yard. As he came closer, Bill could tell that the man wasn't nearly as young as the rest. He was what the saggy-pants gangbangers might call an "OG." Original Gangster. Bill knew that from watching *NCIS: Los Angeles.*

"Aren't you getting a little old to be driving a rice burner?" Bill asked.

"Hah! Aren't you a little old to play *Rambo, First Blood*?"

"Maybe so," Bill admitted. He stretched his back. His head roared with pain. If nothing else, he had a healthy concussion from the round that had gobsmacked him. He reached up and rubbed the spot, now encrusted with a cookie of dried blood. Huge flecks of brown drifted down to the shattered porch.

"You coming or not?" the OG asked.

"I'm sure as hell not letting the neighbors see me in one of your sushi-mobiles," Bill protested.

"I don't give a fuck what you drive, you racist old prick, but we gotta go now."

"Hold on a minute," Bill reached around the door and grabbed a pair of combat boots. He ambled off the porch toward a dead gangbanger laying spread eagle on the weed-choked dirt. Bill whipped out his Leatherman, pried out the saw, sat down on the packed dirt, and began sawing through the dead man's ankle.

"*¡Chingada madre!* What are you doing?" The gangbanger brought his AK up and pointed it at Bill.

Bill stopped sawing and looked up. "He ain't getting any deader, *Vato*. Relax. I'm doing you a favor." He went back to work. After ten seconds of sawing, the severed foot thumped to the ground. Bill slid the dead man's tennis shoe off and chucked it into the crater where the Honda lay on its back. He shimmied off his own cowboy boots and put on his combat boots. During all this time, the surviving gangbangers drifted out from behind cover and watched him, mesmerized.

"You better tell me what the hell you're doing Old Man, or I'm going to pop you right here. That's one of my friends you just cut up."

Bill looked up while lacing his combat boots. "Here in a bit, my son's going to come looking for me. Then he's going to come looking for you. Trust me when I tell you that you don't want him looking for you. He's twice the man I am."

"How will cutting off a man's foot make any difference, Old Timer."

As though it explained anything, Bill stared at the OG while he shoved the severed, dripping foot into one of his cowboy boots. "Because if he thinks I'm dead he probably won't bother coming after you."

Bill tossed the cowboy boot with the foot near the blast mark made by the grenade. Then, he stood up and carefully back tracked around to the rear of the house, erasing his track with a branch blown off the cottonwood tree. He fired up his Land Cruiser and backed it into the barn.

The gangbangers went to work loading the bits and pieces of their friends into a pile while the OG kept an eye on Bill. He'd opened up his vault and loaded supplies into his Cruiser.

"Where'd you get all this shit?" the OG asked when he saw the gun locker crammed with hardware.

"I bought it with money I earned working a job. You ever heard of that? A job?"

The OG laughed. "You're one mean old bastard, aren't you? That's okay. I don't really care. Just remember, we come by here all the time. You screw us on our deal and we can always come back and rape your town. You got it, *ese*?"

"Yeah, *ese*. I got it," Bill snarled. "Take whatever guns and ammo you want, but keep your filthy hands off my food and off my personal effects in the office. Anyone touches that and I'll kill them."

"Nice office. In a barn, even." The OG smiled as he waved men over to carry the weapons. "What are you? CEO of ShitCo?"

CHAPTER 42

NOAH MILLER
BETWEEN O'BANNON AND ELLSWORTH, NELLIS AFB, AREA 2

"I understand about the town, Bill. But these narcos committed mass murder in Artesia. They tried to do the same in Tucson." Noah struggled to get his head around the story—and the fact that his father was alive. Just minutes before, he'd been ninety-nine percent certain that his father's ghost had been riding shotgun with him. Now he was finding out that not only was his father alive, but that he'd become a cartel pipe hitter.

"I'm not going to bullshit you, son. I wasn't there in Artesia, but it wouldn't have mattered. It's not the first time I've served under cocksuckers who wipe out towns. You can judge me if you want, but between the two of us, I'm the one who's been to war."

Noah remembered Captain Spark's face melting off earlier that same day.

"I've been to war too."

Bill poked at the ground with a stick. A strong gibbous moon had risen, blotting out the stars around it like a pool of nothing. The two men could almost see one another's face in the colorless light of that moon.

"Maybe that's true. If so, I'm truly sorry. I did everything I could to keep you out of this."

"I gave you a funeral," Noah smoldered. "I grieved you."

"Hell," Bill looked straight into his son's eyes. "I should be happy anyone cared enough to even raise a glass for my life. I was never much of a human being, I suppose."

Noah sat back on his haunches in the sand. "Yeah, well it's never too late... Where do we go from here?"

"WE aren't going anywhere. I'm going back to the dickheads I work for and you're going to vanish."

Noah stood back up. "You've got to be joking. How the hell..."

"I gave my word and they didn't attack my town. The three things I've got in this world are that town, my talent for war fighting and you." Bill looked up from the ground. "I already steered them away from you once. They had you when you crossed the bridge at Hoover, but I put 'em off your trail."

"Thanks for that, but you can't fight for men invading America. It's our country!"

"It's your country," Bill corrected. "Son, I'm one hundred percent proud of who you've become, and I know you're not going to understand my choice. I knew it the moment I saw your Cruiser parked on the Arizona side of the dam. I'm never going to point a gun at you, but we're on opposite sides of this fight. Get used to it. There are just some things in this world you're not going to understand—like the workings of another man's head. You can drive the same car as me, wear the same boots as me, even track sign like me. But you're not me. There was always going to be a time when you left me behind. That time has come."

Noah shook his head. He supposed Bill was right. Noah would never understand. It was like his right arm had decided to go south while the rest of him went north.

"I'm not going to vanish. I wouldn't be able to look Leah and Katya in the face someday if I didn't see this all the way through. I know what Leah would want me to do and just surviving isn't it."

"May her soul rest in peace." Bill slung his assault rifle over his shoulder and stood up straight.

Noah embraced his father and replied. "I'm not sure Leah's doing much resting. That girl never did know when to lie down."

Bill grunted, pulled away and looked his son in the eyes. "You go ahead and be the man I couldn't be, Noah. That's one hundred percent okay by me." Then, he turned and walked into the desert. His moon shadow faded and vanished.

Noah listened to the light crunch of sand until it disappeared into the endless, rolling dreamscape of the Southwest.

CHAPTER 43

TAVO CASTILLO
FORMER BORDER STATION, UNITED STATES
BORDER PATROL, INTERSTATE 19, NOGALES,
ARIZONA

The squealing brakes of the Humvee woke Tavo from a hundred years' sleep.

"Where am I?" he asked, but he'd already seen the familiar shape of the arched, concrete border crossing at Nogales.

"You're going home."

Saúl sat in the front passenger seat of the Humvee and Tavo sprawled across the back seats. He didn't know the driver by name. Someone had stuffed a small mattress under Tavo, but he could still feel the lump of the center console pressing through. He sat up and his head wobbled on his neck. The pain hit him with a rush.

"Whoa, *Jefe*." Saúl turned in his seat and looked Tavo up and down. "The medic gave you some pretty hard smack. Take it slow, *Canoso*."

"Where are the tanks? The Abrams?" Tavo croaked.

"They're with Beto and Alex outside of Kingston. They scavenged gas there to get them back to the Navajo Depot... I don't know how to tell you this, *hermano*..."

"What?" Tavo tried to drag himself upright, but his severed toe fired shockwaves of pain up the bones of his leg.

"*Canoso.* Sofía is gone." Saùl's eyes filled with tears. "Our Sofí got taken out." Saúl rubbed his stubble, his hand drifting to his eyes. "You heal up, boss, and we'll go hunting that *hijo de puta* who shot her. We'll find him and we'll make his pain our mission in life. I'm so sorry, *hermano.*" Saúl choked on a breath and turned back around in his seat. He stared out the window and twisted his hands around the M4 in his lap, like wringing a wet towel.

Tavo lowered himself back onto the mattress and stared at the black-painted ceiling of the Humvee.

He thought about the night after he shot his mother in the face. He remembered staring at the ceiling over his bed. It had been red, brick tile that arched over his bed and ended in dark timbers.

People had been arguing in the kitchen down the hall from his room—his grandparents. His aunts and uncles. Some voices he didn't know. They argued about Tavo and about his father.

Tavo remembered worrying, who would argue for him if not his father? Who would explain why he had a gun and why he'd pointed it at his mother? Who would tell them about the conquistador game that resulted in the terrible, unthinkable accident? If not his father, then who would be there to speak for him?

The blood on the kitchen floor. Pools of it. The piece of the back of his mother's head on the countertop with hair still clinging to it. The spatter on the ceiling.

Tavo bored into the black ceiling of the Humvee with his eyes, drifting in a sea of pain. He pictured his father. His only mental image was almost forty years old, but it gave his hatred a place to land.

His father had murdered his daughter. He had used her and then sent her to her death. Tavo had made the call, but his father had made that call inevitable.

Tavo didn't know how his father had corrupted his daughter —convinced her to plot against him with the Guatemalan brother he had never met—but Tavo knew that Sofía's murder dangled at the end of a long chain of machinations contrived by that one, malignant disease that had relentlessly cursed his life. His father.

"We'll fuck him up right, *Canoso*," Saùl said as he stared out the window.

In his haze, Tavo imagined Saúl had read his mind; that he meant Tavo's father.

Tavo glared at the black-on-black headliner of the Humvee.

Yes. They would fuck him up right.

CHAPTER 44

TAVO CASTILLO
RANCHO SANTIAGUITO, 65 MILES OUTSIDE OF
HERMOSILLO, SONORA, MEXICO

Isabel, his wife, sorted beans at the kitchen sink, silent in her grief. She stood with her back to Tavo, staring out the kitchen window at the courtyard with its sun-wilted palms and dying flowers. All the men of the ranch had gone to war and the landscaping had suffered as a result.

The ranch house was otherwise silent. The beans pattered into the metal pot.

Tavo sat at the tiled bar. He perched his thundering foot on a stool.

Plunk. plunk. plunk-plunk. plunk.

His wife refused to look at him. Her widening hips and rounding shoulders shuddered. He'd just told her that their daughter had been murdered in Hermosillo. She continued to sort beans, barely pausing at the news.

Plunk. plunk. plunk.

"She's an angel. A perfect angel," Isabel said to the window. "Only a monster would kill such a woman."

Tavo didn't understand how regular people handled grief, but he knew something was wrong with Isabel, something beyond being told that her daughter was dead.

"She wasn't quite the angel you think, Isabel. She tried to have me arrested in Guatemala. She's secretly been in contact with my criminal father in Guatemala through a half-brother and they meant to take my business. They meant to have me dead or in jail."

Plunk. plunk-plunk-plunk.

"You think you're so smart, Gustavo," her voice grew husky, still staring out the window at the withering courtyard. "You think you know everything about everyone."

"Isabel. I did a DNA test and discovered the connection— discovered that I had a half-brother and that he and my father were making a move on me. They tried to have me captured and Sofía helped them—told them where to send the police to take me. Our own daughter... She was beautiful, but she was no angel."

Plunk-plunk-plunk-plunk-plunk.

Isabel stopped sorting and leaned against the sink. She sucked in a breath and her back rose. Tavo waited on her silence, the throbbing of his foot so corpulent that he could feel it in his hands.

His wife whipped away from the sink and lurched toward him. A silver flash winked through the air. A weight slapped into his neck. A keen pain pierced his throat—a pain that cut through the thrumming, dull agony of his ruined toe like a soprano cuts through the choir.

Tavo snatched at his throat, and instead of touching warm flesh, touched cold, wet steel. A huge kitchen knife protruded half-in and half-out of his flesh.

He exhaled and breath spurted out one side of his throat, burbling between his fingers. He gripped his neck with both hands now, trying to hold the breath and blood inside. Both gurgled and foamed through his fingers.

Hail Mary, full of grace... his mind wrestled with the spinning room and the razor's pain as he pitched off the stool and piled onto the tile floor.

"Whaaa..." words bubbled out the side of his throat. His wife stood over him, a second kitchen knife in her hand.

"Do you think you're the only person who can order a DNA test, *Gustavo*? Sofía did one too, found your family and wanted to meet her uncle, you fool. *You animal.* I ordered that test for her for her birthday. She wasn't *conspiring*. She was trying to surprise you by finding your family. And you ordered her murder... Do you think I don't know who you are? Die in your sins, you murderer, you *demonio*."

She kicked the handle of the knife in his throat. Tavo rolled on his back, the pain finally beginning to recede. He stared at the ceiling, unable to blink.

The late sun turned the ceiling red. The bricks of the barrel vault stared back at him. His life a circle of red, brick tile.

"Think not that I am come to send peace on earth: I came not to send peace, but a sword."

Tavo remembered the words, spoken by Christ his Lord. Christ his King. Christ his *Judge*.

The red tile blurred, then faded to gray.

———

"Oh no! Mama! What did you do?" Sofía Castillo threw herself to the floor, covering her father's body and protecting it against the second blade held by her mother. Another knife—a massive chef's knife with a dark, wood handle protruded impossibly from her father's neck. The pool of blood seemed enormous, wrapping around the edge of the island. The room smelled like a butcher's shop.

"He tried to have you killed. God will not blame me for this."

"Oh Mama... No...Papi. Papi," Sofía wept, holding his face in her hands. Blood seeped into her pants, her blouse, her hands. She kissed him on the cheek and pulled herself under him, cradling his loose head in her lap. She wrapped her arms around his dark hair and sobbed.

"That monster did not deserve a daughter like you." Her mother dropped the second knife on the counter and fled the room. She began weeping as she ran down the hallway.

Sofía's tears tapered off. She moved her father's head from her lap and set it on the tile. She stood up out of the bloodletting, stepped to the sink and rinsed her hands. Her clothing, her arms and her hair were drenched in blood.

She walked toward the courtyard and swept up her handbag on the way into the fresh air and the coming cool-down of the late afternoon. Sofía pulled out her satellite phone and speed-dialed.

"Beto. It's over."

"How did you do it?" Beto asked from two thousand miles away.

"I didn't do anything. My mother stabbed him with a kitchen knife. I told her about the killer he sent after me and she put a knife in his throat."

"Where's the assassin?"

"I sent him to help you, *mi amor*," Sofía smiled, thinking that Beto must be outdoors somewhere too, enjoying the same sunset she was enjoying. Beto would be watching it over a column of mighty Abrams tanks rather than over a dying, Mexican courtyard.

Her mighty Abrams tanks.

Sofía shifted to business. "The *sicario's* coming with General Bautista and another 100,000 gallons of gasoline from Monterrey. They should be crossing at Nogales by now. Did you talk to Saùl?"

"Yeah. It took some time to explain," Beto hesitated. "But he understands. He's with the program."

"Good. Call him and have him pick me up at the ranch in fifteen minutes."

"What about Tavo's body?" Beto asked. The discomfiture was obvious in his voice, even through the satellite connection.

"I'll figure it out."

Sofia clacked the satellite phone shut and went to shower.

She'd been planning this so long, it seemed almost strange to have it finished. With the end of one puzzle, comes the beginning of the next, she reminded herself.

First things first: take a shower. Put on some makeup. Put on a fresh, white blouse.

Then, she had a nation to conquer.

CHAPTER 45
SOFI CASTILLO
RANCHO SANTIAGUITO, 65 MILES OUTSIDE OF
HERMOSILLO, SONORA, MEXICO

Sofia Castillo swept into the kitchen with her mind churning. How would she manipulate Saúl into following her command without thinking she was a monster? She needed men like Saúl and she needed his devotion. If Saúl thought she'd engineered the death of her father, he would treat her cautiously, with reservations. She would rather he trust her with blind devotion.

Sofia wasn't ready to give up the role of the innocent. It had paid immense dividends. But, would men follow an innocent into battle? With her lieutenants on the front line and the Catholic faith behind them, she figured they would.

She'd spent a great deal of time with the archbishop's abbot and she'd seen to the archbishop being "relocated" to another parish. She had consolidated the full support of the church and the military in the region. While her father had been chasing gasoline, she'd been stacking the building blocks of empire.

She could hear her mother weeping in the master bedroom. The beans in the sink lay abandoned.

Sofia geared herself up to play the bereaved daughter. Saúl

would probably be in front of the ranch house waiting for her in his Humvee.

She stopped cold when she rounded the counter to the kitchen. The pool of blood remained, but a giant, red smear tracked out of the kitchen and toward the front hallway. Her father's body was no longer on the floor. Sofia followed the contours of dried blood as they weaved right and left through the front hallway and to the foot of the heavy, oak door. A single, bloody handprint marred the plaster wall by the coat rack.

The door had been left ajar.

Saúl's Humvee was nowhere to be seen.

CHAPTER 46
NOAH MILLER
US HIGHWAY 40, NEAR BELLEMONT, ARIZONA

Noah had rallied the people of Flagstaff to the threat of the cartel and the decision had been made to evacuate. Most fled toward Phoenix. Some ran into the mountains. A small group had armed themselves to the teeth and moved north up Highway 89 into Fredonia and Colorado City. The mouth of the rugged Utah mountains seemed as good a place as any to make a stand against an armored column. Noah would likely join them there. For now, he was the watcher on the wall; the lone countryman on the sun-scorched ramparts of southwest America. Though it had faltered, it would forever be his country. He had buried his wife and daughter in this soil, and nothing would ever change that.

The narcos had abandoned Nevada and had scuttled back across Hoover Dam two days after the showdown at the Dry Lake refinery. The nukes remained undiscovered and safely interred in the hinterlands of Nellis Air Force Base.

Noah now shadowed the narco column as it regrouped at the Navajo Army Depot. He would hang around to find out where they would next seek fuel and conquest; his money was on the refineries to the north, Salt Lake City or Wyoming. Or maybe, the cartel would push east into the gas fields of Texas. Either way, Noah's ghosts felt as bullish as ever on tracking these sons of bitches.

Maybe old Bill knew where the narcos were headed, but nothing could be done about that. The old man had surrendered himself to the seductive charms of bitterness. He'd hated so many for so long that he'd lost the ability to hope; at least, that's how Noah explained the loss of his dad to himself. It gave him another reason to hammer the narcos back to Mexico—so perhaps they'd release his father to come home.

Noah had to admit, not long ago, hope had been a stranger to him too. But with his ghosts and his crusade, even while the world twisted in chaos, he felt pretty good about the ground under his feet. He hadn't done the math, but he was pretty sure he hadn't had a drink in over two weeks. Being a good man in a good fight suited him.

Noah leaned across the hood of the Land Cruiser with his binoculars and watched the narcos mull about the depot. He was parked high on the side of the Hashknife Mountains, where he could see them, but they wouldn't likely see him.

It'd killed him to do it, but he'd scrounged some earth-tone spray paint and had given the Cruiser a new look—flat-sheen camouflage. He added a camo net over the Cruiser as well. So far, he'd been sitting on this mountainside for two days and nobody down in the depot seemed to have noticed. Even so, he'd change location tonight after dark.

The cartel was far from dead, he reminded himself. Seven dozen main battle tanks wouldn't just disappear into the desert. Someone would put them to work.

Noah let his binos hang on their harness around his neck. Over the last two weeks, he'd spent so much time with his eyes buried in the binos that they felt like an old friend. He reached into the passenger door, punched the button on the radio and took a chance on a little music.

> Faith is easier said than done
> It crumples in the light of day
> You're beaten and battered, your dreams all but shattered
> But night, it comes. And the Word, it plays...

The tune cut the cool air and Noah turned it down so the sound wouldn't extend past his observation post. He needed to top off his supply of hope and the music never failed to do it for him. Watching tanks had a way of making a man feel insignificant and his wife's cassette tape reminded him of his role in all of this: *the watcher on the walls. The crusader.*

Nobody might ever know the risks he'd taken and the Hail Mary, long-bomb passes that had turned into unlikely victories. But Noah knew, and his wife knew.

Hell. Noah didn't have any idea if the ghosts were real or not —whether God or his girls had put him on this path. It was entirely possible that he'd been carried away in a daydream.

Were they calling him and guiding him from the Great Beyond? Or was he just a sappy, lonely drunk; imagining things to feel better about his personal tragedies.

> I will make my stand,
> No, I won't stay asleep.
> You found me there,
> and pulled me from the deep.

He couldn't give a shit less if it was all fantasy or not. The truth didn't interest him overmuch. He could feel the ghosts living in his bones: Leah, Katya, and maybe the Ancient of Days too. In the end, accepting them was like watching a perfect sunset. Why dither over the why's and wherefores? Why fret about tomorrow? Why not just drink it all in and let the beauty have its way?

A goodness is a goodness. In this new, brutal world, Noah didn't think there would be many goodnesses lying around for the taking. He was sure as hell going to enjoy them while he could.

The truth could pound sand, as far as he was concerned.

Noah tilted the passenger seat forward and searched for a half-drunk water bottle he'd tossed back there the day before. His hand touched steel.

He pulled apart the detritus of the last few days of surveillance to satisfy his curiosity. Laying in the back of the Cruiser, nestled in a blanket, he discovered a .45-70 lever-action Marlin rifle.

Bill's rifle.

A box of rounds lay on the floor beside it. Noah didn't know how long the rifle and the rounds had been there, but he guessed Bill must've slipped it in the back of the Cruiser when the armored column passed by Hoover Dam on their return trip to Arizona.

He chuckled and lifted the cowboy gun out of the vehicle, ran the lever and checked the breach. There was nothing in the chamber, but the tubular magazine was full of fat, blunt cartridges. The brass and blued finish of the gun glowed in the setting sun. Noah shook his head and admired the fine piece of weaponry. A true man's gun.

"You were easier to understand when you were a ghost," Noah spoke softly to the gun. He lifted the rifle to his shoulder and looked down the sights and smiled.

"You beautiful, old bastard."

"Not only did religion rise as a means to hold communities together, but religion also served to propel criminal organizations to geographical reach not witnessed since Genghis Khan and Hannibal. One of the most noteworthy was the Sinaloa cartel who consolidated the Juarez and Gulf cartels just after the Black Autumn collapse.

In order to extend power beyond northern Mexico, the new cartel overlord, Gustavo Castillo, christened the criminal organization Los Caballeros Templarios or Knights Templar. Blending macabre elements of Catholicism, ruthless violence and ancient Templar code, Los Templarios either recruited or exiled all Catholic bishops and archbishops in northern Mexico during the months after the collapse, creating a cartel that seamlessly combined religion and violence in one huge organization. In the vacuum that followed the fall of the Mexican government, dioceses and communities hungered for the Rule of Law and often welcomed the Templarios, especially given their pledge to serve the poor and support the church.

The Cabellero Templario manual required them to 'to help the poor, fight against materialism, not kill for money, and not use drugs.' Of course, none of these pledges blunted the massive and organized campaign of theft and terror the Templarios would launch into the former southwestern United States.

In an unpredictable turn of events, one young widower—an unknown rancher from the border of Mexico, arose to become the Paul Revere of the American southwest and managed to blunt the Templarios' relentless march north. When later asked how he had achieved such military success during a time of utter chaos, Colonel Noah Miller remarked, 'It was strange magic. Perhaps the best way to wage war is to arrive at battle with a heart of peace.'"

The American Dark Ages, by William Bellaher
    North American Textbooks, 2037

A WORD FROM JASON ROSS

Conquistadors and the Black Autumn series of novels take place during the first seventeen days of the Black Autumn Collapse of the United States. Each novel follows a hair-raising struggle to stay alive in a world plunged into chaos— each book from the viewpoint of a different cluster of survivors. As you know, *Conquistadors* follows a ruthless cartel genius—and his even-more-genius daughter—across the American Southwest. *Black Autumn* tracks Green Beret Jeff Kirkham and his family and friends as they battle for their lives while Salt Lake City flips into criminal mayhem. *Black Autumn Travelers* follows three men trekking across the United States against tremendous odds, each man finding his own version of honor in the new, brutal world. And finally, *The Last Air Force One* catches a ride with the President of the United States as he struggles between the needs of a disintegrating nation and his own family aboard the presidential jet that will soon be forced to land somewhere inside the fallen United States.

These novels can be read in any order, as they take place at the same time. Before the end of 2019, we hope to release an anthology of short stories written by Jeff, Jason and other

ReadyMen and women. These too will take place during the seventeen days of the Black Autumn Collapse. Watch for the anthology on Amazon.

Finally, we're preparing to release the first, full sequel in the Black Autumn series in the first few weeks of 2020. *White Wasteland* jumps ahead sixty days as winter descends on Salt Lake City and the Homestead survival compound, and the winter brings disease, tragedy and unfathomable acts of violence. If you thought the anarchy and fighting in the Black Autumn series was a little much, strap in. Things get much worse.

When Jeff and I wrote *Black Autumn Conquistadors*, we asked ourselves, "what happens when a man's mind becomes prisoner to the weapons he covets?" Then, we put the biggest, baddest ground weapon possible in front of the most soulless man on the continent and we asked, "would he kill his own daughter to possess a hundred M1 Abrams tanks?"

My wife weighed in immediately. "There is ***no effing way*** that would ever happen."

Challenge accepted.

We hope you enjoyed witnessing a man descend to hell while another man discovers salvation. Jeff and I kicked around the question of how Paul Revere rose to commit the acts of bravery that would cement his role in history. Then we took a wild guess and brought him forward to a twenty-first century invasion of America.

If you wondered about the music that finally tips Noah over into a life of courage, the lyrics are mostly ours, but the band that inspired them is Third Day—a Christian rock band that could convict any man to seek his higher calling.

After serving almost twenty-nine years in Army Special Forces, Jeff Kirkham continues to help patriots and friends of the United States. Together, he and I along with other ReadyMen members, traveled twice to Guatemala to train the

Kaibil Special Forces and secret service, both times in remote mountain bases. These Guatemalans take up positions on the front line in the war against the drug cartels. Guatemalans take huge personal and national risks to help defeat the drug trade. We have seen it firsthand, and in honor of those sterling friends of the United States, we dedicate *Conquistadors*.

Oh, and the Filadelfia Hotel in Antiqua is easily as beautiful as Tavo Castillo says it is. We highly recommend you visit Antigua, Guatemala—so long as you don't have a devious, criminal mastermind father hiding in Guatemala City waiting to destroy your life and corrupt your children. Otherwise, Guatemala will knock your socks off.

GET EXCLUSIVE BLACK AUTUMN STUFF

Our favorite part of this whole novel-writing-thing is becoming brothers an*d* friends with our readers.

Our dirty secret: we don't write these novels ourselves. We collaborate with scores of experts and fans and we get many of our juiciest ideas from readers. The ReadyMen Group on Facebook worked through several of the scenes in *Conquistadors* with Jeff and I and got them humming. We also took a ton of consultation from veterans on the Abrams tank, military unit disposition and the bizarre practices of munitions storage of the U.S. National Guard. We did not make any of that up, by the way.

Join our newsletter for info on new books and deals—with the understanding that we will occasionally pump you for ideas about The End Of The World As We Know It. We might also throw in a ReadyMan gear deal or two.

GET EXCLUSIVE BLACK AUTUMN STUFF

https://BookHip.com/MLLNTF

Join today and we'll send you *How to Survive a Black Swan Event* at no charge. It's the leanest, meanest preparedness primer ever written and it'll help you and your family prepare for job loss, local disaster or even The Big Enchilada (for less money than the cost of homeowners insurance.)

Join our email list and get *How to Survive* today.

https://BookHip.com/MLLNTF

Made in the USA
Middletown, DE
29 September 2021